DO NOT MARK
THIS BOOK
THERE IS A SLIP AT
THE BACK FOR YOUR

NOWHERE MAN

A note from the publisher

Dear Reader,

If you enjoy riveting stories with engaging characters and strong writing, as I do, you'll love *Nowhere Man*. It's a gripping, edge-of-your-seat financial thriller, packed with surprising twists. I couldn't put it down... And that's not because John's my father or because when I was much younger I named the novel's main character after my favourite video game character! *Nowhere Man* is a great read.

Did you know that big-name authors, John Grisham and J.K. Rowling, got rejected many times by publishers? John Green's own experience of this was one of the many factors that inspired *Pantera Press*, and our aim to become *a great new home for Australia's* next *generation of best-loved authors*. We think we're well on the way.

But there's even more to us... Simply by enjoying our books, you'll also be contributing to our unique approach: *good books doing good things*™. We have a strong 'profits for philanthropy' foundation, focussed on literacy, quality writing, the joys of reading and fostering debate.

So let me mention one program we're thrilled to support: *Let's Read*. It's already helping 100,000 pre-schoolers across Australia develop a love of books and the building blocks for learning how to read and write. We're excited that *Let's Read* now also operates in remote Indigenous communities in Far North Queensland, Cape York, and Torres Strait. *Let's Read* was developed by the *Centre for Community Child Health* and it's being implemented in partnership with *The Smith Family*.

Simply buying this book will help us support these kids. Thank you.

Want to do more? If you visit www.PanteraPress.com/Donate you can personally donate to help *The Smith Family* expand *Let's Read*, find out more about this great program, and also more on the other programs *Pantera Press* supports.

Please enjoy *Nowhere Man*.

And for news about our other books, sample chapters, author interviews and much more, please visit our website: www.PanteraPress.com

Happy reading,

Alison Green

NOWHERE MAN

If only she knew what he knew...

JOHN M. GREEN

First published in 2010 by Pantera Press Pty Limited
www.PanteraPress.com

Text Copyright © John M Green, 2010
John M Green has asserted his moral rights to be identified as the author of this work.

Design and typography Copyright © Pantera Press Pty Limited, 2010
PanteraPress, the three-slashed colophon device, *good books doing good things*, *a great new home for Australia's best-loved authors*, WHY vs WHY, and *making sense of everything* are trademarks of Pantera Press Pty Limited.

This book is copyright, and all rights are reserved.

We welcome your support of the author's rights, so please only buy authorised editions.

This is a work of fiction, though it is based on some real events. Names, characters, organizations, dialogue and incidents are either products of the author's imagination or are used fictitiously, and any resemblance to actual people, living or dead, firms, events or locales is coincidental.

Without the publisher's prior written permission, and without limiting the rights reserved under copyright, none of this book may be scanned, reproduced, stored in, uploaded to or introduced into a retrieval or distribution system, including the internet, or transmitted, copied or made available in any form or by any means (including digital, electronic, mechanical, photocopying, sound or audio recording, or text-to-voice). This book is sold subject to the condition that it shall not, by way of trade or otherwise, be lent, re-sold, hired out, or otherwise circulated in any form of binding or cover other than that in which it is published and without a similar condition being imposed on the subsequent recipient. This edition of this book is not for sale in Europe.

Please send all permission queries to:
Pantera Press, P.O. Box 357 Seaforth. NSW Australia 2092 or info@PanteraPress.com

A Cataloguing-in-Publication entry for this book is available from the National Library of Australia.

ISBN 978-0-9807418-3-4

Editor: Bill Thompson
Cover and internal design: Luke Causby, Blue Cork
Cover Image: PhotoLibrary
Author Photo: Courtesy, Phil Carrick, *The Australian Financial Review*
Typesetting by Kirby Jones
Printed and bound in Australia by Griffin Press

Pantera Press policy is to use papers that are natural, renewable and recyclable products made from wood grown in sustainable forests. The logging and manufacturing processes are expected to conform to the environmental regulations of the country of origin.

For Jenny, Alison & Martin

"Time flies like an arrow. Fruit flies like bananas."
— Groucho Marx (1890-1977)

"The only purpose for which power can be rightfully exercised over any member of a civilised community, against his will, is to prevent harm to others. His own good, either physical or moral, is not sufficient."
— John Stuart Mill (1862)

The end is in the beginning and yet you go on."
— Hamm, in Samuel Beckett's one-act play, *Endgame* (1958)

1

THIS CITY DOESN'T grow on you, it grows in you. It snatches your breath. It scratches its scarlet nails down your back so you squirm for more. Sydney is heaven without dying. But in eight minutes, for Sonya, it would become hell.

The bush track clung alongside the foreshore, a seductive stretch of dirt and rocks and water views. The professor pounded it daily so, even without checking her watch, she knew she'd been running fifty minutes. But after last night, who cared about time?

Dribbles of sweat kept filling her smile lines. It had been their first sex in three weeks, true, but what did she expect after nine, no, ten years. As Sonya was convincing herself once again that Michael wasn't a lousy lover, the lace frond of a fern camouflaged a sandstone outcrop and she almost tripped. Regathering her balance and her pace, she reminded herself that in the long spaces between the sex Michael was still, well, a gentleman; most at ease sniffing a vintage claret or cradling a tumbler of good scotch—no ice, no water—and drawing back on one of his antique smoking pipes. And considerate. The word "companion" didn't endear itself to her, so she pushed it away.

She leapt, almost flew, over a tree root that caught her eye just in time but her shoulder swiped against a split branch of a eucalypt.

To her, Michael was a Mr Cool in a gallant, nineteenth-century kind of way yet "cold fish" was the epithet more often whispered round their circle of friends; these days more a semi-circle, and mostly hers. To them, Michael soaked himself in solitude. "Reserve" was a word conceived for him, or so a friend had said once in Sonya's earshot. It was true he rarely sought friendships and when on odd occasions they were offered, he seldom accepted them.

For him, familiarity bred contentment, albeit one focused on few people and fewer things. Mostly, Michael was a self-contained, tight-lipped man who brushed off the prevailing fondness for approval or intimacy. Cool... yes. Detached at times... oh, yes. But for Sonya, also thoughtful... decent. Integrity and a quiet generosity gently shimmered from him, in soft beats.

He stuck to his guns in most things, even in his business affairs. His work since she'd known him was as a stocks and bonds trader operating from home, a perfect cocoon for his temperament. He'd chosen it well, she decided. Intellectual stimulation, the adrenaline of the markets, and no people. Plus, keeping yourself away from the daily hub-bub helped you filter out the noise and maintain perspective, a lesson he said he had gleaned from his earlier days freelancing as a journalist.

He claimed it was a useful tool in trading on the markets

as well as in everyday life but Sonya was never as convinced about the virtues of isolation. It did have its moments, like when she powered her motor bike down after a day's lecturing and she'd find him at their grey sliver of fence that overlooked the beach, ready for their ritual chat over a freshly-poured wine or whisky. She never knew if it was his first drink since alcohol didn't affect him as much her. Sonya was tall and slim so her vulnerability was a metabolism and fitness thing, nothing to do with her being a blonde as a friend once joked. As she'd head through the house to join Michael at the back fence, she'd try to guess from the wafting aroma what he had cooking. As well as a journalist, he'd also worked as a chef. What jobs hadn't he done? She'd pass by the dining table, usually set for two, often with a spray of fresh tulips. Like last night.

For Sonya tulips went with everything, even her job lecturing in business studies. It wasn't just their cheeky cup shape or their splashes of vivid colour. It was also the history of the manic speculation they'd fired up four centuries ago. Every year, she got a kick out of telling her students how Rembrandt earned less for his 1640s masterpiece, The Nightwatch, than the hammer price a single Viceroy tulip bulb got knocked down for at auction.

There were other kindnesses: gifts, and especially conversations. But Michael kept that side of him to their private world; the modern fetish for public displays of affection, even warmth, repelled him.

Where would she have been without him? Living comfortably on a university salary, for sure, but not in their beach house... well, hers actually... but that was another story. One she had certainly rationalised but never quite worked out.

A barbed sapling brushed against her but she palmed it off, just as she'd done for years to the gibes and gossip. Like Michael she didn't care for the sneering but, truth be told, she yearned that he would occasionally display his emotions so others could see him as she did. Her late mother had always stereotyped him. That he was so reticent, so uptight, because he was British. It wasn't that, Sonya was sure, but there was something. An itch she couldn't scratch.

Sonya knew she should speak to him about it, and she would.

Today.

Six minutes...

Heck, did she really care if he was reserved? Live for the moment! And with him, there were great moments. She brushed back some loose strands of hair, for a change blasé that the whole world could see she had one ear with a lobe and one without. It was an oddity she normally covered up with longer hair, even though Michael claimed he found it endearing.

How often had she engaged in these same arguments with herself? She would definitely raise it all with him today. For sure. What better time, now that he'd agreed, finally, to a baby? Thirty-five on her last birthday, she had certainly been hearing her body. Tick... tick...

The early morning sun slanted through the treetops, leaping from branch to branch like flames. She stopped at the viewing platform, drawing in the crisp sea-spray of the sou'-easterly and watching the wind-shadow skip across the water. An augury perhaps.

Her thoughts lingered, imagining that the rhythmic swell of the water was Michael, his chest rising and falling just as it had been when she'd slipped out of their bed that morning.

Their relationship had always had its edges. Until last night, Michael's stand-off against children, though always gracious, had been as hard as flint. Despite that, compared to the ditch her first marriage had careened into, her decade with Michael was a yellow brick road. There were the unexpected things. Like last night: "Let's go barging on a French canal," he'd said, "before our baby." Before our baby, a phrase lightly tossed in like a vinaigrette, and without any fanfare despite her years of badgering.

Surprisingly, she'd almost not registered it; the mere mention of an overseas trip had thrown her completely off-guard. After they'd quit New York for Sydney nearly nine years ago and despite their, or rather, his money, they'd only ever flown together within Australia. Never internationally. He, on the other hand. God! she thought, as she turned back onto the track, Michael was such a frequent flyer the airport security people probably knew his shoe size. He must have a trillion international frequent flyer miles but, she reminded herself, she had never enjoyed a single one.

His many, too many, business trips were fleeting, always rushed. Inevitably he returned dishevelled, as if he'd just been trekking for thirty days in Nepal rather than on a three-day flit to Los Angeles or some other business capital. In the beginning, she'd stressed herself about these trips—

what wife wouldn't?—but time wore her down and tolerating them simplified her life, despite her mother's finger-wagging: one failed marriage was enough, she'd repeatedly warned.

Four minutes...

A child. Sonya hurtled off the end of the track and her shoes dug into the white sand, so fine and clean it squeaked as it stopped her short. She slipped off her sweatshirt and wrapped it round her waist for her cool-down. Her red leotard top was crimson with sweat and her heartbeat was even outpacing her mind.

She'd come round the headland and this end of the beach was tapped in behind, sheltered from the south. Here the palms and eucalypts stood motionless. The barnacled boats moored in close were rocking imperceptibly from the rising tide and there was scarcely a jangle from their glinting halyards. The sun continued to chin itself above the horizon and paint colour onto the eastern cliffs, giving the final crescent of moon a razzle of gold.

She watched the water nudge against the beach, up and back. It hissed up the sand leaving a froth of lace for the seagulls to trample. As her breath slowed she watched the grey scavengers fluffing up their wings and poking their beaks underneath, picking out lice for their breakfast appetisers. A fledgling with a pink-grey beak and legs and spotted wings scrabbled to the water's edge and dipped its head in and out several times, shaking it in between.

Apart from a drifting foam of cloud, it was a still winter's morning. Sonya strode over the sand for her final stretch, certain this would be a good day... a good year.

But in three minutes, she'd discover how wrong she was.

At the far end of the beach, the familiarity, the odd ordinariness of their grey slatted fence sandwiched between much grander walls caused her to question Michael's sudden new leaf and by the time she reached the boardwalk, she was stamping the sand out of her soles as well as her scepticism.

Once again she questioned how she'd lasted so long with a man so guarded, so private. Obscurity and vagueness about his past hovered around Michael like a cloud of summer sand flies but though it was irritating, years of practice had taught Sonya to swat it off as yet another tolerable eccentricity. No longer. Not from today. Today the itch would be scratched.

She recalled how weeks after she'd moved into his New York apartment on Central Park West, she'd knocked his passport from his desk and two strange dried flowers fluttered out of it to the floor. They were shrivelled, brittle and brown though she guessed they'd once been white. Daisies perhaps. As she slid a page of the passport underneath the wilted blooms, carefully so they wouldn't disintegrate, she'd wondered if they were a memento. But of what? Or whom? She'd never asked. Flipping through the tattered passport that day, she saw some pages were ripped. The corner with his birth-date was gone. Cut or torn, she couldn't tell. But for the first time she saw his full name: Michael Will Hunt. His name was a sentence.

One minute...

She unlatched her gate smack on what she assumed was 7 AM. Courtesy of Ralph their pitch-black Labrador, the time seemed obvious. Ralph was not normally a barker but what usually got him yapping at this time was the racket from the builders a few doors up. Six days a week it was always the same. On the dot of seven the noise dam from the construction site legally sluiced open.

But wait. Apart from Ralph and the squawk of a seagull, and the hiss of the tide, there was no sound. No builders. Not yet. Sonya checked her watch: five before seven.

Something caught her eye and she jerked her head up at the house to see that the glass double-doors of their attic bedroom were ajar, swinging out onto their balcony.

Michael must be up but, at anything before 7:30, that was almost unheard of.

A lorikeet flashed past her, so close the green wingtip brushed her cheek. The bird perched on top of the left-hand balcony door and cocked its head, a scatter of sunlight fluorescing its blues and mauves.

As Sonya unconsciously wiped her cheek, the bird gave a raucous squawk and shot a repulsive stream of grey shit down the glass door panel. Sonya was not religious, yet the smear roused in her an ancient echo of parents daubing blood on their doors to ward away the angel of death.

A scatter of sand flew off her shoe as she kicked open the back gate but Sonya's eyes, puzzled, stayed fixed on the swinging doors upstairs. She almost tumbled over Ralph, needing to stabilise herself against the gate post. She started to reward the big lump of a dog with a scratch under his black muzzle but strangely he didn't roll over and offer his belly as he usually did. He simply pulled away from her and loped back toward the house.

Why was Michael up so early? She bent over, still huffing a little, her hands on her hips, and noticed her toe had jabbed into a small brown mound on the grass. Damn Ralph! She snapped her foot back from it, but on eyeing it closely she saw it was a knock of Michael's pipe tobacco. She squatted to test if he'd already been out here this morning but it was soggy, the same as the grass, and she also noticed how the lone track of her footprints leaving the house an hour earlier still lingered on the dew. No, Michael had not been outside. It was the same with Ralph's paw prints though she could see they were mostly in a crazy circle directly below the bedroom balcony, as if he had been chasing his tail. She tugged her ear, the one with no lobe. Something wasn't right.

Ralph came back to her and snatched at her sleeve, tugging her toward the house. A little jittery, Sonya shook him off, her eyes focused back up at the swaying doors. Even if Michael had opened them and come outside, why would such a stickler for neatness leave them unlatched like this? Maybe the phone had rung or he'd suddenly remembered something inside? She wiped the sudden clamminess of her palms on her sweatshirt.

Every morning when Sonya returned from her run, Ralph would feign sneaking inside under her guard, knowing that inside the house was off-limits—one of Michael's many exasperating rules. But today Ralph showed no sign of playfulness and simply plonked himself at the stoop, covering his head with his paws.

As Sonya headed upstairs, a low growl rumbled from deep in Ralph's throat. Halfway up, her nostrils flared into question as a faint, almost odourless smell insinuated the air. Old socks? Sweat? She ran her fingers through her hair and also over her tights to check if the parrot had deposited anything when it flashed past, but no. She pulled the shoulder of her sweatshirt to her nose, but it wasn't that either. Ralph? She sniffed again and turned her head back to see if he'd snuck in behind her but he was still at the door, watching her through his paws.

She padded up the stairs. At the turn-back, she started to make out murmurings from the bedroom TV. But with the breeze outside picking up, the balcony doors started to bang and the hallway door slammed shut.

"Hey!" she called. "Are you trying to bust the glass?"

There was no response. It must be that the TV was too loud, she decided.

Something held back her hand from turning the door knob. Eventually she turned it and slowly pushed open the door.

But Michael wasn't there. Guessing he'd be in the bathroom, she switched off the TV. But instead of silence or his radio blaring from the bathroom, all she heard were Ralph's growls drifting up from the garden.

Sonya slid open the bathroom door expecting to find Michael semi-dozed and with his undershorts splayed around his ankles. There was no Michael. "This isn't funny," she called out, her cry ricocheting uselessly off the tiles.

The lingering airlessness she'd felt on the stairs was now invading the bedroom as if it was stalking her. Her heartbeats hammered into her ears and her legs felt weak.

She twisted round to Michael's dressing room and yanked its door open so hard it banged against the wall, gouging out a chunk of white plaster which crumbled onto the floor.

Her stomach compressed into a fist that squeezed the air up and out of her lungs. Had Ralph seen something... had he been warning her?

She spun round like a drunk and ran downstairs. The door to Michael's office was wide open. He never left it like that. And that odour... it was stronger, mustier, like the mouldy crust of an overripe brie cheese that's been left out in the air too long. Or truffles... Michael loved black truffles, she remembered. He said he'd spent a season in France once sniffing them out with his own pig. Or maybe it was a dog. Either way, she didn't care. Not now.

Confused and panicked, Sonya stood framed in the doorway. It was more like an office furniture catalogue than Michael's office. His beechwood desk was almost bare, scattered only with a few loose papers. His leather chair was swivelled to face toward the window, as if he had turned his back on her. Even his beloved ashtray was empty. She walked over and lifted it to her nose for a whiff of him but it was cold antiseptic metal.

All that was left was an unplugged computer screen and his music player. She pulled open a desk drawer. Empty. She leant under the desk. A depression in the carpet marked where his computer console had been and a grey power cable snaked itself uselessly from nowhere to nowhere else, neither rearing nor ready to go.

How to explain it, other than the obvious? Maybe her mother had been right all along.

She stared blankly past his chair and out the window, frantic for a flash of inspiration. The edge of a cloud blocked the sun just for a moment and when the gloom passed, a brassy glint sparked up from the floor just between the wall and the desk. In a daze, she stooped for the gold-coloured disk and without thinking slid it into the slot in Michael's sound system as if tidiness were a substitute for action.

Suddenly she tore out to the garage. But both the car and the bike were still there. Unsure if she was pleased or disappointed she circled round the ancient SAAB, its grey enamel absorbing her despair. She unlocked the trunk but it weighed on her fingers. She'd read stories... seen movies... Eventually she lifted it. Apart from an umbrella, an old theatre program and a credit card slip from the supermarket, the space was empty.

She exhaled with a force as if she hadn't taken a new breath since she'd been upstairs in the bedroom. She slapped her side. Of course the vehicles would be here. Michael didn't drive. She drove the SAAB when the two of them were out together or if it was raining. The bike was her work horse, to weave her through peak hour traffic to and from campus. Actually, it was more than that. A twin-cylinder Ducati MH900 *evoluzione*, it was a tomato-red speed machine. But the three hundred kilograms of grunt she loved so much were as cold as she now felt.

As she lumbered back upstairs to their bedroom, she checked her watch. Again. An hour. She'd only been gone an hour.

She stood at the door rocking on the balls of her feet, indecisive, and finally crossed the room to stop the doors banging. Was she imagining it or were they waving farewell? She pushed them open to engage the latches, maybe to let fresh air in to flush the room. She was tempted to clean off the lorikeet shit with a tissue from the box beside the bed but left it there. As a marker.

She turned back into the room and spotted something on the bed, half-tucked under her pillow. It was a note.

Her eyes closed for a moment to calm her raging, thumping pulse but it was futile.

She dragged in her breaths. Her legs had barely the strength to carry her to the edge of the bed. She sat and, pointlessly, one hand tried steadying the other as she read it.

> My darling Sonya,
>
> Sorry our bliss had to end like this—with a scratched note—but I could hardly face you.
>
> We were a great couple. You know that.
>
> And though you'll always have the memory of our last May Day together and our walk to Calvary, without you I'll be ~~knowhere~~.
>
> Your love,
>
> ◆ ▫ ◆
>
> Mike

Blinking back sudden tears, denial scratched at her eyes and her heart. Last night, finally, he'd relented about a child.

And a trip. Hardly actions if he was planning an exit, she argued with herself. He had to be in trouble. Kidnapped, perhaps. But by whom? And why? And why this note but no ransom demand?

Last night. Had it been just a decoy? A cruel lure. To lull her? "The bastard!" she spat out aloud.

Her mother had been right. She had seen through him just like she'd sussed out Charles, Sonya's first husband. Yet now it seemed, she had wasted all those years by staunchly defending shit number two.

"*We were a great couple,*" said the note.

Were... The word slapped her hard.

Her life had already shifted into the past tense.

What would she tell their friends? Her friends, she corrected herself.

She edged herself off the bed. This, she thought, clenching the note in front of her face... this was not Michael. She gripped it harder to prevent her hands trembling but that made it worse.

Her bank loan. What about that? Surely Michael wouldn't just walk out and leave her in the...

She inched to the window and looked out across the water but tears blurred her vision and her mind struggled to focus.

There was something... She stepped back and again lowered herself onto the rim of the bed. She pulled up a corner of the blue bed sheet to wipe her eyes but it was still laced with last night... instead, she crumpled it in her hand and drew it up to her nose.

"*My darling Sonya...*" Her breath caught but knew she had to read on. "*My...*" Her eyes welled up but she pushed herself through the blur. It wasn't his usual old-style copperplate but it was still Michael's handwriting. Yet the words... they weren't his. Michael did not write this.

The maelstrom roiled around her and she fell back on the bed, clawing at the sheet.

He didn't write this...

A baby... The house... He wouldn't leave her.

But he had.

2

SONYA TRIED TO quell the sobs as she snatched for the phone, knocking her charm bracelet and the red tulip from last night to the floor. Even the coppery tang of blood didn't signal how sharply she was biting her lip. The sourness was no longer content down the back of her throat and it started its jolting, revolting, convulsing journey up.

She dropped the phone to the floor as she tore into the bathroom and tossed her head down into the toilet bowl, heaving and hacking her uncertainties.

She kept her head down, as if hiding from the truth.

It was a good thing she'd had her hair cut short.

SONYA had no idea how long she'd been kneeling in the white-tiled room but it was enough for the sun to have shifted behind a tree and for a hairline crack in the designer porcelain to have caught her attention and enough to learn how to spell *Villeroy & Boch*, as if she cared.

She gripped the sides of the toilet and pushed herself up from her cold, numb knees, wary that a cramp could crash her back down.

Light-headed but steady enough, she grabbed a washcloth, wetted it and pressed it to her mouth as she stumbled back to re-read Michael's note. She took it from the pillow where only an hour earlier his head had been and after poring over it twice more, line by line and word by word, she crumpled the page in a confused act of anger and despair and tossed it to the floor, shouting as if to convince herself, "He *was* forced to write this."

She knew she should call the police but worried about what pigeon-hole they'd slot her into. The deluded ranting of deserted wives? What if they were right?

Cautiously she re-entered Michael's dressing room, worried about what she might find there or, more particularly, not find there. Slowly her finger pulled the closet open. His pipe rack was still on top of the shelf unit with four of his six pipes. Michael running off without his treasured pipe collection? Not if his life...

She couldn't finish the thought but while it dangled above her like a blade twisting on a thread, she checked beside the bed. The pipe he'd tapped out last night in the ashtray, before they'd made love—his mahogany Calabash—yes, it was still there, lying next to where she'd rested the tulip and her bracelet. It was a contemplative sweep of a pipe, like a gourd, with a frothy white meerschaum bowl insert, the style Sherlock Holmes drooped out the side of his mouth when he wasn't jabbing himself with cocaine. It was J-curved, like an economy described by spin-doctor politicians, or a saxophone, and she reminisced how this pipe often brought out a soulful mood in Michael. It tended to be the one he reached for when he was relaxed and open, expansive, something which happened so rarely it was a welcome event. Just like last night or so she had thought.

She held the pipe to her nose, closing her eyes as she drew in a last sweet smell of his breath.

She wondered where his sixth pipe was, trying to picture it. It had a round-stem with a squat bowl like two truncated cones joined at their bases. According to Michael who as well as food and wine was a pipe connoisseur, it was a Straight Rhodesian Shell Briar.

So where was it?

"Damn the pipe," she swore as she slumped onto the bed, her head in her hands as she tried to make sense of this. He hadn't taken the other pipes so he was either coming back—yeah, right!—or someone had grabbed him and he'd left them behind as a sign for her.

Unconsciously she picked up the tulip, red as a stripper's lips, and brushed it under her chin, across her bare neck as he had, the aroma faintly waxy and green like cut flower stems. Tulips got into her soul. They compacted their glory for the eyes, their shocking colours leaving little energy for a bouquet. Her eyes clamped shut as if to hang on to only agreeable thoughts but her fingers showed otherwise as they closed around the flower head and crushed it.

Could he have phoned someone? Dropping the petals and the mutilated stem she leant over to the bedside phone, pressed redial and watched the screen flash up a number, but it was the restaurant she'd dialled last night to make their reservation for tonight. To celebrate. If Michael had made a call it wasn't from the house phone. Perhaps from her mobile? Hers, since he didn't have one. She leant back to her own bedside table to get it, scrolled down its calls log and crossed each one off in her mind—all calls she'd made herself.

Repeatedly wiping her mouth with the back of her hand, she kept asking herself questions. If it wasn't a kidnapping—if he'd chosen to go—how did he go? The car and bike were still there and he hadn't phoned for a cab. So someone—a woman?—must have been lurking in a vehicle outside waiting for Sonya to head off on her morning run. Her nails dug into her palms.

Another woman would explain his business trips and why he'd never asked Sonya along... and why he always lurched home like a wreck. "You big fuck!" she shouted, then shot a quick glance round, mortified by her swearing.

This morning had he really been asleep or was he play-acting? Did he sneak the balcony doors open to check when he was leaving? But why bother, since he could've just as easily peeked through the glass. Maybe it was to listen for the gate slamming shut when she returned? Did he wait for her to leave then let his "friend" in? The woman?

No, regardless of what her mother might have said if she'd still been alive, that was not Michael. He must have been taken. Kidnapped. But why? By whom? Michael had no enemies, not a single one so far as she knew. They'd been together for almost a decade so she'd know, right? In any case, apart from her, who on the entire planet did he engage with enough for them to learn to hate him? Dislike him? Easy. But hate him? She shook her head.

Was it his money? He'd certainly done well out of his stocks and bonds trading, amazingly so, as he'd told her, given the depressed bear market the world had suffered the last year or so. Maybe they... somehow they'd fooled him into opening the front door and swept him into a vehicle outside?

But why waste time taking his computer? Was something on it?

Whether he was kidnapped or just a deserting bastard, someone with transport was involved. At least that much was clear.

She ran out front onto the street, but there was no puddle of fresh-leaked sump oil on the drive. There were no tracks or tyre marks where they might have burned rubber speeding off. No telltale computer cables that had fallen out of laden arms. No dropped pipe. Just the morning newspapers rolled up in their tight plastic wrap, like fallen relay batons. Something moved near the bushes. A lizard. An eastern water dragon with its long tail curved round and pointing directly at her. The reptile stared at her, unblinking as if warning her, the black stripes running back from its eyes like eye-liner smudged by tears.

Sonya blinked first, and her eyes started scouring the road surface and the gutters for any clues. She glanced across the road to Tito and Naomi's. She'd have gone over to check if he was there, but she knew the couple were overseas. Naomi, a senior airline cabin attendant, was winging her way to Europe. Tito, a corporate chief executive, had jumped into a cab for the airport last night, on a trip to visit investors.

She knocked at the door of another neighbour. As Jack threw open the door her head was hung so low she noticed his bare feet, but not that he was pulling on a white singlet.

"No 'Good morning, Jack?' " he joked, tucking the top into his pants, but the smile dropped from his face when she lifted her head and he saw her eyes. He turned to call for his wife but Marion's "Who is it?" sang out from the depths of the house beating him to it. "Sonya," he yelled over his shoulder.

"It's Michael. He's gone."

HE chocks his bare ankles into the concrete corner of the cell, wedging his aching back into its cold embrace, habitual, familiar but hardly welcoming. Michael pounds a bug that isn't there into the floor. There is little there at all, except the small silver charm he conceals in his pocket. And memories...

She quivers as the tulip strokes her and closes her eyes letting her lips brush against his. His delusion licks at them too, unaware they have become parched and cracked.

3

"HE WROTE IT, but they're not his words?" said Jack, repeating to Marion what Sonya had just told them. "I don't get your meaning."

He wasn't deriding her but that's how Sonya heard it. "They're not his *normal* words," she snapped, thrusting the note at him. "See?" she finger-punched the page. "It's a clue, a code. He was forced to write this." At last she'd told someone else, and relief flooded over her.

"A code?" asked Marion, retying her white terry towel robe and looking down over Jack's shoulder at the crumpled sheet. She was trying to be more soothing than her just-give-me-the-facts husband, but the tactic didn't work. Sonya snatched the paper from Jack and pointed again, jabbing at the last sentence: *You'll always have the memory of our last May Day together and our walk to Calvary.* "May Day! What the hell is that? It's *help*, that's what."

Jack's emptied fingers tapped his pock-marked cheek just above one of his teenage acne scars. "It's also a, you know, a date," he countered.

"Who does May Day these days? And it's no date that's special for us. I was with you two, remember? And he was in Paris? Not in bloody Calvary, for damn sakes, wherever that is these days."

Jack and Marion did remember. They'd invited Sonya to join them to celebrate their wedding anniversary on May Day, the evening before their big day. Michael was originally supposed to have come too but ended up on an urgent flit to Paris, another of his famous sudden business trips.

"Isn't Calvary where Jesus was crucified?" Jack looked toward Marion since she was the church-goer.

"It means someone's got him," Sonya interrupted. "It's not the Bible thing. It's from the song in *Les Misérables*."

That musical was Michael's bible, thought Jack. He and Marion knew how much Michael loved it judging just by how many times they'd heard the soundtrack blaring out of Michael and Sonya's house, usually when she was out teaching at university. Once in exasperation Jack had even asked Michael if he owned any other music.

Sonya continued, "God, I know it by heart..."

Marian stared Jack down, killing off his predicted retort that anyone within hearing distance of their house would also know it by heart.

Jack cleared his throat. "It's something about a never-ending road to Calvary and, ah, men who know my crime, ah, coming a second time."

Sonya nodded. "There! Maybe he knows these people from before? You know, today could be the second time."

She looked up at Jack. "Well," she challenged his raised eyebrow. "What about this... his signature... 'Mike'. When did you ever—ever!—hear him call himself that?"

Sonya knew she didn't need to be delicate with this couple. Jack had joked about it often enough. "If your name was Michael Hunt," he'd pose with his thumbs thrust into his jacket pockets as Michael often did, "would you seriously call yourself Mike?" To Marion, it was funny even on the first repeat but she soon got bored with it and now always cringed as she waited for Jack's inevitable follow-up lines: "Just say it out loud," he would laugh. "Mike Hunt! Way smart parents, huh?" But he said none of it today, keeping a solemn face, though Marion had kicked him under the table to be certain.

"And that?" he asked, wincing but pointing to the symbols ♦□♦ Michael had written in above his shortened name. "What's that? Two eyes and a nose? He normally signs letters like that?"

"No idea," said Sonya.

4

SONYA KNEW FROM the start that Michael was unique, though a much better version of it than the slime-ball of a first husband she had washed her hands of just before they met.

Ten years ago, once her divorce papers were filed, she'd applied for every post-doctoral fellowship anywhere that bastard couldn't get to her without money. In other words, as far away from Australia as possible. Which was how she got to teach at the business school at Columbia in New York City.

Four years before that when she was twenty-two, her mother had begged her not to marry Charles. Not just because of her age or because she was in line for a university medal—a landmark achievement in their blue-collar family—but because mothers, Sonya later discovered, had a good nose for sniffing out parasitic shits, even if they'd never use such bad language themselves.

AFTER Sonya had been at Columbia only two months, the dean was impressed enough with her work on stock markets to line her up with a public lecture in the auditorium at the New York Stock Exchange: "It'll look good on your résumé," he'd said. But when she got to the top of Broad Street to gaze down on the pale stone castle of capitalism, a seething moat of people blocked her path. After asking a few bystanders, she learned that a nearby building had just had a bomb scare and its occupants were milling around until they were permitted back up. It was a couple of years before the infamous 9/11 attacks and the prevailing mood of the crowd was no more than casual inconvenience, annoyance without fear. People were checking their watches, not each other's faces.

Sonya was scanning over the throng trying to guess which tiny handful, if any, might actually be heading for her talk when a swift tug on her satchel pulled down her shoulder and a tee-shirted kid in battered white sneakers and a red baseball cap ripped off with it. This was her second mugging in three weeks! What was she, she wondered, a shit magnet? Wasn't Mayor Rudy Giuliani boasting only on yesterday's nightly news how he'd already single-handedly eradicated crime from New York City?

The kid cut through the mob using her bag as a knife. Sonya's face contorted in panic and her mouth formed a yell but she couldn't get out a sound. She felt as empty and useless as the godless figure in Munch's painting, *The Scream*. She tried to lunge after the thief but the crowd had closed up behind him. Too late.

Her notes for her talk were in the bag. Her résumé wasn't

looking so good now. Her wallet—her new one—was inside too. Pointlessly her head swivelled round searching for help. Surely someone had seen the crime? But all the gazes were transfixed elsewhere: on the wall-mounted ticker flashing up stock prices, at their watches, to the sky, at their shoes, anywhere but on her, or on him. No eye contact. Not in New York City.

Stretching up on her toes, she spotted the red cap bobbing toward an elderly man in his sixties, maybe seventies, she couldn't tell. The distance plus his speckled grey beard and dark glasses made an intelligent guess impossible. She guessed the thief would go right through him, either shoving him aside or knocking the old fellow down. But the man had witnessed the snatch; somehow she was confident of that. He was a little stooped with a knit jacket, tweed perhaps, draped over his shoulders. She imagined he'd once been tall... decisive... gallant... a decent man who would do something. As the bag-snatcher pushed through, the man withdrew his pipe from his mouth and... he stepped back... He let the creep pass right by without lifting a finger. He even bowed him a civil *¡Hola!* like a matador flourishing his cape but letting the bull charge right through. Damn New Yorkers!

A woman close by Sonya with shiny black hair, wearing a warm Mediterranean complexion and a rank-smelling rayon floral blouse smiled back at her flashing her gap-toothed mouth and lifting Sonya's heart a little. But instead of offering down-to-earth practical help or local advice, the woman simply shrugged and turned her eyes away like almost everyone else.

When Sonya looked back, the red cap—forty, fifty people away—was no longer bobbing and weaving. He'd stopped, his escape blocked by a serious-looking man who strangely also smoked a pipe, his thumbs jammed into his jacket pockets, like a trial lawyer. Probably the only two men in New York still smoking pipes and she got both of them. But this one was younger. A little taller. The thief's confident escape faltered and he attempted small sideways movements, testing his challenger, sizing him up. Sonya gripped herself. Would the gentleman hold firm? She saw him fix a smile on the kid: it was a tranquil, almost carefree gesture. Michael gazed deep into the boy's jumpy eyes and held a hand out for the spoils.

A queer sensation welled up in Sonya… what was it? This man's calm intensity was unnatural. He seemed unfazed, as though he had been watching, waiting for this. It was a feeling that often lingered round Michael. One she would become accustomed to.

Michael forced himself through the crowd to her, holding the recaptured booty above his head in his left hand as if to prevent another marauder's attempt. He passed the bag over to Sonya and politely dipped his head. The woman who'd earlier shrugged resignation cackled though the gaps in her teeth and slapped him on the back. The elderly bearded gentleman waving his own pipe at them as if to say "Job well done" smiled and slowly turned on his heels to melt into the crowd.

"I'm so relieved," she said. "I don't know how…"

"I'm thinking you could use a coffee. A strong one," Michael smiled. "May I?"

"After what you've done?" She caught her watch out of the corner of her eye. "Please... let me."

Worrying about time, Sonya ordered for both of them as Michael held her chair out for her. Before he sat, he formally offered her his hand across the table, and as she took it she noticed that even if his knurled pipe hadn't been peeking out of the pocket of his tweed jacket, his bearing would still have seemed a bit provincial. Her dad was the last of the pipe smokers she'd known, yet today she'd come across two.

Though superficially his eyes were the colour of cold steel, they twinkled at her from their otherwise serene setting in his broad, pale face. She liked the calm strength of that. There was something vaguely academic about him—maybe it was the leather elbow patches—and she wouldn't have been surprised if he'd once had a beard to conceal the small scar on his chin. The harsh, jagged scar oddly emphasised the waviness of his hair, blond on the cusp of grey and his nose with its hawkish thrust added to the impression he was distinguished if not scholarly. He combed front to back with not a single strand out of place. He was clearly particular. Probably mid-thirties, she guessed, ten years on her.

When he stirred his coffee, she noticed the scarred knuckles on his left hand, silently speculating about their cause and wondering if his chin got its scar at the same time.

As they talked, his accent intrigued her. It was elegant and crisp yet nondescript, heading toward an upper Boston lilt, neither American nor British. More Kennedy than Kennedy. She'd have loved to ask where he was from but she wasn't

New York enough to ask straight out so she poked her spoon at her coffee. Later she did ask and, yes he was from Britain but it was "way back". His lack of a definitive accent, when she did probe him, was apparently from his years spent in so many countries.

"How long have you been travelling?" she asked.

He looked up at the sky and smiled, "It seems like centuries," he said, then passed her the small plate of cookies the waiter had brought for them.

From the start Michael was an eloquent raconteur although she bristled at his tendency to skip details and shrug off her attempts to probe. She did manage to extract out of him that as well as Europe and North America, he'd travelled in South America—in Colombia, Cuba, Bolivia, Chile and Argentina—and in Africa, it had been Kenya and Tanganyika.

"Isn't that part of Tanzania?" she asked, a little confused by his use of a long defunct country name.

He grinned and slapped his wrist in mock rebuke.

Asia, he said, had taken him to Cambodia, Japan and Malaya, which he quickly corrected before she did, to Malaysia.

Once, years later, she thought she'd even caught him referring to Siam the pre-1949 name for Thailand, famous for cats and twins and, according to him, a gentle people but unrelenting mosquitoes. His occasional lapses into using outdated names for countries perplexed her.

They'd been talking so long they'd mostly ignored their coffees apart from using them as props to stir and poke. Michael glanced up at the clock on a nearby building and pushed back his chair. "Dr Wheen," he said, acknowledging the recently-awarded doctorate she'd managed to slip into their conversation. It would be another few days before his manners, despite her insistence, licensed him to use her first name. "I have no idea of time," he said, with a lop-sided, wry smile. But she couldn't see the joke.

Not then.

As they stood, Michael asked permission to attend her lecture and Sonya guessed—or rather hoped—that it wasn't just civility or even her topic, a controversial one she hoped back in 1999: "Market Bubbles... When the dot.com will dot.bomb and why."

At the auditorium door with only minutes to go, a distraught official breathed relief. With a firm hand at the small of Sonya's back he marshalled her to the lectern and waved Michael towards one of the many empty seats.

It was a good thing thought Sonya as she stepped up to the lectern that résumés only listed your papers, and not the level of interest they attracted.

5

"HOW MUCH?" SONYA asked Detective Inspector Sorden.

The inspector, a thickset man with wiry salt and pepper hair, looked down at his notepad and repeated the amount. "One hundred and sixty-three million." He'd been on the case only two days but he'd already tracked that down. His forensic team had delivered the goods as far as he was concerned, especially considering Michael's computer was missing and they had to piece everything together through his internet provider.

According to these records, Michael had dispatched his money—an astonishing $163 million—on an electronic trip to a tax haven, and all done just minutes before Sonya returned home to find him gone, "A one-way trip I'm afraid, ma'am."

She noticed him eyeing her warily. If only a fraction of that amount had gone missing, added to Michael's single-mindedness about privacy, most cops would automatically suspect that he, and maybe Sonya, could be perpetrating some insurance mega-scam.

The police work had been impressive. After Sonya had first called them they'd moved fast, checking exchanges, brokers and other finance houses for details of Michael's accounts and trading—and hers she suspected, though she'd done very little of that despite being an associate professor at the business school.

Having run through his findings, Detective Sorden wound his arms backwards so he could shake his jacket off onto the back of his chair. The brown two-button job was crumpled, a bit dated and over-sized as if he'd recently lost weight. His crimson tie was flecked with grey but was otherwise non-descript, its knot pulled loose and low, down near the second button below his shirt collar. With his jacket off, Sonya's eyes locked onto the wash of blue ink that stained his white shirt pocket. This was a man who sorely needed a woman. His police partner, on sick leave with a stomach bug, couldn't possibly be a woman she decided or she'd have nagged him to death about his appearance. Or maybe she had. Sonya knew what her mind was doing: grabbing at any diversion, trying to avoid focusing on the policeman's revelations.

He'd told her that not only had Michael's money gone—an amount far, far more than she'd ever imagined possible—but so had the million-dollar collateral he'd lodged with the bank to secure their house mortgage. She knew that without this security, the three-million-dollar loan—in her name alone—would catapult her into instant default with the bank.

In the two days since Michael's disappearance, she'd already been panicking about it. There was no way now she could even meet the interest payments but this was way worse. Without any collateral, the bank would call for its entire three million right now.

To get her loan originally, the bank had insisted that Michael give his personal guarantee and put up a hard million-dollar deposit.

"How could the collateral be gone?" she asked the inspector, confusion contorting her face. "The bank had security over that money. We signed a mountain of legal..."

"The bank's got a red face, ma'am, but that won't bring the dough back."

Or Michael, she reflected.

Her financial arrangements with Michael were odd, she knew that, but until now she'd never had to explain them to anyone except a fool bank manager.

But Sorden was a cop and he pressed her. "We gotta ask. Can't always tell what's relevant," he smiled, revealing a shred of hamburger meat lodged between his teeth.

She blurted out the facts aware how, well, dumb they sounded. When she and Michael came to Sydney from New York they'd rented the beach house. He'd rented it actually. It was not much more than a timber shack back then. Definitely the worst house on the street, she justified with her working class discomfort over the trappings of wealth she now enjoyed. After a few years they bought it. Well, she did, she clarified. With the bank loan. And his guarantee.

No, she answered, buying it in her name wasn't a tax dodge or anything like that. It was just that Michael got the shakes at the mere idea of owning any major assets. She could never fathom why but he'd never let his name appear on any public register, as if he was afraid to acknowledge his own existence. Though they told everyone they were married, they'd never made it official. The car, the bike... even those were in her name.

She'd suffered Michael's sermon so often: houses, cars, boats... he wouldn't own any of them. Selling them took ages, so the risk was greater that the price could fall away from under you, he'd say. Then there were fees, commissions, taxes and duties, a feeding frenzy for a shark-infested pool of agents, auction houses, lawyers and governments keen to sink their sharpened teeth into your hard-earned money.

Rent everything! It was his article of faith.

Some old quote Sorden had once heard drifted into his head: "If it flies, floats or fucks, rent it, don't buy it." He wasn't about to ask Sonya if she knew who'd said it originally though if he had she could have told him.

Sorden tuned back in as she was finishing off: how Michael craved privacy the same way some people sought celebrity... until they got it. He didn't have a driving licence either, probably for the same reason, which was why she was the driver.

Consequently, she continued, Michael had restricted his investments to trading shares, bonds, commodities and currencies. Their magic according to Michael was that one five-year government bond was as good as any other paying the same rate, provided you chose the right government, since even they could go broke. One share in The Coca-Cola Company was the same as another. And the trading costs were minuscule, especially for big traders.

And in normal times you could buy and sell these assets in the flash of an eye or the click of a mouse. You didn't have to wait the weeks or months like with real estate. And best of all it could be private, anonymous since you didn't have to put your own name on a stockholder register. Michael registered everything in the names of his brokers' nominee companies.

To Sorden none of that was rocket science. He'd been working serious crime for fourteen years so he'd heard most rationalisations about most things and Sonya's was pretty tame, lame even. "Why is any of that relevant to me?" he said, intentionally resisting the urge to scratch his head. He didn't want to look dumb to a professor.

"Okay," said Sonya, rubbing her forehead and trying to push against the load of a three-million-dollar defaulting mortgage, "He wouldn't own anything fixed, but me... I'm the opposite. I've got a thing about impermanence."

"A thing?"

She took in a deep breath. "My parents owned their own house, a semi-detached in Marrickville. It wasn't big, not worth a lot. They bought it with Dad's war veteran's loan," she said quickly, the words stumbling out of her mouth, "but it was theirs, see? And the bank's of course. They always said people had to own their home."

She gave a nervous laugh and looked up from the table noticing a questioning look on Sorden's face. "Vietnam," she said. "Dad was in hospital for ages after he came back. My mother was a nurse there." She watched the detective write something in his spiral notebook. "Then with my first marriage—I was married for four years before I met

Michael—we had no money. I was studying for my doctorate and he was a drop-kick, a loser, always chasing get-rich-quick schemes that kept us poor. Anyhow," she said, "by the time it ended, I had nothing… nothing to show for the whole sorry mess. No husband, no home, no money, no nothing."

No child, either.

Her sobs came out of nowhere.

"HUH?" said Sonya, unsure of what Detective Inspector Sorden had said.

"Mr Hunt? I asked where you first met him."

"Sorry," she said, wiping her eyes. "After the divorce I had to get away. I got offered a one-year teaching fellowship in New York and that's where we met. When my year was up, I returned here and, ah, he came too."

"And the house?"

"The h…? He had some things to tidy up in New York so I flew back to Sydney a few days before him. I stayed with my parents. They were so happy to see me. They're both gone now," she added. "After Michael arrived, he went looking for a place to live, found the beach house and we rented it. I fell in love with it the minute I saw it."

Sorden waited but passed her a tissue packet from his pocket.

"I wanted us, you know, eventually to buy a house, not just rent," she sniffed. "A place we could grow old together. Own it jointly, of course, but no… he wouldn't do that. 'If *you* want to own it, *you* buy it,' he said. 'Oh, sure,' I said, 'on a university pay packet.' As if."

"And…"

"After a couple of years of me hassling, Michael had this brainwave—it's what we ended up doing—that I'd buy the house in my own name. The bank would do it because he'd put up a personal guarantee as well as hard cash for collateral."

And, she pondered, where was she now? No Michael, no money, a massive debt and, it followed almost certainly, no home. No bricks and mortar, as her father used to say.

Charles all over again, but worse. This time, she was thirty-five and the world, not just her world, had turned to shit. A tenured associate professorship was at least some security but the extra money she'd been getting from consulting to big corporations and investment banks was becoming less frequent as the financial crisis worsened. The timing was miserable. Everything was miserable.

"This hundred and… this money," she spluttered, finding it hard to come to grips with her anger as well as the extraordinary sum that Sorden had revealed to her. If Michael had so much money but he wouldn't own the damn house himself, why hadn't he simply given her the dough and she could have bought it for cash? Even if he'd lent it to her…? What had he been thinking? She almost laughed. What a question. She never knew what he was thinking so why was this any different?

Instead, here she was, loaded up with a debt she had no way of repaying and a house the bank would have no hesitation in tossing her out of.

"It was all in offshore companies and trusts," said Sorden. "Nothing in his own name. That gels with what you've been saying. Look, this thing about not using his name...," he shifted in his chair. "Was it because he was hiding from someone?"

6

SONYA NEEDED air. She threw her leg over her Ducati, its vivid red almost a match for the blood coursing into her face. Her passion for motorbikes had started long before boys, when her dad first let her drive his prized 1949 BSA Bantam on a backstreet, illegally of course.

Right now she needed air, lots of it rushing past to cool her, and speed to calm her. With a force that could have crushed a skull she jammed her foot down on the non-existent kick-starter, her good luck ritual ever since riding her dad's Bantam, a futile habit mechanically and now, she realised, also fruitless in the luck stakes. She revved the bike up with the handlebar throttle until she screamed off in a roar of pulse-raising power, leaving behind a stink of burnt rubber and a relationship built on lies.

"THIS won't take long, professor," Derek Minchin said smoothly. It was an oily foot-in-the-door tactic, more befitting a vacuum cleaner salesman than a bank manager. She was wary. Outside of university circles, people only called her "professor" if they wanted something or if it was bad news.

Sonya had only switched off her bike's ignition ten minutes earlier and her head was clear, enough to sense an ambush. "Don't you normally phone first?" she asked but she widened the door for him.

She couldn't place why but she sensed some reticence and discomfort in his demeanour, but dismissed the notion that even a seasoned banker might have a conscience before tossing a grief-stricken woman out on the street.

"The bank has a serious problem," Minchin said, framing his task as impersonally as possible. It's not me, it's them, she imagined him thinking. Even though he looked pale and drawn, Sonya reminded herself that she was the victim and he was the vulture.

"The collateral?" Sonya volunteered. There was no point hiding from it.

"Exactly," he smiled weakly, grateful to be dealing with an educated woman. He slipped a hand inside his pocket. "The bank would like you to pay us out."

"Pay you out," she said, not really asking. The only way to pay them out was to sell up, and that wasn't an option she wanted to consider.

"This is difficult, isn't it?" Minchin pulled his hand back out, empty; he'd forgotten to bring a handkerchief for the sweat already starting to bead on his upper lip.

Soon enough, he got to the bank's bottom line.

"Pay within twenty-one days… or the property goes on the market?" Sonya exhaled. Saying it out loud was harder than knowing it.

"Technically the bank only has to give you a seven-day grace period," he explained, "but of course professor, in the circumstances..." He let it hang.

Sonya was stunned but Minchin knew enough to stay quiet.

As she gathered her thoughts her irritation built, "This house is worth a lot more than what I owe on it," she said, thumping the arm of her chair.

He coughed uneasily into his hand and then straightened his tie, even though it wasn't askew. "Actually, it *doesn't* cover what you owe..."

"Excuse me?" Sonya interrupted. "The loan is three million, right?" Vocalising the amount caused her breath to catch.

He nodded.

"And a house down the street sold a few months ago for six. You do know that?"

"I do." He cleared his throat.

"So why doesn't mine more than cover the loan?"

Minchin responded, "Well, your property has a smaller lot size..."

"But it'd still get more than three million!"

"True. Even in this market we think you'd get around three-and-a-half, four if you're really lucky. But when you add the interest that's been accumulating..."

"Michael paid all the..."

"Not for the last..."

Sonya cut him off, "What are you saying?"

"The *original* arrangement," said Minchin, "was that you'd repay us the three million in a single payment after thirty years—twenty-five or so from now..."

"I know that..."

"...and in the meantime Mr Hunt would pay us the interest due every six months."

"Exactly..."

"Professor, hear me out. Please. For the first year that's what happened. But then he approached us... me, actually, and we changed the arrangement..."

"You mean you changed *my* arrangement..." said Sonya getting even pricklier.

Minchin was on weak ground, he knew that, so he sidestepped. "That first year, the property market had been rising strongly and he asked us to let the interest accumulate. Since we had the million as collateral, his personal guarantee, and the mortgage over the house, we were happy to oblige."

"*You* might've been happy... What you're telling me," Sonya continued, leaning forward so their foreheads almost touched, "is he's paid no interest for..."

"Four years."

"How much is owed?" Sonya asked, her mouth dry and her eyes an inch from his. "The exact amount?"

Minchin hooked his finger under his collar and pulled it away from his throat. "At current rates, roughly $180,000 per year or a total of $720,000 for the four years but..."

"Seven hund...!"

"... it's been compounding, with interest on the unpaid interest..."

"The number?" said Sonya, almost squeaking.

He looked down at a piece of paper he'd been clenching in his fist, "As of this morning, $813,672.23 to be precise. In unpaid interest, that is."

"Holy…," screeched Sonya, throwing herself back in her chair. "Plus the three million?"

He nodded, but kept his eyes fixed on his note.

Sonya got up and opened the window. "How much exactly are you expecting me to pay… in the next twenty-one days that you've so graciously offered me?"

"Nothing, provided you fix an auction date for within a few weeks of that."

"So I have what… five, six weeks?"

He nodded.

She felt an urge to lunge for his throat. "$3.8 million… Jesus. After I pay a selling agent, auction fees, advertising, lawyers… taxes and whatever else there is, I'd be lucky to net anything like that amount."

"Our point exactly," said Minchin, unclasping his hands, ready to rise.

But Sonya walked over and pressed down on his shoulder. "Mr Minchin!" He was sweating so much she could almost see herself reflected in the shine from his scalp. "Without even asking me… the owner of the property… you've done this secret deal with a… a… a man who's vanished. For all you knew, he could have been a bloody con artist. Hell! He doesn't own this house, I do… and you have the gall to sit here telling me this is *my* problem?"

"Look…"

"*You* look. That collateral… those funds… Michael's promise to pay the interest… a promise, I remind you, to protect me as much as your lousy bank. I never would've… never could've taken your loan otherwise."

The bank manager's cheeks were red but Sonya couldn't imagine where the blood was coming from unless he'd sucked it out of a previous client. As Minchin was forced to look up at her, he drew down his upper lip between his teeth and he circled his finger between his collar and one of his chins.

"Mr Minchin," Sonya said, "let me say this in the nicest possible way…" What she desperately wanted to say was *Fuck you and fuck your bank*, but she couldn't. "The missing collateral is your problem, not mine. Now please leave…"

He tried to speak but Sonya stopped him by holding up her finger an inch from his nose. Leaning down, she whispered, "Leave… please."

If he had been wearing a hat Minchin was the old-school type who would still have tipped it goodbye.

7

A DAY LATER when Detective Inspector Sorden next came by, Sonya sensed he was holding something back. It wasn't just that he resisted her questions but his own probing was circuitous, with no apparent pattern. She was certain he had a point but he was taking his time getting to it. In truth he was waiting for a phone call.

"You had no idea how much he was worth?"

"How many times do I…? Look, he never told me how much money we… *he* had. He'd never even discuss his investments with me," said Sonya even telling Sorden about the brass plaque Michael always kept on his desk.

"Can you show it to me?"

"No, it's gone. But it said '*Follow your own mind*'. He said it was to remind him not to let himself get swayed by other people's opinions." She shrugged, "As if he needed a sign! I always wondered if it was all an excuse… part of his privacy paranoia."

Sorden flipped her through the pages in a spreadsheet printout of Michael's trading that his team had pieced together. Michael's record was nothing short of brilliant. She saw that his ability to anticipate markets was unfailing. How could that be, she wondered? And seeing it in print... the extent... the detail... how could he have kept all that from her?

Worse, what else didn't she know?

But Sorden pressed on. He pointed out that most of Michael's trading had been in options, whether over bonds, shares, currencies or commodities. Sonya reeled back when she saw his enormous gold and oil plays. Not only were the amounts he traded huge but he won every time. On one trade, he'd earned himself a $10 million profit.

"Hang on," said Sonya, perplexed. "There's not one loss-making trade here. There's no way you can do that. No matter how smart you are."

Sorden had hit the same quandary himself, the reason why he'd put his three-man forensics team on the job to see what they'd missed. But there was nothing more. After all their work their simple conclusion was that either Michael was a unique trader, a one-of-a-kind, or he had amazing luck. Sorden had briefly wondered if Michael was some sort of well-connected insider trader, illegally dealing off confidential information, but he dismissed the notion. With most of Michael's trades in commodities, currencies and bonds, Sorden knew that inside knowledge was virtually impossible.

But what intrigued Sorden and his team, even more than Michael's infallibility, was that his winnings "only" amounted to $163 million. But Sorden didn't mention that to Sonya. "We looked for losing trades, sure we did," he said. "But this is everything." Suddenly, he saw Sonya's back stiffen. "What is it?" he asked.

"Nothing," she lied. What caught her eye was a single line on one of the spreadsheets: an options trade in ZipChip Corporation. According to the entry, Michael had bought them only two weeks earlier. It was his timing that first shocked her. That date... it was just after he'd bawled her out for buying ZipChip shares herself, for her superannuation fund. The two of them had been enjoying a lunchtime barbecue with their neighbours, Tito and Naomi Wells. Well, Sonya had been enjoying it. Michael tolerated it. Tito was ZipChip's new chief executive. She and Michael had been standing at the buffet while Tito and Naomi were inside fixing drinks, and when Sonya told Michael about her share purchase he grabbed her, something he'd never done before.

Sorden saw her rubbing her arm. "Are you okay?" But before she could answer, his mobile phone rang and he jumped up to take it by the window.

Why, she wondered, would Michael buy ZipChip options when he'd only just scorched her for buying the shares herself? She pulled the spreadsheet closer. Ah, she noticed, they were 'put' options, the options you buy if you think a stock price is about to fall. He was right. Of course! In those two weeks ZipChip had dropped, though far less than the overall market.

Why did he buy put options, and why then? It was almost too much to think about but, still, she tried putting the pieces together. Yes, he was a top trader, a secretive and apparently unbelievably wealthy man who took frequent and short "business" trips. Sorden, it was obvious to her, thought Michael had skipped off with another woman. No kidnap, no fraud, no crime. Just utterly wretched heartbreak.

But she... she knew otherwise. Everything could equally point to financial fraudsters who'd tracked his trading and kidnapped him. If Sorden could reconstruct it all so easily—without access to Michael's computer—so could sophisticated criminals. Perhaps one of his brokers was involved? She would mention it to Sorden when he got off the phone.

But if there was another woman why had she been so blind? She brought her charm bracelet up to her mouth. Because she'd become complacent? Because she'd craved security... for bricks and mortar... for a child...?

She heard Sorden finishing his call. "Coffee?" she asked as she stood up. Anything for some thinking space.

Sorden coughed. "Professor?"

She was already filling the tank on the espresso machine with fresh water. "Hmm?" she replied, her nerves sharpened.

He coughed again. "I... er... need to double-check Mr Hunt's trips with you."

"What about them?" Sonya switched on the espresso machine to warm the cups stacked on top and returned to the table where Sorden was now leaning back against his jacket.

He slid across to her the list of Michael's trips she'd constructed with him on his previous visit. "You're still certain of these?" he asked.

"Why wouldn't I be?"

He cleared his throat and when he spoke it was soft. "That call I took just now? No one by the name of Michael

Will Hunt either left or entered the country on any of those dates..."

"Maybe I got them slightly..."

"...or any dates near them."

"They're idiots! Check with the airlines... or with Immigration." Sonya twisted her bracelet. Michael had given it to her. At least he had the second time.

Originally the antique was a gift from Sonya's mother. In the *something old, something new* tradition she had clasped it round Sonya's wrist on her wedding day to Charles. But when Sonya was mugged in New York the time before she met Michael, the punk had not only snatched her wallet but ripped off her bracelet.

Four weeks later, with a flute of Krug champagne, Michael presented her with a small box, neatly wrapped in red damask paper and tied with a black silk ribbon. When she'd opened the lid, she stuttered, "W-where'd you get this?" She'd lightly fingered the chain, sliding it round to examine the charms one-by-one, all miniature busts of scientists, writers, and other historical figures. They were all there back then, including her favourite, Adam Smith the moral philosopher. It wasn't a bust of Smith since he'd apparently refused to sit for artists. Instead, it was a ruffled eighteenth-century shirt sleeve cast in silver with a hand in clear perspex: his famous "invisible hand". She'd found it rummaging one day in a second-hand jeweller's in New York.

Michael had shrugged. "I've been fossicking all over the city for something close to what you described. But the same one? What are the odds of that?"

The invisible hand. Out of habit, her fingers were feeling for it even though she knew it had since fallen off somewhere. She'd first noticed it missing the day Michael had gone, when she picked up the bracelet from her bedside table. Over the years other charms had broken or fallen off but they usually turned up under the bed or a sofa. But not this time. Not yet.

"We *have* checked with the airlines *and* with Immigration. That's what that call was about. He didn't leave the country at all, not under any names we have for him."

"Names?" she asked, her cloud of suspicion growing even darker.

"Michael Will Hunt... Michael Hunt. And Mike...," he hesitated, a faint blush tinged his cheeks. "Is there any other name?" he asked, watching her carefully for the slightest sign of guilt or nerves.

She turned away, glancing out the window, a weak shrug suggesting she wasn't so sure. She wasn't certain of much right now.

Again, he coughed. "See, the thing is, professor... Mr Hunt hasn't got a passport."

"He's British," she said, recalling the two flowers that had fluttered out of the old one she'd chanced upon a decade ago.

"You said that last time. But the Brits have no record of him either. We checked with the Americans and the Canadians, too. Nothing. I'm sorry," the inspector said. He leant back, and folded his arms over his chest, "So if he didn't go overseas when he claimed to, where did he go?"

Sonya put the energy required to answer Sorden's question into giving her bracelet a workout, rubbing one of the charms—Karl Marx—so hard that the detective could see the bead of blood ooze from her thumb.

Again and again her mind swept over Michael's so-called trips and his clearly lame excuses, excuses that even at the time didn't make sense but which she'd always been too ready to accept at face value.

She was oblivious to the blood now coating Marx's beard, as red as the tulip Michael had brought to their bed for their last night together.

8

M*OST PEOPLE TRUDGE their years, plodding one day at a time but Michael had surged through his. What he'd crammed into his life was from everywhere. A scoop from now... a chunk from then. But that was once...*

Whenever it was, his body was now wasted... his spirit sapped. Randomly, he would wake in any one of twelve different environments. "Environments," they claimed, were better than a cell but not to him.

On the cold cracked concrete beneath his shabby cot, feeble echoes of his blood shrivelled into flaking rusty curls, like the stray shreds of tobacco he once tamped into his beloved pipes. He dropped his hand to the floor to feel one of them but, as before, his fingertips passed right through them. Like the environment itself, they were a hologram.

His dim, grey eyes hauled themselves up from the floor, way up, to check whether the square of tempered glass was still there, so crusted with pigeon shit it mocked the skylight it was supposed to be.

He'd named this environment "Dante". He picked a name for them all, to make them more familiar, less frightening, but the tactic only partially worked.

The far corner of the cell was bare but it wouldn't last. He waited... he had nothing better to do. And out of nowhere the TV screen appeared and he watched, again and again, a ten-minute loop of what had happened during the morning he'd gone. As always it was stuck on repeat, the same loop... Sonya, naked, slips out of bed, careful not to wake him... she dresses quietly and leaves for her run... then the two men somehow materialise beside him.

Why hadn't he foreseen it? He knew the answer: hubris... the arrogance of knowing everything, yet grasping nothing.

He wrenched himself up and stood next to the chair. Yes, it was really there. After three deep breaths he picked it up and hurled it at the screen, but as with every previous time it passed right through it and vanished behind it. The loathsome clip droned on.

A tear of regret—maybe guilt—might have seeped from an eye if they weren't so dried out. But instead, self-loathing clawed his chewed nails into his thigh, scraping deep into his rail-track scars and oozing another penitent drizzle of blood down his leg.

9

THE *AMERICAN LAWYER* magazine rated Black + Lieberman as the major league law firm that generated the highest profits-per-partner in the southern hemisphere. The firm rivalled the US and UK mega-firms even in their best years.

Al MacAntar had become quite a wheel in the world of corporate law and was next-in-line as B+L's senior partner. Despite his thirty-eight years, his sun-starved complexion and prematurely sparse hair led most clients to assume he was a learned decade or two older, an image-crafting error he was happy to cultivate. When two months earlier the International Bar Association honoured Al by electing him chair of its worldwide corporate law section, he celebrated by boosting his charge-out rates twenty-percent even in the face of the weakening global economy.

For years Al had kidded himself that his legal success was an extra chip that might help win Sonya over but he'd never got close to putting it to the test. His first big chance was when she needed her divorce from Charles and he was the lawyer she turned to. Back then he was a senior associate but conveniently, because of professional ethics and his own lack of family law expertise, he fixed up one of the firm's specialists to handle her case. That way he could snuggle by her side as her confidante and help navigate her through it, all the while inveigling himself into the gap left by Charles. But his plan was foiled when she packed herself off to New York.

The years since hadn't changed Al much though he'd masterfully honed his hangdog jowls and his roly-poly humour into convenient tools of his trade. His close professional colleagues admired him as an artist when it came to negotiation, always amused by his practised air of a slow-witted pushover with people who didn't know him.

With Sonya Al couldn't pretend. He might be able to put together the biggest, toughest, most complex deals but she was his bugbear. He'd tried so many times, even as far back as university. It had become an endearing joke between them. Except for Al it wasn't funny.

BLACK+Lieberman's main conference room sat thirty at a pinch, though today Al was ensconced there with only Sonya and Karen Longly, his brightest associate whose red hair, rouged cheeks and deep olive skin made Sonya look as pallid and lifeless as putty.

Only yesterday in the same room Al had tied up a multi-billion-dollar biotech merger codenamed Project Helium. All big corporate deals had codenames. But that was yesterday. Today was no day for games, at least not that sort. Not given how miserable Sonya looked.

Al had recently levered Karen Longly out of the firm's criminal law department to come work with him. It had been a battle to spring her but it had been worth it already. Al needed the fiery redhead's mind and he didn't object to her body.

To suit Al the three of them sat at the top end of the long table within arm's reach of the mini-bar. Standing at attention in a neat row in front of Al were three Coke bottles, all Diet, two of them already empty. Sonya was nestling the same bottle of mineral water Al had offered her when they'd commenced an hour earlier, and Karen was onto her second coffee. Judging by the cappuccinos, macchiatos, and other assorted espressos on offer from the firm's natty black-tied waiter, and the donuts, danishes and cookies piled up before them on large platters, Sonya wasn't sure whether this law firm was servicing its clients or its partners, some of whom she'd noticed were even pudgier than Al. Whether it was to keep her figure or because she didn't like them, Sonya couldn't tell, but Karen ate none of the treats, instead staying focused on the work in front of them.

Even with the plush red velvet drapes pulled back the harbour vista from this high-rise floor didn't rate a moment's glance. In yesterday's highly-charged final negotiations for Project Helium, the overseas executives oohed and aahed over the view but, unlike Sonya, they were playing with other people's money—their stockholders'—so they didn't seem to mind wasting time on banter, even if Al was gouging them $900 per hour to listen to their jokes.

His fee for yesterday's deal brought his tally for the year up to double his budget. It was a backslapping effort in any year let alone this dreadful one so he could easily justify pushing an entire day's work aside to focus on Sonya. With mixed motives—a steady hand for an old friend in trouble, as well as a chance finally to wangle his way into her heart— Al was hunched almost single-mindedly over the items scattered across the table: spreadsheets, a giant-sized blue legal document, assorted law books and a laptop computer. Like a crumpled English bulldog spotting a new bone, Al's doleful features were fixed on the memo Karen had been up all night writing for him.

Sonya rose to get herself another mineral water from the bar fridge concealed in a sideboard that Al had shown her earlier. She hadn't seen Al for almost a year and from her vantage point above the bad comb-over that his futile vanity had gelled across his head, she wondered how he'd lost so much hair so quickly.

Al was the endearing type eternally exuding the clumpiness of a feather doona no matter how hard he tried to spruce himself up. He was wearing his jacket and, Sonya noticed, there was a lot more of Al these days for it to try wrapping itself around. He'd even worn suits when they met at university and no one did that except for the part-time students who had day jobs. Back then, she even imagined he slept in a suit, though she resisted all his attempts for her to find out for herself.

His fleshy lips were wrapped around a cigar-shaped black pen. Sonya slipped back quietly into her seat and unwound the cap of her bottle of water. The two women watched silently as Al slid the pen thoughtfully in and out of his mouth, in between occasional ink flourishes on some of the many pages he was reading for the first time.

"Son, the..." Al hesitated when he looked up over the top of his glasses and noticed Sonya grimace. "Sorry. Old habits. Son...*ya*," he corrected himself. "Your situation is pretty shit, but," he said, smiling at her, "you're one heck of a smart lady and you're right, we can give these bankers a major poke."

"How major?"

"Karie?"

Karen rested her top teeth on her thumb. Unlike Sonya she didn't have the age or the guts to insist that Al call her by her full name. Karen was already furious with him for last night, when he'd pulled her off the memorandum she was drafting for a hostile takeover offer and he didn't need to make it worse by calling her some cutesy name. She loathed the habit just like Sonya hated the diminutive "Son" that he kept calling her. But Al was Karen's boss and one of the firm's big wigs and "Karie" was way better than "Care Bear" which he'd actually used once, thankfully not in front of anyone else.

"How major?" said Karen lifting her head up and looking over Sonya's shoulder to avoid her eyes. "It's a long shot, but we might just get a court to say that the unpaid interest is the bank's problem, not yours."

"A court?" Sonya spluttered. "What'll that cost? And how long..."

"Son... Sonya, give it a rest, okay. Let's hear Karie out."

"Basically," Karen continued, "your claim has legs... that

they should never have altered the original arrangement without your consent. Technically, the documents," said Karen pointing to the blue legal papers, "allow them to do whatever they like, even what they've done, but the circumstances here are so unusual. Your parameters at the outset were so particular. They're spelled out in your emails back and forth with the bank five years ago, so we doubt they can rely on the relevant clause... clause... er... 56.10.11, I think...." She ran her finger down one of the pages. "No," she blushed as if she'd committed a cardinal sin. "It's 56.10.12... Anyway, they can't rely on that to protect them. Legally, what we're talking about is called an 'estoppel'. It's a fancy way..."

"I know," said Sonya, "it's when their own knowledge and actions stop them exercising their contractual rights."

"That's it. And even if we're wrong, it's worth a shot."

Sonya's fingers were tapping the table. "Karen, if I can cut through...?"

The young lawyer nodded.

"You're saying that maybe we can stick the bank for all the interest up to now... the money Michael should've been paying, right?"

Al and Karen nodded simultaneously.

"That's great..." said Sonya.

From her ever so slight wince, Al was sure there was a but coming.

"No, really," she continued, "it *is* great and you guys are amazing but what about the interest payments? You know, the not-so-small matter of the ninety grand every six months I have to pay from now on. How do we... I... deal with that?"

Al turned his head toward his associate. "Karie?"

She cocked her brow realising Al had flicked to her so she would be the one bearing the bad news. "Bottom line?" said Karen. "Sonya, either you pay it when it's due or you lose the house. One or the other. No leeway."

"But how do I find that sort of money every six months?" she said, more to herself than to the lawyers.

Al knew he had to step in. "You have to, Son…ya," he said. "Best case? You sell the house, we win the suit on the *old* interest payments and you pocket the difference between what you get for the house and the three million you owe the bank. If you're lucky, maybe you net a half million and you move on. Worst case? We lose our suit and you have to pay over the whole $3.8 million to the bank, but with costs it would be way more."

"If I do that, I walk away with nothing," said Sonya. "What are my odds on your best case?"

Al fiddled with his jowls. "Hmm… 60-40… maybe 70-30… in your favour, of course… those sort of odds. Karie?"

"In that ballpark," said Karen, shifting in her chair. She wasn't keen to disagree openly with her boss but she didn't want to come across as a wimp either. In her memo she'd already assessed it 50-50.

"How long before we'd know for sure?" asked Sonya.

"Six months," said Al, scratching his nose with the top of his pen. "And that's provided we actually pay the next instalment, as a sort of good faith thing."

"If it blows out beyond six months? What about the ninety grand due after this one?"

"We'd have to pay that," Al replied, reaching across the table and taking a plate-sized chocolate-chip cookie and stuffing as much of it into his mouth as he could as if to say he had no more to add.

"I could sell up all the stocks in my retirement fund…"

"And the house," Karen ventured, looking to Al for support since they'd actually discussed this before the meeting, but Al kept munching to avoid confrontation.

"That's just the point," Sonya said. "I don't *want* to sell it." Not only would she be left with nothing, like ten years ago, but it was her only remaining connection with Michael. With no house, it would be a pitiful repeat of history.

"I don't want you to sell it either but, well, you may have to," Al finally said, some crumbs spraying out of his mouth. "Karie, organise a formal real estate valuation so we can see where we are."

Based on what Sonya had told them about her conversation with the bank manager, Karen knew that if Sonya sold the stupid house right now and they won on the interest, she'd clear herself a whopping half-million dollars. So why the hell were they wasting time on this? Because, as she reminded herself, her panting boss had the hots for this woman. From the moment he'd called Karen into his office last night to work on Sonya's case she'd noticed his ears wiggling as if they were antennas scanning the vicinity for his perfect match's arrival.

Karen reached over to a small pile of papers in the middle of the table. She pulled them across to her and flicked through them with an air of exasperation as if they were a sun-faded stack of parking tickets that someone had tossed onto a car's dash.

"The stocks in my superannuation fund are listed in there," said Sonya. "I could sell all of them, I suppose. They're worth around $200,000 today. A few months back I could've got close to $400,000 for them, but I'm no Robinson Crusoe there, am I?"

"Anything else?" Al said, keeping the discussion on track. His own stock portfolio had also taken a hammering these last few months. Nobody he knew had escaped unscathed from the dramas raging in the stock markets since late the previous year.

"There's my cash management account," she said. "The yellow sheet, there," she added, pointing halfway down the pile.

Karen slid it out. "There's fifty thousand in that."

"Any insurance policies?" Al asked. "You know," he cleared his throat, "on Michael?"

"None." It was one of Sorden's first questions, so she was surprised it had taken Al so long.

Al made a note. "Anything else?"

"Well, I got a lawyer's letter from London recently... an aunt—my mother's sister—she died a few months ago and apparently left me something in her estate, but they're waiting on probate to work out how much... and when." She extracted a page from the papers and handed it to Al.

He skimmed it and nodded. "Okay... we've got a house worth maybe three-and-a-half and there's another quarter million in liquid assets—the fifty in cash plus the two hundred in stocks, okay? Technically you can't sell the stuff in your superannuation fund, but... close your ears, Karie...

bugger it, Sonya. All up, there's $3.75 million we can play with right now..." He saw the scowl on her face and quickly added, "you know... only if we're forced to." Then he continued, "Son, what have we got on the liability side? Apart from the interest... there's the three million you owe the bank. What else?"

"Nothing... but what about your legal fees?"

He raised his finger. "Karie, when's the next interest payment due?"

"The ninety grand? Two weeks Tuesday."

"Tuesday week, actually," Sonya corrected her.

Karen's sympathy for her boss's heartthrob was fading fast. Here they were futzing with this sad but trifling case when they had much weightier work to do, namely what Karen had come to this firm for: the really big stuff like white-collar corporate crime where she'd been working until recently. And now with Al on corporate and securities law... initial public offerings, the big corporate deals like the biotech merger they'd just closed and the hostile takeover they were set to launch next week. That was why she was here, not shit like this. Her friends in other firms weren't as lucky. Most of them were twiddling their thumbs with the corporate work drying up. These days after-work drinks were all about how the action was shifting to insolvency. Bo-ring. At least she thought so. But Al's department, Mergers and Acquisitions, was well-placed although with the worsening economic climate he'd started joking they should rename it Dirges and Dispositions. "We clean up either way," he said.

Pity the poor clients Karen thought at the time. She had been electrified by Al's performance during Project Helium's final negotiations. By noon the entire merger was stitched up. He'd even taken both sides to lunch and made a point of pulling out his own credit card to pay for it though Karen suspected the bill would still finish up charged to the client's account, probably as photocopying or a few extra hours at Al's extortionate billing rate.

But Karen was learning fast that if you became sidekick to one of the big gun partners in these mega-firms you had to expect your saddle bags getting weighed down occasionally by working for their pals. Worse, she knew these piddly little jobs rated for zilch at bonus time but still, showing a cooperative attitude to your boss was critical if you wanted to land a role on the big deals.

"I can't sell the house." Sonya bit her lip and dropped her head to her hands. The other two held their breath as they waited for the sobs. But they didn't arrive.

This time Al raised an eyebrow and said, "Look, your retirement funds will be enough to keep things going, at least till we work something else out. We can always put in a hardship case to the tax office." He passed Sonya the box of tissues Karen had thoughtfully brought in with her. "Like I said, we need to make a good faith payment to the bank while we litigate the crap out of them."

Karen had pulled off one of the pages from the document pile and was skimming down the list of assets in Sonya's superannuation fund when she almost choked. She circled something with her pen and, silent but wide-eyed in warning, pushed the sheet across the table to Al.

He saw it immediately. "Son, three-quarters... $150,000 of this is in stock in ZipChip Corporation," he said.

Sonya thought Al was going to criticise her for putting so many eggs in one basket. A fair criticism but it was a calculated risk she'd taken. One that Michael, too, had slammed her for.

But that wasn't what Al meant. "Listen, I'm no investment adviser," he said, "but if I were you I wouldn't be selling those shares."

Sonya didn't see the glower that Karen shot at Al as she jumped up and excused herself from the room almost knocking her chair to the floor. They both watched her fly out of the room, her hair and temper ablaze.

Precariously Al leant back on his swivel chair and reached over to the sideboard to answer the phone which had not yet actually started to ring. When it did, he spoke in monosyllables and shambled out of his chair. "Back in a minute," he said.

Confidentiality was everything in a firm like this. After fees, anyhow. Karen was thankful for the extra soundproofing as Al went ballistic, standing inches away from her in the room next to Sonya's. Karen didn't need witnesses right now.

"Al, for chrissakes," she bravely butted in, staring right into his eyes, her shortness though not her stature boosted by her try-hard Blahnik four-inch-heels. "We've got a client about to launch a hostile take-over for ZipChip and you go telling Sonya to hang onto her shares so she can get a higher price later?"

Al's corpulent features were swelling even more. "Who the hell are you to tell me...?"

Karen said nothing, unsure where he was headed.

If a clock had been on the wall you would've heard it ticking, unless you were Karen who couldn't hear anything over the blood beating at her brain. Her heels didn't help her stand any straighter either. She nervously slid her hair behind her ear. "What you did in there, it's not ethical."

"Miss Longly, if you want to keep a desk at B+L so you can afford to keep buying those ridiculous shoes," he said smirking, "you'd better understand that this is the law business not the morals business. If you want to be in the morals business, go take an oath of poverty. In case you hadn't noticed, we don't do poverty round here."

He stormed out of the room, muttering to himself that she should take an oath of chastity as well, or words to that effect.

FOR the rest of the morning Sonya noticed a veneer of tension had slithered between the two lawyers but she didn't dare ask.

After they'd gone through everything several times over, Al recommended that she sell her shares—all except the ZipChip stock—to raise fifty thousand toward the next interest bill and, to make the full ninety, he offered to top up the extra forty himself.

"But I've got another fifty in my cash management account," Sonya said.

"Keep it there. You never know what expenses we'll have if we go to court. I'm lending you the balance, that's final." Even he could see she was uneasy about his offer. "Don't worry, Son...ya; I won't treat you like a bank would... though, hey, I'd love to," he winked.

Standing behind him, Karen felt like putting two fingers in her mouth, but she knew better.

10

SONYA'S NIGHTS HAD become even more unsettled than her days. Despite Al's obvious enthusiasm to fill the breach she chose an alternative, wine and sleeping pills. It had been like this for a week.

She woke, woozy and coughing, and her ears were throbbing. There'd be no run for her this morning, that was for sure.

Her clouded eyes finally narrowed in on the bedroom clock: 3:12 AM. "Jesus," she wrapped the quilted bed cover round her more tightly. Vaguely, she felt pounding through her desensitised fog. She lay still but the thumping sensation wouldn't leave her so she pulled herself up onto her pillow to drain the blood from her head. Even with socks on, and her tatty blue woollen sweater she started to shiver.

The pounding... what was it? An alarm? Faintly, she heard Ralph yelping.

Michael? She patted the bed, absurdly hopeful.

Was there an intruder? She bounded out of bed but her mind was out of whack with her legs. She slipped on the parquetry and she tumbled backwards. She remained confused and though the sleeping pill cloud was dissipating her mind was still sluggish.

Slowly, she pulled her legs up inside her sweater and her hands pressed against her ears, but still the cacophony and confusion roared.

It *was* an alarm, yet it was too loud to be a car in the street.

Was it her smoke alarm?

She tried to sniff but phlegm plugged her nostrils. Straining her eyes in the dark she imagined a wisp of smoke floating in the night air. She stood again unsteady and holding herself against the wall. After taking her robe she snatched a handful of tissues from her bedside table and blew her nose. An acrid taste coated her tongue.

It *was* smoke.

She flicked on a light and forcing her legs and head to cooperate she stumbled downstairs and burst out the front door where the air was thick with the stink. Out here it wasn't cold—the air was singeing hot and it glowed with a fiery red haze. Then blue.

The roar of the fire cracked into her fug like random shots from an automatic weapon. From behind, and with no warning bark, Ralph buffeted her forward and Sonya imagined he was pushing her out the gate to where it was safe. "Good dog," she mumbled, groping her way through the smoke to the street.

A police vehicle was screeching to a halt behind two fire trucks. A third was barrelling down the steeply inclined narrow roadway.

The teams of fire-fighters split ready for their pre-set

routines. Some connected the trucks to the water mains, others snaked the hoses across the road. Three weighed themselves down with oxygen tanks and masks.

The smoke and the towering fire trucks parked in front of Sonya's gate obscured her sightlines.

"Over here!" she shrieked but the violent staccato of sirens and cracks of fire outwailed her. "Help, please. Here!"

She could get no one's attention. It was like a nightmare. It was.

The whole street was up watching and fearful. The cautious were hosing their roofs to prevent a spark or some red-hot debris spreading the inferno to their own properties.

Police patrolled up and down to keep milling observers out of harm's—and the fire-fighters'—way. Still fuzzy from her tablets, Sonya stood herself directly in front of a man-in-blue, her stinging eyes pleading for help.

"Lady, they're trying to get the fire down so it doesn't spread. Then they can go in for the people."

"I'm the only one in there," she sobbed, pointing back to her house.

He looked at her strangely, as if wondering what drug was she on, then shook his head. "Not there, ma'am. There!" he said, pointing over his shoulder across the street. Suddenly he understood her confused panic. "You've had a scare, haven't you?" He put his arm round her and walked her toward her gate. "Why don't you go back inside and make yourself a cup of tea? And keep your windows closed, okay?"

He left her at her gate.

Coughing and flustered, her eyes smarting from the smoke, Sonya now saw it wasn't her house on fire, but the relief was fleeting: it was Tito's and Naomi's. She gasped in terror.

Alone at her front gate, she stared at the enraged flames tearing through her friends' upper floor. Room-by-room, windows burst in explosive blasts of shards and splinters as the fire rampaged. A tiny fragment—glass or wood, she didn't know—shot into her face just below her right eye. "My God," she said, touching it with her finger, though it wasn't for anyone to hear. A drop of blood dissolved into her tears.

Instinct told her to ignore the policeman and run past him through the trucks and across the road. The watchful cop had a premonition and walked back to her. "Ma'am, stay behind this line. Please?" he said. "We've got plenty to do without rescuing people who *aren't* in danger!"

The tongues of flame darted high, licking the fronds of the Wells's palm trees like they were lime ice-creams and once done they moved on, greedy for more.

Marion, Sonya's neighbour, came rushing up to her. Wordless, they hugged and watched the fire fighters get the blaze under control. When the heat dropped enough, she saw three men in yellow suits, oxygen tanks and masks burst through the front door for the second time. They'd tried a few minutes earlier but the fire had overwhelmed them.

Sonya and Marion moved next to one of the fire trucks to shield themselves from the blistering heat. Marion's husband, Jack, brought their son, Willie, who was gripping Jack's track pants and cuddling his yellow stuffed toy with his other arm. This was a night Willie and Big Bird would go on talking about for a long while.

Every so often the static on the fire truck radio scratched into life. "Living room... okay," the rescue team leader reported. "No *Vogue* photo shoots in this place," another cut in, unaware his black humour had an unexpected audience.

Sonya saw Marion shudder at the joke but neither of them tut-tutted or voiced any criticism. They knew that in a high-stress job like this, levity was a useful cover for fear.

Jack hoisted Willie up into his arms. But as they all huddled beside the truck, the next message caught the group off-guard with its brutality and its finality. "Chief... no survivors."

Jack drew Willie even closer and Marion circled her arms around them. Sonya bit into her fist.

"Body count?" It was the chief.

Marion lifted her head from Jack's shoulder to listen.

"Two. Main bedroom. Smoke asphyxiation by the looks of it."

Willie giggled at something Big Bird had confided to him and grabbed Jack's nose, giving it a mischievous tug.

SONYA sat alone in her kitchen even though Jack and Marion had invited her to be with them. She switched on early-morning TV as a diversion but realised what a mistake that was when the screen panned back from the smoking wreck on the other side of her street. A reporter was on-camera with the fire chief beside him. Sonya tapped up the volume control on her remote:

> "Last night, fire swept through this luxury harbourside mansion, the home of corporate boss, Tito Wells. Chief executive of technology company ZipChip, Wells and his wife died in the blaze wrapped in each other's arms..."

THE 10 AM news repeated the story and by the time the finance report came on air the stock market had already opened. In the first five minutes ZipChip's share price had plunged 25 percent.

Sonya's barbecue conversation with Michael a few weeks earlier rushed back to her... his strange anger when she mentioned she'd bought ZipChip stock. He'd grabbed her arm, not roughly but firmly, and pulled her aside where no one could hear them. *"Share prices can collapse, damn it,"* he'd warned her. *"Do you want to lose half your money?"*

With a shiver of trepidation she recalled how, according to the trading records the police had reconstructed, Michael had bought put options over ZipChip stock. He'd gone much further than mere social chitchat over this. He'd spent big money betting on the ZipChip stock price falling. Now she could see he'd been just as prescient on this as on everything else.

The front gate buzzed. Checking the video monitor, she couldn't make out who it was as her face was turned away from the camera. It was a woman, she could tell that, and she was looking back toward the still-smoking ruin across the street. She was in uniform, dark blue, so Sonya guessed she was a police officer or a fire-fighter giving residents the all-clear. But as the woman turned to face the camera, Sonya inhaled sharply. "Naomi!" she shouted into the handset before dropping it and running out to the gate.

The crying women rushed into each other's arms. Ralph came bounding up too and nuzzled in between them as they hugged while inside the telephone handset swung back and forth on its cord.

NAOMI, Tito Wells's wife, had been scheduled to fly home the previous night but a mechanical fault forced an unscheduled stop in New Zealand and they'd only landed in Sydney that morning. Jumping into a cab to head home, she had no inkling about the fire.

When her ride was a few streets away, she first sniffed the reek of smoke. "That smell? Is it your engine?" she asked the taxi driver.

He wound down his window and quickly rolled it back up switching the air-conditioning onto recycle. "Fire, I'd say."

When they pulled into the street the fire trucks had gone but some police and fire investigation vehicles were still scattered over the grass verges. The taxi slithered through the puddles they'd left behind, its tyres slurping like long strips of Velcro being ripped apart, just like Naomi's life was about to be.

The police vehicles blocked where her house was at the end of the cul-de-sac and the cab had no choice but to pull up a block back.

Naomi couldn't make out what was happening but she knew it wasn't good. There was some movement down the street as a towering police rescue truck began to reverse and for the first time she could see beyond it...

She staggered out of the cab gasping for breath and the smoky air only made it worse. The charred and gutted wreck of her home was crawling with sour-faced investigators. She stumbled to the property with her black travel bag faltering behind her, its wheels reluctant to follow.

An officer blocked her path, mistaking her for yet another voyeur.

"This is my house. My husband is..."

For reasons Naomi at first couldn't fathom the officer smiled and her own hysteria didn't make the situation any easier. She fumbled in her purse then shoved her airline photo ID into the investigator's face. The snap had been taken when she had black hair but the police officer was only focused on her surname—Wells—and not the fact she was now a brunette. "My husband...?"

He dropped his smile, and his eyes. Naomi knew instantly. Her hands fell to her side and she began to sway.

The man grabbed her arms to steady her, conscious of his double burden: informing Naomi of her husband's death, as well as broaching the delicate subject of establishing exactly who they had found dead in his bed beside him.

THE two friends took refuge in Sonya's kitchen, Naomi quiet at the table and Sonya fussing by preparing hot drinks, cool drinks, wiping previously cleaned countertops and both avoiding the question that dangled between them: the identity of the second fire-victim.

Naomi stared into her glass. It was as empty as she felt. The TV was background hum, its sound low but not muted. Tito was dead. The horror… the shock of arriving home to it was still beyond her comprehension. And having to explain the circumstances—his bedmate—to the police, it was too much. Sonya hadn't asked. Not yet, but she knew she would. What was she going to say?

A flicker of flames on the screen caught her attention and without asking Sonya she notched up the volume. It was the business news and the reporter was now fronting the stock exchange.

"The stock price of technology company, ZipChip," *he said*, "is reeling today after a raging house fire killed chief executive, Mr Tito Wells.

"Earlier today, officials reported that Mrs Wells also died in the blaze but, only moments ago, in a shock revelation from police headquarters, we learned that the second body was not that of Mrs Wells, but…" *he paused, his eyebrow cocked for emphasis*, "a second ZipChip executive."

Sonya glanced at Naomi whose grim eyes were fixed on the screen, her body shaking silently.

Tilting his head in the direction of the stock exchange ticker behind him, the reporter continued:

> "Today, the market is up but right on the opening bell, ZipChip plunged a massive 25 percent to only $9 from last night's $12 close, and the stock is still tumbling..."

He paused for effect, pretending to turn to someone off-camera, nodded and continued:

> "$6... as I speak, it's now $6," *he said, effecting a dramatic incredulity.* "In the first two hours of trading, 50 percent has been wiped off ZipChip shares."

Michael's warning: "*Share prices can collapse, damn it. Do you want to lose half your money?*" Half her money? Exactly what Sonya had just lost. Yesterday, her ZipChip stock was worth $150,000 even after the recent downswing. One day later, it was teetering at $75,000.

How had Michael known? What was he? The question made her nauseous. Or was it the alcohol? She did have one drink when she came back inside after the fire. Or maybe it was three. Almost zombie-like she walked over and switched off the TV as if Naomi wasn't there.

How much had Michael known? And if he *had* known something, why hadn't he done anything to stop it?

If only for her sanity, Sonya forced herself to snap out of

her despondency to consider Naomi's despair and humiliation. Tito dying in bed with a work colleague; well, more than a colleague.

Sonya didn't feel equipped for this. With her mouth pressed together and her brow furrowed all she could do was look across at her friend in puzzlement, hoping the silence would do the job for her.

Naomi wiped under her eyes with her fingertips and cleared her throat. She reached into her bag. "Sonya," she said, blowing her nose on the handkerchief, "It's complicated…"

Sonya's scalp tightened.

"…the woman was Tito's marketing director. Her name is… *was* Carmen… Carmen Lynch."

Sonya sighed though respectfully kept it to herself.

As if she'd been reading Sonya's mind, Naomi whispered to the tabletop, "What will you think…?" Her eyes came up to meet Sonya's and she took a deep breath. "If I'd made it home last night as I was supposed to, there would've been three bodies in that bed."

Sonya went to speak but her tongue stuck to the roof of her mouth.

EXHAUSTED, Naomi returned from another round of police interrogation late in the afternoon and slumped into a lounge chair. She was wearing some of Sonya's clothes—a pair of white jeans and a black roll-neck mohair sweater—since her own carry-on spares were in the washing machine.

Sonya handed her a tumbler of scotch—a Johnnie Walker Blue—splashed with soda.

"It was a fire bomb they said... traces anyhow... under the house..."

Sonya's hand flew to her mouth. "What do they...?"

"... think?" Naomi shrugged. "I can't..."

Sonya knew she'd find out later. "I've been thinking. You've got no family here so stay here with me, you know, till something gets worked out?" She sighed, "I could use the company." Sharing her house with Michael's dwindling stock of whisky and wine as her only companions was getting less appealing by the day.

Naomi raised a knuckle to her lip as if she were suppressing a thought.

"What?" asked Sonya.

"They... they asked questions..."

"About Carmen?"

"About Michael."

Sonya blanched. She became light-headed and giddy. Flash... the image that came to her was Naomi and Tito, with Michael. The three of them in a disgusting tangle, surely not. It stabbed at her, blinded her, sickened her. "You didn't! Not with Mi..."

"No!" shouted Naomi, slamming down her drink, the whisky splashing onto the table. "Jesus, no. But they asked if we did," her voice cracked. "And if I did stay... here with you..."

11

TWO DAYS AFTER Tito's funeral, a police badge filled the screen of Sonya's video intercom. "Mrs Wells isn't here," Sonya said into the handset, assuming they were looking for Naomi. She'd flown to Chicago the previous afternoon to stay with her sister.

"Professor, it's you we want to talk to."

"MURDER?" Sonya's lungs were scorching. She was constricted, unable to speak or breathe. She pressed one hand up against the wall to steady herself and clamped the other to her chest. Absent-mindedly she noticed a brown ant that was missing a leg struggling up the window glass. Her eyes floated back to Sorden and she stared in a vague unfocused way. "Michael's been *murdered*?"

"No. Your neighbour. Mr Wells, and his... er... friend."

"Why would you want to talk to me about that?"

"It's routine."

She'd seen enough TV crime shows to know that routine

never meant routine. And she didn't know why but her barbecue conversation with Michael about ZipChip thumped back into her head. "If Tito's been murdered, are you saying Michael is... connected?"

Sorden didn't respond.

"You think *Michael* murdered Tito?"

"I don't think anything," he said. "I just have a few questions."

Sonya got to her feet and flicked back her hair, short lank strands drained of life. She turned toward the wall for a second to wipe her eyes so he wouldn't see and again she spied the five-legged ant limping up the glass. "I can't deal with your 'routine' questions," she said, hooking her fingers into air quotes. "First Michael... gone... and all that money... and two weeks later two of my friends... one of my friends... Oh, God. And now you waltz in here... and you want to ask me... routine... Yeah, right."

"You're upset..."

"I'm upset, but I'm not stupid."

The cop shuffled his feet. It wasn't out of embarrassment; he'd been in these situations frequently enough. No, he wanted Sonya to babble on; rambling witnesses were gold.

She wiped the back of her hand across her forehead, "What, are you suggesting? That Michael was in that... that love triangle?" She paused, as if for breath, and her eye flickered, a nerve twitch, "Wouldn't be a triangle then, would it?" Sonya slammed her fist against the window, angry with herself for being flippant and squashed the ant. The silence fell hard on her. The detective stood waiting.

Suddenly she cracked and an unfamiliar temper charged up through her veins. Her face was afire and she felt scarcely in control of her voice. "How can you stand here, in my house, saying these things?"

He shuffled his feet some more.

"I want you to leave," she said, replaying how she had dealt with the bank manager.

This wasn't what the detective expected. "Professor, we need to talk. Please."

"No, you please. Please leave. You want to talk? Talk to my lawyer."

"And... who-o might that be-e?" Sorden oofed each time Sonya's open palms shunted him toward the door.

"MacAntar. Alan MacAntar. Mac-An-Tar," each syllable-stress punching his stomach in time with her vehemence. "He's in the phone book," she scowled, shoving him to the door.

She slammed it shut with her fists finally sealing the panel, her face pressed against the cool wood and she felt swamped, buried, unable to move, her last surges of energy drained as if an undertow had sucked her deep beneath a crashing surf.

Sorden bolted up the path, side-stepping past Ralph who didn't know whether to bite him or sympathise.

12

"ALL I KNOW about homicide is what I've seen on TV and what I dream about inflicting on my law partners," Al laughed. But Sonya didn't see the joke, nor did Karen Longly who twisted with embarrassment.

Al was trying to make light of things since Sonya's appearance had shocked him. She looked wrung out, far worse than on her previous visit, with her blond hair hanging dull and scraggly as if it hadn't met shampoo for days. She had been so distraught on the phone the lawyers had driven out to her house.

"I called in Lex Talionis like I said," Al reminded her. Talionis was one of his criminal law partners. "Karie used to work with him before she joined me…"

Sonya nodded.

"He's in court or I would've brought him with us, but he still wheedled out some of the story in the recess. This is one heck of a situation, Sonya," he said. "But it does look like Michael, you know… over a long period… that he's…"

"…lied… I know."

"Like all those times he told you he was going overseas, well, he didn't. Ever."

Sonya nodded absently and wiped her nose on her sleeve.

Al and Karen exchanged glances and Al continued, "The police checked back... way back. There's no record of him ever entering the country, let alone nine years ago. Nothing then, nothing since."

Sonya jolted, "Excuse me?"

Despite her haze, Sonya knew that if they didn't have a record of Michael's first arrival into Australia and she personally knew it to be true, their other records had to be suspect as well.

Her mind wound back to when she flew to Australia with him... Damn it she recalled. He had flown in separately a few days later. And because he'd arrived a day sooner than she'd expected, she didn't get to meet him at the airport either. At the time she enjoyed the spontaneity, the surprise, and had never imagined there was anything suspicious about it. Not till now.

Al interrupted her thoughts. "Sonya, that's not half of it."

Her shoulders were defeated, her expression numb.

"Michael's not huge on people skills, right?" said Al as an observation rather than a question. "Doesn't make friendships easily."

"This is something I don't know?" said Sonya, almost dismissively.

To Al her voice was raspy like a drunk's, but it was more from crying. He went on, "What if, only two weeks after, ah, someone disappears one of his friends—one of his very, very few friends—dies in a mysterious fire with his lover and..."

"Al, come on."

He held up his hand, "Hear me out. According to the cops, not long before Michael vanished he bought ZipChip put options."

So, Sonya noted, the cops had finally twigged that Michael's put option trade might have some significance though the insight hardly warmed her. She fingered the tangles in her hair but it did nothing to improve her appearance. "What are they saying?" she asked. "That he bought the put options wanting the stock price to collapse and he killed Tito to make sure of it?"

The way Al pursed his lips told her that was indeed their theory.

"But they're wrong," said Karen, "and Lex told them so. If their wacko theory held up how come he sold the put options the day he left you, right? At that point they weren't even worth what he'd paid for them two weeks earlier, whereas if he'd kept them till after Wells died when the stock tanked, they'd have been worth almost $4 million dollars."

More than enough to repay the loan and the outstanding interest entirely, Sonya noted. But she had a feeling about this: that Michael hadn't *wanted* the ZipChip price to plunge, though somehow he *knew* it would.

Sonya slid back into her chair, the soft leather feeling uncomfortably hard and cold. "If the cops' theory of deserting husband ridden with guilt is right... if he wanted to look after me... he would've just left behind four million of his far more than ample money. He wouldn't have bought put options and he wouldn't have murdered anybody. In any case, as Karen says, he didn't even keep those options so there's nothing for me to get my hands on anyway."

Sonya was convincing but she hadn't convinced herself. Whichever way she looked at it, it was a losing bet: either Michael was a murderer, something she couldn't contemplate, or he was an infallible clairvoyant, something she couldn't countenance.

AFTER the lawyers left, Sonya walked out onto the beach over the boardwalk that separated the houses from the sand and headed down to the water's edge. She gazed across through the moored boats to... nothing. So what if she'd simply missed her menstrual period? One missed one hardly guaranteed a pregnancy. Maybe it was just late. It could be anything... the stress.

But what if she were pregnant? It was what she'd wanted for years.

Her lip curled as if attempting a smile that would not come.

13

"TELL ME THE ethics of keeping Sonya as a client," Karen asked as they drove back to the city in Al's metallic gold sports car. With him at the wheel of his precious Porsche 911 turbo cabriolet she felt safer raising the touchy subject than she would have back at the office. "We've got a serious conflict Al... There's the Michael thing with the ZipChip options... she owns ZipChip shares herself and..."

"Hey, you're not still on that red herring are you?"

She could see that Al was about to froth up again about the place of morals in the law so she held up her hand. "It's a plain question of a conflict of interests... Sonya owns ZipChip shares, her missing partner almost made a killing—pardon the pun—from ZipChip put options and the police," her voice rose, "are investigating him to find out if he *killed* the two most senior executives in the company! Gees, Al, and on top of that, B+L—our firm, you and I, and now Lex—are actively counselling Sonya on all of this at the same time as we—you and I!—are advising a client about to launch a hostile take-over for the same damn company. This isn't a re-run of *Boston Legal*," she added.

They were still ten minutes from the office but Al pulled over to the kerb and with one elbow on the steering wheel turned sideways and loomed over her. "Sorry this offends your pretty rules of neatness Karie, but life's a bitch. It's messy. So what do you suggest, huh? That I call up Sonya and say, hey, sorry old girl I have to dump you, a life-long friend, in your darkest hour because I have a client who wants to buy some damn fucking company? You saw how this is affecting her..."

"If you want us to keep helping her, fine, but I don't see how we can do that and stay on the takeover."

"You're not serious," he said, but he could see she was. "Karie, our takeover fees will be eight, maybe nine million. That vow of poverty... you didn't actually take it, did you?"

"THEY'RE wrong," said Karen.

"Longly," Al said with force, "lay off, okay? You raised an issue... We took it to the firm's ethics committee... If you don't like the decision..."

"I don't..."

"Listen, I've spoken with Joe." Joe Jimenez was president of Pahokee Networks, their Florida-based client planning to bid for ZipChip. "He's happy with the approach. 'It keeps it all in the family,' he says."

The lawyer knew he was baiting his associate. "In fact it was his idea... that we hold back from doing any further work for Sonya till next week until after the bid's announced. Then we tell her and see if *she's* got a problem with us continuing to act, but I'm sure she won't. Just as Joe hasn't."

"I don't like this."

"Fuck, Karie! This is work. Since when does *like* come into it?"

14

THE NEWSPAPER HEADLINE stared up at Sonya—*Raid on ZipChip*—and as she read on her adrenaline pumped with the good news, for the first time in a long time. A company she'd never heard of, Pahokee Networks, had snapped up a strategic 15 percent of ZipChip stock the previous afternoon and launched a hostile takeover bid at $8 a share.

If this turned into a hard fought takeover battle as she hoped her shares might even push back to what she'd actually paid for them, no mean feat in a market that had already been suffering wild mood swings, mostly downwards. She logged onto ZipChip's web-site:

Announcement to Stock Exchange & Media
FOR IMMEDIATE RELEASE
ZipChip rejects cheap foreign takeover attempt

The directors of leading Australian technology group, ZipChip Corporation, today rejected the unsolicited takeover bid from Pahokee Networks Inc, a little known firm from the Florida backwaters.

"ZipChip has a long and proud record," said Mr Raymond Mansfield, ZipChip's founder, chairman and currently acting chief executive officer.

"This contemptibly opportunistic offer ignores the true value and the outstanding prospects of the successful company I have returned to lead.

"These market raiders add nothing to ZipChip. Not only do they lack a profitable track record, they have no technology of substance of their own.

"Their derisory $8.00 bid reeks of slick opportunism, coming so soon after the tragic deaths of ZipChip's two most senior executives," Mr Mansfield continued.

Only two weeks ago, before ZipChip's then CEO and Marketing Director died, ZipChip shares were trading at $12.00, one-and-a-half times higher than Pahokee Networks' bid.

"Shareholders should reject this contemptible offer, just as my fellow directors and I will do for our own stock," Mr Mansfield said. "And, because the ZipChip board hold 18% of the stock," Mr Mansfield added, "this offer is doomed to fail."

Sonya's arm shot out in an air punch. "Go for it, Mr Chairman," she shouted to herself and to Ralph who, until then, had been enjoying the novelty of lying at her feet inside the house.

After years of observing them, Sonya knew how takeover defences worked: play tough, pump up the price for all it's worth and then bring home the bacon. At least she hoped that's what ZipChip's strategy was.

She logged onto the stock exchange website, to see what Pahokee Networks had said in their own announcement:

For Immediate Release
PAHOKEE NETWORKS BIDS FOR ZIPCHIP
— $8 all-cash offer —

Pahokee Networks Inc, a $5billion corporation listed on America's NASDAQ exchange, today announced an A$8 per share all cash takeover bid for ZipChip Corporation, an Australian-based technology multinational.

Pahokee is Zipchip's single largest stockholder, owning 15% of the company which it readily acquired on-market this afternoon at prices between $6.50 and $7.50.

Pahokee's offer price of $8 per share is a 33% premium above what ZipChip stock was trading at before Pahokee started buying its shares on-market.

"ZipChip has a fine business but it's been plagued by board and management clashes," said Mr Joe Jimenez, Pahokee's president.

"ZipChip delivered poor results last year and looks set to do so again unless the vacuum can be filled," Mr Jimenez said. "First, six months ago, the company lost its highly regarded CEO, Mr Nathan Klim, when he resigned suddenly. And recently, his successor Mr Tito Wells and marketing director Ms Carmen Lynch died in a tragic fire."

"The market has already recognised our offer as full and generous: 15% of ZipChip's stock rushed into our hands today at prices well under our bid price. We are now ZipChip's largest single shareholder and we are confident of success."

Pahokee's offer is subject to...

Sonya couldn't help but see at the foot of the release that Pahokee Network's advisers included B+L, Al's law firm.

"You were next on my list," Al lied. "My last 48 hours have been crazy."

"The ZipChip takeover?"

"Until we announced, I couldn't tell you... cone of silence and all that. But, hey, this is good for you: eight bucks sure outpays six."

Al explained how the firm's ethics committee had okayed him staying her adviser as well as Pahokee's so long as she agreed. "I already discussed it with Pahokee's president. He's relaxed about it... totally. My only handcuff is I can't advise you what to do with your ZipChip shares given I'll have inside information."

"What happens next?" she asked.

Al misunderstood her. "Like I said, my lips are sealed... but usually, you know, the big investors sit back and wait right till the end to make sure they don't miss out on anything, you know, like a price rise to clean it all up." He added, "But, hey, I'm not telling you anything you couldn't get anywhere else."

She could almost feel the breeze from Al's wink. What he meant, she was sure, was Pahokee would up the ante if that's what it took to get ZipChip's board of directors onside.

15

SONYA'S RUSH FROM the ZipChip takeover was only brief and her lead blanket soon dropped back over her. Michael was still gone. The money was still owing. There was the pregnancy, or at least the possibility, and she didn't even know any more if that was a good thing or not. Her cold sweats and nightmares were still with her.

Some days she'd even get close to taking the easy way out. Not suicide though it had once flashed into her mind, but selling the house and pocketing whatever money she'd clear after her court case against the bank... shove all this behind her... move somewhere else... start a new life... And not have the baby... if there was one. She'd bought the tester from the pharmacy but couldn't face opening the packet.

Her mind was like jelly, gummed up and clouded with none of her thoughts able to break free from the others. Fretting over the house and the money gave her the chance to avoid thinking too much about the chance of a child. And anyhow, she'd missed a period before.

The house. Why couldn't she just let it go? She glanced

out the window. The serenity... the boats swaying on the almost motionless water... the stainless steel halyards clinking... a scoop of five pelicans splaying their webbed feet forward ready to skid to a stop as if they were out-of-control cartoon characters desperately braking as they approached the crumbling edge of an abyss.

Just like she was.

The sky was so wide here... and so high. It drew her eyes up... far from her torments. That big, teasing luminescence of the Australian sky. Tingling as a razor on your skin... It was a different light... true blue with a tint of lavender. That was how Michael had once painted it for her.

She lowered her gaze to the ungainly white pelicans: their ten black eyes fixed on an unsuspecting school of taylor fish frothing and jumping toward them.

THREE AM. Again. She couldn't get past it. Her bed was soaked in sweat. A wisp of lost memory hovered like a dust mote before her bleary eyes... Michael... in a dank cell. Scratching to get out. Calling her name. She couldn't quite remember. She slid out of bed, her body shaking.

She fingered her silver charm bracelet. She must be pregnant. This was her metabolism, not her mind.

It was what she'd wanted, yet it was the last thing she needed.

MICHAEL *wound his thoughts back to the day he'd brought her the antique charm bracelet, 'replacing' the one stolen only weeks before they'd first met.*

He remembered wrapping it... each fold of the flocked damask paper, each knot in the silk ribbon. But Sonya didn't know that.

"W-where'd you get this?" she'd stuttered.

He rubbed her charm of the invisible hand in his pocket, out of sight, and this time his smile was broken, more of a tic.

He'd found it, he'd told her.

Just like he hoped she had found his disk.

16

CLARITY BEGAN TO slice through the haze of dawn. Sonya knew that Al and his lawyer's tricks would only get her so far. It was obvious she'd have to stump up with a significant amount for the bank or she'd have no choice but to put the house up for auction. She wasn't the only one she was fighting for now she thought, even though she'd still avoided taking the test.

She knew she had to refocus. The university's mid-year break was long over but with little sleep she'd been lecturing on auto-pilot. It was obvious to her so she guessed her students would have noticed. Throwing herself back into her work was more than just an obligation; she decided it would be a tonic.

The ZipChip takeover had also got her thinking about share trading again. Despite her knowledge of markets she'd only tried it a few times in the past and usually lost more than she'd made, both in money and confidence. Michael had the gift, she didn't.

Her ZipChip stock purchase hadn't been for a fast buck. She'd bought into ZipChip as a long-term investment, a buy-and-hold... something to put in her bottom drawer, though a fat lot of good that had done her!

But now everything was different. She needed to make money.

A lot of it. And fast.

MAYBE Sonya's luck was changing. The dean's 'All Staff' email applauded Steven, one of her academic colleagues, for his great work, and regretted his decision to "resign to pursue other interests". Sure, like unemployment, thought Sonya. The dean was silent on the real reasons: Steven's embarrassingly large losses from his options trading and his impending bankruptcy. Having a bankrupt stock market trader teaching about markets would make the school a laughing stock. The dean was determined to bury the issue, even if it meant doing the same to an academic who'd give fifteen years' devoted service to the school.

But Steven's tragedy meant Sonya wangled his classes which meant extra money, starting right now. It was nowhere near enough to dig her out of her hole but everything helped. It also meant new lecture notes and new students to get acquainted with. A fresh start. More on her mind. She was engaged, busy.

For three days solid, including the weekend, she'd worked up her notes for the new classes and was just backing them up onto a DVD when an irritating alert flashed up onto her screen:

> **WARNING!**
> **BACKUP INCOMPLETE**
>
> Your backup disk is full
>
> Insert a new disk and click OK to complete backup
>
> OK

Without looking she stretched her hand up to the shelf above her desk for the box of blanks she kept there but when she probed inside, it was empty. She yanked the box down and tossed it in the bin under her desk.

She scurried round the house searching for a disk, perhaps one she could over-write and although she couldn't put a finger on why she did it—since everything inside was gone—impulse led her to Michael's office.

She hesitated at the door, having hardly set a foot inside it after he left. Her memory of that overcast but still morning welled up before her just as a passing cloud cast a shadow of gloom through the window. It froze her thoughts back on the image of the disk she'd found on the floor that day, the one she'd slotted into his sound system. What had Michael been listening to?

It was almost always *Les Miz*—the Broadway soundtrack, the London one, Sydney's, the Tenth Anniversary recording, the Complete Symphonic recording, even the Czech Revival recording. He had even more of these recordings than he owned pipes. She hadn't played a single one of them since he'd gone. When he returned... that would be the time, but not before.

Her finger tapped the eject button and she watched the CD/DVD drawer slide open. It wasn't a music disk at all. It was a data disk.

Back in her study she slid it into her computer drive, pressed OK and waited through the usual whir, hoping it would have some excess capacity.

"Damn," she mumbled as another warning flashed up: Michael's DVD was also full. What was loaded on it? Maybe she could delete some of it to make space for her notes.

Her computer displayed the disk's name, curiously, *FOLLOW YOUR OWN MIND*, just like the plaque that used to be on his desk. She clicked to open it and after the computer chugged for a moment she saw its contents were split between two main folders, DATA and KW.

Clicking on the DATA folder, it opened up into six sub-folders:

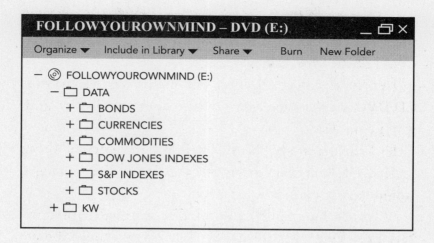

She guessed they'd be data records he used for trading.

She clicked open the S&P INDEXES folder first, focussing on the sub-file for Standard & Poor's famous S&P 500 index, the one that tracked 500 of the largest American companies.

She watched a line chart begin to ink its way across her screen and graph the index's turbulent path from its start date in 1957. She'd seen this chart often enough but it was the time-frame along the horizontal axis that raised her eyebrows.

Scrolling across the chart from left to right she was perplexed to find that it continued way past the date that Michael had vanished, the last time he could possibly have entered data or downloaded an up-to-the-minute version of the chart. No, it streaked forward from there, and not merely to the day—in August 2008—when Sonya was scratching her head over it, but into 2009, 2010, 2011 and even further.

But it wasn't what she saw years out that snagged her attention. If his chart was right or even close to it, what was going to happen in just a few weeks scared the hell out of her.

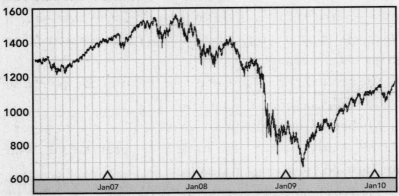

What would hit the world, or at least the US, was an extraordinary market rout, a cliff face of a crash far worse than the one everyone had been moaning about for the past year.

She quickly searched for Standard & Poor's website, clicked on the icon for its official S&P 500 Index chart and downloaded it.

She split her screen into two, positioning the official chart she'd just downloaded immediately above Michael's version and compared them, date-point by date-point. Sure enough, right up to yesterday's close the two charts were identical, not a single divergent spike or trough anywhere. For the entire period up to the present the charts were indistinguishable. But how was this possible? For the charts to match up until Michael disappeared was to be expected.

But... and a shiver ran up her spine as if someone had scratched their nails down a blackboard... but not finding a single zig or zag of difference since that date was ridiculous. As ridiculous as the quake the chart predicted was about to rock the world yet again. Markets had been bad the last year—everyone in the industrial world knew that—but if Michael's chart was right or even close to it, they were going to get cataclysmic.

She printed both charts and took them to the kitchen to study while she brewed some tea.

Michael was a chartist, an investor who tried to predict future market prices by examining past trends with sophisticated mathematical tools.

That was what he'd done here, she decided: after he downloaded the official price chart himself, just like she'd just done, he did his own modelling on it and plonked his predictions at the chart's tail end so he could see how his theory panned out.

So what she was staring at was Michael's *forecast* for the S&P 500 index for the next few years.

She dribbled some milk into her cup. She knew very well that chartists had a mixed following. She was one of the doubters, which meant she'd often had to bite her lip with Michael. She accepted there was some science in it, a mix of mathematics and psychology, but she couldn't get over her scepticism that it skated too close to hocus-pocus. Half-jokingly she'd once asked him, "Why not simply use a crystal ball?"

But now she remembered his strange grin when he said, "Maybe I do."

That was then. Now she'd seen the reality: that at least recently, Michael's predictions had been *perfectly* accurate. Not just in the trading records Sorden's forensics team had scratched together, but according to this chart, for the whole period since the moment he'd vanished. Weeks on end.

No matter how good he was, unblemished accuracy like this was inconceivable. She knew that the longer time ran on after making the predictions, the less likely they'd be even close. The odds weren't just improbable, they were impossible. It *was* witchcraft… flimflam… Something.

She repeated her S&P 500 experiment with some of the other charts on his disk. Michael had split his STOCKS subfolder into regions, with companies from the US, Europe and Australia. Sonya pulled up various samples, each time also downloading the official charts from the web to compare.

All these experiments played out identically: she'd roll forward along a chart's date line—there were varying end-dates—and, without exception, from the day Michael disappeared to now, each of his charts tracked precisely what had transpired in the real world.

She churned out copies of the charts on her printer and held each matching pair up to the light, one behind the other, but there was never a discrepancy, not even a small one.

She struggled for a credible explanation, one that didn't involve Michael being able to see into the future. After all, if he had been clairvoyant there was no way he could've been kidnapped. But Sorden's theory… no, she wasn't going there, not now.

The most rational explanation she came up with was that clicking on one of the charts on his disk somehow triggered it to update itself, perhaps by automatically logging itself onto an on-line data provider hidden in the background, and then, maybe, Michael's predictive software, perhaps embedded in the disk, took over... and added the new "real" data to base his predictions on from that time forward. While that theory could explain the inexplicable, it contained too many maybes to be correct.

FOR hours, painstakingly, she checked pairs of charts against each other. Her back and shoulders were aching and concentration had pounded a dull throbbing into her head. Needing a stretch, a chance to clear her head, she walked out onto the small balcony overlooking the bay. The light wind and its sharp tang of brine refreshed her face. She arched her back and sucked in the salty air, holding it in till the weight on her shoulders lifted.

A storm seemed to be brewing in the east with dark clouds tumbling toward her from the headland opposite. Light rain started to dimple the water extinguishing the pinpricks of light that were winking from it.

Ralph ambled out onto the balcony and nudged against her leg enjoying every minute of the changed house rules. Since Michael had gone, Ralph got to roam free in the house and be her company sitting at her feet when she was working or watching TV.

As she leant down to give his black coat a stroke, she was struck by something and ran back to her computer, leaving Ralph rolling on his back with no one to tickle his belly.

She yanked out her modem plug severing her link to the internet or with any part of the outside world. To make certain, she tried opening up Google, then her email, and both times the computer confirmed it was disconnected from the internet. Excellent! Next she clicked onto Michael's disk and opened his stock charts for two well-known global corporations: General Motors and Microsoft. Without an external internet source, neither the disk nor any embedded software could surreptitiously update these charts. She printed out hard copies of both charts, handwriting "without internet" on each one, and she also left them open in separate windows on her screen.

Satisfied that the versions she'd printed were identical to those on her monitor, she replugged her modem and re-linked herself to the outside world. For a backup check, she clicked onto the financial website, Bloomberg.com, and found their charts for General Motors and Microsoft and printed them as well.

Now, with printouts of Michael's raw charts as well as the official ones she once more applied her split screen technique. Again, for the full period from the Michael's disappearance to yesterday, his "without internet" charts traced the official charts she'd just freshly downloaded with perfect accuracy. To make certain even more, she took the four printed sheets and getting up to stand at the window, she held them up one-against-one in the light, comparing the "with" and "without" versions. There wasn't a single jot of difference.

Even the best meteorologists in the world couldn't accurately predict the next day's weather day-after-day, so how could Michael have got all these prices, *all* of them, so perfect? She chewed on her lip.

Maybe, she thought, she just had to roll with it... suspend disbelief, like in a movie, or a religion. Billions of people had faith in things there was no hard evidence for and here, before her very eyes, she was staring at what seemed like very solid evidence. Mystifying, for sure, but real. The only thing missing was a credible explanation. Tell that to the Pope, she told herself.

Next, she scanned the disk to see if there was a price chart for ZipChip. There was, and she followed it from past to present, from left to right, and saw a very familiar path unfold: a slight fall to $12 just after she'd bought in, then, her finger lined up the date, the fire when the stock price halved. And, there, a sudden spike with the $8 takeover bid.

As she started to scroll further to the right, something thickened in her throat. If what she saw proved correct, over the following two weeks ZipChip would hover around its current price of $8.90, a little above the bid price. But when she scrolled a couple of weeks further on, to just before the takeover bid was due to close, she uttered, "Shit!" The price lifted, first to around $10 and two days later it got another spurt, rocketing to $15, more than she'd originally paid. She'd not only recoup her money, she'd make a profit.

Fifteen dollars! What would cause that? she wondered, giving Ralph a scratch as if seeking inspiration from him. Pahokee surely wouldn't increase their offer to ten and raise it again two days later?

Suddenly, she recalled Al's wink, his not-so-subtle hint that she should sit on her hands until the close.

SONYA watched and waited; this would be the perfect test for Michael's disk. One week before the ZipChip takeover was set to close, Pahokee Networks publicly announced a two-week extension and—yes!—they increased their bid price to $9.50. "To wrap it all up", as Al told her when she phoned him. But only $9.50? She scratched her head. Michael's chart was showing a closing price of $10.

The day still had a few hours' trading left and by its close the market did shoot up, settling 50 cents higher... at $10. On chart. On time.

Next morning, over coffee and treating herself to a blueberry bagel, Sonya was devouring the business press when Al phoned her, "It's in the bag," he said. "We're putting the heat on ZipChip's board now. There's no more money in it, Son, but an offer of $9.50 is still $9.50..." He detected a reticence in her silence. "If you want to do better than that, you ought to think about selling on market to the arbs... the arbitrageurs," he elaborated as if a business professor wouldn't have a clue. "They're buying on-market at $10 hoping there's more in it, the crazy bastards, but when they realise that Pahokee's $9.50 is the best price they'll ever see, the market price will fall back."

Al's advice didn't gel. Not with Michael's chart. She was confused, "Al... Pahokee could increase again, assuming they wanted to, right?"

"No way," said Al. "We publicly announced this increase as final and under the rules final means final."

"But what if... I don't know... if someone else comes along and offers more?"

Al didn't answer directly but even so, he was adamant. "There's no one out there. Not in this market. This is it..."

She thought for a moment; she could sell out now and take $10 but, if Michael's chart was tipping correctly, she'd make a whopping $5 a share extra by just sitting pat for two days. "Al, I'm hanging on till the end."

TWO days later, Sonya woke, wincing with severe stomach cramps. It was the strain... the anticipation. It had to be since it was the day she was hoping ZipChip would be flying to $15, and her $150,000 worth of stock which had at one point withered to $75,000 was going to rocket to a stunning $190,000. It wouldn't solve her financial problems, not even close, but every dollar would help.

It was strange but she had expected to feel relieved, possibly even exhilarated; not knotted up like this. She pressed against her stomach wondering if it truly was the strain. Maybe it was the makings of a baby—she was still avoiding the test, as if not knowing kept her options open.

A spasm ran through her, starting from the pit of her stomach. Instinctively, she rolled onto her side bringing up her knees to reduce the pressure and then she felt it... the familiar stickiness. This wasn't the dread of anticipation... and it wasn't a baby...

For weeks she'd been keeping the possibility at bay. She knew it was weird since she'd pined for a baby for years, but with everything... no Michael... the debt... her new load at university... it was easier to just let it happen. But now was different.

The certainty she wasn't pregnant hit her hard. She didn't know what to think, not that she had known before. At first her mind shifted into automatic pilot. She couldn't focus on anything, except an absence, a nothing, a zero.

Eventually, she stood bowed, damaged, under the shower rose, her head down, the water streaming over her. Drying herself was desultory, a rub here, a swipe there, a pat down... With her hair still dripping like bunting after a rained-out parade she mindlessly stripped her bed.

Slowly, as she wandered about the house, she wafted out of the fog and, despite her shower, felt clammy again. Not down there—she'd taken care of that—but her chest. It was her tee-shirt, front and back. The back was damp. She'd expected that from her hair. The front of her shirt was drenched. She looked down and it was as if the red cotton had corroded to rust. She must have been sobbing for over half an hour.

17

THE ALL-NIGHTER in the law firm's conference room reeked of the testosterone of a contest almost won.

The flat-screen TV on the wall silently beaming Bloomberg, the financial news channel, as well as a live stock market feed flashed up a news bulletin that stock market trading in ZipChip shares had been temporarily suspended. Al MacAntar and everyone else round the table knew that a stock went into a trading halt only if there was an important announcement pending.

"Let's take a book on it," Morris jumped in. Morris Pierce was Pahokee Networks' lead banker on the takeover bid but so far as Al knew Morris was no shoot-from-the-hip gambler. He was one of the country's most respected investment bankers these days. It was a fast-shrinking group, Al smirked to himself. Morris was early forties, a little older than Al, svelte and with a sickening lush head of black hair, quite a contrast to the lawyer.

Morris's trademark attire was a cool blue shirt under a subtle grey woollen suit, always two-button and bought off-the-rack, something Al had never been able to do, especially not in any Zegna, Armani or Valentino store where the slim-cut was the depressing convention. Morris also had his famous collection of silk ties: Karen had told Al that the gossip was he owned around 300, never wearing one twice in any year.

Despite the whole room having worked through the night Morris kept true to his brand though he loosened up enough to unbutton his jacket as he sauntered over to the whiteboard. The red marker he'd picked up squealed down the whiteboard making three columns. Down the left-most, he listed the names of everyone in the room, scrawling his own last. He headed the middle column: "A: ZipChip Capitulates." The last one was: "B: ZipChip Fights to Death."

"Okay. Fifty bucks a throw," said Morris turning back to the room. "Winner takes all. Two or more winners, they split the cash. Angus…," he called to his offsider, "collect the dough as we go."

Angus stood up and headed to where the first person on the list was seated. It was Joe Jiminez, Pahokee Network's always casually-dressed president. "The boss always goes first, Joe," Morris said, needling his and Al's client.

"They capitulate," Joe shrugged and reached into his jeans pocket for the money. Morris marked a cross alongside Joe's name in the "A" column. Angus palmed the $50 note and moved on to each of the others in turn.

By the end, seven were predicting ZipChip's surrender and six that ZipChip would defend to the end. One person had slipped out of the room for a comfort break, or so she said, but in truth Karen Longly wasn't wasting fifty bucks for a stupid boys' game when she could better spend it as a down payment on new shoes.

"And you, Morris?" Al asked. Al's bet was ZipChip would surrender at $9.50, although his heart and his pocket were hoping the fight would continue since he'd gouge more fees for his firm that way.

"Me? A rival bidder… Option C," said Morris. "ZipChip's been way too quiet since we punched out our increase. Not a peep." He buttoned his jacket and walked back toward his chair.

"You've been saying that," Joe nodded. "Run me through how we play this if you're right?"

"It depends on their price, Joe. They come in too low, we jump them immediately with another price hike of our own. We've got to block them soaking up any stock. That's our edge. That 15 percent we snapped up will be hard for them to beat. I've got a press release drafted, ready for an increase. All we have to do is fill in our new price. But they come in too high, we stall, make them think we're going to overbid them and we negotiate a deal, maybe force them up again, sell, pocket their dough, have a party and you fly home to Florida, disappointed but richer."

Al was about to say something but Morris's mobile phone rang. As he talked, Morris walked back over to the window and stared out over Sydney Harbour, seeing beyond his success fee to what it could buy. To the others his body was silhouetted and even when he turned back to them his face was in shadow so they couldn't see his smile. Not a bad day, he chuckled. The bonus he'd get for this deal alone—

provided his employer, a European bank, stayed solvent—could buy him any one of those boats scooting across the water, but who needed boats? He had always thought of himself as a private jet sort of guy and he suspected a few of them would be hitting the second-hand market pretty soon, especially if world's financial woes got any worse.

He placed his hand over the mouthpiece and nodded to Joe, "It's Kramer." Kramer was ZipChip's adviser. "Unless we give him an increase in the next five minutes they're going public with announcing a higher offer at $12.50… from IXJ would you believe?"

Joe snapped, "What bank in its right mind would finance those fucks? And at that price? Jes-us!"

"Bank? Right mind? There is such an animal these days?" said Al, not entirely joking and worrying about how Morris could even be thinking about increasing the bid after Joe's public statement that the offer was final. He was about to say so when Morris interrupted.

"Angus, my winnings." Morris held out his hand but he continued cold as ice, "Joe, at $12.50 we're done, right?" The analysis Morris had presented to the full Pahokee Networks' board in Florida a month earlier estimated $15 of value for ZipChip on a most optimistic case, assuming they were deal-crazy enough to pay away every cent of the synergies, the benefits from putting the two companies together. Joe's board had said a flat "no" to that and set an upper price ceiling of $12.45 hoping they wouldn't have to go even that high.

"What are these guys smoking'? Twelve-fifty?" Joe turned to his chief financial officer, "Hell… Christie, what's our profit if we pull out now?" She was already punching the numbers into her hand-held calculator.

"Our average entry-price, $7.50," she said, without looking up. "At IXJ's $12.50 we make a gross profit of five bucks per share and across our... 20.25 million shares, it's just over a hundred... less costs of 15 to 20." She looked over at Morris. "We come out $80 million ahead, give or take."

"Not bad for a few weeks' wor..."

Morris interrupted, waving his phone, but with his finger over the microphone. "Kramer wants our move."

"Tifi," said Joe, as he slipped a cigar out of his shirt pocket, a Cuban. Unlike back in Florida, Cubans weren't embargoed here but as Al had reminded him several times already smoking anything in the building was, even for clients.

"Tifi?" asked Morris.

"T-I-F-I," said Joe, spelling it out and drawing the cigar under his nose. "Tell 'im: fuck 'im," he explained. "We're done. We're out."

Morris removed his finger from the mouthpiece. "TIFI," he told Kramer. "...You shittin' me you don't know what that means? It means you get your IXJ patsies up to fifteen bucks then we're out, the company's all theirs, and you get your big fat success fee."

Both Joe and Al gaped at Morris in horror.

"AL, I'm glad I waited," Sonya gushed over the phone. "Fifteen dollars!"

"Yeah," his voice flat.

"Did you think it would go this high?" she asked.

Al's bravado had fled him. "Me? No way."

But Sonya had expected it.

While Al blathered on about the drama of the bid's final minutes, her eyes stayed riveted on Michael's chart, the sheet of paper laid out before her like a treasure map with X marking $15.

18

BY MID-MORNING THE early buds had shaken off the night's frost. Their petals unfurled, yawning welcome to the glare of the day. The sky was a smouldering golden-blue with a single stripe of clouds scudding across from the north-east. Sonya stood at the window and drew in the bouquet from the honeysuckle that Michael had planted two years earlier.

She was about to close the glass but decided crisp was good so she wrapped her knit jacket round her and headed back to her desk.

As she did every day of the eight weeks he'd been missing, she thought of him... What drove her was the conviction that there must be a good explanation, that he would return and that she'd be waiting for him... here.

After the ZipChip take-over proved his disk data—to the date and to the dollar—she relied on it more and more and gingerly took the next step: using it for actual stock trading. She was already making money. Daily, she'd click open his DATA directory on the disk and skim through it, her sole intellectual input being a random choice of what stock to buy for her next trade. She only took small positions for short periods. It was all she had the stomach for. Looking ahead a few days on the charts and trading off them was all the pressure she could take.

But today, her mouse slipped and she accidentally clicked on the KW folder, the other directory on his disk. Until now she'd never opened it; the data charts had been more than enough to keep her absorbed.

She noticed that not only did the KW folder sap a massive seven gigabytes of the dual-layered disk but it contained a single file, a program: kw.exe.

Curious, she double-clicked. Her fingers tapped while it started up.

Aagh! A stupid computer game. It even commenced with the regulation drums beating... and the classic corn ball, resonant voice: *"Get ready and brace yourself for the tour of your lifetime... if you dare."* Yadda, yadda.

She tugged at her earlobe. Michael wasn't into computer games. He simply wasn't the type and neither was she. As if she'd get infected by it she quickly clicked the exit button and went back to familiar territory: her charts. Well, Michael's charts.

Even after the proof of Michael's prowess from the ZipChip takeover and her subsequent test trades Sonya maintained caution. While the charts had worked flawlessly so far, as they'd apparently done for him, she knew there was no way they'd maintain perfect foresight. Not every time. It wasn't possible. And it would be just her luck that she'd be the victim when they failed.

In the first few skittish days she kept her trades cautiously small, staying on edge for when the whole thing went belly up. But the strange thing was it didn't. As her confidence grew, so did the size of her trades. It was uncanny, alarming even: no matter what stock or bond she selected or what market index, they performed right in line with Michael's predictions. She was already amassing some healthy profits. And needed to.

Since the close of the ZipChip bid stock markets had become even more volatile.

Her mind flew back to the first chart she'd opened those many weeks before, the S&P 500 chart, and she wondered why she'd not thought of it before. She pulled it up again and, yes, for the next six months starting in just a week in mid-September, through the Obama-McCain US presidential elections in November and even several months beyond, the world was going to get ugly.

Yet, though she knew the charts had been spot-on so far, accurate to the day and to the cent, the market trajectory snaking down her screen was way too extreme. The prediction simply had to be wrong.

She pulled up other charts, index charts, individual stock charts. The world—virtually every market everywhere—was headed for Armageddon at the same time with chilling declines of 30 to 50 percent, some even more. And that, she noted, was even after most of the world markets had already plunged a shocking 20 percent from their record highs only a year earlier.

She zeroed in on individual stocks for the next month—if she didn't have some serious money by October, November at the latest, Al was getting worried he wouldn't be able to keep her bank at bay.

She saw that even in that short time, some stocks had—would have—momentous swings. If she was going to rescue herself, she needed to move. She needed the world to collapse and she started working up the idea of how she'd play it.

It was the chart for Merrill Lynch the international investment bank which first caught her eye. What loomed for it over the next few weeks was a stock price saw-tooth of unthinkable ferocity. She pored over every shift in the bank's price chart as if she were peering down a microscope. Since its all-time high a mere two years earlier, the famous Thundering Herd, according to the chart, would stampede off a cliff with almost 85 percent of its value obliterated.

How it would play out intrigued her... shocked her. Assuming it was accurate. In one week's time, Wall Street's famous financial powerhouse would face an abyss... an out-and-out vertical spiral of 40 percent down in two short terrifying days. Even more incredibly, and without a pause a monster updraft would haul it up again by more than 80 percent, where it would just as suddenly peak, hovering briefly in mid-air, before gravity took over, dumping the once-prestigious financial firm and sending it into a terrifying 60-percent freefall.

This was breathtaking. This was Merrill Lynch. The world's financial troubles were bad but could they really get this bad? In all her years of teaching about markets, all her research, she'd never come across anything as severe across the globe. There were parallels with the 1930s, for sure, but this was unbelievable. This was now. It was everywhere. It was huge.

Yet there it was, right in front of her, one of the world's financial titans lurching down, up, down as if it was on a bungy cord, but if it were true not one second of it would be fun for anyone.

She rechecked the other stock charts she'd flicked over for the same period. The carnage was spattered everywhere. Virtually no one was spared. But looking quickly, she couldn't find a chart as volatile as Merrill Lynch, except for one other investment bank, Lehman Brothers, but to Sonya that chart clearly had something amiss. Its price line collapsed and then just stopped. She didn't understand it. Not unless Lehman went bust. Overnight. It was unimaginable.

The professor's mind drifted to the consequences of what she was looking at… wealth wiped out on an unimaginable scale… hundreds of thousands of jobs gone. There wouldn't be just a ripple effect from Wall Street to Main Street… this would be a shockwave. And all the various charts she again started clicking through showed it would race unabated all around the globe crushing firms and markets in its wake no matter where they were or how strong they were.

What on earth could trigger a calamity of such unthinkable magnitude, she pondered, feeling an urge to tell someone.

Suddenly she blinked. This was her make-or-break time, her one chance to throw her own bank off her back and make enough extra money to fund a real search for Michael since, so far, the police had got nowhere.

Keep focused… don't get sidetracked…

This couldn't be true… but what if it was?

To stop her arguing with herself, she got busy adding up every cent she could lay her hands on: $340,000 after her recent trading. Not peanuts by most people's standards, but for what she was aiming to do, it wasn't anything like enough.

She calculated her likely winnings. If she traded into the Merrill Lynch rollercoaster, she'd make heaps but nowhere near enough and not quick enough. She drummed her fingers on her calculator keys, contemplating how bleak her mission seemed.

What if, she wondered, what if she leveraged herself up using options, like Michael had done so successfully? She terrified herself. What if she did it and she was more like Steven, her busted university colleague who had done it so spectacularly unsuccessfully.

Stock options were notorious. While she'd lectured on their benefits and perils for years, she didn't have any real experience of them. Her lectures weren't on how you traded them, merely the pitfalls when you got them wrong. Even the Enron whiz-masters had got mixed up with options. When Bear Stearns had collapsed everyone was talking about the noxious influence of their options and derivatives holdings. And now there was a lot of attention on Lehman Brothers. She'd scanned the web for news and saw report after report claiming the firm was overburdened with exotic options and other toxic assets, masses of sub-prime mortgage derivatives and five trillion dollars worth of credit default swaps. Maybe it would go bust?

Options had a lot to answer for. And here she was seriously contemplating that she'd become an options trader herself. Was she kidding?

Michael had played options superbly, she knew that, but there were still plenty of Nobel Prize-winners, corporate titans and stock market gurus who'd screwed up big-time.

As she could. As Steven had.

But she wasn't going to, was she? She would win. Options would be her firepower.

She'd seen Michael's success first hand in some of the trading sheets Sorden had left with her. With one of his trades he'd grown a single $500,000 bet into $10 million in just a few weeks. It was a 20-to-1 shot and it came through. Her kitty was $340,000. If he could do it...

She pored over a stack of borrowed university texts and soaked up whatever she could snatch from all over the web. Sonya had to be scrupulous, not miss a thing. This had to be right. Perfect.

She picked up the trader's jargon. A lot of it she'd heard before and she was a quick learner. She threw around terms, to herself to start with, like *in-the-money*, *at-the-money* or *out-of-the-money*. Cutting through the gibberish she knew the basics were pretty simple, but get them wrong and it could be fatal. In her own lectures her standard spiel was that playing options was like betting on a 50-to-1 long shot. You place your wager and if the stock does what you pray it will you collect big-time... a massive multiple of your money. But if your stock stumbles at the final stretch you tear up every single cent you handed over the counter. Just like at the track.

Playing options was a win or lose game, virtually nothing in between. That was terrifying. Yet if she made this play... her pen slipped out of her clammy fingers.

What she was planning was foolhardy speculation, she told herself. No it wasn't, she slapped the desk as if it was her face. Not with Michael's charts it wasn't.

To clear her head of the competing voices she headed out to the beach. A few mothers in sweaters were digging in the sand with their toddlers, the naked kids oblivious to the springtime cold snap. As one little girl waddled to the water's edge, her mother instantly scrambled to her feet carelessly demolishing the turrets off their McSandcastle.

The family scenes did nothing to calm Sonya's dread. Not quite talking aloud, she told herself she needed to come to grips with the intricacies of trading, all the practicalities. For example, she knew that option prices didn't move precisely in parallel with stock prices and that would, she knew, screw with her calculations since Michael's charts only forecast stock prices, not option prices. Any major divergence and Sonya could get wiped out. And what about liquidity? She knew that it wasn't always possible to buy or sell the options you wanted when you wanted them, even if you were prepared to pay their technically correct prices.

Kicking the cool sand with her toes she reminded herself how the massively bigger American options markets were far more liquid than Australia's so, easy, she'd trade there.

Decision one was made. And given it was the Merrill Lynch price data she'd been most keyed up about, Merrill Lynch would be her play.

Decision two.

TWENTY, thirty times per day she rehearsed, agonising over every micro-detail. She knew all the moves and the timing and the amounts. Everything. Every cent she owned, and some she didn't, she'd be betting on this. She was even taking a hit on her credit card: $10,000 to round her kitty up to $350,000.

The trepidation was staring her down. Her gut knotted with worry that she might miscalculate. She checked again and again. And again.

Despite finding no more errors, her confidence was as shaky as her late father's alcoholic hand.

A website she found claimed she could know it all for just $99:

"TRADE LIKE THE PROS!" it screeched. "*The Ultimate, Simulated On-line Floor Trading Experience... Get prepped for the trading event of a lifetime...*" it urged, as shrill as the stupid game on Michael's disk she'd opened up earlier.

"*The bell will ring, the ticker will start and the orders will flow,*" it claimed. "*Using our state-of-the-art, fully electronic trading system, you'll be coached by real options exchange floor traders on how to place options trades and execute strategies just like the pros! This simulated floor trading session will set you up for profit.*"

She downloaded the course on the spot and laboriously worked through every one of its simulations, passing each with flying colours and handing Ralph down at her feet a dog biscuit each time as a reward.

She knew she was as prepped as she'd ever be and was ready to launch herself headlong into a wild, real-time casino.

SONYA lurched between terror and ecstasy. The ecstasy that, against all conventional odds, she might win versus the terror that her decisions were based on a mere puff: a computer disk that supposedly predicted future stock prices. Right! Explain that to the bankruptcy judge or the dean when he fired her. The terror that she'd never done this before... that for her it was on such a huge scale... that she was playing with an infamous security: options, that people far smarter than she was had gone belly-up on... that she was throwing down every single cent she could find to do it, plus some, and risking the lot... everything...

This was all or nothing, and every jittery part of her knew it.

Karen Longly's nagging voice broke into Sonya's already throbbing head: sell up the house and walk away... Sure, Karen, she thought, but then I'd start with nothing all over again.

Focus! More dummy runs, again and again, day and night, double-checking, triple-checking, and...

It was a mad ritual but the big day was looming.

19

SONYA JERKED AWAKE at 5 AM. Her eyes wide open she saw her bedcovers were strewn over the floor. Her dream... what was it about?

What the hell was it? It was something important.

Currency! She'd neglected currency risks. Jesus! All her Little Miss Clever calculations and she'd totally ignored how she'd be exchanging currencies, twice in fact; once when she opened her broker account—since all her options trades would be in US dollars—and again when she was done and would be converting her profits—if there were any—back into Australian dollars. Worse, she'd be exposed to US dollars over a few weeks and she was completely at sea as to how the exchange rate would fare during that time.

Normally currencies were stable enough not to worry over short periods but lately the exchange rate had become such a big issue it was a major feature on each night's news. In just the last six weeks the Australian dollar had plummeted by a startling 18 percent against the US dollar. "It can't go any lower than this," one radio expert pontificated. "At 80 US cents, the Aussie dollar has hit bottom," he continued. "From here it's a weakening greenback and a strengthening Aussie as the US heads into recession. The A$ is going up from here."

The recent dramatic fall of the Australian dollar had already sent shock waves through importers and holiday makers who were now being hit with paying 18 percent more for exactly the same computers, cars or overseas vacations they could have bought only two months ago.

What if the currencies made another wild swing while Sonya was loaded up on US dollars? It could blow her entire strategy.

She shot out of bed as if it was about to explode and ran cold and naked to her desk, not even stopping for her robe. Her screen-saver was swirling at her when she pulled up her chair. These days she never switched off her computer.

Michael's disk contained charts on currencies too, and she tracked them forward for the next couple of months. Holy…!

The Australian dollar was set to drop further, like a stone, by a massive 30 percent on top of the tumble it had already suffered. "It can't go any lower than this," she smirked, remembering the so-called currency expert's precise words. It would and it would be a bloodbath.

"Don't panic," she said aloud, lacing her fingers together and banging her hands against the edge of her desk. Protection! She'd have to buy currency protection, a hedge. It would cost, she knew that, but it wouldn't cost 30 percent, not even remotely.

Just as she started punching out her night broker's phone number to get a price on a currency hedge, her tired eyes sparked as it dawned on her that the currency slump she was looking at actually went in her favour. For her, this would be good news. Great news.

Apart from converting her Australian funds into US dollars as quickly as possible, ahead of the imminent cliff dive, she didn't have to do a single extra thing. Whatever US dollar profit she'd make from her options trades would be worth an extra 30 percent to her when she swapped the funds back into Australian dollars afterwards.

Sonya was prepped for battle though she felt nothing like it, her mind and body already duelling for what little remained of her energy. The whole world was headed for ruin and she was the only one alive who knew it... who actually knew it!

Her weak smile flagged the ache that gnawed at her insides. Yes, it was other people's misery she was aiming to profit from.

Trading options in the US meant she'd be night trading, another factor she had initially overlooked. The Chicago Board Options Exchange rang its opening bell at 8:30 AM, fine if you lived in America but an uncivilised 1:30 AM start for Sonya.

The whole period she'd be trading she'd be a nocturnal stalker, hunched over her screen, watching, waiting, her phone to the ready while most people she knew would be curled up snug in their beds. Well, not so warm and not so snug, she realised. More likely, they'd be tossing and turning and suffering nightmares and panic attacks as the stock market terror unfolded. While she would be gorging they'd be despairing as their wealth and their jobs flushed away from them.

THE final task on her list was to concoct an excuse for cutting classes. The police investigation was taking its toll on her she lied, though she wished it had been true. The fact was she'd hardly heard a thing from Sorden lately. As far as she knew his investigations had gone into a black hole. Much like Michael.

She told her dean how her lawyers and bankers were making stressful demands on her, that she needed her full mental capacity to sort out the mess her life had involuntarily become.

His sympathetic eyes peered over his half-moon glasses and he held up his hand to stop her, saying, "Take all the time you need. I'll work out a fix, even if I have to take your classes myself."

Sonya tensed with guilt over her deception but it was brief, only until she threw her leg over her bike to ride home. She had work to do.

20

It took only a minute but as Sonya drew her head in from the window and closed it, her nose and lips were tingling. It was 2 AM and the September moon was a sliver of fingernail no bigger than those she'd been biting off her shaking hands. To still them she pressed her fingers against the edge of her desk until her knuckles bleached white and the tiny muscles ached.

Her diaphragm clenched as she lifted the handset to phone her broker, her local link to the Chicago exchange. Bruce, in Sydney, was also a night owl.

Her eyes were drawn back out the window. All life was out there somewhere yet tonight it was unseen.

A weak, discomfiting laugh sputtered up her dry throat just as Bruce came on line and she quickly babbled her mammoth order at him as if he were a short order cook in a greasy diner. Hearing him gasp didn't help her and her teeth clamped her lower lip while she prayed he'd just do as she'd asked.

"Huh? Merrill Lynch? You sure about that?"

From the jolt in his voice Sonya could almost see his eyes bulging. "I'm sure," she croaked, sounding anything but.

"This is one really big trade," he said, stressing each of the last three words as if they were in capital letters and she was a five-year-old. "Ever done anything as big as this before? Maybe with another broker?"

While he waited for her answer—she was slow to work up her lie—he clicked around his screen to access his firm's latest equity research on Merrill Lynch. He skimmed the key points set out in a convenient bullet point list made for moments like this. Not liking what he saw, he continued, "Look, they've been hammered lately for sure, but now they're on an upswing. This is a bad time to be shelling out to buy put options. According to our research, this stock is on a rocket. No way is it going down…"

He left the statement hang which was exactly what Sonya felt he was doing to her.

Bruce's mind spun. Over the past few nights, he'd been trading options for Sonya in small licks. He didn't know it but they'd been practice trades—and for a novice she'd done brilliantly. She was a quick pickup of the tricks that most new traders missed or found difficult to master. Despite her misgivings the on-line "*TRADE LIKE THE PROS*!" course she'd taken had done the trick.

What Bruce had tonight was a Sonya totally different to the tentative, careful one whose penny-ante micro-trading had annoyed the hell out of him… This one was a wacko, prepared to toss every single cent in her account onto the single spin of a roulette wheel, one that he thought was rigged against her. One giant options play. All on red when, to him, the market for Merrill Lynch looked the complete opposite.

If this went bad and she lost everything, his boss would demand answers. From him. Did you give her the right advice, Bruce? Was she aware of the risks, Bruce? She ever done this before, Bruce? What the fuck were you doing, Bruce? And worse of all, Bruce nodded to himself, You're fucking fired, Bruce. Job-wise, this was no time to be an optimist. In this environment, optimism was when a broker took a cut lunch to work and expected to eat it at his desk.

His fingers ran through his gelled hair as he worked hard to sweet-talk the little lady out of her lunacy.

Sonya did start to waver. To calm her hands, she put her phone on loudspeaker. Her fingers drummed and dithered against her thigh and she rubbed her other hand across her forehead. Her stomach was twisting like a car body in a wrecker's crusher. With Bruce banging on in her ear and beating down her resolve she tuned him out and focused on her plaque. She'd made a replica of Michael's in case she needed it: *Follow your own mind*.

She picked up the phone, took a deep breath, and loudly, too loudly, interrupted the barrage, "Stop. No advice, okay. Just execution," the broking jargon that he should simply take her order without asking questions or giving advice.

Yeah, but it's not just *your* execution he worried though he comforted himself a little because all client calls were taped. Broking houses knew from long experience that taping calls was the best way to resolve most "I said/she said" customer disputes.

Keeping his eyes fixed on the butterfly tattoo fluttering to his left on Jacquie's shoulder over at the wheat desk, he spoke into his headpiece as formally and clearly as the gum he'd been chewing would allow. "Ms Wheen," he began, unaware she was a PhD let alone a professor. 'University employee' was what she'd scrawled on her client agreement form. "I'm very uncomfortable with your order. It's extremely risky. Extremely risky," he repeated, as if she needed him to. "Going toe-to-toe against the market isn't a smart call at the best of times. You know what they say, the trend is your friend? Well, like I've been telling you, Merrill is on the upswing yet here you're wanting to bet your whole account that it's gonna dump, and dump quick."

The air heaved into Sonya's chest, straining her lungs against her ribs. In the blackness outside her window a faint tap-tapping sound approached, but against the thumps of the pulse in her ears she couldn't hear the possum tightrope-walking across the power line to its lair in her roof.

She focused on Michael's plaque then squeezed her eyes shut. "Do it," she told Bruce. "Just do it," she added for her own emphasis and threw down the phone as if it was coated in poison. Her breath burst out of her like a deflating balloon.

It was a Friday in Chicago, Saturday her time. It would be three more days before she'd have any idea if this massive punt was going to work. Today would be an up day for Merrill Lynch. Michael's stock chart predicted that and she knew Bruce would keep reminding her of it. But that was precisely why she chose to lay her bet today. With the market mood for Merrill somewhat buoyant the contrarian put options she wanted would be dirt cheap.

Bruce didn't call back. How long was he going to take to confirm he'd executed her order? She kept checking her watch. Two minutes. Five. Ten. It was unbearable. When she'd been doing her small practice trades it had taken him a couple of minutes at most, and often he'd kept her on the line while he did it.

Fifteen minutes later, her nerves snapped when the phone rang. Before he said anything, she shouted, "What did we get done at?" It was the shorthand trader talk for, "What price did you buy my put options at."

"Ms Wheen, I... I'm really worried. I've been on the phone to our research analyst... in New York. He backs me up on this... that it's the worst time to buy Merrill puts. You'll do all your dough, every cent, if you go ahead with this trade."

She stifled a scream and kept her voice tight and cold, "You haven't... done what I asked?"

"He knows this stock ma'am, and he's got a 'strong buy' recommendation on it."

To Sonya there were only two types of experts. Those who didn't know the future and those who didn't know they didn't know.

"Let me ask you again," she said. "You haven't done what I asked?"

"Er, no," came his sheepish reply. "I mean, if you insist... but I think..."

Follow your own mind she yelled at herself, but with him she raised her voice only a little, "I'm not asking you to think, alright? If you don't execute my trade now... right now... and I lose this opportunity..."

She didn't have to complete the threat. He knew what she meant. She'd sue the hell out of his firm and he'd never get to eat another cut lunch at his desk or, in his case, another midnight McDonald's.

Sonya held her breath a moment, easy since a tight band was already constricting her chest. "Just... do it. Do you hear me?" She'd almost sworn at him and as she was slamming down the phone the telltale beep that the call was taped made her glad she hadn't.

Her whole body was trembling. She could feel the wetness oozing under her arms and around the back of her neck. She squeezed her eyes shut and bit the side of her index finger so hard her tongue reeled back from the acrid taste of blood. With a groan she exhaled and waited, again. In raw panic.

SHE dialled through to Bruce only a second before he was going to call her, his phone finger already poised above the keypad.

"It's done," he said.

Sonya had expected a rush of relief but the heat that steamed from her pores was only a hint of the fire that would stew her over the next two weeks threatening her resolve.

She was fixated for the whole six-and-a-half hours the Chicago exchange, the CBOE, was open for trading that day. Even after it was closed she relived the day minute-by-minute. She couldn't eat, only pecking at food. Her main sensation was a numb terror that she, and Michael's chart, were wrong and the broker's research analyst was right.

Early evening, feeling totally drained, she slipped one of Michael's shirts over her tee-shirt and took Ralph out on the beach for some air and a run. The air for her and the run for him. She hadn't run, not once, since Michael had gone. While the dog pounded along the sand chasing the froth of each wave in and out, two black herons were paddling close to shore, but turned away.

She clambered onto the pink-yellow sandstone jutting into the water at the end of the beach, careful to keep her bare feet clear of the razor-edged oyster shells. The last time she'd come out here was with Michael, at sunset with two glasses of wine. Tonight, though cool, the still air was heavy. Briny and thick. She glanced around expecting to see dead clumps of washed-up seaweed but looking left, near the point, the low tide had exposed a sprawling mat of leathery sea squirts, cunjevoi, and a fisherman was slicing bits off one to use for bait.

CHICAGO'S weekend, Sonya's Sunday and Monday, was a trader's no-man's-land with little to offer her except worry. When the news broke on TV, she worried even more, watching agog as a grim-mouthed US Treasury Secretary Hank Paulson announced a rescue of the giant mortgage twins, Fannie Mae and Freddie Mac, semi-government firms which he said touched half of America's massive pool of home mortgages, millions of which were already infamously under stress. According to the news anchor, this was one of the largest government bailouts in history and done "to avert a major blow to global financial stability." Her head was shaking in disbelief. A short six months ago the term *sub-prime* was so uncommon it meant second-grade meat but now the words were on everyone's lips and its aftertaste was poisoning the entire global financial system.

Sonya reeled. What would this do to the markets when they reopened? Appease them? Shock them with the fear that this was worse than they thought... that there was more? How could she even think of trading into such precarious times? One bad scenario after another played itself out in her mind.

Ralph, sensing her distress, licked her hand. Good old Ralph, she muttered. He nuzzled into her lap as she stroked his back. She reminded herself that while she didn't have a clue why markets and stocks were going to move, she just knew that they would, which way and by how much.

Even though the why didn't matter, she couldn't help guessing. Merrill's stock price would rise the next trading day, as Michael's chart showed, because investors would be relieved that the weekend bailout had averted another financial crisis. But why, she wondered, would it then go into freefall on Tuesday, as she needed it to, to turn her put options into big money? She stopped herself. The only certainties right now were that the world as she knew it was in total frenzy and that she was going to come out on top... provided she could hold her nerve.

On Chicago's Monday, tracking Michael's prediction perfectly, Merrill's stock price continued rising, a move which strangely comforted her despite it slamming down on the value of her put options. Just one more day she kept reminding herself. During her last conversation with Bruce she swore at him and hated herself for it. What was she turning into, she worried, her hand trembling as she lifted it from the phone. To ease the pressure she stopped taking his calls. The last thing she needed was his badgering again and again to sell out while she could still get something for her options, before they were worthless.

But then it was Tuesday. Beautiful, wonderful Tuesday, as she thought of it, but Black Tuesday if you were a Merrill Lynch investor or employee. For the rest of that week, Merrill shares plummeted. Yes! thought Sonya, cold to the suffering of many thousands of others, but not so cold, or calm, that she could smile.

Mid-week Lehman Brothers posted a gigantic loss for its three months to August, almost $4 billion, sending not only its own shares, but also Merrill's into even more of a dive. The chart hadn't lied. Commentators were openly speculating over Lehman's survival, an implausible possibility even to Sonya not long before, but some were even daring to ask if Merrill Lynch itself would still be standing. Contagion was the new buzz-word and investment banking was the new dirty word.

Sonya hadn't contemplated what Merrill Lynch becoming insolvent would do to her options but she comforted herself that Michael's chart showed Merrill would keep trading long past her options plays. Whereas, more ominously, the price line for Lehman Brothers virtually fell off the page in three days' time. She now knew that what she saw being played out in a single line in front of her was the once venerable firm of Lehman Brothers hitting the wall.

Halfway through Sonya's first option play with Merrill already down 20 percent Bruce called to tell her how much her options were now worth, but she knew that already.

To Sonya, Bruce's call was bizarre. He was almost gloating, as if he'd been the genius who'd counselled her into taking this trade in the first place. Ignoring their earlier fiery conversations, he told her almost proudly that his firm's research analyst—the same one who'd previously had a "buy" on Merrill and had warned her against put options—was now calling Merrill a "strong sell".

He would have been great as Noah's adviser, she steamed. Noah and the animals would have drowned but the analyst could hold his head above water and warn everyone there was a flood. Late, but accurate.

Sonya's nerves were too taut to stay contemptuous for long. Hell still had plenty of time yet to freeze over for her. This time she listened politely, her ill-mannered gestures silent and unseen except by Ralph who cocked his head in bewilderment.

By the end of the first harrowing week Merrill shares had melted a third of their value, from $27 to a mere $18, and looked like they were still on a relentless downhill trajectory. When the shares slipped even further—to 40 percent down—Sonya phoned Bruce, this time an easy call to make, or so she thought. "Close me out... Yes, sell my puts... Yes, all of them."

"You're kidding me, right? Why now? That turkey's going way down, everyone says so."

Bruce was right, she knew that from her charts, but it wasn't going to happen just yet. *Follow your own mind*. She held firm. "Bruce, you don't lose money taking a profit," she said. "If I want your advice, I'll ask, okay? Sell my put options now. Right now." And once again she hung up, exhausted.

Why did she feel so lousy? If she sold the options at their current market price, she'd just made... she totted it up for the fifth time... a $4 million profit. Deducting the tax she'd eventually have to pay on her gains would cut that by around half, call it $2 million, but the coming move in the exchange rate would boost it back up 25 percent. Though $2.5 million wasn't enough to pay off her bank, that day was getting closer. And yet, she wasn't thrilled. She wasn't excited. She was utterly drained.

But she didn't have time for that.

Bruce called back to confirm the sale and just as he was about to hang up, Sonya said, "Wait, now I want you to buy me some Merrill call options." She picked the options she wanted from the screen in front of her.

Bruce restrained himself. "How many contracts?" he asked her simply.

"However many my account will pay for. The lot. The whole four million. Every cent."

Bruce muted the phone to give the screen jockey next to him the low-down. "Mate! This lady's totally fucked in the head," he said, pointing to his headset and contorting his face as if someone had farted. "With all the shit going down out there she's made fuckin' four bars on Merrill puts—yeah, her!—and now she wants to piss it all down the toilet on Merrill calls for fuck's sake! Can you believe this fuckin' loon?"

His desk mate shrugged thinking so what if Bruce had told his client their banking analyst had a strong sell on Merrill and so what if the crazy woman wanted short-dated call options. He'd been in the game longer than Bruce and he'd seen more fortunes come and go than rock stars in and out of rehab. He pulled himself another strip of gum and turned another page of his girlie magazine to ogle some more.

Bruce almost screamed at him, "Like why the hell does she think Merrill's going to fly out of the crapper all of a sudden? What the fuck does she know that we don't, huh?"

Both brokers knew the markets were a bloodbath out there and how everything pointed to Merrill continuing on its dive yet here was a client wanting to bet it was going to turn up and turn up big. Big deal thought Bruce's colleague as he popped the gum in his mouth and turned his iPod up loud enough that Bruce could hear the tinny sound from his own seat, a signal their conversation was over.

"Hey, Ms Wheen, you can't seriously be expecting Merrill to rally anytime soon. You'll be killed." Bruce's stomach twisted as if it was dropping the whole thirty floors from his dealing desk to the deserted 5 AM Sydney streetscape below. "I can't let you do this."

With her own stomach as tight as his, Sonya did as best she could, "Isn't that what you told me last week?"

"But that was luc…" He realised what he was about to say and let his ill-advised comment hang. What the heck! It's her money. It's on the fucking tape.

Luck. Maybe it was luck, she thought. She had made $4 million, $2.5 million after tax and currency, but... what if this next trade didn't work? What if it had all been a fluke the first time round as Bruce had been about to say?

BY lunchtime Bruce was at the local brokers' haunt with an arm around Jacquie from the wheat desk and chortling about his crazy client who'd just won and likely lost a fortune in the space of a mere week. He raised his beer, "I'll miss her commissions but... but what the heck... cheers," he toasted, and drained his beer.

"FEEL like dinner? While I've still got some money left to burn," Al laughed, though not too loudly. The financial crisis was seriously impacting his firm and his income as a partner. Many clients had stopped paying their bills. Numerous others had pulled back from deals his firm had been working on for months and for the first time in years they were worried about cash flow, which he now half-joked was the movement your money made as it flushed down the toilet. Floors of lawyers were twiddling their thumbs. Al needed a friendly face.

Even while she held the phone to her ear, Sonya continued reviewing her charts. She didn't know the pressure Al was under and she didn't feel like social chit-chat tonight, with him or anyone else.

21

WEEKENDS DIDN'T ROLL up or roll by. Not for Sonya. Not for Al. Nor for anyone even remotely embroiled in financial markets.

Normally weekends were a respite from the day-to-day but not now. Weekends, when overseas markets were closed—Sunday and Monday for Sonya—had swiftly become the choice time for governments and regulators globally to slam bad banks into good ones or broadcast multi-billion-dollar bailouts; astonishing announcements individually, but taken together, tectonic with kick-on effects that impacted virtually every person on the planet, whether they realised it or not. Sonya had seen the charts. She knew that this was no mere gorilla tearing down the gilded towers of London and New York; this King Kong was rampaging in everyone's backyard.

This Sunday the news bulletins were reeling with the high drama of traffic snarls grid-locking Manhattan as limousine after blacked-out limousine ferried over-stressed bankers in and out of the US Federal Reserve. TV news crews were camped outside Lehman Brothers and Merrill Lynch… and

Goldman Sachs... all angling for a hint of what was going down.

By 1 AM Monday, New York-time—Sonya's mid-afternoon Tuesday—the awful secret was out. Lehman Brothers had filed for bankruptcy, the largest insolvency in world history citing $768 billion of bank and bond debt and assets of $639 billion, a deficiency of $129 billion. Billion. A bust bigger than the total national output of oil-rich Kuwait or, closer to home, New Zealand.

From the single line sky-diving off the bottom of Michael's chart, Sonya had drawn the correct but shocking conclusion: this stalwart of Wall Street since it started trading in the 1850s was no more.

But good news came the same day, for Sonya as well as her Merrill Lynch options, when Bank of America, its superhero red and blue logo flapping, leapt off its building in a single bound with a $50 billion rescue package under its cape and snatched Merrill Lynch away from a Lehman-like fate with only moments to spare, or so some said.

So Bruce, she smirked, this lady's going to be killed, is she? Sonya finally let herself smile. Even her red, dry eyes had their first hint of a glimmer in over a week.

She hunkered in front of her computer screen as usual, her supply of coffee going cold while mesmerised she watched Merrill stock fluctuate between $17 and $23, precisely what she expected.

But by Monday night in the US, the financial news was again chilling. After leaving Lehman to hang out to dry, US authorities stunned the world again by tossing a $20 billion lifeline to the global insurance behemoth American

International Group whose stock price had been heading so far south it was about to crash through the ice. Across the Atlantic Britain's biggest mortgage bank, HBOS, saw its Scots' heritage of financial conservatism disappearing as its stock price nose-dived 35 percent.

A mere two days later, AIG's $20 billion lifeline had not only blown into an $85 billion taxpayer-funded bailout but President George W. Bush stepped in to take control of the once proud bastion of capitalism. Sonya was agog... the most aggressively self-professed free-market administration in history had just effectively nationalised one of the world's most significant financial institutions.

And in London the beleaguered bank HBOS, its share price already on its knees, halved in value and after just one day's negotiation announced an agreed £12 billion rescue bid from rival Lloyds TSB bank.

By Friday of that week, to halt fears of bank runs in their tracks, Britain was tossing government guarantees at all its banks and the US Treasury Secretary was working night and day on a $700 billion bank bailout. According to one radio report Sonya heard, $700 billion was enough to buy every single item that the hard-working people of Singapore plus Hong Kong plus the oil-rich Saudi Arabia produced during that entire year.

Yet despite all this dire news, and courtesy of Bank of America's rescue bid, Merrill's share price had rocketed up to $30, an eye-popping spike in just five days. Sonya would have liked to punch the air but she was too exhausted, though not so much she couldn't call Bruce. "You heard me, yes, sell my options... sell them now," she almost screamed, the pressure on her was so intense. "Yes, damn it. All of them."

This time Bruce didn't press. Though he calculated that Merrill Lynch shares had risen a whopping 83 percent from its low, her $4 million punt had ballooned 750 percent to $30 million dollars. All due to the magic leverage of options. Investment guru Warren Buffet, the so-called Sage of Omaha, frequently panned options denouncing them as financial weapons of mass destruction. But he didn't own Michael's charts. Some sage.

When Bruce's email came through with her account summary, Sonya saw how much she'd made, down to the cent: US$30,195,242.88 after brokerage. All in glorious black and white. No red. Not now. $30 million plus. She worked out in her head what that meant: around US$15 million after tax or $18 million Australian. $18 million!

Sonya rippled. She had done it. While people were losing fortunes, real fortunes, she was winning, and now grinning, even though she knew that was almost indecent in the face of such widespread bedlam.

She had one more options play left. But when she got through to Bruce he mentioned a development she hadn't expected. "What short-selling ban?"

He started to explain what short-selling was: a high-risk trading strategy where you sell stock you don't own when it's high, hoping to buy it back later when it falls.

"I know what short-selling is," Sonya snapped. "What's this ban?"

According to Bruce, the US and UK market regulators had posted coordinated temporary bans to stop punters short-selling any financial stock—including Merrill Lynch—and it was rumoured other countries would follow, even Australia.

"Will that stop me trading put options?" Michael's chart had told Sonya the Merrill share price was set for yet another plunge—from $30 down to $12 over the next three weeks—and she'd been planning to bet half her $30 million pot on it by buying fresh put options. Betting the whole thirty, she had decided, was too risky no matter what the charts forecast.

This was uncharted waters for everyone so Bruce didn't have a clue what the impact of the ban would be. "I'll check," he volunteered.

While she hung on Sonya made an instant decision. She'd made more than enough money; enough to clear her debts, keep the house, hire her own investigator and still never work for the rest of her life if she didn't want to. But even though the charts had been spot-on perfect so far, the startling streak of company busts and government actions had shaken her—who knew what could unfold next?—and she simply didn't have the stomach to roll the dice even one more time, not for the three weeks of nail-biting her next bet would take. She was done. No way could she go through it again… not in this turbulence.

Telling Bruce to keep $3.5 million aside, she got him to invest the rest for her in US government treasury bonds. With everything happening in the financial sector she was nervous about leaving it on deposit with any banks anywhere until she'd be converting it back into Australian currency in a few weeks. Although she hadn't planned on it her chart for treasury bonds showed she'd make an additional profit of five percent in that short period, an annualised profit of close to 90 percent. She whistled as she guessed, correctly as it would turn out, that central banks were set to make yet another round of rate cuts in their attempts to hose down the crisis.

She had other plans for the balance she'd kept separate. She got Bruce to convert it into Aussie dollars: $4.25 million at the prevailing exchange rate.

Sonya's head was exploding. She'd managed to keep everything together so far but now she was drained. In the bathroom mirror her eyes were drawn and criss-crossed with red and her skin was pasty and her hair limp. She popped two sleeping tablets, then a third, disconnected her phone as well as the front gate buzzer, left out plenty of food and water for Ralph, stuck in some earplugs and collapsed on her bed.

"SHE'S a fucking guru," was the line Bruce was spinning to his drinking buddies and Sonya now soon discovered the downside of Michael's charts. For three nights running, Bruce kept pestering her.

Her big plays were done but she still didn't have the energy or the inclination to be rude to him. She explained her trading days were over for a while but he didn't believe her, guessing she was still scanning the markets, primed to pounce, or worse he was in dread that she had dumped him and was already dealing through another broker. It had happened before.

Things had taken a turn for the worse in Bruce's firm. Even though markets were volatile, normally music for a broker's ears, they were so wild that most of their clients were sitting on their hands, too spooked to play.

A couple of Bruce's mates from other broking houses were already drowning their sorrows after being fired, not a fate his payments on his speed boat or his Maserati could bear. Sonya was his main hope for a stream of commission and his boss was breathing down his neck to suck more business from her. But again and again, all he got was her answering machine. Given the shell-shocked faces and cancelled eyes staring into their drinks all over town, it was no longer the size of this year's bonus that was important to him. The only bonus he was focused on was simply having a job.

Bruce's messages went on and on and she couldn't bring herself to listen to them in full, eventually simply erasing them, desperate to avoid the distraction, needing time out to map her crucial next steps.

She hadn't told a soul about her plans, not even Al. She knew he'd try to stop her but she had to follow her own mind. She hadn't told him or anyone about her winning streak either, and wasn't planning to. The cover story she'd concocted would keep prying questions to a minimum or she hoped so.

She was going to take the next steps on her own, without charts, without help from anyone else. Needing to claw back the self-esteem that being left in the lurch by Michael had crushed out of her, she planned her next move as meticulously as her trading.

22

GRITTING HER TEETH behind her fake smile and smoothing the line on her new silk suit Sonya followed Derek Minchin into his office.

She scanned the chintzy paraphernalia scattered over his desk: the obligatory family photo frame, the twenty-year fountain pen and the thirty-year gold clock. Suspecting trouble, Minchin shifted the knot on his ten-year tie, fretting over even seeing her without her lawyer being present, what with the court case and all. But she'd just shown up, no appointment, following in behind him through the doors, so he had no chance to call the bank's legal department.

He pasted on his own bogus smile and barely touched her hand, as if she were a scabrous plague victim. Yet within minutes he was all over her like a summer heat rash and his face was flush probably, thought Sonya, with blood he'd sucked out of another customer's veins.

"Professor... of course, I'm deeply sorry for your loss," he said, his eyes dipped in faux sympathy about her recently-departed aunt. "But where there's a Will there's a relative," he joked tastelessly referring to Sonya's lie that her British aunt had left her enough to pay out the bank's loan in full.

Sonya watched as the relief flowed into his previously ashen face. Eventually after a few more forced smiles and small talk she opened her purse, extracted a slip of paper and handed him the money order. For $3 million. No more, no less. It was the full amount of her loan but not a penny of the interest the bank had allowed Michael to build up—$813,672.23 or whatever it had grown to since.

She stayed silent until Minchin's disappointment burbled to his mouth then, fixing her eyes on his, she raised her finger. "This is what I owe. This is all you'll get. If you accept that," she said "it's quits between us. Just send my lawyer the loan discharge and the title deeds," she said, gathering up her things and walking out, deaf to his bleating about the interest that Michael, or she, still owed.

"IS something funny?" the waiter asked her as he set Sonya's cappuccino down in front of her.

She'd been chuckling aloud over a joke Al had told her when they last discussed Minchin. "No, just enjoying the day," she replied, spooning some froth into her mouth and looking away from him up to the cloudless sky.

"A bank customer," Al had said, "is at the counter asking to speak to the manager but she's told, 'I'm sorry, ma'am, but he died yesterday.' After several days the bewildered receptionist says, 'Ma'am, four times you've called in asking for the bank manager, and four times I've told you he's dead.

Why do you keep asking?' 'Because I love hearing it,' the customer says, smiling."

"YOU did what?" spluttered Al.

Sonya's new silk suit was black and classy and it set off her rosy glow. A few nights' sleep and a few days' suntan were possible when you didn't have to be holed up in front of a computer all day and night. She passed Al the letter from the London law firm confirming they'd sent her a telegraphic transfer to settle her aunt's estate. Fortunately for Sonya's fairy-tale, the letter, a real one, didn't mention the true amount: a meagre £276.

Al dragged his pen down the page. "How much did you get? In Aussie dollars?"

"Around five million…" Another lie.

"Some aunt!"

"No one knew she was rich," Sonya added, this time truthfully.

"Okay, okay, so you got this money and without consulting me, you walk into the bank and hand Minchin a take-it-or-leave-it for three million…" He saw her squirming, so he put her at ease. "Don't get me wrong. It was brilliant, but did it work?"

Without waiting for an answer, Al picked up the phone and dialled the bank's lawyers. After the briefest of conversations, he slapped his desk, turned back to her and shook his head, muting the phone against his shoulder, "They're still chasing you for the unpaid interest."

Sonya's plan was set. "Offer them half," she said. "Tell them that's it, my final offer and it's only on the table for 48 hours. It's that or we see them in court. And Al, tell them I mean it."

Another TIFI, he smiled.

SONYA'S decks were clear. The bank had taken the two full days but they did capitulate. Her tactics had worked and after a few more days' legal mumbo-jumbo the title deeds to the house were hers. For the few minutes she held the weighty old parchment before handing it back to Al to keep in his firm's strongroom, she was in bliss.

Her dean had extended her leave of absence. She'd contemplated going the whole hog and quitting but ties, which she had too few of these days, still mattered.

Finding out what had happened to Michael at last could become her uninterrupted priority. And now she could afford it, she hired her own investigator, an expensive consultant who Al's firm frequently used for tracking down fraudsters and for dredging up hard-to-get information. Activities teetering at the edge and which a prestigious law firm couldn't be seen doing itself but needed to get done.

23

WITH THE INVESTIGATOR reviewing all the old ground, at least what she'd been prepared to disclose, one question at the back of Sonya's mind could now surface: how had Michael been so prescient, not about himself—if only! No, how did he get his foresight about markets? She'd assumed he'd created some whiz-bang predictive price program but what intrigued her was why he'd never bragged about it. Or sold it.

At first she couldn't fathom it but then it dawned on her. What had she said to anyone? Nothing. And why? Because they'd all think she was nuts. It was precisely why she'd cobbled together the story about her aunt. Why would Michael be any different?

Suddenly her mind conjured up his disk and with so much time on her hands she wondered if the computer game she'd found on it might offer her some clue.

She clicked it open, once again getting that same melodramatic drumbeat followed by the theatrically deep voice:

> "Get ready and brace yourself for the tour of your lifetime... if you dare."

Though wincing at the cornball cliché—had Michael really enjoyed this crap—this time she *would* dare and within seconds she was figuratively belted up inside the cockpit of a tiny plane, shooting round the globe at supersonic speeds, flying high and diving low... zooming in to spy close-up on towns and cities beneath. She could even fly up streets without the wings clipping the buildings. Not even little Willy two doors up had any video game as wild or as realistic as this.

As she turbo-charged round Europe, maybe two seconds per scene, centuries spun before her eyes. One moment she was streaking above a crowded English port seething with creaking square-rigged vessels flying the Union Jack and she saw one, the Mayflower, weigh anchor. Then she was zooming over filthy cobbled streets littered with horse-drawn carts and street vendors. A wild-eyed man astride a toppling barricade swept his tricolour flag to and fro. Was that French he was shouting? The image triggered a memory of a rousing scene from the musical Michael always raved about and her eyes misted up. She left the intro running and slipped downstairs, missing Gustav Eiffel's tower being erected, Bartholdi's Statue of Liberty being assembled in New York and several other enactments of history.

Flicking through their music albums—she hadn't been in the mood to play much lately so the disks were still in Michael's obsessive alphabetical order—she pulled out *Les Miz*, the New York cast version, slid it into the player and returned to her study as the music rang through the house's speaker system. By the time she got back to the game all the drumbeats had faded and, fluttering from the sparkling tip of an enormous building she didn't recognise, a banner was unfurled. *Know-Ware*, it flapped... Something stirred within her. But she couldn't place it. A faint memory floated just out of her sight, her mind unable to catch it.

A box popped up onto her screen requesting a password. She guessed *Michael* but that wasn't it. Next she tried *Michael Hunt* but that didn't work either. With her hands folded under her chin she contemplated what else he might have chosen. People often used birthdays but that would be a joke in his case. She tried their house alarm system code and, yes, she was in.

"*Hi, Michael*," said the game's text-to-voice synthesiser, its soft robotic voice startling her. "*It's been a few months.*"

"Wha...?"

It spoke again: "*Hello-o-o. Mi-chael. Are you the-ere? Please answer... Oh, I see... your computer lacks voice recognition.*"

Another pop-up flashed onto her screen but the space next to Player was already completed: *Michael Will Hunt*. She shuddered when she saw her own name typed in the space reserved for the Second Player.

She pushed back her chair and stood. Hardly aware of her surrounds, she stumbled around the house, dazed and hoping to make sense of this. When Ralph's bark brought her back she was on her balcony overlooking the beach with the dog gawking up from below, his tail swiping the grass. Ralph wanted his walk she guessed. On her way out she passed Michael's study door and stood motionless, as if entering it might invite danger.

RALPH shot out the gate scampering over the boardwalk onto the sand and down the shoreline, his loping paw prints punching the smooth white sand that the receding tide had been planing back the last hour or two. As Sonya ambled along the water's edge her mind tripped through the possibilities. Had Michael intended to share the game with her? Had he left the disk behind so she'd find it?

After thirty minutes' walk, she'd come up with no answers, only questions. She whistled to Ralph up the beach ahead of her and pointed back to the house. Ralph twisted his head back, panting with his tongue hanging out, but bounded on, oblivious to the stranded starfish his paw crushed into the sand as well as the phone ringing in Sonya's pocket.

24

AL TOSSED HIS Porsche keys onto Sonya's desk and pulled up the chair so he was sitting in front of her computer screen. Door-to-door it had taken him only twenty minutes and the adrenaline was still charging through his body, as much from anticipating her reaction to what he had to show her as from the hair-raising trip.

All that Sonya knew from his earlier call was that the investigator had discovered something that Al couldn't easily explain over the phone. Or wouldn't, she suspected.

The lawyer reached into his jacket pocket and pulled out a photocopied sheet of paper, unfolded it and set it down on the desk. When he looked up, Sonya's eyes were closed. Even though it was weeks since she had last physically confronted Michael's note, she knew the text as if it had been burned into her eyes. Yet the letter itself still had a physical pull on her, demanding that she read it again. Something tightened in Al's throat as he watched her lips move with each painful word:

My darling Sonya,

Sorry our bliss had to end like this—with a scratched note—but I could hardly face you.

We were a great couple. You know that.

And though you'll always have the memory of our last May Day together and our walk to Calvary, without you I'll be k̶nowhere.

Your love,

♦ ☐ ♦

Mike

He saw her head jolt, unaware it was a flicker of a connection. It was the strange mistake in the letter: "*…without you I'll be k̶nowhere.*" The letter 'k' that Michael had struck out was no mistake at all. It was a clue. A clue to the disk, and his computer program, *Know-Ware*. She was certain now that her theory, as Detective Inspector Sorden, and occasionally Al, had labelled it—that Michael had been kidnapped—was no theory at all.

It was why Al must have rushed over, she speculated, her mind racing ahead trying to work out how much he knew and how much he didn't.

Al had expected the letter to distress her, and the rapid movements in her eyes told him he'd been right. He placed his hand on hers for a moment. "Let me show you something," he said, forcing her to focus on her screen.

He opened up Microsoft Word, the typing program but started fiddling with reformatting the font style. Font? Who gives a shit about font? On edge now, she almost spat the question at him but rather than offend him she balled her hand into a tight fist. But as Al tapped three times on her keyboard, her hand went limp.

Staring at her from the screen was the shockingly recognisable symbol on Michael's letter: ♦ ☐ ♦

"What…" she started, but Al held up a finger to his lips and, with his other hand driving his computer mouse, block-selected the symbols and again tinkered with the font-style. When he pressed OK, Sonya gasped, "Holy…!" but she couldn't finish her exclamation.

Somehow that final click of the mouse transformed the senseless symbols into a chilling sequence of letters: S O S.

Sonya's hand flew to cover her mouth but her eyes stayed fixed on the screen as she tried to process what Al was showing her.

For several seconds, neither spoke until Al broke the silence. Barely. "You were right," he said, his voice a whisper. "Michael didn't leave you… he was taken."

AL left Sonya's and headed straight to Sorden. Sonya was hoping… praying… that the breakthrough would lead the police, or her investigator, down some new path that would bring Michael back. And this way, she didn't have to mention anything about *Know-Ware*, although if she had, she wouldn't have known what to say.

She grabbed a bottle of mineral water from the fridge and, barefoot, stepped out again onto the beach, recapping what Al had told her. The symbols on Michael's letter had puzzled the investigator in the same way they'd puzzled her, but he played out his intrigue and found he could type them using Wingdings, the common font for symbols. As Al told it, for no reason the investigator could explain, it dawned on him to switch the font from Wingdings into one of the standard fonts for text, a five-click process that transformed the cryptic symbols into the universal distress call, the Morse code for Mayday. "Our last May Day together…," Michael had written.

When she got halfway down the sand she stopped to roll her jeans up above her knees. The white grains were warm and squeaked through her toes as she padded over them to the waterline. With only a few weeks to the official start of summer, the water was still bracing, but exhilarating, and she waded in till it was calf-high and took a swig from the bottle.

It was four in the afternoon and, she reminded herself, only two hours till she needed to get ready for the dinner Al had insisted on before he left. He had almost called it a celebration, but thankfully had checked himself. "To mark the discovery," was how he put it.

She held the water bottle up to her cheek so her face would feel as cold as her feet, and then flipped the container and watched the liquid gurgle and plop into the wave a dinghy had created in its wake. She nodded, as if the wasteful splash had triggered a connection to something in her mind.

Moving back up the sand she realised she hadn't seen her dog anywhere. "Ralph," she called, and within a second she heard the slipping and sliding of the large black labrador as he bounded along the terracotta-tiled pathway down the side of the house and out the open gate onto the beach.

On the sand, she sat and cuddled him across her lap for what seemed like ages, deciding to share her dilemma with him, as if he might be able to help her resolve it. "The disk… *Know-Ware*… I didn't tell Al anything. Should I?"

BACK inside her study Sonya sat quietly. After replaying the ♦□♦/sos trick that Al had shown her a couple of times to make sure it was real, she clicked her mouse on *Know-Ware*. Everything was starting to add up but, apart from Michael, she was still missing what had happened to him, information she hoped she now had the means to acquire.

The computer welcomed her, "*Sonya, this is your first time, so greetings… If you choose to, you'll be joining me on an adventure such as you've never enjoyed before… Will you join me?*"

She paused. That computer voice. There was something about it. But while she was reflecting, he—it—pressed her: "*Well… will you join me?*"

It didn't sound like Michael's voice but she'd swear the impatience did echo his own. Her head began to swirl. The new clue in Michael's note proved in her mind that he'd been kidnapped or kil… abducted anyway, so the disk—possibly this game—could easily contain something more. That was the decision she'd made while rambling to Ralph: she wouldn't share the disk's existence with Al or anyone. Maybe later, but not now. She had to find out more herself first.

Sonya clicked on YES and the computer responded: "Know-Ware *has systems-checked your computer. You need an upgrade. You also need GPS—Global Positioning System. If you have a portable GPS, please connect it to your computer. If not, please type in your location.*"

Her neighbour Jack had one of those talking road maps in his car and Marion even had one on her phone, but GPS in a desktop computer? Why would anyone need that? Strangely, she sensed the computer was about to hassle her again so she tapped in the details it asked for: her house number, street name, suburb, city, state, country.

"*Thank you. Since you've never played before, please choose your level by clicking one of these buttons*:

From 3D through Realtime to 10D. She supposed 10D meant ten-dimensional. Curious, she clicked on it, ignoring the warning written below it. The computer voice laughed, out loud, a bit creepy like in a scary movie: "*It says don't even think about it. Try 3D.*"

"Couldn't you have suggested that the first time?" she snapped back. As soon as she'd said it, she shook her head, "I'm talking to a computer?" But the weirdness didn't stop her from clicking 3D/Holovision, whatever that might be.

"*When do you want to go?*" the computer asked next, flashing up a box with a date and time left blank, ready to be filled in. "When", it had asked; not where. If she hadn't just seen Michael's SOS message, this would have been light entertainment but, leaning back in her swivel chair to that precarious balance point where the slightest nudge could send her toppling backwards, she closed her eyes... *Without you I'll be knowhere*, Michael had written.

"*When do you want to go?*" it repeated, an edge of insistence in its tone.

She drew in a breath... When else? She typed in the date he'd gone missing and wiped her mouth, uneasy about what would come next.

"*Sorry, Sonya. In 3D, you can't go back in time or you might try to change history which is against the rules, ha ha. So try another time... in the future.*"

Sonya clicked *Let's Go* once she'd typed in 6 AM for the following day. The screen sputtered and went black for a second or two. It started pixelating and, out of the tiny digital squares that were tiling across the screen, an image started materialising... a spinning globe. The Earth. The moon—no, it was a satellite—was orbiting around it. A long thin cone of light shot out from the satellite, beaming a white circle of light down onto the planet's surface, crisscrossing the world until Australia moved into view. The beam jerked itself across to the east coast, onto Sydney. Then, the white disc switched to black, and from a circle to a tiny square which grew and grew in a faltering sequence of growth spurts until the blurry image reached full screen size:

Sonya gazed with awe as it sharpened into… her house. A full-colour three-dimensional image of her home. She'd seen the still images on Google Maps, one an aerial shot and another a flat streetview photo, but they were nothing like this.

"If you like 3D, wait till you see Holovision. But for that you'd need packets more computer power, specifically a…"

In computer jargon, the voice explained what she needed, and like most jargon it was incomprehensible: what was a quantum computer anyway, let alone a Quip?

If she'd bothered to click on the hyperlink the computer would have told her that a Quip would one day be what we'd all be calling the quantum computer equivalent of a chip, though no one had got around to naming it that yet. Instead, it added: *"Quips won't be in mass production for years, so no Holovision for you. Sorry."*

The game had a distinct personality, Sonya noted. If Michael had created this, it revealed a side to him—a lighter side—she'd rarely seen. Instinctively, she moved her cursor round the screen. She drew in her breath, "My God!" Circling her computer mouse had a profound effect: as if she were remotely driving a video camera, moving her point of view right round the house, just like in those shoot-'em-up video games. Her fingers swirled the perspective round and round a few times to get the hang of it, moving 'herself' around the perimeter of her virtual house, stopping here and there, turning round to experience different angles; smelling the roses, almost.

Suddenly, a jagged flash cracked across the screen. Reflexively, she snapped her hand away from her mouse in case of an electric shock. "Hell," she screeched, her hand covering her mouth. The flash stopped as abruptly as it had started, though a vague static haze kept flickering down the screen. Her monitor was shorting; it had to be. Damn. Carefully, she tapped it, but the static continued. She jiggled the cable connection at the back and crawled under the desktop to look at its other end but that wasn't the problem: it was plugged in securely at both ends. When she popped her head back up, a car was on-screen, driving down her street with its windshield wipers arcing swiftly.

The flash hadn't been a short. It was lightning.

She swivelled round to sneak a look outside her window and saw the spring evening was as cloudless as it had been when she'd been out on the beach. There wasn't even a hint of rain.

But there didn't need to be, she realised. Her computer was supposedly viewing the weather for the next morning.

She swivelled back and, planting her elbows on the desk, she leant forward resting her head on her fists trying to fathom this. Eventually, a smile replaced her concentrated frown. Of course! Michael had taken a video of the house and copied the clip into the program. He'd even, she thought approvingly, captured minute details like the rolled-up newspapers on their drive. Cute. Probably, her thought developed, he'd loaded in a whole series of clips, each from a different time of day... it wouldn't be hard.

She shifted off her elbows and slid her cursor toward the newspapers on the driveway.

Hang on, she thought to herself, taking her hand off her mouse. To have captured this specific clip, Michael needed to be videoing from up on their roof, yet he didn't do ladders, not even to change the light bulbs; that was always her chore.

Just at that moment, her calendar flashed up a reminder that it was only an hour before her dinner with Al, almost past time to get ready. She started to log off and as she did another box popped up on the screen...

"Protected by itself and by the laws of nature?" She screwed up her face in disbelief. This had to be a joke. Even so, despite the clock ticking toward her dinner engagement she had to learn more about this mysterious program. Just a quick internet search. It wouldn't take long, she kidded herself... as people always do.

Exiting the game to open her search tool, her nose twitched: uncomfortably, a cheesy stuffiness, a fusty yet odourless smell, invaded her space. Something vaguely familiar insinuated her memory, but it slipped by and once her search engine opened up, she forgot about it and typed in *Know-Ware*. Heavens!—over eight million entries. She skimmed through the first few pages but there was nothing about a computer program like this.

Even narrowing down the search to "Know-Ware"+game brought it down to 3,000 entries. Scrolling... scrolling... 25 percent of the entries were simply appalling spelling: *dose anyone know ware I can get ufo pants in toronto?*

Looking again at the time, she pressed her finger against her bottom lip, debating with herself what else she might try. She settled on doing a quick search for the copyright's owner. It was very quick. Google didn't even list a single entry for Venari Inc.

25

SONYA SCANNED THE restaurant. Al's table was way out back in the cobbled courtyard, nestled under a rustic pergola. As usual, he had chosen it for mood and food, the cutesy phrase he'd used so many times it was no longer amusing, or threatening.

After apologising for being late, she asked about Al's visit to the police, disappointed and deflated to hear they'd dismissed the investigator's new information.

"Why didn't you call to tell me," she asked, as the waiter poured her a glass of the wine Al was already drinking. Judging from the level in the bottle, Al was onto his third glass.

"Better face-to-face," he said. "Their point," he said, raising his glass and clinking it against hers, "is that Michael is already on every missing persons' list there is. Not much more they can do."

Later, as they were putting down their dessert spoons, Al delivered his come-on. "We've been 'just' good friends," his fingers air-quoted, "for years, right?" He topped up her glass with the honey-coloured botrytis riesling he'd selected to go with the soufflé. "With us," he continued, "it's been like... like trying to catch a puff of smoke with my fingers."

He'd rehearsed his speech—so much was obvious to her—and despite the gentle evening temperature, his forced attempts at nonchalance were squeezing the sweat beads out of him as if his pudgy feet were roasting over coals beneath the table.

A waiter overheard Al's pitch as he brushed past to collect a credit card waving from a nearby table and, while swiping it in the machine at the front counter he whispered to the owner out of the corner of his mouth, "The fat, bald guy? Table 15? Must be his third time here this month. Same table, same wine, different woman, but same damn luck. By now, you'd think he'd work out his little formula sucks, wouldn't you?"

"I hope not, and actually it's the fourth time. *Cherchez la femme*, I say," and the proprietor toasted Al with the glass of cabernet merlot he kept hidden but always topped up behind the menus.

Al wasn't completely stupid; he knew what he was doing was insensitive but when the investigator had shown him the SOS trick that afternoon, it sent him into a panic and he almost kept the news from Sonya. He had imagined that he was making progress with her and now this investigator found something to stop it. This was his last chance he decided, wrongly. The truth was he'd never had a chance with her, and never would.

He picked at the last specks of soufflé clinging round the rim of his dish and said, "After Charles... before you went to New York... I'd hoped we'd get something going... I don't know if you ever really knew... And now Michael's gone..."

Sonya couldn't fathom how Al could be so indelicate but she stayed polite. If it hadn't been for Al sticking by her she would never have had the time to trade out of trouble. "Al," Sonya forced a smile and reached her hand across the table, "you're my dearest friend. Always there when I need you. Today, with Michael's disappearance... back when I split with Charles. Your support these last months..."

"It's me, isn't it?" he interrupted.

Sonya tried hard for her smile to appear genuine, not patronising; a kind, tender smile. "Of course it's you. I mean, how could I, er, be..." it was a safe word, she decided, "how could I *be* with my lifelong patron saint?"

When working for a client, Al was confident and decisive. Yet when he represented himself he became vaguely self-deprecating with an engaging habit of giving a light brush to serious subjects. "Heck, you can't blame me for trying," he shrugged.

As the waiter delivered their coffees, Sonya asked, "Al, does anyone at your firm do trademarks?"

He put on a genuinely cheery face. "Do dogs lick their balls? We got a whole department does it." He cracked up at his unintended lawyer joke. "Sorry," he coughed, wiping his eyes. "Why trademarks?"

"Er... there's a computer program I need to find out about... who makes it, that kind of thing? It's, er, a potential investment," she said, hoping to avoid him probing deeper.

"I'll get an intern onto it," he nodded and dug his hand

into his voluminous pants to search for his phone, bumping the table and splashing the coffees, not giving a damn that he'd be calling someone at 11 PM. At his firm, there were people there round the clock, though not the partners, of course.

"Two Sambucas!" he called to the waiter, not asking Sonya if she wanted one. If she didn't, he'd have both.

26

THE HAZY GREY cracked through Sonya's curtains but to her sensitive pupils it was a piercing flash. Shaking off the Sambucas, her eyes blinked into a vapid kind of pre-wakefulness and, as she dragged herself downstairs for a caffeine heart-starter, the simple rat-tat of her two morning papers both thudded onto her eardrums and her driveway.

She leant against the frame of the front doorway and squinted skywards to the rain clouds hanging heavy like her head, thankful that her need for a coffee meant she'd save the papers from a soaking.

How much had they drunk last night? Al had ordered shot after shot of the anise-flavoured liqueur. "Small, but potent. Like me," he'd joked as he puffed out the blue flame and shot back the last one, their fifth she seemed to recall through the fog, or maybe their sixth.

A blade of lightning sliced the sky and as she scurried out the front drive to rescue the newspapers, unsteady on her feet, the thunder rumbled and the rain started flicking onto her face.

LATER, hours later, Sonya sat at her computer and saw the bags hanging under her eyes look back at her from the brassy shine of the plaque she'd perched on top of her screen: *Follow your own mind*? Follow, yes, but today wasn't a day for decisions. She tightened the belt of her white cotton robe.

"*Welcome back, Sonya. Would you like to reopen your saved session from yesterday?*"

And when *Know-Ware* opened up out on the drive with that morning's newspapers starting to get spattered with rain, it was strangely startling. Her expression twisted into a spectre of unease as she watched what definitely looked like herself dashing out to collect the papers and her same toe snubbing the same stone like it had that morning.

Tentatively, she moved her mouse cursor over one of the rolled-up newspapers and its front page popped open to fill her screen. It was Rupert Murdoch's *The Australian* and yes, it carried that same day's date. Which it would, she calmed herself, since the game would undoubtedly be synchronising itself with her computer's internal clock. It would, wouldn't it?

But the headlines! They were… She tore back down to the kitchen ignoring the hangover still clanging around in her head and, with the flat of her hand, she ironed the real newspaper out, almost knocking over the empty mug she'd left sitting on top of it. She hadn't imagined it: the headlines—the real headlines—*were* similar to what she'd just seen on-screen.

No... the headlines weren't just similar, they were identical.

She took the paper and her other one, *The Sydney Morning Herald*, and once back at her desk she opened up their two screen clones. They were both perfect matches. Each page one was identical to the one on her screen.

She tried to open page two, but *Know-Ware* wouldn't allow it: *"For more, you need Realtime."*

Despite the ache behind her eyes, Sonya focused intensely, first saving and closing her Level 3D session, then clicking to open a new one in Realtime. But, like before, she couldn't get it to work and the computer nagged her with the technical details of the hardware needed for that to happen.

Desperate for some head space, she got up and walked outside, oblivious to the rain soaking her hair and her robe. It was one thing to imagine Michael loading an interactive video clip of their house onto the disk, but conjuring up scenes that actually occurred later in real life and newspaper stories that actually didn't exist at the time...? That was imposs...

But she'd seen them herself.

AL picked up his private line with such a detached grunt that Sonya guessed she was interrupting. "Any luck on the trademark?" she said, trying to keep it short.

"Bloody interns..." he said, and without apology he clicked her on hold, tuning her in to a classic rock radio station playing an instrumental version of *Yesterday*.

An apt song, she was thinking when the DJ cut in: "*So... as I was asking... for $100 dollars cash... name the band that Sir Paul McCartney was in... before Wings?*"

To Sonya, the question alone was comical enough—well, she *was* in her thirties!—but the answers phoned in were more so:

"*Rolling Stones?*"

"Forget it. Next caller... Tom."

"*Kiss?*"

"No way. Hey, listeners, this band claimed to be bigger'n Jesus. Yeah, Sharon..."

"*Genesis?*"

"Wrong book, girl. Someone else... How 'bout you. Bill?"

"*Oasis?*"

"Try a generation earlier, buddy..."

Al clicked back on. "No luck," he said. "Our IP people—you know, intellectual property—they couldn't find a thing. There's nothing under Venari Inc. Plenty under *Know-Ware*, as you said... but nothing relevant. Anyhow, we can't find the game you're looking for. Any other leads?"

"None. And I should've started off with this, but thanks for dinner."

After they hung up, she clicked her mouse over *Know-Ware's* exit button and, as her session closed, her nose gave another twitch. It was the same weird smell that loitered, hung in the air. That stuffy feeling she'd noticed yesterday, but today it triggered something.

She powered down her computer and left her desk in the hope that a swim might clear her haze, but she never made it. Her measured steps down the staircase did it, reminding her... it was exactly where she'd first detected that smell... only moments before she discovered Michael had gone. She'd never experienced it before that time or since. Except when she exited *Know-Ware*.

Within seconds, she was back in her study booting up her computer, opening *Know-Ware* and then immediately switching it off. But nothing happened. There was no reek of cheesy socks... no odour of a closed up, dank room.

Baffled, she tapped her fingers together repeatedly as if that would force out an answer. She glanced about the room to see if anything else might spur an idea: her pens, her plaque, the double stack of textbooks on options trading, an open box of stale crispbreads, her university notes, two half-empty coffee mugs, an unopened pack of cigarettes.

Her eyes went back to the options books, stuck with hundreds of curled up bits of torn white paper as page-markers.

Almost mechanically, Sonya re-opened *Know-Ware* again, re-entered her saved session and this time, waltzed herself around the garden with her cursor, placed it over the newspapers briefly and only then saved the session and closed it down.

The smell.

Shit!

SO much of what Sonya had come across these last weeks was weird, so why was it so strange for a computer to generate a smell, even if it was the same one she'd sniffed when Michael vanished? She fiddled with her bracelet, her fingers settling on Einstein.

She'd heard of *Scratch 'n Sniff* technology. Who hadn't? It had been used for perfume ads in glossy fashion magazines for years so maybe, somehow, someone had cracked it for computers. She hopped onto the internet, and yes, developers all over the world were indeed vying to crack a *click-&-sniff* protocol for computers. One firm was already marketing a prototype but to get it to work you had to plug a special aroma box into your computer's USB port. Another more pedestrian explanation she found was that some computer casings emitted an irritating odour of triphenyl phosphate when they heated up. But this wasn't her computer; she scanned the specifications on-line and they expressly excluded this chemical.

She rubbed her forehead. Damn the smell.

What about the newspapers? What about seeing herself ahead of time? What about the stock prices? The explanation that was pummelling at her brain was ridiculous, she knew that. But what if it wasn't?

SCIENTIFIC proof required repeatability. If an experiment couldn't be repeated, it wasn't proof, it was a coincidence. Sonya managed to repeat the same madness two days running. It wasn't crazy.

Reading about the devastating earthquake in China hours before it happened. Knowing that the President of the United States had paid a surprise visit to Afghanistan half a day before any news media anywhere had reported it. None of that was crazy. Unexplainable, yes. But she'd seen it with her own eyes.

Sonya jiggled her bracelet, slowly accepting the uncomfortable notion that Michael had left his disk for her intentionally, hidden it behind the desk for her to find. To help her. And to help her find him.

To save him.

27

AS SONYA CONTINUED exploring her new gift for knowing tomorrow today, the downsides soon became apparent. While it was uplifting, a relief, to know ahead of time that the missing five-year-old son of hysterical parents would be found unharmed in a dilapidated shed three blocks from their home, the burden of that knowledge weighed down on her. Should she phone the police... his parents... to tell them how and where to end their agony earlier? She should, she knew, but she didn't, fearing the consequences.

It got worse for her when she read that Sri Lanka had suffered—actually, would later that day suffer—a massive landslide claiming almost a thousand souls, wiping out an entire coastal village that had managed, miraculously, to survive the Christmas 2004 tsunami. She could save these lives, but she felt she couldn't... she shouldn't. She sat for hours, often with her head in her hands or banging the desk in frustration.

Her personal responsibility taunted her. What if she knew ahead of time—a day before it happened—that Iran was launching a barrage of nuclear missiles on Israel? Or North Korea on Japan?

She didn't need her PhD to grasp how *Know-Ware*, if she put it into the wrong hands, could be misused and manipulated, how it could become an excuse for virtually anything. How about, she pondered, police arresting criminals for *future* crimes, offences they hadn't yet committed?

For her, it had become spell-binding to look forward a day but for the police it would be an early-warning tool, to scan for murders and robberies to be able to stop them. What evidence would they present in court as proof of the crimes? A *Know-Ware* clip of something that hadn't yet happened. Proof? *She* knew it was proof, but she also saw how easy it would be for the corrupt or unprincipled to digitally manufacture it. With *Know-Ware* at their fingertips, she imagined how even leaders motivated by good intentions, let alone tyrants and demagogues, could easily concoct a rationale for war, or arrests, with no one actually knowing the real truth. ("If we don't do this, they'll do that... We've seen it... Trust us!")

For Sonya, no longer was this merely an astonishing point-and-click program. When she read about people dying... they died, but she froze when she thought about putting *Know-Ware* into hands other than her own. Despite the strains tearing at her conscience, she couldn't bring herself to tell a soul about any of it. Now she understood why Michael had kept it under wraps, even from her. Until he had no choice.

Even so, as she daily read of some tragedy or shocking crime, her hand itched for the phone, but each time she held back, forcing herself to play it out in her mind... First, there'd be the disbelieving face-twists... "You say *what's* gonna happen?"... then a day later the event would shatter people's lives... and then, after two, three, maybe four of her predictions ruled out any further brush-offs that they were mere coincidences they, the police... the government, they'd confiscate *Know-Ware* for examination and testing... And then they would have it, and use it.

It wasn't just the authorities she was baulking at. Her own trading profits proved *Know-Ware's* extraordinary monetary value, and if that potential leaked out there'd be those who'd come after it. They might kill for it... might kill *her* for it. Might kill *with* it.

She worried about what *Know-Ware* could do to markets, to whole economies if the data, which so far she alone possessed, were widely available? Think about it, she told herself. If a single person could see far enough ahead, and saw Microsoft stock rising by $50, say, in a year's time, they wouldn't buy in now, they'd wait the full year until just before the rise, hanging onto their money in the meantime. But if a second person also saw it coming but suspected the first person would be buying on that slightly earlier day, they'd barge in even earlier and buy the day before that. And if there were yet others, they'd elbow in to buy a day even earlier, and so on, until the $50 rise would be an unexplained wave crashing backwards in time. Markets could move years ahead of when they were supposed to.

Cause and effect would be turned on its head. Economies would be in disarray. Fraudsters and charlatans and rumour-mongers would abound. The world was already suffering financial instability of previously unimaginable dimensions. This could be worse. Not just corporations, but entire markets could easily collapse and whole economies.

And what about military and counter-intelligence? Sonya pondered that, looking out the window nervously. If they could clamp their Kevlar-lined mitts on this, what lengths would those agencies go to, to bag it for themselves?

And terrorists…?

She felt like a slab of raw meat waiting for the dogs to pounce. The only thing that stopped her seizing up was her decision to keep *Know-Ware* a secret.

It was uncivil she knew, but far from thoughtless. While this disk could do plenty of good—she'd experienced some of that herself—its potential for catastrophe was greater, and she'd read enough about physics to know that nature trends toward entropy—inevitable decline—so it was rational to assume the worst.

Suddenly, she jumped in her chair. But it was only Ralph nuzzling her lap.

28

HER FEET FINALLY hit the sand. Sonya had been back running every morning for a week. Reinstating her rituals was healthy, she knew, but it was also defensive. Routine helped her manage her fears.

Little Willie was up ahead in a red Big Bird tee-shirt and flappy board shorts so long they fell past his knees. With Ralph bounding beside him, he dashed from the hole they'd been digging together in the sand to the surf. As the pair splashed around, Sonya smiled as Willy filled his blue bucket with water and ran back up to dump his load in the hole, scratching his head as to why, no matter how many bucketfuls, the hole did not fill. Each time he poured, he watched the water soak straight down and vanish, leaving only a stain in the sand.

She popped up to see Willie's mother who was waving from her terrace. After a cooling glass of orange juice, the two women leant back on Marion's old-style deckchairs to chat. Like Sonya, Marion was a tennis tragic and, with Argentina and Spain playing the Davis Cup grand-finals the next day, Marion was betting on a home team advantage.

Sonya's eyes scanned down to the beach. Willie was hunched over Ralph's back, his head nuzzling into the dog's haunches, giving him a gigantic hug. It was a wide stretch for the boy's short arms.

Because her mind was distracted by the endearing scene, Sonya let her guard down. "Sad about Acasuso's muscle strain, don't you think?" As soon as the words had escaped, she knew she had said too much and her mouth clamped shut, her buttocks clenched and she bit her lip, the sour taste and the alarm surging through her.

Marion, a tennis fan who could replay every point of a match, jerked her head toward Sonya. "What strain?"

Sonya quickly checked her watch, "Sorry," she said, jumping to her feet, almost knocking over her glass. "Sorry," she repeated. "Got to run... get ready. The lawyers... You know what they're like if you're late... They bill you anyway!"

NEXT morning, Sonya switched off the live tennis broadcast early, and tore straight out to the garage to go for a spin instead of her run. The moment Argentina's José Acasuso walked off court before the fifth set with an abdominal muscle strain, her heart started thumping against her ribs. She'd known since yesterday that in the sixth set Spain's Fernando Verdasco would slap a forehand winner down the line, drop to his knees and pitch onto his barrel chest to kiss the surface of the court. She had to escape, to avoid Marion who, in a matter of minutes, would be banging on the door.

After two hours pulping the freeways, Sonya turned the key in her front door. But even before the engine roar had left her ears, her phone started ringing and she knew she couldn't avoid answering it forever.

"The game!" Marion said breathlessly as if she'd lost the last set herself. "It played exactly like you said!"

To slow her racing pulse, Sonya placed her riding gloves on the table one-by-one, straightened her back and focused her eyes on a buzzing mosquito zeroing in on her bare hand. At first, she said nothing, just breathed.

Marion insisted, "Yesterday... you knew. How?"

"Ah... I'm a clairvoyant?" Sonya said, forcing a weak chuckle and straining to prevent a guilty inflexion in her voice. For 24 hours, she'd been sweating this conversation. She'd even composed a list of retorts, but this one, patently ridiculous and slightly humorous to make light of the question so it would float away, seemed the best, the most likely to close down the whole subject. Better than her second favourite: the airy-fairy, "women's intuition". Outright denial—"I don't know what you're talking about"—had limped onto the list as number eight but only just.

Telling the truth wasn't an option. Letting even Marion in on the truth could ultimately be fatal, as it was for the mosquito on her hand once she'd put down the phone.

While Sonya picked off the bug and absently kept looking at the blood on the back of her hand, snippets of old conversations drifted back to her: "How long have you been travelling?" she'd asked Michael once.

"It seems like centuries," she remembered him saying, a hint of mischief lighting up his eyes.

All his little jokes about time. And travel.

His trips.

While one heavy cloud was lifting, another was building.

29

GRADUALLY OVER TWELVE months, Sonya almost returned to normal. As normal as anyone who'd gone from bankruptcy to millionaire, hardly a normal shift in any economic climate let alone the crisis which was still rocking the globe. As normal as anyone who traded markets in the most volatile, frightening times in recent history but who held a perfect track record. As normal as anyone who could read bad news one day ahead of time but struggled with her conscience because she could do nothing about it. As normal when, no matter what she did or how much she spent, she still had no idea what had happened to Michael.

Apart from discovering the SOS code, her investigator had turned up a fat zero, a failure which didn't embarrass him out of sending her his monthly bills, and a failure which left Michael still on the official missing person's list and wanted for questioning by the police for the arson that killed Tito Wells.

What she told her neighbour when she asked her on short notice to care for Ralph was partially true, that she needed some time away. But Marion agreed almost without thinking, not just because Willie would be over the moon, but because for months she had been nudging Sonya about a fresh start. She'd been circumspect enough never to use those words though, knowing they'd drop a heavy curtain on a sour ending. Marion knew Sonya didn't want closure. She wanted to find Michael.

IT was Sonya's first white Christmas in eleven years. Well, it was whitish and despite New York doing its best to sparkle its welcome through the cab window, her trip into Manhattan from JFK airport was a terror of swerves and sways and skids and brakes, and several times the side window or the driver's security screen got far too close to smacking the side of her head or her nose. Sonya read as much of the passengers' laughable bill of rights sticker plastered on the back of the driver's seat as his jolts and lurches permitted. Who was the New York City Taxi and Limousine Commission trying to kid? No matter how much she pounded on the scratched bullet-proof perspex that separated them, her driver didn't cock his head or even acknowledge it with a tic.

Even if "please slow down" was in a language he could understand, and that seemed unlikely, the boom box plonked beside him on top of what could have been his complete scraggy wardrobe was doof-doof-doofing at such a blast he couldn't have heard an elephant trumpeting in the lane next to him.

Within the first ten unnerving minutes of their ride, she'd calculated he'd violated a full fifty percent of her so-called passenger's rights. By the time he squealed up outside Erica Whitman's apartment building on Park Avenue his foot slammed the brakes for thankfully the last time as he skidded across the ice to a stop, wringing out of her any last speck of the indulgence of flying First Class for the first time in her life. Even the glittering last couple of miles, the famous annual commemorative Christmas lights streaming down the middle of Park Avenue, had been a harrowing, strobing, jerking blur.

Wallis Place was one of New York's pre-war grand dames, a blood-red Park Avenue brick building up around the 80s, regally set back from the boulevard as if it presided over it. The instant her cab screeched up kerbside she saw, when she'd opened her eyes again, that Erica had divorced well. Sporting a gold and navy uniform, the doorman strode out under the emerald green awning and opened the cab door, tipping his cap just like in the movies.

The elevator inside radiated old-money charm, though she decided its sepia-stained mirrors offered a handy mask for the worry lines on the Wall Street trophy wives who still lived here, despite many of their husbands no longer having a day job. For unemployed bankers, their plight was even worse than a divorce, at least according to a satirical magazine Sonya had read on the plane: they lost their cars, their boats, their homes, their jobs, and half their money, yet they still had their wives.

Erica Whitman, on the other hand, had the home but not the husband.

George, the doorman, confirmed what Sonya already knew, that Erica had a doctor's appointment and that meanwhile Sonya should make herself feel at home. Holding Sonya's bag in one hand—she would have wheeled it, but apparently doormen don't wheel, they carry—George shouldered Erica's solid oak door open, revealing an expanse of oriental-style furnishings in sumptuous brocades. Placing Sonya's bag near the door to the second bedroom, he crossed the salon to let in the light by pushing aside the damask curtains and then slid open the double-glazed doors leading onto the terrace, helping Sonya over the step to brave the cold.

When she'd been nine floors down, especially in the cab with her eyes clamped shut, Sonya hadn't taken in how broad the road was. "You almost need a packed lunch to get you across it," she said.

From here, she could soak up Park Avenue's full dusk vista: the reds, whites and flashing oranges of the cars and the greens, but mostly reds of the traffic lights that kept them at a crawl. Thousands of tiny pearl white bulbs strung over the hawthorn and cherry trees that split the Avenue down the middle from 97th to her right and 48th way to her left.

George explained the median strip lights were a tradition harking back to the end of World War II when a Mrs Stephen C. Clark and some of her friends who'd all lost sons and daughters first installed lit trees along the Avenue as a memorial to all New Yorkers who had given their lives. Sonya instantly thought of her father. Though he'd died decades after he'd come home from Vietnam, he was as surely a casualty of war as anyone.

THE phone. She stepped too swiftly onto the floor, her heel only half making the bathmat, causing her to slip, though not fall. She grabbed for the towel and patted herself down quickly as she raced into her room, still dripping, to pick up.

"Dr Wheen." It was George, the doorman. "Mrs Whitman is on her way up. She's back a bit early, ma'am."

Erica... early? How things change she thought as she shook her head. If she'd had the phone number for the *Guinness Book of World Records* she might've called them. She smiled, recalling a cavalcade of instances she'd be waiting somewhere about to give up and Erica would arrive in a whirl of wind and words and too-bright scarves, oblivious to her friend's frustration and totally mesmerised with whatever amazing manuscript had just enveloped her. Erica was a book editor, an Australian in New York, but she'd stayed, found love and eventually wealth. A year ago she lost the love but, it seemed as Sonya looked around, not much of the wealth.

She heard the door open and, buttoning her shirt as she ran, rushed through the apartment to greet her friend.

But this wasn't Erica. Sonya's air froze around her.

Her Erica was small, true, elfin with a spring in her step and a sparkle in her eyes. This Erica wasn't just thin, she was sunken-chested and stooped, her complexion sallow and her eyes, that once had flamed with passion, were dim. This Erica still wore her trademark scarves but she no longer fussed with them; it seemed from her ill-fitting and otherwise drab clothes, she didn't fuss with much at all. It was when Erica removed her woollen cap and held it to her chest that Sonya could no longer deny what her own eyes had been telling her.

At first the two women stood quietly, weakly holding hands, Sonya afraid that Erica's might break. After a few silent moments, led by Erica who by now was accustomed to the shocked distancing of first reactions, the two friends hugged.

"You didn't tell me," Sonya whispered.

AS Erica poked at her food, Sonya wondered why her friend had insisted they go to a restaurant. In the circumstances, she hardly ate more herself. "Two months? We email once, twice a month for ten years and you wait till now to spring on me that you've only got two months to liv…" Sonya said, hurt, though knowing she didn't have the right to be. "What if I hadn't come to New York?"

"Sonya… with what you've been… I—I didn't want to add to your burden."

Sonya's fork played with her food. She felt like screaming but knew that was Erica's prerogative. "Well," she said, redirecting the conversation, "what does Richard say?" He had been Erica's husband.

Erica tried to draw her wasted body up to its full length in her chair, "The Philandering Dick? He can choke over it when he reads the obituary."

"You haven't told him?"

They divorced before Erica showed any symptoms. After years of struggle, with Erica pulling in the main wage, he'd finally cracked his dream, pulling in the big money when the movie he co-produced became a box-office smash. But instead of sharing the glory with the woman who'd supported him during his long, spluttering non-career, he upped and left her for the west coast and, within three weeks, was shacked up with a Hollywood starlet he'd met while she was waiting tables. "Between roles, she'd told him, but more likely between sheets," Erica had emailed Sonya at the time.

"At first, when he walked out on me, I thought I had the black dog, you know, depression... no appetite, weight loss, stomach pain, nausea. But then I started itching... went yellow. Jaundice, it turned out. And that's when I..." It was pancreatic cancer, one of the most virulent.

"Erica," said Sonya taking her friend's hands from across the table, "you should tell him."

"Yeah... well," Erica mumbled, looking down at their clasped hands, drawing energy from them. She looked up, her eyes blank. "And you, Sonya? You don't keep any secrets?"

Sonya drew herself back so quickly it startled her friend, and her own eyes fell to the table.

"Hit a nerve, have I?" Erica pressed, relieved the focus had moved off her.

Sonya hadn't flown to the States to confide in Erica. It was to find someone she didn't yet know: a scientist attending a high-powered conference at Princeton University. "I'm a bit jet-lagged," said Sonya. "Mind if we go?"

On the way back to the apartment after their pathetic attempt at dinner, Sonya noticed Erica tense up when she asked after her mother. "Is she still in LA with her brother?"

Erica explained how her mother was flying over to stay with her shortly. "For the end," she said.

Sonya was sorry she'd asked. No parent expected their child, especially an only child, to die before they did.

Back at Wallis Place, Sonya insisted she make some tea, black in Erica's case. Once she joined her on the sofa, Sonya decided to lighten the mood and upended her purse, tipping two objects onto the silk cushion between them. Erica picked them up, delicately holding them to the light as if they were rare treasures. One was a little bigger than a mobile phone. The other was a thin hollow tube about as long as the width of a sheet of letter paper.

"This blue is very cold-looking," Erica remarked, pulling her scarf around herself, though Sonya was unsure if it was a joke. Erica dug into her pants to pull out her mobile. "See? Mine's blue but it's a breezy blue, not like this iceberg of yours. Brrr," she said, shoving hers back in her pocket as if to keep it warm.

"I guess that's why they chose that shade," said Sonya. "Because of the brand name... it's called an IcePaC."

"Cute. So," said Erica, holding it up, "it's a cell phone, right?"

"There's a phone in it, but it's more than that."

"What? Like a BlackBerry or an iPhone?"

"That bit you're holding is a phone but it's really the guts of a computer... it's called the IceQuB." She pronounced it ice-cube. "And it's got a hard-drive, speakers, email, internet, GPS, software, all that... the works. Incredible, huh?"

Erica shrugged.

Its miniature size camouflaged the fact that it pumped far more power than any other portable computer Sonya had been able to find.

She didn't mention to Erica that for almost all of the past year she'd been trying to find a device powerful enough to operate the higher levels of *Know-Ware*. Nor did she mention the cost. It was more than Erica had said she'd spent on her treatment. As a bonus, in addition to the power and the features, all its grunt was crammed into this tiny package. Despite its size, its on-board utilities meant Sonya could conduct any business any time, anywhere.

By now, Sonya wasn't much in the market for stocks and bonds. She dabbled, but it wasn't with the spirit or conviction, or terror, of her first serious foray. How much money did she need, she'd asked herself? It was a question she often wondered if Michael had asked himself.

But she was in the market for one of the world's leading physicists. Despite all of the IcePac's technological whiz-bangery, *Know-Ware* was still blocked, still stuck at previewing only one day ahead, unable to view the past, and useless in helping her find Michael.

"It's really a super-turbo-charged PC in a tiny, tiny box. And it can do all this other stuff. You don't need wires or cables..."

"Neither does a BlackBerry or an iPhone," Erica interrupted, still unsure why this device was such a big deal.

"If you press this button," said Sonya, "it shoots out an invisible beam and you can use it like a laser pointer on the screen instead of fidgeting with a mouse and a cursor. Simple as anything."

"And this rolled-up tubey thing?" Erica said, pointing to it but losing interest as the fatigue started to weigh her down.

"I told you... it's the screen... they call it the IceTuB. Whatever."

"Jesus, what's with this? Ice pack, Ice cube, ice tube. Next you'll tell me it has its own porn website: iceboob.com."

Sonya smiled, guessing Erica didn't crack too many jokes these days. She took the tube and unrolled it. When flat, it clicked itself into a sheet that was thinner than a credit card and a bit larger than a normal letter page. It was translucent and, once clicked flat, fairly stiff weighing less than a handful of loose change. Sonya pulled out two plastic tabs hinged at its base and slanted it back on the coffee table, like a book stand.

"That's the screen?" asked Erica, finally a little incredulous, her finger running across the top of it and half-expecting to get a paper cut it was so thin.

"It's some kind of light-emitting plastic," said Sonya. "Super high tech."

Emboldened, Erica picked it up, and turned it over in her hands.

Suddenly, Sonya snapped, "ICY! On!"

Erica dropped it in fright. "Jesus, Sonya...!" She picked it up off the floor, "*I see on*? What the hell was that for?"

"Not *I see*," said Sonya. "But *icy* as in... icy cold. It's my password. The point is... it's voice-activated. I just say my magic word and tell it what to do; I don't have to type a thing."

While Sonya was explaining, Erica watched mesmerised as the flimsy-looking screen flickered to life. Her thin mouth dropped in awe as a series of bright icons materialised. "The colour's amazing...," she said, her mouth open just long enough for Sonya to notice her gums, bright red and slashed with white ulcers.

Sonya took a deep breath to stop her welling reaction to her friend's decline and pointed the phone unit toward the screen, to an icon labelled *Demo*. Light relief came a split-second later when a video presentation flashed up and a deep voice boomed that this screen—what it called an active matrix back-plane substrate—was the "ultimate rollable flat-screen." It was, it proclaimed, impregnated with millions of electro-luminescent blue, green and red pixels, and all it took was a minuscule electric charge to make each of the dots—conjugated polymer light-emitting diodes—glow. These pixels weren't backlit like a conventional screen or the iPad that Apple was about to release; they radiated their own light. These miniature bulbs shone the right colour at the right time, virtually eliminating heat radiation and internal fans, cutting battery power to a fraction.

"ICY! Screen off!" said Sonya, and the plastic went blank.

"Where's the keyboard?"

"It doesn't need one. You just talk to it. It got used to my voice after only an hour. But, if you're desperate, you can use a virtual one with this little touch pad on the back."

"Show me something cool," said Erica. "Cool, get it?"

"ICY! Phone Erica!" and almost instantly a ring tone trilled out of Erica's pocket, Simon and Garfunkel's *I am a Rock*.

Erica pulled her phone out again and pressed it to take the call. "Erica Whitman," she answered, expecting it was merely a coincidence and that it would really be her mother, probably packing early for the trip over and asking whether she should bring one coat or two. Instead, her name in her own voice echoed out of the box nestled in the palm of Sonya's hand.

Sonya leant over and spoke into Erica's phone slowly, "Time to go to bed, okay? If I'm beat, you must be more so."

Erica, teasing, held her chunky older-style mobile phone up near Sonya's hand to compare the devices more closely. "They're twins, almost."

"Okay, one last trick for the night... hang up your phone."

Erica did it and Sonya continued, saying each word separately and clearly, "ICY! Music! Station one! TV! Volume ten!"

Erica decided that Sonya obviously knew something because of the way she quickly tossed the cube onto the sofa opposite. As it bounced off the gold silk and onto the scarf Erica had tossed there, some gangsta rap started pumping out of the tiny but incredibly powerful speakers. A second later, the music was also coming from Erica's TV speakers.

With her fingers plugging her own ears, Sonya shouted, "ICY! Video on!" With that, the small screen, and simultaneously the TV, lit up to a clip of a heavily jewelled rapper strutting in time to the track with twenty dancers, all women, all barely clothed. With Erica's mouth still agape, Sonya shouted, "ICY! Off!" and the TV flashed blank and the computer screen sputtered back to its earlier translucency. The sound went dead and they could hear the rush of the room's air-conditioning and the banging on the ceiling from the apartment below.

SONYA woke to the crisp rustle of the starched sheets. At 6 AM, which was 10 PM on her confused body-clock, it looked like the last luscious hours of slumber would elude her. Her mouth was as parched as a dry river bed and her tongue kept sticking to the roof, which felt coated with sand. This wasn't the after-effects of alcohol; Erica didn't drink any more, and last night Sonya hadn't either. She slipped out of bed for some water.

After gulping down her second glass, she padded to the front door for the morning papers, but it was still too early and it was only then she recalled George telling her that he normally dropped them at the door at 6:30. In truth, it was of no real consequence. She'd already scanned them on the plane yesterday, but it had become a habit: look today, check tomorrow. She'd been doing it almost every day once she discovered she could. Tomorrow's news today… It had become an obsession, as it would for anyone, she kept telling herself.

She headed down to the gym on the third floor. As she pounded on the treadmill she again mused on her office-in-a-purse. She could be anywhere. Any country, any city, on a beach, in a cab, on a plane, in a hotel room, it didn't matter. She could do email, talk and, if she felt like it, which she didn't, access her stock market feed, download broker research, and so on. None of that was magic these days, since even her students' iPhones could manage all that. But the real benefit, the real joy, and frustration, was engaging *Know-Ware*. Eat that, iPad! She chuckled.

It was only a year earlier she had first listened, *really* listened, to that emotionless, automated decree—"*Get ready and brace yourself for the tour of your lifetime...*" Even though her IcePaC didn't have the capacity for a virtual jump forward of more than one day or for any backwards slip in time at all, it did have the juice to experience *Know-Ware's* big sound and magical effects almost as if you were watching a big-budget 3D movie without the special glasses... as if you were really there. As if.

Sonya had returned to teaching at university two semesters ago. At a low ebb because her search for Michael had stagnated, she desperately needed to occupy her mind, and her time. By that stage her trading was sporadic and rote. The thrill, the urgency—what she'd initially felt as the terror—had gone. She no longer needed to worry about her brokers hassling her so much; several had become so dispirited by the overall market gloom that the only two positions they could bring themselves to recommend to her were in cash or foetal.

The last couple of months, since the start of the university's long summer holidays, she was opening up *Know-Ware* daily, again hunting for something new, some twist or trick, some technique. It was dispiriting but not enough that she stopped asking around. She'd done so much useless internet searching that Yahoo! had almost lost its exclamation mark. Yet no matter where she went or what she tried she'd never seen anything remotely similar anywhere.

If the program hadn't come from Michael, where had it come from? She'd asked Jeeves, and Yahoo! and Google and every other search engine she could find, and did it again and again every few days in case one of them found something new.

She'd asked herself the question a thousand times and she asked it now another five or six hundred, once for each stride on the treadmill. Michael had picked it up somewhere... or made it himself. It had to be either of those. Without stopping, she took a slurp of water from her bottle... but if he'd found it, where had he found it... or, given what she now knew, *when* had he found it.

Each time she came up with the same answer. And every time she considered it, she couldn't help but spin her head around taking quick furtive glances to make sure no one was mocking her. Or worse.

30

LEANING BACK ON the sofa, her hair wrapped in a towel after her shower, Sonya logged onto the website she'd tripped over only the prior week. It was her real reason for rushing to the US.

> ...+ princetons time travel conference...
> best ever with hawking, kaku, zontsmann + other gurus"
> "howdyu register?"
> "http://www.cs.princeton.edu/research/colloquia/timeconf
> —or u can email to timeconf@cs.princeton.edu

But she'd read all this before, so she clicked open her email hoping that the Ivy League university had formally accepted her application for conference registration. She'd taken a risk flying over before she'd been confirmed but these days Sonya could afford to take risks.

She'd thought about confiding more to Erica last night... about the data... about *Know-Ware*... but no, that was one risk she wouldn't take. Erica wouldn't be human if she didn't start dreaming how it could change her own life, building false hopes. Sonya wasn't going to let herself be the cause of that heartbreak.

Yes! Her registration was confirmed, and she was now an official delegate to Princeton University's elite International Conference on the Physics and Metaphysics of Time. But her flush of excitement waned when she read the agenda had changed.

She got a sinking feeling… what if the professors she had flown all this way to meet had cancelled? She scanned the details and was relieved to see they were still on the list. Three full days of cosmology, quantum theory, thermodynamics and philosophy. Even for an educated person like Sonya, a PhD herself, most of the lecture titles were mumbo-jumbo jargon, topics like "*Stochastically Branching Space-time Topology*"—whatever that meant.

The changes were better than she expected. One of the professors she'd marked as a potential, Professor René Zontsmann, was now also slated to give the after-dinner speech for the opening night event: "*Pop goes your Grandfather: Resolving Theories and Paradoxes.*" The title of this talk was far more appealing than his grimly-titled paper for the following day: "*Quantum Phases, Dissipation and Decoherence.*"

She hoped that someone at this gabfest would be able to help her crack her puzzle. Maybe this Professor Zontsmann.

MIDNIGHT, and the labs at Princeton's Centre for Integrative Computational Research & Strategy were almost deserted, most of the academics having scattered for bed. But CICRS's director, Professor Sam Sing had just returned after dining at home alone. It was a clear January night, biting cold, but no snow.

He'd walked back to CICRS from his apartment to take in the night air because his bike had to stay in the repair shop for another day, its pistons being lovingly rebored. Clearing a spot on his desk for his hat, a genuine ten-gallon Stetson, he hoisted it off his jet-black hair and set it down.

While his terminal was logging on, his finger tenderly circled his hat's snakeskin band, feeling its scaly roughness. With his black hair and smooth skin, Sam could pass for thirty and in the clubs he liked to frequent he let people believe it.

A gifted mathematician, he'd escaped from mainland China to Hong Kong, migrating to the States at fifteen after winning a scholarship to MIT where it didn't take long for his pioneering work in cryptology to be noticed.

These days, being on the consulting payroll to several Fortune 500 corporations, he had plenty of money to indulge his other passions: travel, the animal thrill of road speed, and gourmet Chinese food which, according to his colleagues, was normally an oxymoron unless you lucked into some of Sam's cooking. Though Sam was equal to any Chinese chef in the country, he rationed his cooking, especially his exclusive dinner parties, preening himself that their scarcity swelled the demand.

And Princeton hadn't blinked an eye at his eccentric obsession with cowboy apparel when it appointed him foundation head of the new CICRS or, as Sam had cheekily rechristened it, Kick-Ass. Its express mission was to push the edges of computer simulation and mathematical algorithms to advance humankind. If anyone could get the inter-disciplinary institute up and running and attract the world's top researchers, it was Sam.

The standard array of icons flashed up onto his monitor. Secreted in the bottom-right corner were two extra icons, invisible until Sam slid his cursor over them.

He clicked on the cartoon-style binoculars and a scaled monochromatic line-diagram snapped open on his screen: it was CICRS's floor-plan with every workstation precisely plotted, each tagged with the name of the relevant staff member or PhD student allocated to it. He'd only installed this surveillance program two nights earlier, but still needed to check it for bugs, ideally when no one was around, like now. He moused his cursor round the screen and smiled, satisfied, as it passed over work-space after work-space, altering its colour from the standard white-with-blue-outline to a blazing fire-truck red.

31

SONYA FELT OUT-of-place as she stood in front of the Princeton notice board, chewing over the list of legitimate registrants and exhibitors. Fingering her charm bracelet like an anxious child would fondle the satin edging on her security blanket, she swung her head to the right as if someone had unexpectedly tapped her shoulder and she launched off, bumping through the throng till she reached what had caught her eye: the trade show.

Crammed with flashing lights, screens and a sprawling hoard of historic time-travel trivia, the gothic McCosh Hall had to be shaking to its Indiana limestone foundations with something so... well, tacky, but Sonya knew that these days even the Ivy League had to press up against the edges to attract funding, since their endowment funds had lost billions in the financial crisis. Princeton's alone, she'd read, had lost a whopping $3.7 billion in the last year.

She hustled herself through a clutter of tables and stands for computer gaming and software companies peddling their wares with displays of artefacts and memorabilia and other aficionado's highlights of a well-trodden realm.

After twenty minutes' searching, she got no closer to finding anything remotely like *Know-Ware*, not even a close predecessor.

As Sonya forged on through the stands, her steps became shorter and more precise. Each stop to query an attendant or salesman became briefer. Part way through, and already conditioned for another no, she'd refined her ritual so she could mutter her spiel and walk past almost without a pause: "Have you heard of *Know-Ware*, a time-travel game? Very realistic."

"There's a *Marvel* comic set in a place called Knowhere?"

"No, this is by Venari Inc."

After forty minutes of disappointment but still clinging, her last stop was at a stand remarkable only for its low-tech setup. The attendant's blond hair stuck up like a half-sucked mango, as if he'd just extracted one of his piano-potential fingers from a power socket. After her standard question, he steepled his fingers in thought, burying a couple of them into his wispy moustache, then after tapping something she didn't see into his clunky-looking computer his fingers resumed their contemplative spire. He sat a while, focusing his Coke-bottle glasses on the screen.

"Can you come over here?" he said eventually.

Sonya sidled around his trestle table to see his screen jam-packed with reference numbers and prices.

"If this *Know-Ware* is anything to do with time-travel and it was sold anywhere, anytime, on this planet, my little search system here would find it, but there's nothing… nothing at all."

32

"TONIGHT, ON BEHALF of everyone, I thank you, Professor Zontsmann, for your entertaining and stimulating address, a perfect opening for our conference..."

It had been obvious throughout his after-dinner speech that the compact professor was stressed. As an academic herself, Sonya was used to speaking to large often hyper-critical audiences so what, she wondered, had been his problem?

During the speech he kept pulling back the sleeves on his tuxedo jacket. That, together with the jacket's drooping shoulders suggested to Sonya that he'd once been an even stockier man and perhaps he was recovering from a recent illness. The more pedestrian but correct answer was he'd rented the last tux on the rack and his stress came not so much from the bad fit but from a scientist's stage fright at having to make soufflés out of his normally impenetrable academic molasses.

Professor Zontsmann nodded in response to the applause, his half-moon eyeglasses almost sliding off his nose. He pushed them back up, surreptitiously wiping off the sweat with the extended cuff of his sleeve. After he had stepped down from behind the lectern and shuffled back into the relative anonymity of the official table for his coffee and more backslapping, Sonya noticed he was wearing caramel suede loafers.

"Great speech, René."

"You had'em eating out of the palm of your hand."

He pulled his sleeves back to look at his hands, "Would've tasted a bit salty," he said, his natural self-deprecation as close to a smile as he could muster, and wiped his hands on his slacks.

Apart from the official table, the table seating was random. At Sonya's table, Peter Something—his jacket lapel had been flopping over the surname on his name tag the whole evening—said, "Frankly, I'm amazed old René had it in him."

"You know him?" Sonya asked, a little too hopefully she decided.

"René?" he laughed. "Sure, back at Cornell. We were like this…," he said, holding up his right hand and crossing his fingers to signify intimacy. "I teach philosophy there… You liked his talk?"

"I did, yes…" She was going to add that she hadn't expected to follow even a word but her dinner companion interrupted her.

"Hey, they're serving drinks over there," he pointed. "Anyone wanna join me?" he said, pushing back his chair, and narrowly avoiding tripping a waiter.

"I'm there," chipped in another, which got all the chairs apart from Sonya's to scrape back on the limestone floor. Rather than be left alone, she followed hesitantly, aware from her own campus experience that standing between an academic and a free drink was risky, though not as dangerous as blocking their way to a research grant.

To be sociable, she cupped some water in a cognac snifter, and clumped herself with four others from her table.

"René! Over here... over here." Peter Something kept waving and calling until the after-dinner speaker came over.

"Hello, ah..."

"Cornell...? Philosophy...?"

Sonya smiled as Zontsmann twisted, trying subtly to read Pete's surname off his impossible tag. He failed.

"Pete! Sure," lied Zontsmann and, to camouflage his embarrassment, he slid off his spectacles to hurr a breath on them and wipe them clean on a handkerchief. "New eyeglasses—just getting used to 'em... So...," he added as filler, "been a while, huh?"

"René, that was some speech. Your little fan club here," he said, sweeping his arm to encompass Sonya and the others, "we loved it."

"Make it humorous, they said. Me! Zontsmann! Frankly, I was scared stiff up there..."

"It didn't show, Professor," smiled Sonya, stretching the truth.

"Really? Why, thank you." He paused. "Your accent? Let me guess... Kiwi?"

She smiled, shaking her head, "Australian. From Sydney," and she stuck out her hand for him to shake. "Sonya Wheen."

He pulled back his sleeve and reciprocated. "Sydney, you say? Which school?"

He steered clear of reading her nametag—these days, just getting accused of ogling breasts could land a professor in a legal minefield, though he did notice the white label was quite stark against her cobalt blue silk dress. She'd been reluctant to pin it to her new Versace outfit, and so had clipped it with a hairpin through a button hole.

"No, no… Sydney, the city. I'm actually at University of New South Wales, in the business school there. I taught at Columbia before that."

Zontsmann's eyes remained on Sonya but his mouth seemed unable to connect with his brain. Absently, he rolled his jacket sleeve back forming a cuff, and for a second his eyes flicked to the unusual pendant dangling from her neck.

Pete from Cornell became agitated that his old friend was ignoring him, "Jane! Hi," he called gesturing to yet another imaginary friend. "Sorry, guys. I'll catch you both up later," he said as he peeled off, his arm waving. The others also took his cue, so Zontsmann and Sonya were temporarily left alone.

"Are you here for the whole conference?" he asked, one suede shoe standing uncomfortably on the other.

"It depends. My interest here is quite narrow."

"Business angles, I guess. You'd like Anna; she's speaking tomorrow. Anna Ptyxis? You know her, right?"

Sonya shook her head. "Business is my discipline, but it's not why I'm here."

"Tell me more."

She wanted to tell him. His credentials were perfect—she'd pored over them on his Princeton webpage even before she flew over—and even from their brief chat so far she had the feeling he wasn't the type who'd laugh her off the planet as soon as she told him. But even so, she remained coy. "It's a long story."

"Physicists are great with stories," he said, "but I'll let you into a trade secret: we make them sound important by calling them theories or hypotheses. Why not try me?"

This had all seemed a lot easier when she'd imagined it from Sydney. With the expert actually in her sights, she felt anxious. "You're making fun of me," she said, her head dropping in embarrassment.

"Not at all," said René. "I guess what I..."

"You guess what, Professor Amazing After-Dinner Speaker?" whooped a shortish man who broke into their conversation, his only accoutrement missing was his horse. His boots, buckle and bolo string tie with a jade clasp said cowboy, despite his Chinese features and ever-so-slight accent. "It's lucky for you, René, that Stephen Hawking hasn't arrived yet, or he'd have chucked something at you—tried, anyhow," he laughed. "Excuse me," he said, seemingly noticing Sonya for the first time. "Who's your... er... friend?" he asked.

Zontsmann had no reason to blush, not yet anyway, but that didn't prevent it. "Ah, this is Sonya... Wheen," he said, checking from her nametag, but only briefly, that he remembered it right. "From Australia. Sonya, meet my very brash colleague, Sam... Sam Sing. Believe it or not, Sam's a professor here," Zontsmann added. "He heads up our new Centre for Integrative Computational Research & Strategy—CICRS... *Kick-ass*, as we prefer to call it. A typical geek, don't you think?" he said, slapping Sing on the back.

"Gook, maybe," Professor Sing chuckled, to both Sonya's and Zontsmann's astonishment. "Bruce Lee meets Lone Ranger meets Albert Einstein... that's me," he added. "Hey, René... Anna's after-dinner after-party? It goes without saying you'll be there, right?"

Sonya thought she saw Sing wink. She didn't know what was being said silently between them, but she guessed.

"Anna won't mind if you bring your, er, friend, I'm sure."

"Sonya, you want to come?" asked Zontsmann. "It's at Anna Ptyxis's... she's the one I was just talking about."

Except for the sense there was something between Zontsmann and this woman, Sonya would have said yes, to get to know him better and check out other possibilities, but she decided she had three days for all that and didn't need her efforts to be muddied by a jealous scene at a drunken party. "Thanks, really, but I'll give it a miss."

"So, René, see you there?" Sing winked again, not even subtly this time.

"I'll be there... but later," said Zontsmann.

"Then so long, pardner," Sing said, and he cantered off into the crowd.

Sonya's peaked eyebrows betrayed her so, without being asked, Zontsmann volunteered a swift rundown on Sing's history, something he had obviously recited many times to other astounded visitors.

"From his, er, manner," said René, "you wouldn't guess it, but he's a consultant, and very highly sought-after, to a swag of Fortune 500 corporations. Only a clutch of them left, I suppose, ha ha! But you being in business, you'd know all about that." He smiled at his own joke. "We all do consulting, but he's made an art of it. Given how much he adores travel, he's never short of a trip to some exotic location... and university pay packets alone don't stretch that far, let me tell you... but, of course, I'm preaching to the converted," he added, almost slapping himself for the faux pas. "Like I said, Sam's just moved up to head Kick-ass. It's super-advanced inter-disciplinary work... we use the very latest in computer simulations and mathematical algorithms..."

"We?"

"I work there part-time."

Sonya noted that for later. She was about to ask about Sam's atypical attire for a black-tie event, certainly odd for a man of his apparent eminence, when she again noticed René's suede loafers, so decided it was more diplomatic not to broach the subject of dress at all.

René continued, filling the lull, "Enough about Sam. Er, you sure you won't come to Anna's?"

She knew she should go, but the pink blush tinting his cheeks made her baulk. "I'm suffering jet lag," she smiled but, before pulling away added, "Could we catch up tomorrow morning... at the conference?" It would be less compromising, she felt.

"Ah, sure," he said, unsure how he should take the signal. He'd only just started seeing women again, Anna in particular, though it wasn't so much seeing her as sleeping with her. He forced a smile. "Maybe I could be your translator," he ventured. "You know, to help you wade through all the jargon? What if we catch up ahead of the first session, say for breakfast?" He could leave Anna's early.

"René, I..." Personal involvements weren't what she was looking for, but equally she didn't want to appear ill-mannered. Here was precisely the person she'd hoped to find here. She touched his sleeve. "Sure," she said with kind eyes, but not quite a smile, "Until breakfast."

TWO hours later, with René's lips lubricated by far too many celebratory drinks, he whistled as he strolled over to Anna's, a white two-story clapboard only two blocks from campus. He was so pumped by his fleeting celebrity, and the alcohol, that the night chill didn't bite. By the time he arrived, Anna's place was teeming with aging partygoers bustling, standing, sprawling and shouting over blaring music that together with whatever they'd been drinking made their sagging bodies feel 20 years younger but look 10 years older.

As René pushed open the door, a man he'd never met cheered him in. "Professor," the stranger smiled, and with one hand he helped René off with his coat and jacket and even his overshoes. With the other he shoved a glass of indeterminate white wine at him, spilling enough to two-tone one of René's caramel suede loafers. With his nose pink from the cold, it made René look as if he'd just snuck in after a Big Top clown gig. "Sorry, man," the other man laughed, not sorry at all.

René slid from cluster to cluster looking for Anna. Apart from the usual Princeton crowd, they were mostly people he'd hung around with for years at one conference or another, and he played along with the forced high-fives and backslaps and repeated toasts, pretending to relish his fleeting notoriety. And while his wine wasn't being topped-up at quite the speed of light, it was getting close and the grey matter in his head was expanding rapidly into a throb.

When he finally located Anna, she was on the floor, her head resting on her knees, and surrounded by an eager coterie of hangers-on, including Sam Sing.

Sam was first to notice René approaching and jumped up to welcome the hero, oblivious to the half-full wine bottle bracketed between his knees. Fortunately, Anna snatched it from mid-air just in time.

Sam grabbed René's shoulder and started shouting to the crowd in his best mock-Chinese Ringling Bros. spruiker voice, "Ray-dee and Gen-tel-men. To-nigh, we have glay preasure in ple-senting to you, at huge expen, Lené de Lemarkable... Zontsmann the Zensational... The Physical Physicist." Sam swept his loose arm in a wide arc suggesting an urgent need to clear a spot on the tiled floor for the man of the moment, but now, switching into the genteel air of an English aristocrat, he whispered to René, "Don't fret, my old sod, with Anna's excellent under-floor heating your bulging hemorrhoids are in good hands... so to speak." He glanced at René's shoes, one still stained darker than the other. Uncharacteristically, Sam remained silent, as if noting the fashion for future consideration.

"Great party," René nodded to Anna as he tried to sit gracefully, but when his backside smacked the tiles he tipped backwards. At first, Anna couldn't help but laugh and the wine she had just chugged direct from Sam's bottle sprayed out all over him. Once she wiped her chin, she patted René down and flicked back her hair, baring her long pale neck. Waist length, her hair only just cleared the floor. As usual, she'd changed into her uniform of too-tight blue jeans and knee-high boots, tonight topped with a clinging black singlet that showed off far too much of her fake tan, and, so far as René could tell, that the central heating wasn't set high enough.

"Seriously seminal speech, my friend," she slurred, winking one of her strangely pale blue eyes at him.

"Er, thanks. It was a bit of fun," he lied.

Anna leant into his ear, "I adore people who have fun…"

A jolt ran through him. It had to be the alcohol, he supposed. Anna was upfront, always, full of the pique of sexual and every other kind of tease, but not usually in public.

Though there wasn't even a drizzle of wine left for her to wipe off, she languorously drew the back of her hand across her mouth, letting the tip of her finger hesitate at her lips for a second too long. The inference was unmistakable.

Suddenly, a hard-rocking sound shattered the air and Anna sprang up from the floor, yanking René's hand to lead him into the room she'd earlier cleared of furniture for dancing. "My favourite formula for my favourite physicist. Come… let's dance," she said, trying to pull him up.

René, still down on the floor, squirmed, "I'd love to, but I don't, er, dance."

"We'll see about that," she said, pulling harder.

"Re-eally," he insisted as she tugged, "I'm… I'm bushed."

"Then let me pump up your, er, adrenaline."

Sam leant back on his elbows and smirked.

As Anna dragged René along behind her, she explained that this was a classic from *Midnight Oil*, one of the famous Australian rock band's best. She'd first heard them by pure chance, she babbled, in the 1990s in New York. She'd been hoofing along Sixth Avenue searching for a café that wouldn't set her back a whole year's funding grant for a sandwich when the band, aboard a rumbling flattop truck, screeched to a halt outside the Exxon building. Powering up their amps from a diesel generator, they blasted into a protest about the *Exxon Valdez* Alaskan oil spill, sparking local traffic chaos and a worldwide blitz of controversy. "Their record sales probably didn't suffer any, either," Anna told René, tapping the tip of her nose with her forefinger. "They broke up a few years ago, when the lead singer became a politician. Like Bruce Springsteen going into Congress," she said. "I doubt that would work."

She kept a grip on his hand, tugging him to the sitting room where she shut the door behind them. In the closed space the music was ear-splitting and the driving bass and percussion pounded so strongly he was glad he didn't yet need the pacemaker his father had.

Anna dimmed the lighting and René noticed through the gloom a few others were already flapping and flouncing round the floor. One, a middle-aged professor he knew from MIT was wrapped in a slinky ankle-length dress that looked like a silvery chain mail. She swung her body this way and that, rotating her shoulders almost hypnotically, her eyes roaming in a vain hunt for approval from people who could hardly see. "*Peo-ple... wast-ing away in par-a-dise...*" She was not exactly what the songwriter had intended, but it worked for René.

While Anna broke her grip briefly to flick the music player onto repeat mode, René took the opportunity to hyperventilate. He knew Anna was a natural dancer, in bed as well, which is where he knew this would end up, again.

Anna began slowly, rhythmically. The pulsing drums were hypnotic. For her. René was wooden. He could see her eyes were fixed on him... not on his eyes, but somewhere lower. He wasn't sure where, but he could guess. He wasn't going to check in case it might encourage her. He jigged and jerked around the floor trying to look everywhere but at Anna; at the walls, the ceiling, and inevitably—he couldn't help himself—her breasts. Damn it. It was Zontsmann's First Law of Gravity: every male retina travelling near the earth's surface at any velocity will eventually accelerate at 32 feet per second squared right into the nearest pair of tits. He'd struggled to avoid it with Sonya earlier, but now it was hopeless. Eventually, Zontsmann's law proved its immutability.

Anna's sound system had as much grunt as she did and, as the rock band's rhythm section developed more kick than even René's beloved New York Giants, Anna's seductive, trancelike, swishing and swaying segued into mystifying outstretched open hand movements that did little for his unease. When the full line of brass erupted, Anna ground herself into him. René was a frozen mix of fright and misgiving but he was thawing—though not all of him—and he was trying to occupy his mind with the lyrics: "*Daytime telly, blue rinse dawn,*" whatever the hell that meant.

The wall of brass blasted to a climax. Anna surged with the music to a new urgency and René sweated over embarrassing himself on the floor. He prayed this would be over soon and strove for control until the false finish tricked him and he momentarily relaxed. Anna took the crash of the final percussion solo as a signal to peel away from him and stomp eccentrically around the floor, ignoring everyone around her, including him. Just before what he'd shortly learn was the final throw of the drumsticks forty-five seconds later, she was back at him, this time from behind, her breasts pressing into his back, her hands gripping each of his thighs with her thumbs pressing into his groin. She knew this track; every note, every rhythm. She locked her body into position, her thighs driving his forward in rhythmic pulses. In the dim light, her head pressed into the hollow between his shoulder blades, and her hands slid up his body to caress his chest.

René surrendered. What else could a man do? He turned to face her, allowing himself to be held. He needed this. He pushed her hair back off her neck and brushed his lips from her shoulder, letting his tongue slide up to her ear.

It was a moment or two before he noticed the music had paused. The two of them stood there, swaying. Anna lifted her head and her tongue pushed itself into his mouth, exploring deeply. When the track started again, she drove her tongue in even harder. Then, quietly, she gripped one of René's hands and led him off.

The song had done its job for her; it usually did.

RENÉ woke slowly and reality began to filter into the room. He slipped his twisted wire-frame half-moons back over his ears so he could glance at his watch, spluttering several expletives when he did so; he'd slept much later than he expected. Anna? She was in the shower; he could hear the water running. He slithered out of her bed and faltered over the carpet into the fogged up bathroom, sliding the shower door half open to talk to her. The steam tumbled out onto him and she spoke before he did. "I was hoping you'd get up..." she winked. "Get up again, that is," and her eyes prowled up him, and down him. Sliding the glass wide open, she added, "Want to slip into something a little more comfortable? Me, for instance?"

Two weeks earlier, Anna had snared him at a weak moment. And again two nights ago, and now as well. It was pathetic, he knew that, and sure, he'd be late for breakfast with Sonya but still, a man had to shower. "I've got a quick phone call to make... but keep the water running."

"YOU saved me a seat," René whispered, sliding into the third row next to Sonya. She passed him a croissant in a bag she'd salvaged from the cafeteria after he phoned her to apologise he'd miss breakfast. In a way, Sonya had been more relieved than annoyed, preferring to keep things at a more professional level.

The flaky pastry smelt good, rich and buttery, and he was hungry but it reminded him of why he was late. The crazing on his eyeballs was desperately trying to hide behind the thick black Buddy Holly frames he'd picked up when he'd slipped home to change. They were his old glasses, unbent by Anna's frolics.

Sonya spoke out of the side of her mouth, "Must've been a good party." She regretted the comment immediately and locked her embarrassed eyes on the lectern so she didn't see René's own awkwardness when he tugged up his collar to conceal the hickey on his neck.

Once the sessions got momentum, the discomfort between them settled quickly. It was perfect for Sonya; she had her own attentive interpreter at her side, a bit dozy at times, but maybe that was how all geniuses behaved. Sonya hadn't planned on sitting through all the morning sessions but with René's whispers translating the technobabble, she was glad she had.

By lunchtime, as he swept her round the frosty lawn to the dining hall where everyone lined up cafeteria-style, she was feeling confident he was who she'd been looking for. She was about to edge into the subject when a soft but insistent English accent intruded, "Excuse me, Professor Zontsmann. Rees is my name... From *The Economist* in London. Could we have a chat?"

"An economist? Look, I'm here with a friend..." René said, excusing himself and tipping his head toward Sonya.

"No, it's *The Economist*, a newspaper... well, we call it a newspaper, but it's really a magazine. I write for the Science and Technology section. It won't take long..." the Brit persisted, a toothy Etonian smile gracing his face.

"After lunch maybe?" René suggested, a little too quickly. "Say, at two? Assuming Professor Wheen here..."

"René," said Sonya. "I'll skip your interview if you don't mind. Anna Ptyxis is on after lunch with her ethics paper—and," she joked, "according to you, I won't need an interpreter for her."

Both Sonya and the journalist wondered why René's face went grey.

"I'm sorry, Professor Zontsmann," Rees continued. "Actually, I need to catch Professor Ptyxis's paper as well, though 'performance' might be a more apt description, don't you think? Perhaps we could meet during the afternoon coffee break?"

"Fine." It wasn't really fine since René had actually been relieved by the prospect of avoiding Anna's session and the risk of public humiliation. Her talks were notorious.

The journalist smiled and walked off with his tray.

"Sonya, maybe I'd better sit out Anna's talk. You know, prepare for my interview."

"Prepare? I don't imagine you'd need to prepare a thing."

René shrugged as Sonya loaded her tray and after they paid, he scouted a table in the far corner. As she followed, Sonya couldn't help note how poles apart René and Michael were, not that there was any reason to compare. Michael was lean and tall, imposing, pale with sharp grey eyes and a sweep of once blond hair, with streaks of distinguished grey. He walked with purpose whereas René ambled. And where Michael was light, René was dark, swarthy, with brown, almost black eyes that on another would have been a harsh impenetrable barrier, but on him Sonya had found them, she had to admit, warm and calming despite being a little bloodshot this morning. And all that with an air of snug dishevelment, his jumble of clothing—all browns—draping loosely over his stocky frame, much as his tux had done the previous evening.

Over their lunch trays, René displayed an easy, courtly gentility and thoughtfulness. He pressed Sonya, of course, about why a business professor from Australia was at a conference on the science of time, a tried and true academic code he explained for time-travel. It was an obvious question now she was here but she hadn't rehearsed her answer.

"It's always fascinated me," she stumbled, looking down at her plate as if she'd find the answer there, buying time as her mind darted around. It was a weak, spiritless attempt but she had to be sure about him before she could trust him with the truth. "What about you?" she asked, deflecting the conversation away from herself. "How'd one of the world's leading physicists get into this?"

René trotted out his standard potted history, close enough to the truth. As Sonya downed her coffee, he caught a glimpse of her watch and, relieved, said, "Hey, all we've done is talk about me and it's almost two. We better go quickly. Anna's session's about to start." This was one time he was desperate not to be observed coming in late, especially with another woman. As the two of them entered, he decided the best way to get through the next hour was to find someone tall to slouch behind. Very tall.

The Economist

Science and technology — The Economist January

Time to travel
Einstein's theory of relatives

What if Albert Einstein had vaulted through time and filched his ideas from the future? He might have saved on brainpower, but he should not have done it

THIS is Princeton, an American Ivy League university where Albert Einstein worked. It is also the venue for an International Conference on the Physics and Metaphysics of Time for which you can read 'time-travel'. Truly.

The campus is buzzing with swarms of scientists, sci-fi freaks and voyeurs all gorging on whatever pollen they can sniff out. Here, a Nobel laureate known only to the cognoscenti, and there, a shiny silver De Lorean TDV (temporal displacement vehicle)—a time-travelling car from the *Back to the Future* movie trilogy.

A big screen loops an interview with Gene Roddenberry, the late creator of *Star Trek*, a TV series. Nearby, clunking and whirring is a chair-like apparatus that George Pal featured in his 1960 film of H.G. Wells's book, *The Time Machine*. Harking from the pre-Spielberg clockwork epoch, it's a jam of quaint spinning wheels and giant gears. If this congregation had been convened back when the contraption was still brand new, its sponsor might have been the magazine *Popular Mechanics*. Today, *Quantum Mechanics* would be more apt.

Until recently, scientists studying time-travel have cowered in the closet, reluctant to come out for fear of ridicule (and funding cuts), cloaking their research with jargon: abstruse terms like closed time-like curves, wormholes, alternate universes; all just furtive code-names for time-travel. But judging from the speaker line-up, a science Who's▶▶

Who, the secret has gained respectability: Stephen Hawking, Paul Davies, Richard Gott, David Deutsch, Michio Kaku and more.

Pop goes your grandpa

An unexpected highlight is a springy low-key Princeton physics professor, René Zontsmann, delivering two papers: an insightful exploration of quantum esoterica, *Decoherence and Dissipation*, and a light speech entitled *Pop Goes Your Grandfather*, a reference to the classic yet callous grandfather paradox about travelling back in time to kill your maternal grandparents before your mother is born. Thus you weren't born, so you couldn't have actually gone back to do it. Which means you *were* born.... And so on.

When Cambridge scholar Stephen Hawking pondered such paradoxes a few years ago, he posited that since we never see any tourists from the future, time-travel could never be. But he later changed his mind, proposing a Chronology Protection Police to explain away their absence.

Dr Zontsmann, too, similarly pooh-poohs the dearth of camera-snappers and he provokes at least three thoughtful *Ahas!* along the way. Consumer choice: if you had the chance, where—or when—would you go? Back to the birth (or death) of Moses, Christ, Buddha or Mohammed? Maybe, but if you knew what the future held in store, with its infinite drawcard, you and millions of others might snub all of the well-documented, more 'traditional' travel spots. Besides, the past is finite, and you'd probably worry there'd be no room at the inn. Where would you stay? Where would you eat? Whereas in the future...

Secondly, Zontsmann postulates we'll need a few new laws and, just as Hawking does, a Time Protection Agency. Or a God.

And last, maybe we don't see any tourists because our observation powers are wanting—they are there, waving and snapping, but they remain invisible to us because they are either fleeting quantum phenomena or are taking their vacations in alternate universes.

Food forethought

If Zontsmann is right, the potential beyond time-tourism is extraordinary. Famine could be eradicated forever, for example. Those lush epochs before humankind and before the Ice Ages could be tilled and sown as farms to feed all future generations.

But watch out, he warns, and not just for dinosaurs. Wouldn't lazy free-riders from future centuries work the ancient lands to exhaustion? The physicist has an economist's answer to avoid that: put a price on the past's resources to ration them. This suggests truly retrospective legislation. And if future lawmakers can't or won't pass these laws, it may be left to the generals to wage intergenerational food wars.

Without such laws, having our cake and eating it might not be possible.

Groundhog DIY

If students fail their finals, they could travel back a week, study some more and try again. Should Zontsmann's new laws ban that? No. Educational standards should rise. And so might the calibre of campus bar-stool pick-up lines.

Que sera sera

But, unless something does manage these things for us, might we find ourselves stumbling over a lot of dead ancestors killed by descendants trying to disprove the grandfather paradox.

Zontsmann suggests that history is pre-determined and that we have no free will: what will be, will be. So, maybe we can still enjoy our time-trips assured of our grandparents' safety, no matter what evil inflames us; and that we didn't have to fight them on the beaches because Hitler would have lost anyhow… somehow.

Future stock

Also at this conference is Anna Ptyxis, a tough-talking Princeton philosophy professor who is against leaving this to physicists, or even to chance. Instead, she advocates human law-making, now, well ahead of time.

She twists the movie *Back to the Future II* where Biff the bad guy returns from the future with a sports almanac crammed with future racetrack results.

Under Dr Ptyxis' direction, we have a scene change and Biff is no longer a punter on the nags but comes equipped with all the NY Stock Exchange's data for the next 25 years. Should Biff trade on this knowledge, she asks? Is it insider trading? How, she poses, is Biff morally different to a pharmaceutical executive aware—unlike the market—of a cancer cure?

If there is a difference, she claims, it doesn't matter. Yes, the pharma knows both that the stock price will go up and why, whereas Biff has no idea, nor does he care. To Ptyxis, it's the same degree of guilt as if the executive phoned her father to tip him off to buy the shares, and when he asks her "Why?" she offers the classic shifty dismissal, "Don't ask."

Ptyxis insists that if physics ever really does permit us to discover accurate future prices but doesn't automatically block us from using them, the laws of man must.

Perhaps she is right. Time will tell. ■

34

"RENÉ. ABOUT ANNA'S paper..."

"She's crazy," he said, laughing over his cup of green tea. "We're a zillion years, regrettably, from building any sort of time machine and Anna wants to regulate us already. You heard my talk... that if one day we *do* work out how to do it, physics will automatically thwart these causality violations: we won't be *able* to make ourselves rich from tripping to the future and we won't be *able* to kill our grandfathers, God forbid. Yeah, God forbid. If there is a God, He or She will prevent it and, if there's not, physics will do the job.

"If physics won't?" Sonya pressed.

"That's when I'll start to worry," he smiled, mistaking the guilt on her face for concern.

"You should start worrying now."

He looked at her strangely, "Excuse me?"

"I need to show you something," she said, taking his arm.

FOR the three days of the conference, most of it over a weekend, Princeton had allocated some of the visiting delegates, people like Sonya, to any of the rooms in the upper-class residential colleges which students had temporarily vacated for the short winter break. Sonya's was tiny: a single bed, a closet and a desk. Despite the central heating, it smelled damp and cold, and musty, as if the thousands of books that past students had leafed through late at night had remained behind long after their owners had graduated.

Not having much alternative, she took René to her room. As she set up her IcePaC on the desk, René sat, sagging into the edge of her bed. "So," he started, "That's your cell phone?"

Sonya had already decided she'd have to reveal more to René than she'd shown Erica, and to explain it was a computer, she opened up one of Michael's stock charts. *Know-Ware* itself would come later… She'd take this one step at a time.

"Nice, er, graph," he smiled cautiously, wondering where this was leading.

"It's charting the stock price movements for General Motors." She nudged the screen a little more toward him. "On the vertical axis, there," she pointed, "you have the stock prices, and across here, on the horizontal axis, you have time. Yes?"

He nodded, having seen similar charts before; his ex-wife Rachel's brother was a Wall Street investment banker, with the emphasis on 'was' from what he'd heard; a blowhard who even talked in charts. Bor-ring.

"Scroll to the right, René, across the dates... here, along the horizontal axis." She handed him the IcePaC and indicated the finger touch pad.

"Oops. Not so easy, is it?" he said. "There... okay, the chart goes back a long way. Is that it?"

She thumbed in the other direction. "To the right..."

"Oh, yeah, you said forward. What's this... a dot.com stock or a motor car company? Whew!" René was whistling over the chart's mountain shape with its big, almost $100 peak back in 2000 and a pretty much relentless decline ever since, even despite the government's bail outs. "My former brother-in-law, he loved cars... big ones, fast ones... buying new ones all the time, but me, I've never thought cars were much of an investment," he said. "Looks like the stupid old scientist is the one with the good judgment, huh? Hey, this thing of yours... it scrolls ahead... wow...! almost what?... ten years. Hey! That'd be neat... just like in Anna's talk, huh? So, what is this, Sonya? Some sort of simulation? An extrapolation?"

"That's what I need your help to find out. My husband...," she sucked in a breath and blew it all out at once. This was crunch time. "He disappeared over a year ago and, ah, he left this chart behind... charts, actually... lots of them. They were all on a disk," she said touching with the pendant hanging round her neck. She sat down on the mattress beside him, her eyes dropping for just a moment too long.

René squirmed about being shoulder-to-shoulder, alone, in a tight college room with an extremely engaging woman, even if she did seem to be nuts. As their shoulders pressed, he didn't need to calculate the gravitational and magnetic effects of a drooping mattress on two seated individuals. "Why don't I sit on the chair?" he said, pushing himself up.

Sonya wasn't listening, intent on what she was about to say, and how to say it. "The point is that when you check all his charts against actual market prices," she said as the mattress bounced her, "they match what happens in real life. Perfectly."

"Anyone can get up-to-the-minute stock price data these days," he said, snapping his fingers to show how easy it was, though personally he had no idea.

"Not these charts," she said, pointing. "They're 100 percent accurate. Forget the hindsight. No, these... as each day passes, they stay right on the button. Incredible, but a fact."

He squeezed his lower lip between his thumb and forefinger. "You're saying this chart predicts *future* stock prices... just like Anna was saying? Sonya... come on!" He stood up. "You're making fun of me, right?" He looked round to see if there was a camera anywhere recording him being made a fool of. "I'm not being *Punked* or something, am I? You know like *Candid Camera*?"

"Of course not. René, listen... please. I thought Michael was a chartist..."

"The 19th century political movement?" René was a history buff whose forte was the giants of science, and this momentous century was the one that sprouted Doppler, Darwin, Kelvin... many others. It was his favourite.

"No. Michael's type of chartist is a trader who studies the behaviour of stocks and markets. They examine trading histories—charts—to discern a market's trend, and then they trade with it... '*the trend's your friend*' is one of their maxims," she said. "If you're into the 19th century, René, you'll know what Mark Twain said, '*History doesn't repeat, but it rhymes*'. It's a pretty simple idea—a market gets a momentum and you trade with it—you know, swim with the tide?"

"A good scientific principle," he nodded, looking at the door.

Sonya sensed she was losing him. "When I first came across these charts," she pressed on, "I guessed that he'd designed some clever system for approximating price prediction. But the problem—or the beauty—is that whatever chart I've looked at... it's perfect... accurate to the cent... every day with every stock. And that's got to be..."

"...impossible? Of course, it's impossible."

Sonya's mouth firmed, "Impossible... but real. Which is why I need your help." She watched as he ran his fingers through his thinning hair, as she'd seen him do a few times already. She took a breath and launched into her story about her trading wins, though not the whole thing. But his rising eyebrows didn't tell her if she'd sparked his genuine interest or he was trying to be polite before rushing out the door.

"Okay," said René, "can I copy this to a new file in case I screw something up?" he asked. "I don't want to ruin your data..."

"No need. I've got a backup," she said.

"Maybe there's some algorithm that connects the data... If there is," he added, "and it does what you say it does, that would be some formula..." He started tapping on the

IcePaC's virtual screen. "No, that doesn't work... Let me try something else..." He wasn't even remotely convinced. It had to be some charlatan trick but for the moment he would just humour the lady until he could prove it.

After several minutes, Sonya's legs had gone numb so she got up to stroll around, or rather stretch given the closeness of the room, but she kept quiet, letting René study the data uninterrupted. He fiddled for a half hour, um-ing and ah-ing every few minutes, and Sonya craned intently from on high, expecting each contemplative grunt to burst into a shout of "*Eureka!*" or whatever modern-day scientific geniuses scream out when they discover something big that has commercial application, probably "*Call my lawyer and a private equity fund!*"

Eventually, René stood up. He stretched his back and rubbed his legs. Sonya sat back on the bed to give him room and waited for him to speak. "I'm getting nowhere," he said in a chance play on words. "This is no prediction system: it's not even a system... It's just data... prices and dates." Just as he had expected. "There's not a single thing buried in here pointing to how the data got created. If something spat this out, it's somewhere else, maybe on the actual disk you copied it from..."

"No, I copied everything across." She could feel she was losing him again.

"Or maybe it's on a disk you didn't find. Even so, why it's perfect, if in fact it is..."

"It is. I promise you..."

"Okay, it is. But why it's perfect beats me."

She wiped her eye. "You know in Anna's talk..."

"Sonya," he said. "You surely don't believe these charts are from the future, do you?"

She thumped the air as if she had made a mistake to trust him. But then she looked up and stared at him, a new resolve on her face. "René, you're right. What system on earth could perfectly predict stock prices?"

He shoved his hands into his pockets and shrugged.

"Could you invent something like that, René? Could anyone… here at Princeton? Or anywhere?"

"Er…," he mumbled. "No."

35

THREE MESSAGES FROM Anna were blinking on René's office voicemail next morning. He'd already had five messages at home. She only wants dinner, he pondered... yeah, right. Married twelve years, he'd been faithful right to the end—okay, apart from two itchy days in the proverbial year seven. Even though his marriage was over, it wasn't long gone and being seduced by Anna these last few times still caused him a degree of awkwardness.

He reflected on how vulnerable he'd been, fresh from his split with Rachel—well, six months wasn't exactly long, was it?—and she had got him just after his gruelling speech.

Without realising it, he traced his nipple through his brown check cotton shirt and shivered just thinking about what Anna might next have in store. She did attract him, he admitted... as a person. It wasn't just the sex; he was sure of it. He leant back into his chair... Her mind... clearly brilliant, if you liked that weird track it ran on... Her sense of humour and taste in music? Pass, and pass. And her conversational ability? Well, maybe it was just the sex.

And at the same time, there was Sonya with her bizarre data and crazy theory to go with it. Just as he was about to ruminate over the charts again, his phone rang. "Anna?" he asked.

"It's Sonya. Am I interrupting? I can call back…"

"No, it's fine."

"René. Last night… I wasn't totally frank. I need to see you again."

In fact, he'd thought the evening had ended strangely, as if she'd left something hanging. "Won't I see you at the conference?

"I mean in private. This evening? Please?"

What an easy choice, he mused. Option one, a slow nuzzle as Anna unbuttons your shirt and peels it off your shoulders… she lightly toys with the hairs on your chest, flicking at your nipples with her searching tongue, unbuckling your belt, and pushing you back onto her bed… torturing you with a drizzle of almond blossom honey over your chest, rubbing it in with her circling fingertips and deliciously pressing you with the soft, warm mounds of…

Or option two: tedious numbing hours studying meaningless computer crap in a desperate woman's futile search for a man she loves but who's clearly dumped her.

It was a simple choice. "What time?" he asked her, gritting his teeth. He and Sonya settled on an early meal at his old undergraduate eating club on Prospect Avenue: unexciting, but quick. The conference organisers had made special arrangements for delegates to have access to the eating clubs.

Maybe, he hoped, he could fit Anna in after. Or was it the

other way round? He stroked his stubble wondering, and reached into his desk drawer for his razor.

AS 5 PM approached, René's nerves tightened. He'd avoided Anna all day, had only the briefest conversation with Sonya, and had raced home for his weekly call with his father in Florida. With the strong winds that blew up in the early afternoon—outside, it was howling—he'd have preferred to go straight to the eating club but he never missed these calls. He wasn't a daddy's boy. Alzheimer's had taken its grip on his father the last three years, and the doctors had told René that habits were important.

By contrast, the sky that morning had been so clear he'd almost skipped to the campus with the friendly snapping chill at his back urging him on. He'd felt alive. The freshness had prickled his nerves and frozen his pores, and he didn't care. He'd snuck a boyish jig over a snowdrift on a drive and finished it with a razzle-dazzle kick of white powder spraying into the air. Not just Anna but a new scientific challenge, well maybe, if he could convince himself that Sonya wasn't some whack job, delightful but insane.

If he'd still been married to Rachel... He slapped his thigh. Not in celebration, more in self-reproach. He still felt guilty, as if he'd walked out on her. The truth was that if Rachel phoned up right now wanting to rekindle the flame, he'd hurl himself at her instantly. No question.

After his depressing call with his father, made more painful because the old man kept asking after Rachel, René peeked through the drapes. This was no evening to be dining out. In the short time he'd been home, the snow had become treacherous, hitting his window almost horizontally.

He phoned Sonya. "Yeah... incredible snowstorm, for sure. You phoned a cab? Why not get them to drop you here? I'll throw something together in the food department... nothing elaborate, I'm afraid... but it'll save on the frostbite."

Though the physics professor could slice through a theory and dice any fractal, he would never win any awards for his culinary skills. That was Sam Sing's department. René's specialty, pretty much his only dish, was eggs. He'd fry up some thinly-sliced white onions till they were transparent, toss in a slurp of Madeira and caramelise the rings till they were golden, careful to avoid charcoaling. The heady, thick, sweet aroma always drove him nuts. As he'd spoon the onions round the pan with the same wooden one his dad, once a cook, had presented to him when he'd moved to Florida, he would marvel at how eye-stingers like onions packed so much sugar. Then, he'd slide a whisked up concoction of eggs into the skillet, a dollop of cream and three dashes of Tabasco per egg, swirl it round with the onions and, when it was starting to firm but still runny, he'd crumble rock salt and a sprinkling of parmesan cheese and chives over the top or, since he was out of chives, some dried thyme. Simple but scrumptious.

Rachel had always said so.

"RENÉ," said Sonya, stabbing her fork at the eggs. "These *are* really delicious."

She liked his eggs! "If those charts are what you think," René said, pointing his own fork toward her IcePaC, "and somehow your Michael did steal them... from the future," he almost choked as he said it, "you're not seriously fretting about laws that exist only in Anna's imagination?"

"She makes a point..."

"Look, if all this was true, forget about being a criminal, you'd be showered with confetti... You'd get a presidential pardon, for goodness' sakes, possibly an interview on *Oprah*, though that'd be harder to swing. But frankly you're jumping the gun. People have theorised for centuries about time-travel. We've spent millions on it, maybe billions—research grants, bequests, subsidies... all that."

"And you? What do you think? In your speech the other night..."

"The truth? I've garnered a pretty good supplement out of it... as you can see," he said, spreading his arms in a semi-dramatic flourish that mocked the sparse comforts of his apartment. If he had put his fork down first, he wouldn't have slopped the slimy wad of egg onto the floor. "But I'll let you into our little academic guild secret if you promise not to tell," he said, leaning down to pick up the food. "It won't happen. Not in our lifetimes, and not in our children's lifetimes... if ever. What you and I will discover—of this I'm certain—is that Michael was one incredibly gifted... what did you call him?... yeah, chartist. Simple as that. There's no other rational explanation." He ended the discussion, so far as he was concerned by shoving a fresh forkload of eggs into his mouth.

Sonya was astounded that one of the world's most eminent experts could be so cavalier about his own work, dismissing it as idle fantasy, as a tacky contrivance to attract grant money. He would change his tune, she knew, when he saw what was hidden up her sleeve.

René wiped the sides of his mouth on his napkin. "On the phone, you said you hadn't been totally frank. What, you're on vacation from an alternate universe?"

She smiled, finally making the decision she'd been wrestling with. "I'll just have to show you," she said, reaching over for her IcePaC.

"Not more charts!" he squealed, the back of his hand pressed against his forehead in mock terror.

"No charts," she promised as she cleared some space on the dining table.

René refilled their glasses with the Californian cabernet he'd dug out of the extensive five-bottle cellar he kept tucked away at the bottom of his closet. The wine had a rich blackberry nose with hints of cherry and dark earth—at least that's what the label claimed. That might have been the aroma once, René thought as he poured, but it wasn't now, probably why Rachel had left the bottle behind.

While Sonya was setting herself up, René put together a platter of dried fruit segments and a grainy parmigiano. Eggs, onions, cream, and now cheese and dried fruit. No wonder his doctor kept nagging he had a cholesterol problem, and hardly the diet for an asthmatic.

AT first, when *Know-Ware* boomed into the room, René bit his lip so as not to laugh.

"I'm braced," he said, unable to contain himself, almost giggling. "It's a computer game, right?"

Sonya ignored the sarcasm—to be fair, she'd been exactly the same at first. She set *Know-Ware's* destination time for the following afternoon.

She watched René more than the screen. Even though the screen was showing what would happen in this same room in 24 hours' time, with René it was like seeing her own mouth gaping in awe when it had been her first time. She held back, waiting for his inevitable question.

"You scanned in a video clip, right?" he asked.

"Wrong. Have I ever been here before?"

"Hmm. Fact: no satellite in existence today," he glanced up to the ceiling, "has a camera that can shoot with this degree of definition, let alone come inside... And this is supposed to be when, tomorrow afternoon?"

She nodded.

René pondered. "How about you re-set it for five minutes from now?"

"Why?"

"Because..." He fiddled with his watch, setting the stopwatch, then got up and took a black and yellow striped cushion from the sofa. "Because in precisely five minutes I'm going to open that window and fling this cushion out onto the snow and, if what you say is true, I want to see me do it, you know, *before* I do it."

Sonya gave the idea an appreciative nod and did what he asked. She also manoeuvred the viewing aspect—she was expert at this now—to focus on his window from the front sidewalk, but far enough back so they could see the snow in the garden below. This boldly striped cushion plunging onto the white powder would leave an impression, for sure. René's curtains were drawn to retain the heat inside. On screen the bare grey tree branches were swaying like the arms of ghosts, poking their hands into the white windstorm.

They watched the screen and an image of René did push the curtains apart.

"That's me. Really me. How the hell did you do that?" he said, dropping his head to check that the on-screen René was wearing the same shirt and tie he was wearing right then.

"I didn't," she insisted, though she could tell he didn't believe her.

She clicked fast-forward and they both watched as his image hovered at the window—the computer timer said it was for 30 seconds—but there was no sign of the cushion. The drapes fell back across the window and René's image vanished from the screen.

Without a word but with a smugness plastered on his face like a character in a French farce, the real René saw he had three minutes before he needed to enact the cushion throw in real life. So he collected the dishes from the table, stacked them on his arm and carried them out to the kitchen. Sonya stayed at the table waiting but also watching. To the clatter of plates in the sink, a smile crept onto her face but she decided not to call him back instead clicking at her computer's controls to save the clip of what she'd just seen.

Finally he emerged, wiping his hands on a dish towel as his watch buzzed his five-minute alarm. "Time's up." He dropped the cloth on the sofa and picked up the cushion again, taking it over to the window and drawing back the drapes. Needing both hands to open the window, he tucked the pillow under his left arm. He twisted the catch and pushed, but the window was stuck. "Damn, it's iced."

He let the drapes swing back and leant down to set the cushion on the floor before heading into his bathroom. A moment passed. He returned with a green pouch that was dangling an electrical cord. "Hair dryer," he explained, adding with a smile, "not that my excuse for hair needs one." He unzipped the pack inserting the plug into a socket near the window. "I'm going to melt the ice. Then," he drummed his fingers on the glass, "I'll complete my mission."

When finally he'd flung the window open and the cushion out, a frigid blast of air blew a spray of snow about six feet inside. He yanked the window shut and shivered back to the dining table. "That wind chill... it must be... I don't know, what? Minus fifty? And now I've got to go out there to retrieve my stupid cushion, just to prove a point."

"Before you go, have a look at this," Sonya said, pointing to the IcePaC, then brushing some snowflakes off his eyebrows. "I left it running when you went into the kitchen, then I saved it."

She clicked on *Replay Saved Game* and sat back with her arms crossed as René watched himself slide the curtains aside, fiddle with the window, then back away and, a long minute later return to blow a hairdryer at the edges of the frame. The corners of her mouth twitched as she watched him watching himself do exactly what he'd just done.

She leant forward, "It's not just a mish-mash of data, is it?"

René pulled his asthma inhaler out of his pocket, and puffed on it.

Twice.

36

"YOU'RE STAYING LONGER?" Erica teased when Sonya phoned her. "Found a gorgeous young Einstein, have we?"

"Sort of," said Sonya, brushing over the truth. The excuse she'd given Erica for going to Princeton had been a conference on the interplay of science and business—a field Sonya claimed to be developing a subject in to teach next year.

With the conference over and students returning to campus, Sonya booked a room at Princeton's local Nassau Inn. It was big enough to squeeze in four dorm rooms like the one she'd occupied the last few days and instead of a sagging mattress, a firm queen-sized four-poster took centre-stage.

***

RENÉ had cleared his other commitments. "One thing that's bothering me... Actually, it's not the only thing, but... Look, if Michael had this... this program... so he could look into the future, surely he would've checked out what was coming at him and dodged it before 'they' got him, right?"

"I've wondered the same thing," she said, squeezing her ear lobe. "The best answer I've come up with is that he got careless. Familiarity can easily inspire over-confidence."

René scratched his head, careful to replace the strands across his thinning pate. "Sonya, what I've got to do—and please, don't take this the wrong way—so I can test this properly, I have to eliminate your influence. Hold on..." he said, raising his finger to stop her interrupting, "it's not that I don't trust you, but scientific rigor insists on replicability in control situations."

She knew this was coming. Like René, she had her own control condition and she, too, wasn't going to budge on it. "Fine, but the deal is you've got to work on it here..."

"In your hotel room..."

"... so no one else can observe you. I'm not going to risk someone else finding out about this... not yet."

Her screen was already displaying a rich image of her room, with the clock in the bottom corner ticking over the following morning's time.

"Okay," he said, his eyes glued to the screen. Tomorrow's Sonya had pulled up the quilted bed-covers, just as she had today. A white terry robe was thrown over the period reproduction sofa, and her suitcase rested on the luggage stand exactly where it was at that moment, although tomorrow's bag was yawning wide-open. She wasn't visible on-screen and the bathroom door was slightly ajar. René's eyebrow raised a telltale twitch.

"Relax. I've set it to after I've already dressed."

"Shame I missed the early show," he said, instantly regretting it.

It grated with Sonya, true, but she let it slip, not wanting to do anything to derail his interest. She kept her focus on the screen where they both saw the front door of her room swing open and Sonya enter from the hallway lugging a weighty plastic bag. She slid a pile of newspapers out of it onto her bedspread and arranged them in a tile pattern, splayed across her screen like a grid of thumbnail images.

In his heart of hearts, René was hoping that somehow Sonya was faking, that she was a masterful con-artist. At this stage, the alternative was too momentous for even him to comprehend fully.

"Click on one of those newspapers," she said, nudging his hand toward the IcePaC. It was hardly his normal paper of choice, but he selected *The Wall Street Journal*, mainly because its front page was so densely packed. On this small screen, other than the paper's stippled and hatched portraits and its many headlines, the rest was a blur.

"There... '*85,000 jobs disappear from economy in December.*' That'll send the markets into a spin," he nodded sagely, but clueless.

Sonya, on the other hand, started to ponder how it would affect her stock holdings, but reminded herself not to bother. She knew exactly where they'd end up, so this was only noise.

René explained his methodology. He would use both an electronic method and a manual control backup. First, he would save the actual screen front pages onto her IcePaC and also onto the portable flash drive he'd brought with him. Importantly, the drive was his, not hers; Sonya understood the importance of that without him saying so, and since she didn't have a printer, he could print them out at home so he'd have an unchangeable hard copy of the images to line up the next day against the real front pages. "No, I won't do it at the university... Yes, that's a promise."

IT wasn't just *The Wall Street Journal*; for René, daily papers in general weren't a staple of his reading habits. But today he purchased four of them, stopping his cab on his way to Sonya's hotel at a combined newsstand/coffee bar. He'd left his car garaged since the 'copy' of this morning's local paper he'd printed last night had predicted an afternoon snowstorm even worse than the last one. He slipped all but one of the papers on the seat next to him with the two coffees he'd bought perched, carefully, on top of them.

What struck him first from the paper on his lap was the headline confirming the drop in jobs—the same headline he'd seen a full day earlier; he'd also seen it reported last night on TV. And *then* it was unexpected... huge news, judging by the news anchors scrambling around for experts to explain what it meant, and the added pressure it put on President Obama to point to something positive out of the administration's $787 billion spending stimulus. The other headlines also mirrored what he'd seen the previous day. He wondered if the articles below them were also identical, but he decided to leave that for when he got to Sonya's, despite the printouts he'd made being stuffed in his bag. They'd do it together, he decided; he owed her that, though if the cab driver hadn't been so chatty he could easily have succumbed to the temptation.

"That job slump, man. It sure looks bad," said the driver, taking his eyes off the road to look back at René. "Damn shock after all that dough Obama tossed into the economy, don'tcha think?"

"Not really," replied René as he kept scanning the papers, his lack of concentration slipping him up where Sonya had already trained herself not to.

"Whadya mean? You knew it was comin'? You a seer or somethin'?"

"A seer? Heavens, no," said René, starting a sweat despite the cold outside. "I, er, I heard something about it somewhere... you know... around."

By the time he buzzed himself at Sonya's hotel room, the exact scene she'd conjured up for him the previous day was awaiting him: she was dressed, of course, and the bed was already tiled with her own freshly purchased copies of the papers. He thought of them as *her* papers, the reason he'd purchased his own. Replicability. To prevent even the possibility of manipulation. Not that he expected her to cheat—actually he did, just a little—but he had to be certain.

René tossed *his* papers onto the floor and slipped his sheath of printouts from his satchel on top of them. "So," he said, offering Sonya the spare coffee he'd brought with him, "Let's start with... what? *The Wall Street Journal*?"

Sonya reached for her copy. "Looks like the real thing," she laughed a little nervously, holding it up to the light as if she were testing for a counterfeit $100 bill.

René motioned for her to put it back on the bed, and leant down for his own purchased copy as well as the printout. A part of him hankered that *his* newspaper would be different. Life would be simpler if this was just some prank, some fraud; not better, just simpler.

He laid them out side-by-side on the coffee table, noticing a slight tic in Sonya's cheek. Was it anxiety over being exposed? He hoped not.

He scanned the pages and yes, the two looked similar, apart from the coffee-stain, proving the cup was not as spill-proof as the newsstand guy claimed.

With his left index finger on the real *Journal* and his right on his printout, he zigzagged down the page. They weren't just similar; they were word-for-word identical. Not just the headlines, but the articles themselves. Thousands of words. This was no joke. No fraud. But how? What other rational hypothesis could there possibly be? If there was one, he didn't have a clue what it was.

He noticed that Sonya was hanging back. She seemed to appreciate his precautions: the printouts and the additional independently-acquired papers. He'd been concerned she might take offence, but she didn't seem to. Then in a move that reminded him of the cushion incident, the first time he'd seen the future, he ambled to the window, removed his black-rimmed glasses and contemplated his next steps, grateful for the silence that Sonya was affording him.

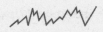

UP to now, pre-René, the best that Sonya could winkle out of *Know-Ware* was to fast-forward by 24 hours.

"No, I've told you. Not the university," Sonya jumped in before he could even finish.

"Actually, I was going to suggest we do it back at my apartment. I may need to access to, well, I have no idea what, but the thing is... whatever we need, I can probably get it by logging into my research database from there... I've got a secure link direct into the university's network."

FOR two hours with Sonya peering over his shoulder at his desk, René had been fiddling with the computer's code but no matter what he tried, he wasn't making any advances.

After he'd burrowed even deeper into the IcePaC's operating system to disable some power-hungry features and activate others, René had a semblance of victory: he managed to stretch *Know-Ware's* reach out by an additional six hours. He looked up at Sonya expecting accolades, perhaps an excited slap on the back, but she was almost mauling her earlobe. "More," she said, her eyes pleading. "René, I need more... especially to have it go back."

Shrugging, he re-examined the computer's specifications. "This thing is incredibly powerful but it's not a candle to the super-computers at Kick-ass," he said. "I know you don't like hearing this, but if you really want to see what happened to him, you have to let me work on this there."

He tried outglaring her but Sonya wasn't one to play dare. Her refusal was sharp and firm.

"Sonya, just my fiddling with your IcePaC, me alone, gave us six extra hours. And as I keep telling you, I know squat about encryption and code-breaking algorithms," he continued, "and this *Know-Ware* is packed full of them. I checked the code. If you really want to do this... my honest opinion...? It's hopeless without reinforcements."

"Like who?"

He cautioned himself to appear calm, not to scare her off. "Like Professor Sing," he said casually. "Sam Sing. Remember him?"

"The Chinese cowboy? You've...," but she paused and her eyes turned away from René. "Look, there's something odd about..."

"Sam isn't..."

"For me, he is."

"You're making a... "

"Mistakes are mine to make."

The phone interrupted their face-off. It was past midnight and René, not in the habit of receiving calls so late, prayed it wasn't his father's nursing home. That was a call he'd been dreading more and more after the accelerating deterioration he'd been noticing lately in their weekly chats.

"I'm cold," said Anna, her voice husky and tempting.

Embarrassed, René turned his back to his guest and whispered into the phone, "It's very late."

"It's never *too* late, René," she cooed.

"I'll call you back."

Sonya was puzzled.

"It's a cruel world, Sonya. Science respects neither time nor place," he shrugged. "It was a colleague, but I'll deal with, er, him shortly." René wasn't a good liar but Sonya was too tired to notice the red creeping up from under his collar. "Listen, we've been at this since six," he huffed, feigning exhaustion and initiating *Know-Ware's* exit process. "Tomorrow... 9 AM?"

Sonya nodded. "Here, right?"

"I guess," he said, his nose twitching. It was the sour odour they now experienced routinely whenever they closed the game down. If it wasn't triphenyl phosphate from an overheated computer casing, he didn't know what it was, but it was downright unpleasant.

With his apartment smelling so badly, he thought, what choice did he have except to hot foot it over to Anna's. Once Sonya left, that is.

For Sonya, the strange smell was to be savoured since it connected her to Michael. And for so long as she could inhale it, foul or not, she sensed hope. She closed her eyes to sample it: the sour-sweet aroma of Michael's last moments at home. Not one other person on the planet could possibly garnish this perfume with a vocabulary of fragrance, but not a single person shared her memory, or her need.

"Sonya?" René pointed to the box displayed on the screen.

"I saw this before," he recalled, "but I never paid attention to the small print. The name *Venari*... it's kind of familiar." With a rough swipe of the back of his hand he brushed his stubbled chin; repeating the move several times to help him scrape at a memory. "There's something about that name..."

Sonya shrugged. It had been one of the first dead-ends she'd tried to go down. As she began to stack the dinner plates, René offered to drop her at her hotel but she insisted on a cab since, at that hour, no way would she accept him driving her.

If she'd known he'd be driving anyway, maybe, but he wasn't going to be telling her that. He phoned for a cab.

"Princeton Cabs... Please hold... Your call is important to us. The next available operator will be with you momentarily... Princeton Cabs... Please h..."

"I'm on hold," he called out over the clatter from the kitchen. A couple of minutes later, he shouted again, "The whole town must be calling for cabs... I'm still on hold. Listen, I'm happy to drive y..." but before he could finish the sentence, the cab operator came on line.

"Princeton Cabs, good evening. We're not operating tonight..."

"Excuse me?" René said.

"Freak snowstorm, sir. Have you looked outside?"

"But..."

"It's undrivable, sir."

"Sonya, the blizzard's so bad, all cabs are cancelled. Come look."

She was wiping her hands on a tea towel as she came out of the kitchen.

"You'll have to stay here...," he coughed. "You know, stay till it clears. We could keep working," he added, to demonstrate his fine intentions and to mask his disappointment over missing seeing Anna.

They reopened *Know-Ware* but after yet another hour of getting nothing new, they'd had enough. René offered to sleep on the couch.

"I've got a better idea."

"Er, you do?" said René, misinterpreting her. This, coming after Anna's earlier invitation, got his heart pounding so much he could've smashed the walls of Jericho by simply leaning against them.

"*I'll* take the couch," she said, unaware of his palpitations.

"Sure... fine." He jumped up and pulled spare sheets, a blanket and a pillow from his closet and made himself busy.

"I don't wear pyjamas," he apologised, handing her his robe.

"Shouldn't you be calling your colleague back?" Sonya asked, pointing to the phone.

He swallowed and, after closing his study door behind him, made the call. "Anna, there's a blizzard out there."

"I got one here, too," she said. "I was hoping you'd know what to do about it."

What René was hoping was that his awkward erection would subside before he re-entered his living room. "It'll have to wait, Anna. I can't come."

"Makes two of us." She hung up on him.

He stood in his study a while, waiting, and by the time he thought it safe to reappear, Sonya was in his robe and had made fresh coffee.

"Ah!" He inhaled the steaming aroma of the freshly ground beans. "Now, that's an odour to die for."

René often said things that came out differently to what he intended and Sonya saw he regretted saying this as soon as it had slipped off his tongue. In good spirits she let it slide and rather than sleeping, they sat talking until three. First about *Know-Ware* but after she refused a further three times to involve Sam Sing or anyone else, they changed topics. Last time it was Rachel who'd been the mainstay of the conversation, this time it was Michael. He was, after all, the reason for all this.

Sonya skimmed over Michael's background, what little she now realised she knew of it, worrying how thin her knowledge must seem out of context and strangely concerned that René would think less of her for being so ignorant of her husband's past.

"It's not that I didn't ask. His replies were well... vague... large; never specific... Of course I was curious, but it was a strain to keep pressing... When he spoke of the past it was always with a... a kind of dismissive disinterest. Like it didn't matter. What did matter to him was now, where he was, what he was doing... He didn't even talk about the future. No plans. Not often anyway... There were some things from the past he did talk about though... like when he was a travel writer and some of the places..."

"Like where?"

"Like... like Botswana. You know, I always thought it was strange but a few times he called it Bechuanaland. It wasn't called by that name since the sixties. And now with *Know-Ware*, it sort of makes sense, don't you think?"

"Sense? Hmm... Where else did he talk about?"

"France. He raved about the canals, and once in a while said how we should go on a barge trip, but we never..."

"A barge trip?"

"He had this favourite canal a couple of hundred miles from Paris. The Nivernais, I think..."

"You're kidding me, right?"

"Kidding? Wh...?"

"Because that's where Rachel and I spent our honeymoon, floating on a barge. Hey, I've got some photos..." He scurried off for them, and Sonya went back into the kitchen for more coffee, sensing they'd be up quite a bit longer.

René's photos knocked her off-guard. She hadn't expected his wedding album.

"When Rachel left me, I insisted on a complete copy. If I had nothing else to show for it, I could at least keep my memories." He thought he picked up on her discomfort, "I'll flick through to the canal shots..."

"No, René. Can I see them all? The wedding, too?"

Apart from Hollywood movies, this was as close as Sonya had got to a real Jewish wedding, so she prodded him with questions.

He explained he was an atheist, well, maybe more of an agnostic, hardly unusual in his line of work, but it was Rachel who'd insisted on the full religious ceremony. He would've settled for a simple civil service with a few friends, he said, but Rachel pressed, claiming it was to please her aging parents. "An excuse."

The René who Sonya saw smiling at the album may well have been twelve years younger but he was as ruffled and rumpled as today—the stereotypic physicist.

And Rachel? Sonya saw a woman of flawless classical beauty. She envied the full, almost blue-black hair that brushed the side of her face. With her high cheekbones and dark piercing eyes, Rachel seemed both strong and alluring. Maybe, thought Sonya, it was that hint of strength that was so compelling. Standing taller than René, Rachel wore the poise of a woman who was comfortable with her beauty without being driven by it. She was nothing like what Sonya had visualised from René's ramblings, making her wonder what his mental image of Michael was like. "It must've been a fabulous wedding."

"It was," he said, lifting his watery eyes from the photos but Sonya kept hers there, not wishing to embarrass him.

Rachel was much younger than René. She looked to be in her early twenties, whereas René had been perhaps ten years older at the time. Divergences as they got older? Pangs for lost opportunities? The lack of children?

"She complained I never let go of the trivial," he said, flicking over a few pages. "That I didn't care about what was important, what was important to her, anyhow. Hey, enough of that... Here's the Nivernais." He wiped his eye and without missing a beat went on to explain the canal's turbulent history, how it took over 80 years on-and-off to build it, from the late 1700s on.

Though she'd heard much of it before, from Michael, she listened without interruption, as if it were Michael talking through another voice, similar to what she'd started assuming he was doing through *Know-Ware*.

"We rented our barge at this ancient little town called Auxerre... in Burgundy. Heard of it?"

Sonya couldn't say she had. "You took a photo of a supermarket?" she laughed.

René coughed then jabbed his finger at the contents of the shopping cart, "We stocked up for our boat with this white Chablis, these amazing pre-cured meats... and Rachel just went crazy about these wedges of cheese... the pack had a picture of a laughing cow."

According to René it took their barge a full week at the regulation 8-knot maximum to navigate to their destination, a mere 80 road miles away at Décize. A week to travel what would have taken only a couple of hours if they'd gone by car.

"So why go by boat?"

"Slows down time. For a week you live in a world where little of any moment happens. Where one of your most critical decisions is choosing your breakfast... pushing into the crowded pâtisserie, inhaling the yeasty aroma of freshly baked pastries. *Brioches, monsieur? Croissants?* Now there's a decision! Or deciding where to tie up your barge for lunch so you can crunch into your crusty baguette stuffed with cheese and local ham? Or where you rope up for the night? We loved wandering the tiny villages, you know, hunting for bric-a-brac, patrolling the street markets for strawberries..." He went silent for a moment.

"You loved it," she said, realising he still pined for Rachel as much as she did for Michael.

He smiled. A distant smile. "You're cast off from your normal hurly-burly," he said, more for himself than for her. "You get immersed in the mundane, yet you find it liberating."

In some small ways, René was like Michael, she decided.

The self-drive barge in the photos was what René called a péniche. A white boat, hunched low in the water, with a wide beam you could walk around and, according to René, it was easy to handle. A blessing since he and Rachel had only ever skippered a rowboat and navigating the often narrow canal, and especially the locks, was no cinch.

There was a shot of René at the wheel, sporting a jaunty yachtsman's air. Probably he saw himself as a debonair James Bond type, but to Sonya he had a little more of the wild-eyed Kramer from *Seinfeld* about him. The roof above his steering position was slid full back to reveal clear blue summer skies, and a rush of fresh air was rumbling through the curls dangling below his skipper's cap. Back then, René had curls.

"Quite waspish, don't you think," he smiled, with his fingers taking a patrician swipe of his imaginary captain's brim.

In another shot, Rachel was riding a bicycle along the canal path; it was one of the bikes supplied with the barge. Look, no hands, she seemed to be saying. René told how before lunch some days they'd tie up and ride carefree down the miles of *chemins d'halage,* haulage tracks that hugged the canal where a century or more ago heavily-yoked beasts of burden would plod, their ropes dragging log barges from lock to lock on their journey to supply Paris with its winter fuel.

The locks—*écluses*—fascinated Sonya. Michael had gushed about them, but René's snapshots attested to how flawed the picture in her mind had been. As she looked on, an old thought started bubbling: that despite decades of travelling, Michael had no photos. None. No videos either. Not even any souvenirs or trinkets. "It's all about memories," he'd say. And tapping the side of his head, he'd add, "Memories never break, never get lost."

He had been glib, she knew that, but she swallowed it, just like his many other foibles and eccentricities. But now, sitting here with René, the implausibility staggered her, though she mentioned nothing of it to him.

The first photo of a lock showed the canal narrowing into a neck just wide enough to take one boat, though long enough for two or three to be lined up, stern to bow. The sides of this lock were lined with stone, and heavy metal gates sealed each end. Hand-operated, the gates descended all the way to the silty canal bed. Metal bollards, like teat-shaped baby pacifiers, sat along the tops of the side walls, patiently awaiting ropes to be slung over to secure the boats from smashing side-to-side during the lock's emptying or filling flushes.

Sonya imagined the *éclusière's* children running in and out of the tiny stone lock-houses that huddled next to most of the locks. Rachel must have been smitten with the lock-houses, Sonya guessed—she'd snapped virtually every one.

Unlike other canals, the lock gates on the Nivernais were not motorised back then, so it was back-breaking work.

Most of these multi-ton gates were decades old, and to open and close them travellers had to emulate slaves heaving around a grind stone. In the photo René had turned to, Rachel was straining with her arms stretched rigid, pushing against a red-painted crossbar, her body at an almost 30-degree angle and the toes of her sneakers pressing back against slippery grey gravel. Sonya could almost feel the sweat beading on the young woman's brow.

Over the page, the scene moved to the slow-changing countryside: acres of pastures waiting for the quiet herds of drowsy white charolais to munch their way through. Occasionally, a few cows would winch their bowed heads up from the grass and blink their huge eyes into the camera. Haste had escaped these parts for centuries.

Next were acres of lofty sunflowers. The massive golden flowers reared toward René's camera, their haughty black faces surrounded by giant yellow petals, attuned to the day's slow rhythm.

But René felt his stomach flutter as he came to his favourite shot. Rachel… so sensuous… stretching under a low draw-bridge made of iron and wooden slats, and hoisting it up so he could manoeuvre their barge underneath. René adored this shot. He'd taken it just as he drifted the barge under the bridge, before he pulled to the side so she could leap back on board.

Suddenly he gasped, "I knew it. There!" His pudgy finger was jabbing at the photo, at the side of the stone bridge-supports, beneath Rachel's feet. It was a faded, timeworn advertising placard, and from the vaguely visible style of art nouveau lettering and the costumes and feather boas of the tourists who were faintly waving from it, it had to be from the early 1900s.

Sonya hunched her head close to it. "What?"

With a burst of energy Sonya wouldn't have associated with René, he hopped over to his study and returned, almost running, waving a magnifying glass at her. "Here!" he said, puffing. "See for yourself."

"It's hard to read... so faded... *bâteaux Venari*." Sonya's hand flew to her mouth, and her own breathing stopped.

René watched her face swivel toward him, like a soul suddenly lost in hell. "Maybe it's nothing," he said, trying to be soothing but failing miserably. She didn't object when he slipped the magnifying glass out of her hand. Holding it to his own eyes, he said, "Ah... '*Les voyages... en bâteaux Venari.*' What's that mean?" he asked. "Voyages in Venari boats? Venari boat trips? What the hell does *venari* mean? Maybe it's some French word?" He glanced at Sonya and thought he detected a shrug. "I'll check," he said, standing again.

Sonya blinked, slowly, like the cows in the photos.

"Come." He took her hand and led her into his study. In Michael's study everything had been squarely in its place whereas René's was comfortably dishevelled, like its occupant. Papers were piled in toppling mini-towers, the floor was spread with books, most closed with cards and bits of paper or pens stuck between pages to mark relevant re-entry points.

The silence cracked with the phone but despite the time, he didn't answer it, letting it go to the answering machine in the kitchen. He quickly went for the door, closing it so

Sonya would not hear the message then, logging his clunky PC onto his favourite translation website, his saviour when reading foreign research papers, he typed in 'venari' and a moment later got the answer:

```
Text translated:   venari
Language:          Latin
Root:              venare; uenare—to hunt
Translation:       I will hunt.
```

Sonya whispered, "Michael's name..." Her face already drained by exhaustion from lack of sleep leached into a sickly pallor. René said nothing but noticed she seemed to be wheezing. He fumbled in his pocket for his blue inhaler and offered her a puff but with a whip of her wrist she sent it flying to the floor and her head fell to her hands and she started to sob.

THE tissues were crumpled in a pile in front of her. It was nearly five in the morning, and while the blizzard had passed, a greater storm was still swirling inside René's apartment.

"René, his surname was... is Hunt. Wheen is my maiden name," Sonya explained. "I never changed my name, not when I got married the first time, nor with Michael. His full name is Michael Will Hunt. *I will hunt*. Get it? Venari..."

"Holy...!"

"That means *he* created *Know-Ware*, right? That *he* is Venari Inc."

Both withdrew into contemplative silences, knowing they were at a crossroads but wavering over which turn to take next.

René broke first, and put his hand on her shoulder. "We've got to get more resources."

37

"THIS IS WHERE Sam's the head," René said as they huddled under the protective awning to the sound of the snow ploughs doing their final scrapes to clear the roads. René indicated the plaque for the Centre for Integrative Computational Research & Strategy. It was still so new, so polished, that instead of noticing Sonya flinch at the mention of Sam's name, what caught his guilty eye between the orange flashes from the snow ploughs was the reflection of Anna's hickey creeping up from under his turtleneck.

Hunching a little and rolling up the collar, he continued as if nothing was awry. "They've just moved in… Before, the Centre commandeered a floor of the computer science building," he waved toward the squat building further along Olden Street, "but that got too cramped. As an honorary professor here I get to use the facilities any time… within reason." René was collaborating with CICRS on a cosmology project investigating the initial conditions of the universe.

He'd already explained how CICRS's massive computers had the absolute latest in advanced technology, much of it developed at Princeton. The university had been at the forefront of computing with Alan Turing and John von Neumann and, he said, it wasn't letting its reputation slip.

It was 5:30 AM. "No one turns up this early," he'd told her, promising they'd be able to grab time on CICRS's computers without interruptions; not from Sam, not from anyone. Sonya was still point-blank rejecting any notion of outside help, but she relented on using the university's computers if they could do it without witnesses. Their cover story, if anyone did show up, was that René was testing some new algorithms he'd just developed. And Sonya's presence? That he was being hospitable to an overseas colleague, though they had joked how others would read a far less innocent excuse into it. An excuse René could, he was starting to think, be happily guilty of.

She was insistent that he do nothing to risk someone gleaning their real purpose. Instinct, and paranoia, told her that widening the net would only arouse trouble. In René's apartment, they'd debated this over and over and while he understood her concerns he argued strongly, and repeatedly, that a well-chosen team, Sam especially, would help find a solution, but Sonya took a hard-line and, ultimately, René gave up.

They quickly scouted round the building to check it was empty, and Sonya passed her IcePaC to him. They'd agreed to load a copy of *Know-Ware* temporarily onto the network—a big step for her—and while he started logging himself in, Sonya excused herself to use the restroom.

He copied *Know-Ware* onto the network quickly and, keen to lose no time, opened it straight up. He clicked *Mute* to avoid the aural salvo that by now he knew would blast them and then projected it up onto the huge screen that covered the whole span of the wall of the lab. Much of the work here was done in small groups so wall display was often the most convenient way to foster discussion. It was far better than phalanxes of co-researchers smashing elbows as they huddled round pesky desk monitors or sat at separate desks shouting at each other across the room. Out of the silence, he heard the click of Sonya's shoes from down the corridor, but when he looked up he was shocked to see it was Sam.

"Wha's up, René?" he said, cradling his bike helmet.

René was petrified Sonya would accuse him of a set up. Though flustered, he maintained enough presence of mind to disappear *Know-Ware* off the screen. Almost instantly, the wall went blank. He knew that if he was to maintain any semblance of Sonya's trust, he had to get rid of Sam, and pronto. "Oh, just some new algorithms I've been working on. But you? Why are you here so early?"

"I've got to write my monthly drudge report for the board. Paperwork! The burden of the researcher-turned-bureaucrat." Sam shot a glance at the wall screen. He thought he'd seen something when he pushed into the room through the glass doors, but now it was blank.

René watched Sam's eyes linger on the screen, praying he wouldn't notice the taskbar down near the skirting board, spelling out the word *Know-Ware* and indicating that a file or a program with that name was open.

"Enjoy your, er, algorithms," Sam winked over his shoulder as he walked off. With the cheeky way he swung his helmet as the door closed behind him, René suspected Sam had seen it.

WHAT René had told Sonya about Sam was dead right: not that he'd shown up—René certainly didn't fess up to that—but that he was imaginative and resourceful.

Once out of René's eyeshot, it was simple for Sam to slake his thirst. Using a digital crowbar he'd designed himself, he jimmied into the network computer. A screen, the identical one that René and Sonya were seeing themselves, popped onto his own:

"Sonya, when do you want to go?"

Sonya? The name rang a bell and Sam was intrigued. He let it mull as he saw a date being typed in, one that was four days off. His screen—and the wall display that René and Sonya were watching—cut to an aerial shot, high above the earth, as if from a satellite. It cast a narrow beam down onto the east coast of the United States, and the screen zoomed in stages toward what seemed like Princeton, New Jersey.

As the screen zeroed in tighter and tighter, Sam watched it pinpoint the CICRS building from on high and zoom down onto it, plunging in through the roof and breaking into the room he'd just seen René in.

It was the next image that gave Sam a real start: it showed Sam himself. Sam's brow—the real Sam's—furrowed and quietly contemplated his next move, fiddling with the strap of his helmet as he rocked it to and fro on his desk. He didn't have to be the genius he was to decide to copy René's files, though he should have been a more cautious one.

In the other room, Sonya's face flashed with alarm. "What's that?" she said. A dialogue box had fluttered momentarily on the big screen. She'd thought it said something like *Copy Files*, but she was unsure. "Where'd that come from?"

"No idea," said René, hoping it wasn't Sam up to no good, and worrying why Sam would be sitting in this room in four days, since his own workspace was down the corridor.

For Sam, even the fleeting appearance of the dialogue box was frustrating; he thought he'd got this glitch out of his surveillance tool a week ago. Alerting his targets wasn't especially smart, so he scratched a reminder on his pad to put in a permanent patch.

Even though Sam had access to the most sophisticated 1,024-bit code-breaking software—one of his PhD students had designed it only weeks before—and this one could crack the most complex encryption imaginable, now was clearly not that time. If he went ahead, René would know. He killed his surveillance.

"You did it," said Sonya, punching the air and almost throwing her arms around René.

"The parallel computers did it. Four days, first up. I told you this'd be worth doing. I want to try to ramp this thing into Holovision mode, whatever that is or, if we can't do that, we'll try to push it even further into the future."

"We need to go back!" said Sonya.

"Hmm," René mumbled. "Before we try that, I want to

see what this Holovision thing is. Just for a minute, okay?" He typed in the date and time for the following morning.

If Sam had still been watching, he would have seen himself, wearing his black leather motorbike jacket, arriving for work, early again, but this time motivated to try peeking at the files he'd just tried to copy. He could have witnessed himself, just as Sonya and René were—not on the wall screen, but in a ghostly 3D image—walking into the room, removing his riding gloves and stuffing them into his jacket pocket.

"Holy fu... er, gosh," gasped René. "It's so real." It wasn't just the reality that perturbed him, but why Sam was sitting there again. He said nothing about that.

The holovised version of Sam walked over to where Sonya was sitting, and dumped the helmet he'd been cradling in his elbow onto her chair, or rather her lap, letting it glide straight through her astonished body in a translucent sort of way.

She brought her hands forward gingerly to touch the vague image. René held back, out of discretion, and he watched as her tentative hands passed right through the helmet. "It's air... just air," she whispered at the same time as Sam's own ghostly 3-D image decided to remove his jacket and throw it over the back of her hurriedly vacated chair, swapping it for the conservative crisp white cotton coat he affected inside CICRS. As the seconds ticked by, the holovised Sam intensified itself into a near solid.

Cautiously, Sonya's hand edged toward him again as if to make sure he *wasn't* real. She even ventured a tentative "Hello?" but Sam ignored her, of course.

All they could do was observe; nothing they did could influence Sam or make him react. He acted out what he was predestined to do, they assumed; a true vision from tomorrow, totally ignorant they were spying on him, a turnabout that escaped them.

'Sam' sat at the computer ready to work. Ready for mischief, really, but they didn't know that. As his virtual fingers typed on the keyboard, his image began to flicker, sputtering to and fro between near-corporeality and the merest cloud of vapour. For five seconds this played out until his image puffed into nothingness, and Sonya and René just stared at each other, unable to speak.

38

SONYA STRADDLED HIM, *hitching like he was a bronco. With one hand, she twisted his nipples, fast and rough, and pulled at his short chest hairs, then raked her nails down his stomach. Her other arm was stretched behind her, her fingers between his splayed legs, massaging and manipulating him, feeling the raw energy as she bucked.*

Michael's eyes were clamped, his body perched at that metastable point teetering between ecstasy and agony. Each pitch drew Sonya up him higher, tingling and teasing him. She'd pause, he'd tense, and she'd crash back down.

She hovered her breasts, out of reach of his tongue but not his fingers, and when she felt the explosion surge through him she leant forward and crushed one onto his lips.

She was pressed against him, their sweat sticking them together. They lay prone, motionless, silent for minutes, enjoying the private thrill of sensing the other's heartbeat, occasionally both in tune. When her pulse subsided, Sonya peeled off him like Scotch tape and lay next to him, her face pressed down into the pillow, her arm thrown over his chest staking her claim.

THEY looped this clip for Michael, this once private moment, over and over. It was not charity, but torture. They flashed it onto the screen when he least expected it, and they'd run it again and again, twenty... thirty times.

To Michael, it wasn't erotic. It had become obscene. It condemned him for what he saw as his real crime. Not what they'd arrested him for. But hubris. With Know-Ware, *he had possessed the tool that could have guaranteed their future together, yet he had arrogantly failed to use it.*

"Why didn't I check, just once?" he shouted, to the amusement of those monitoring him, and he dug his nails into his thigh.

39

"IT'S SAM," SAID René, pressing his palm over the mouthpiece. "He's asking me, er us, for dinner tonight."

"What do you mean… us? Shit, René! You've told him, haven't you?" Sonya sucked her lips over her teeth.

After the Holovision breakthrough, and now being able to jump up to four days forward, they'd stalled on progress. After two more dawn sessions, they still couldn't get *Know-Ware* to go backwards, not even by a single minute.

And meanwhile, René had kept nagging Sonya about asking Sam for help. At first, he thought her resistance was just paranoia.

"I haven't said a word," he insisted, technically true. "And he, ah, cooks great Chinese…"

"You've said nothing?" she pressed, not letting him change the subject.

"Nothing."

Sonya nodded, though she was sure she'd regret going.

"Eight o'clock?" René said into the phone. "Done." He replaced the handset. "Sam's Chinese is to die for, really."

OUTSIDE, it was so bitter, so cold, that the shadows cast by the street lamps seemed to stick frozen to the sidewalk. The huddled pair scurried out of René's building, anxious to keep moving and avoid the fate of these gloomy shapes and, six long, cold minutes later, the two were in the corridor outside Sam's door, cross-slapping their arms.

The spaghetti-Western Clint Eastwood couldn't have outfitted Sam better, Sonya thought as he swung the door open. He was kitted out in a washed-out denim shirt strung with a Western-style bolo tie, not the same one he'd worn at the opening night dinner. This one had a Wyatt Earp clasp holding it together and his stove-pipe jeans sported a hefty silver Texan belt-buckle, polished so it shimmered, spotlighting the toes of his hand-tooled boots. The only thing missing was a 'Howdy, pardner' hat-sweep though Sonya's eye did catch a cream-colored Stetson dangling off a wall hook in the hall.

Sam whisked away their coats, scarves and hats, excusing himself to hang them in the closet. As René followed after him, Sonya wandered into the living room and let her eyes rummage around. The apartment was somewhat larger than René's and the elegant soft furnishings and cool colours gave it a calm spacious feel. A picture on the opposite wall captured her attention. Was it a guitar or a violin? she wondered. Maybe a woman? She'd seen something like it before somewhere, she was certain, and stepped over to examine it close up. Wow! This, she had certainly seen—in art books or a museum somewhere—but she'd never seen a real Picasso in anyone's living room before.

"A gift from one of my consulting clients," Sam volunteered as he sauntered back in with his arm round René's shoulder.

"Lehman Brothers, wasn't it?" René asked, with a snide hint of envy but followed by a brush of his nose as if the name didn't bear mentioning in polite company.

"Corporations are here today, gone tomorrow, yet good art lives on," Sam shrugged then swung open the door to the dining room. He grabbed the bottle of lightly chilled sauvignon blanc he'd left on the table. "This will complement our meal."

Sonya noticed it was a New Zealand wine. Michael had a case of the same label in their cellar. He knew wines and when it came to sauvignon blanc, he swore that tiny New Zealand produced some of the world's best. "You're into wines?" she said, though as she said it, she realised her tone was a little too sceptical, and she cringed about it as it became clear during the evening that Sam's talents weren't limited to science or even wine. He was a charming, even hilarious raconteur, and his cooking was indeed superb as René had said.

"... *Les Misérables*, so I'm back to New York for a couple of days to see it with Erica. She's a friend."

"When?" asked Sam.

"Wednesday night," Sonya said hesitantly, hoping he wasn't asking because he wanted to tag along.

René pushed his chopsticks under some steamed rice and lifted it to his mouth. Though he accepted that with a friend dying of cancer Sonya would have to juggle her priorities, he couldn't comprehend why, point-blank, she'd refused to leave *Know-Ware* with him, not even a copy. Now he had to wait till she got back from New York.

"If you need somewhere to stay," Sam said, passing Sonya the small pancakes for yet another serving of Peking Duck, "you're welcome to my pad there. It's in TriBeCa. I use it," he said, rolling his own pancake round a slice of duck, some spring onion and hoi sin sauce, "when I'm there for a client... or for a party. I love parties, don't you? And it saves me the drive—it's a good 90 minutes getting back here... and that's if you're lucky with the traffic." He popped the duck into his mouth.

"Thanks, but I'm staying with Erica, on the Upper East Side."

"Sam's a major party animal," said René, "if you hadn't worked that out."

She hadn't, but smiled anyway, and excused herself to go to the bathroom, curious why such a party animal hosted a dinner for only three.

"Never been to Australia," Sam was telling René when Sonya returned. "Almost everywhere, but not there."

As Sonya took her seat, René explained that Sam was always off to exotic locations, "Not bad for a lowly-paid university professor."

"Without my wonderful clients, you think I afford all this...?" Sam waved his arm. Though elegant, and larger than René's, the apartment wasn't even close to a Donald Trump scale, apart from the Picasso.

"Sam, you've got this, your New York place, your bike, your vacations. And all that dough you save on ex-wives."

"Ah, women..." Sam said, closing his eyes dreamily and crossing his hands with his palms over his heart. "Despite his copious wealth and extraordinary good looks," he winked, "where did Sam go wrong?" He bowed his head toward his wine glass and lifted a finger to his face to mime a tear running down his cheek.

40

MICHAEL HAD BENT the rules, he'd smashed them, which was how they saw it when they'd finally tracked him down. Despite his jaunts into times past and future, Michael had managed to keep himself hidden from them for years... decades of elapsed time. He'd known it couldn't last. And it hadn't...

DAMN rules! Who the hell are they to set the rules? He spits his disdain to the floor, his glob of phlegm just missing a startled cockroach that scurries back to its hole.

Once, he'd gone too far... and been noticed. Just once! That was why they'd come for him...

DESPITE his unkempt appearance, and his escape being blocked by a high-voltage wire-mesh barrier, an aura of unnatural calm radiates from him. He is younger... much *younger. His coat is grimy, the sleeves smeared with green; his hair a little wild, and grey—whether through dust and muck or because time has leached its colour to match his eyes. His face, though set in concentration, is ghastly pale; his chin marked with a brown cut—a cut half healed; and his expression is haggard and drawn, though not from worry. For a moment he hesitates, and his eyes squeeze shut as if they are dazzled by a sharp light. When they open, he cracks a smile.*

The broad hilltop three hundred yards behind him is capped with a squat, sprawling research facility. It houses the world's most sophisticated developer of quantum computer technology, a firm that only five years earlier, through the wild-fire success of its revolutionary 2020-Quip, shook off its bankruptcy. Rapidly, quantum-based 'quips' supplanted computer chips, and PCs have become QCs: quantum computers. Even the early QCs, loaded with a mere 30 qubits, could thrash the best super-computers, though they still suffer irksome reliability problems. But happily Microsoft is still there to blame.

The stranger has just intruded on the facility to acquire the Quip he needs to power the device strapped to his sleeve. He slots the one-of-a-kind prototype into the apparatus, knowing it gives him 10^{20} times more grunt than even the most powerful Quips previously available. After today, this new one won't be reproduced for years: it will stay his, and his alone. It will keep him safe. For a while.

His contented smile pinches. A cacophony of sirens erupts and he glances back at the hilltop he has just strolled down. The roiling smoke-belching cloud is already consuming the building. Thick silvery tubes—robotic fire hoses—begin to telescope out of the earth and, as if unaided, they draw themselves up to majestic heights.

A hundred people, maybe more, come scooting out from under the swirling plume. Their eyes sting. Their throats scream for air. When they've escaped, many stop and bend over, hands pressed to thighs, gasping, choking. Some turn back to see the churning black curtain. Some look round for other faces, shouting words he can't hear over the shrieking fire alarms. A few take charge throwing their right arms back and over in 'come on, let's go' gestures, and they are all off, charging down the hill, many toward where he is standing unseen.

When the fire hosepipes stop their rapid rise, the stranger observes that each tip is bending to aim itself back into the building, like swaying cobras ready to strike. Their heads rear up and fierce gushes of thick spray spew toward the source of the smoke.

"Stupid," he laughs. The fools are reacting precisely how he expects them to since they don't know he's disabled the emergency shutdown system. Inside the complex, the sprays burst open, wrecking everything. All the precision-tuned electrical and electronic equipment—still powered up and running, when they shouldn't be—spark, short and fuse, including the top-secret research database and the unique process software.

Oh, he also injected a computer virus into the system, just to be sure—its job to insert a few lines of erroneous code into the operating system so it can never reboot. Ever.

They won't be making these Quips for anyone, he thinks—he knows—not for a very long time.

He also knows that, like all well-planned systems, this one is fully backed-up at an external site, in this case, 100 miles away. There, the vigilant management has built a complete mini-version of this facility, a fully functioning enough-to-keep-us-going factory with the essential equipment. Those few with the presence to think about it as they escape the building above him recall this fact with relief, comforted that their vast research effort, their jobs, as well as their stock options will be safe; the firm might lose the equipment at this facility, even the building itself, but insurance will cover that. What is critical, foremost, is protection of the irreplaceable research data and an alternate workplace, albeit cramped, set up and ready to relocate to immediately in the case of an emergency. The most precious thing they'll lose is time, they are thinking, but because of the back-up facility, it won't be long.

He smirks: Synchronicity! Funny how two such similar fire storms can occur in two locations, 100 miles apart, on the same day and at the same time. Well, it will be the same time when he gets there.

"Hasta la vista, baby*," he chuckles to himself with a vaguely Austrian accent, not quite recalling why.*

He swings his gaze back at the fence with an impatient sigh and a peaked eyebrow. He brings his forearm round as if he's about to look at his watch, but instead he taps a square glowing on his matte-black sleeve device.

If any of those running down the hill catch sight of him, they would see him vanish; but to his eyes, they are the ones to disappear, as is the electrified fence currently barring his escape. The wire mesh shimmers, then it sparks and sputters—in a way, it curtsies before him—and he steps across the line where it will one day stand.

He strolls over to where he'd left his vehicle some time before.

Some time, indeed.

॰॰॰

IF only he'd checked.

41

OUTSIDE Wallis Place, Sonya went to hail a cab but Erica yanked her arm down. "The subway's only a couple of blocks," she said indicating to Lexington Avenue and, pulling up her hood, she led Sonya toward the station.

The mutual hustle for warmth swept them briskly down the shiny wet sidewalk. The frosty duo huddled at the corner traffic lights, waiting for the pale green WALK sign to glow, and while they stood there in the drizzle, neither woman noticed a black Ducati pulling out of the oncoming traffic to their left. The motorbike swerved perilously close to the curb and slowed to a barely-moving roll as it neared them.

In readiness for the WALK sign, Sonya hitched her purse higher onto her shoulder. She sensed movement and her eye caught the black bike rolling forward. Instantly she recognised it as a Ducati, a 1750cc. carbon fibre, fuel-injected speed machine. She'd go for a spin on this baby anytime, she smiled. The bike came to a stop at the lights. Erica noticed it, too, but her reaction was wary, not admiring; unlike Sonya she stepped back from the curb.

A split second before the pedestrian signal flashed to green, when Sonya's front foot was starting to poise over the gutter, the bike thundered into life. It reared onto the fat treads of its alloy-rimmed back wheel and hurtled toward them, throwing the pair off-balance. The rider thrust out his gloved right hand and snatched Sonya's bag from her, almost tearing off her arm as she gripped onto the strap, dragging back against the bike's acceleration.

"My IcePaC's in there," Sonya screamed to Erica.

Erica grabbed onto Sonya's waist, her frail arms clinging on as best they could. The women were losing the tug-of-war, the strap of Sonya's bag burned through her fingers, slipping till the bag itself thumped against the heel of her hand and, after the engine revved into the red zone, the sudden jolt snapped her grip open.

Erica, seeing the bag about to fly, ignored her infirmity and letting Sonya go, lunged at the driver, grabbing for his arm, hoping to pull him off the bike. She missed but got her gloved fingers into an open sleeve pocket and held on grimly. She tried a low kick at his leg, but the bike jerked forward and she missed, her foot smashing itself into the wheel. The biker swerved to break loose and lurched forward. But Erica, amazed she was doing this, held tight. She hadn't had a burst of adrenaline like this for ages.

As the rider pulled away, Sonya could hear his pocket stitching give way under Erica's fingers—a staccato pop-pop-pop—and the final snap flung her friend back onto the wet oily blacktop.

From the ground, Erica pulled her mobile phone from her pocket. "Damn. The screen's cracked. Must've broken in the fall." Under the yellow cone of the streetlight, she punched in 911, praying it would work despite the shattered panel.

Erica put one hand over the mouthpiece, "They're running a check on the plate... Yes, I'm here... You're kidding..."

She slipped the phone into her pocket and got to her feet. "That bike... reported stolen an hour ago," she said, her eyes wide in disbelief. "Odds are it'll turn up ditched in some back alley, but they want us to take this to the station." Pinched between her thumb and forefinger, she limply held up the rider's leather pocket away from her face, as if it was her cancer.

With Sonya's IcePaC, purse, theatre tickets, and one of her credit cards gone—she'd left the others with her passport in Erica's apartment safe—neither woman was in a mood for entertainment, not even *Les Miz*. After dropping the leather patch at the police station on East 67th, they moped back to Erica's.

Sonya called up American Express and cancelled the card, but Erica could see she was brooding. "Hey, it's no big deal. You've got insurance, don't you?"

"It's not the money... Fuck!" she said uncharacteristically, and slammed her fist on the sofa armrest.

"THAT'S the real reason I went up to Princeton," Sonya sighed. She hadn't wanted to tell Erica about *Know-Ware*, but Erica had pressed and in truth Sonya was relieved. René wasn't here. She needed to trust someone, to have another shoulder to lean on, and Erica's was as resilient as any she'd seen in a very long time. If you only had a couple of months to live, Sonya concluded, most other things probably wouldn't seem so bad. "But you can't tell anybody. Promise?"

"Like who?" asked Erica. "Anyhow, they'd put it down as the ravings of morphine." Morphine or not, Erica couldn't help but wonder if it was Sonya who was raving.

"SO that's it?" said René, the distress in his voice ringing down the phone line. "But didn't you tell me you'd left the original disk back in Sydney? You could get it FedExed over."

Sonya had left Michael's original disk for safe-keeping inside the vault at Al's law firm. She stood for a moment. Suddenly Erica, who was sitting on the sofa, saw Sonya yank down on her pendant, splitting it in two. "Actually," said Sonya talking to René, but holding it so Erica could see a USB plug sticking out of the piece cradled in her hand, "I've got another copy on a flash memory drive."

So, thought Erica, she'd now have the chance to check Sonya's absurd story for herself. She held out her hand for the tiny computer storage device and examined it. Sterling silver, she whistled after seeing the famous silversmith mark. When she'd seen it hanging from Sonya's neck, she'd assumed it was just a pendant. "A Tiffany flash drive! What'll they think of next?"

THE police had been right. They found the bike, abandoned near a subway entrance. The thief had dumped it there before padding down the stairs and according to the grainy security video, had they bothered to examine it, which they didn't, he'd hopped onto the first train that came by. He'd gone to a great deal of trouble to cover his tracks, disembarking at the first subway stop to change lines, then making another couple of train-switches before he rose back up to the street, hailing a Yellow Cab to Times Square, where he hopped into a second cab to take him downtown to a block from his apartment.

He sipped a glass of his favourite sauvignon blanc and hunched over the spoils he'd rigged up in front of him.

It hadn't taken him long to work out the intricacies of the IcePaC—the product's website made that easy. But *Know-Ware*, annoyingly, was demanding a password the thief didn't have. Not yet.

On his own laptop, he clicked onto an icon of a hammer smashing down on a security safe, with the word 'Cracker' beneath it.

He smiled, his gold tooth glinting in the screen's glow.

"RENÉ," said Sonya, "you... we..." she held her pendant off her neck towards him, "if you can make *Know-Ware* go backwards, we can find out who did this. You've got to find a way."

René had just arrived after a tortuous two-hour trip through the pelting rain, all the more stressful since one of his ancient Ford Escort rattler's windscreen wipers was not working. "To have even a chance at that, I'd need the Princeton mainframes but the snatch happened here in New York so that wouldn't..."

"If you can make *Know-Ware* go back at Princeton, surely it'll be easy to repeat it here?"

René leant back into the sofa, the cream cushions enveloping him, making him feel even more tired than he thought he was. "You want me to drive straight back to Princeton after I've just spent...?"

Sonya nodded.

"But I just got here..." he said, raising his watch to emphasise how late it was.

Sonya's glowered at him.

"Tomorrow morning, first thing, please?"

"We can't afford any lost time, René. Whoever has it... they might..." Sonya bit her lip under the stress and suddenly rose to her feet. "Let's go!"

"What can we do tonight? Even if we left this minute, we wouldn't get there till after midnight, and we'd—I'd—be stuffed. Sonya, I need a clear head for this. I could just nap here... on the sofa... and in the morning... early... we could all drive back."

Sonya still stared, and he knew he was beaten but, just as he was about to give in, Erica groaned. Sonya's and René's eyes flew across the room to where she was bent over double.

"Erica!" screamed Sonya rushing over. "René, phone for an ambulance."

Erica held up one of her hands; the other remaining in place pressed across her chest. "I'll be fine," she said and slowly straightened up. "I'm good, really." But her twisted face told a different story.

Sonya took her elbow and escorted her over to the sofa. "What can I get you?" she asked as Erica fell back onto the cushions.

"In my bag... pills..." She attempted what looked like a smile, but Sonya knew it wasn't.

René ran for the water while Sonya rummaged in her bag.

"I'm sorry," Erica said weakly after she popped two of the pills. "With all the excitement, I forgot my medication... Argh!" she cried as the burning spasm drove her head down to her knees.

42

RENÉ GRIPPED SONYA'S flash drive, reminding himself that other scientists would kill for this opportunity.

Kill. As he sloped over the tiles to his workstation, the word shivered up his spine. It was six in the morning. Sonya had compromised so he got a few hours' sleep on the sofa before he left at four. Sonya didn't want to wake Erica, so she stayed behind with her.

His steps echoed in the eerie chill of institutional emptiness. Even the white noise of the central heating made him edgy.

He pulled the tip off Sonya's flash memory pendant revealing the USB plug and slotted it into his computer. He waited for it to register. And waited. The drive hadn't connected. Had he damaged it... perhaps knocked it against his car when it was in his pocket? Maybe got it wet when he ran into CICRS?

He pressed both eyes closed and placed his nervous palms on the desktop, and breathed slowly and deeply, the same breaths his therapist had taught him after Rachel left. After thirty seconds, he should have been more at ease but he felt as relaxed as a man standing on the ledge of a forty-storey building. This was potentially the most significant scientific breakthrough of all time, literally, and somehow he, Professor René Nicholai Zontsmann, had screwed it up.

He pulled the drive out, and lowered his glasses onto the tip of his nose so he could examine it closely… as if he knew what to look for. He was a physicist, he reminded himself, not a computer nerd. Even so, he gave the plug a hurr of his hot breath, wiped it with his tie then re-inserted it, crossing his fingers.

The weight of impending failure pressed in on him and though he'd only been at CICRS a short time, anyone arriving would guess from the hour, from the heavy bags under his eyes and his wild hair that he'd been working all weekend unbroken. He kept repeating the routine: plug in, wait, pull out, plug in, wait, but each ended with the same inoperable outcome.

His ear twitched and he looked up. Dave Jackson was a fellow professor, though his renown came from never wasting time completing anything except grant applications. "Love your shirt," said René, relieved it wasn't Sam.

Dave was oblivious to most external influences, including peer pressure, stress and, it seemed, the cold. It was so cold inside CICRS, René had kept his coat on, yet Dave was parading around in blue jeans and a flimsy cotton tee-shirt printed with "I'm an Infomaniac' on the front and 'Let's Futz' on the back. Dave was tall, six foot three, and wispy thin. René always thought of him as a praying mantis reared on its back legs. His shirt flapped straight down from his pointy shoulders over his hips as if there was no body inside, like a billowing empty ghost sheet. His straggly untrimmed beard was mottled but René cringed when he saw, close-up, that the discoloration was not just due to the march of age but rather a recent meal.

The pleasantries were quick and predictable. "Found any new grants out there?" René asked.

"Dave knows all," said his colleague, encircling his soft hands over an invisible crystal ball with a theatrical hint of mystery. Dave enjoyed playing to his caricature. "If there's grant money, Dave will find it." He picked into his beard and popped something disgusting into his mouth. Satisfied, he walked off leaving René with an additional reason for his stomach to be churning.

He withdrew the drive again and held it direct under the desk light to scrutinise it even more closely but it still looked fine. An idea struck him. He scrabbled around in the drawer for a second flash drive and plugged it in. Yes! It too failed to register. He fist-punched the air, for the first time in his life thrilled that a computer was faulty. The problem was with the terminal, not the flash drive. Surging with relief, he jumped up to find someone else's console, entering the next room and passing by Sam's workstation.

Most days, Sam arrived before his assistant, Marina, but today she was in early. "Hey," René asked, smiling a little uneasily. "Sam must be a slave-driver if you're in here at this time."

"He phoned me last night. He's sick, can you believe it?" she said, her brow slightly cocked. "Asked me to come in to finish the monthly report. It's due in by nine," she tipped her head toward her computer.

René knew why she was perplexed: not once in the years he'd known him had Sam ever called in sick. Even with his eyes veined and blood-shot, and his nostrils drizzling buckets of slimy viscous mucus, he'd still be at his desk working, oblivious to his own discomfort and indifferent to those around him who might be worried about infection. "No wimps won the West," was one of his favourite sayings.

René feigned as much empathy as his bucking system could muster, but he was relieved.

"I've got a problem with my console," he told Marina. "I'll just try this out on Sam's, okay?" and he held up Sonya's flash drive as he sat in front of Sam's computer before Marina could say no.

In neat rows, Sam's screen displayed CICRS's familiar standard array of network icons, but way down in the bottom right corner René noticed two new icons that flashed up when he'd moved his cursor over the area: a graphic of a hammer smashing a security safe, labelled *Cracker*, and a cartoon-like set of binoculars labelled *Overview*. He checked Marina wasn't watching him, and he clicked on the *Overview* icon.

A scaled blueprint popped up, a plan of each floor of the CICRS building with every workstation plotted and tagged with the name of the relevant staff member or PhD student allocated to it. René moused Sam's cursor round the screen and was intrigued how, when it passed over a work-space, it changed colour from white with a blue outline to a solid red. He located Dave Jackson's workstation and the arrow engorged itself—like Dave would if he could—and then a text box appeared informing him that Dave had logged onto that computer at 3 AM. He clicked onto Dave's workstation outline to see if anything more would happen. It did. A dialogue box appeared:

> "Note to Sam: Complete patch to block Surveillance Alert from appearing on workstation monitor. Meantime, click the BLISSFUL IGNORANCE button below within two seconds."

René's eyes tightened. Sam was invading his colleagues' privacy? René couldn't imagine a single reason for it, but he clicked on the amber *Blissful Ignorance* button anyway and watched as a new window opened up on his screen. This was definitely Dave Jackson he was eavesdropping on: Dave was in the midst of an internet search for "philanthropic foundations +tax returns." He watched for a few moments then clicked the spy window closed.

René felt sick. Sam could easily have spied on them the other day. This was going from bad to really bad. What if Sam had monitored them? René didn't want to think about it. Sam was his respected colleague... his friend.

But Sam rode bikes. He had a place in New York. He knew Sonya was going out to the theatre that night. And maybe, with this snoop tool, he knew something about what they'd been doing. Maybe it was to get intelligence on Sonya that he invited them both to dinner. In the struggle between denial and fear, and fear winning, René decided to focus on the flash drive. He plugged it into one of the ports on Sam's console and it opened up on the first attempt.

The first thump of the drums from out of nowhere had startled Marina—and René—but he swiftly muted the volume, though not quick enough. He shrugged at her and luckily, she buried her head back into her own time-sensitive work. The last thing René wanted was to attract a crowd of voyeurs hoping to brace themselves for the ride of their lives.

He typed in Sonya's password and, as usual, *Know-Ware* sought details of when he wanted to go. This time, with the backing of the super-computers, all running in parallel, he would try accessing the past: aiming for last night.

Damn it!

```
"In 3D/Holovision you can't go back
earlier than your first entry point."
```

Just checking, he twitched. He'd have to try Realtime mode, so he clicked on that:

```
"You need a different password for
Realtime."
```

This wasn't a surprise. He knew from prior attempts that Sonya's normal password didn't work, and that after three failed attempts it would shut itself down. He stood, hoping for inspiration, and once again ran his stumpy fingers through his hair making him look even more like a wild man.

Pacing the vinyl tiles up and down the corridor, his soft-soled loafers felt like they were pounding. Everything jarred this morning. To the few others who'd also straggled in, he was just another academic who had ambled over to the water cooler, preoccupied, locked in esoteric thought—nothing unusual in this place. He cradled the white paper cup in both hands, walked back and gently placed it on Sam's desk and stared at it, noticing there was something vaguely origami about it.

Sam's screen was still pressing him for a password. Then it hit him: among Sam's many talents, he was an expert in cryptography. René clicked on the *Cracker* icon.

```
"Sammy, your password?"
```

René was screwed, he knew that, but he still groaned at the elegance of Sam's code-breaker needing a code for itself.

43

MID-MORNING, ERICA was still sleeping off her pills and Sonya hung around the apartment, anxious for word from René as well as the NYPD.

She went over and over the facts. Apart from Michael, only two other people in the world knew about *Know-Ware*—René and now Erica. Erica couldn't be a suspect, no way and despite their short acquaintance, Sonya had total confidence in René.

The phone rang. "Son. It's me." It was Al MacAntar, her lawyer from Sydney. "I tried your mobile but it's not answering."

"It must be the middle of the night over there," she said, avoiding his hidden question. "Or are you here… in New York?"

"I'm here," he said, clarifying nothing, then added, "Sydney, I mean, and yes, it's not even sparrow's fart. I've just got back to my desk after one of those all-nighters and…"

"Al, it's great to hear from you—but this is a lousy time." She decided to tell him, not everything, just enough. "I was mugged last night. I can't really talk... I'm waiting for the police to call back."

"Mug...? I didn't think that happened in New York any mo... are you okay?"

"I'll phone you back, maybe tomorrow?"

"It's just that Lex—my criminal law partner?—he's left a note here, on my desk..."

Sonya could hear the rustle of paper over the line.

"Apparently, the police found some new evidence about the fire at your neighbours' place."

Not this; not now... It had been more than a year, and the police had got nowhere on the arson investigation, and while sure, courtesy of her own investigator's work, they'd come to a strained acceptance Michael was kidnapped rather than a deserter, they'd found not a thing more.

Why would Al be calling her? Her mind swirled with the worst. Her eyes closed, as if she could shut it out. "Not Mich..."

Al jumped in, "I have no idea. All the note says is they've got new evidence. It's 2 AM here so I can't exactly raise anyone. It'll be six, seven hours before I'll be any wiser. I'll ring back when I've got more."

WHAT if they'd turned up evidence that Michael had lit the fire? Sorden, the detective, had tried this on before, but back then he was speculating. It was totally circumstantial. Now, they had hard evidence... of what, she didn't have a clue. But why tell Lex? And why did he want to tell her?

Sonya rocked Erica awake. She needed to talk. Bleary-eyed, Erica pushed herself back onto her pillow, not noticing Sonya was shaking until she heard it in her voice as she told her what had just happened.

"It means squat, surely," said Erica. "Anyway, what else can you do except wait till the lawyer calls you back?" Her mouth was dry. "Let's have some tea."

Sonya was pouring when René phoned. He'd had no luck. Despite everything he tried, he said, he couldn't crack the system. Every attempt to shift *Know-Ware* into reverse had failed.

Sonya gazed out the window for a moment. "Maybe you *should* ask Sam after all?"

"Er... He's not in. But," René added, too quickly, "I've got another colleague over at Los Alamos, in New Mexico..."

"Someone I haven't even met? What's wrong with Sam all of a sudden?"

René was fretting. If he told her... He knew he had to tell her, but not now, not like this, over the phone. He decided to keep trying a little longer; he needed some good news to temper the inevitable explosion.

IT was two hours later. "YOU sound breathless, René," said Sonya, thinking she'd even heard a puff of his asthma inhaler over the line. René was wound-up about something. Had he cracked it?

"I kept trying... trying everything... but I couldn't make it go back one second, no matter what. So I started hunting round some of the university databases and the on-line research library." He coughed, with a slight wheeze. "I was looking for ideas, but I, er, I found something else... some old newspaper and magazine articles."

"Old?"

"The earliest is from 1925, from a French newspaper, *Le Temps*. It's headed '*Les Canaux à Bois*,' the wood canals..."

"This is no time to reminisce..."

"Let me finish. The by-line on the story... the person who wrote it?" he coughed again. "It was, ah, Michel Venari." The phone seemed to go dead. He shook the handset. "You still there? Hello?"

"I'm..."

"There's more," he said. "In *The New Yorker*, a 1938 issue, there's a piece called '*It's Nivernais or Never*.' It's also about the canal..."

"So?"

"This one was written by M. W. Hunt."

Sonya's legs were suddenly weak. She lowered herself to the arm of the sofa.

"There's one more: another article about canal vacations. It's thirty-plus years later, in *Atlantic Monthly*..."

"And...?"

"A Michael Hunt wrote it."

From her silence, René guessed that Sonya's neck hairs were crackling just as his had, and were still.

THE doorman stood at the apartment door with the pages René had faxed through flapping from his hand. Sonya snatched them, letting the door close on him without a thank you.

"These have to be flukes," Erica said, picking up and waving the *Le Temps* piece. "If your Michael was this Michel Venari, he'd be over a hundred years old. Gimme a break!"

Initially, Sonya stifled her response. The coincidences were bizarre, crazy, ridiculous, but so were the charts, and the disk, and *Know-Ware*, and reading tomorrow's papers today, and the holovision of Sam...

"Or," Sonya said, avoiding Erica's eyes, "this *Know-Ware* program doesn't only *see* the future; somehow it takes you there."

"And Michael should've stayed there, given what he's put you through," Erica snapped, saying what Sonya knew she should be thinking.

44

"Lex says he won't have anything solid from the police until tomorrow at the earliest." Given Al had no real news, other than the possibility that there would be news, his real reason for calling Sonya back empty-handed was out of concern about the mugging.

"Does he know anything… even if it's not solid? Is it about Michael?"

"I have no idea, nor does he…"

"Jesus, Al. It's over a year, "she said, but when the doorbell chimed, she asked him to stay on hold.

In the fish-eye peephole lens, René bulged grotesquely. Layered in his habitually unfashionable variegations of brown he looked like a crumpled paper bag with the head of a pink jelly baby poking out the top. He leant his toothy smile forward into the lens—not a good sign, she thought.

"René?" she said opening the door, puzzled to see him. She waved him in while she headed back to the phone. "Al," she said, "Someone's come. I've got to go. Sorry. But call me… as soon as you hear something."

René was here to confess about Sam. In person. But he didn't want witnesses, and his eyes buzzed around the room for signs of Erica—what he now knew as her telltale scarf—and was relieved. Even so, he couldn't bring himself to say anything about Sam at first.

He began with the hard copies he'd brought of the three articles he'd previously faxed through. They had mileage, he'd decided earlier. They were his Sonya softeners. But as he nervously worked up to raising his suspicions about Sam, the sweat ringing the top of his shirt collar started closing in on him like a noose.

The doorbell rang.

"It's Erica," said Sonya as she stood up and pointed to the clump of keys resting on the coffee table. "She left her keys when she went out for donuts."

René slumped back with his eyes closed and felt everything envelop him, wishing *Know-Ware* could disappear him into the sofa permanently.

Over her shoulder, Sonya asked, "René? What were you about to tell me?"

He cracked open his eyes. He'd really wanted to do this without a witness. "Sam..."

"Sam?" said Sonya, her hand frozen on the door knob.

René could have lied again, but he began what he'd been bottling up.

The doorbell rang again, longer this time.

"He knew," she muttered. It was a statement, not a question, and the emptiness in her voice bowed René's head far lower than if she had screamed at him.

She opened the door.

"Hello-o!" Erica almost sang when she saw René but quickly felt the silence from the other two hanging unfinished in the room, and stopped, knowing not to break it.

Sonya eventually spoke, "René?"

"In front of...?"

Sonya gave a curt nod, and sat opposite him, patting the sofa for Erica to join her. Sonya's eyes fierce and determined, as if she were lining up to be head shooter in a firing squad.

After she heard the story, Erica, taking some pity on René turned to Sonya. "There's no certainty Sam was the one, you know. What evidence there is," she said, "is pretty circumstantial."

"Erica!" said Sonya, exasperated she was taking René's side.

"Look," Erica continued, "what've we got here? This Sam guy, he rides motorbikes. Big deal... so do you. There must be thousands of bikes in New York. And he's got a place here on Manhattan... So? How many fit that bill? Okay, it gets a bit sticky since he knew we were going to the theatre, and maybe... but it's only a maybe... he did spy on you when you were at Princeton... but that doesn't make him the thief."

"He's never called in sick before," said Sonya, her jaw clenched.

"Okay, assume it *was* him... It's hardly René's fault that a respected colleague, someone he's known for years, turns out to be bad. What about Tiger Woods, the golfing holy of holies for chrissakes? The question is what do we do about it? Sitting around glaring at each other won't get your stuff back."

René wiped his hands on his pants.

"Phone him," said Erica, shoving the hand-piece at him. She had wolfed down one of the donuts when she was alone in the elevator and the sugar hit was having an effect.

René slid his address book out of his back pocket and waved it, a half-smile almost coming to his lips but when he saw Sonya's scowl, it fell away. "I'll try his Princeton apartment first, but if he answers I'll hang up. We'll know where he is... and we can decide what to do next."

He dialled, and after ten rings it diverted to Sam's answering machine. René hung up and tried Sam's TriBeCa number. Again, there was no answer, but there was no answering machine either. The call simply rang out.

René rocked back and forth. "CICRS!" He dialled the Centre, but even if anyone was working late they didn't choose to pick up. "I'll tell you what I'm thinking..." he said, replacing the phone. "If it *was* Sam, maybe he took the IcePaC back to his apartment in TriBeCa, you know, to get *Know-Ware* up and running..."

"And?"

"The draw to use Princeton's super-computers would be seductive... at least that's my theory. So maybe he's back there, or heading back there right now. I've got my car in the parking garage round the corner... I say we shoot back to find out." René was no fan of driving at the best of times, and another two-hour trip in his old Ford Escort, 90 minutes if they were lucky, wasn't his idea of fun but he felt it was the only way.

"And if he's not there?" said Erica, asking the question they were all thinking and no one had an answer to.

45

SAM SITS ALONE, astride his chair. His professional white lab coat belies his true intent and, with an intentional cliché of expectant preparation, he cracks his knuckles one-by-one, and taps *Enter* on his keyboard.

The *Know-Ware* drum roll instantly jars, even though he already knew to turn down the volume, and he eagerly braces himself for the password request. On cue, a pop-up box asks for it and he licks his lips as his code-breaker automatically cuts in to supply it.

Cracking a smile so wide it reveals his gold tooth, he presses *Enter* again, but completely mutes the sound, just in case.

Sam has fed the enormous horsepower from Princeton's sprawling computer network into running *Know-Ware*. René had wanted to try this but didn't have the access code. Sam isn't entitled to it either but his code-breaker has busted through the firewalls for him, and not for the first time. He'd be fired if anyone knew what he is doing but, he chuckles to himself, they'll never find out.

This time, *Know-Ware* immediately enters Realtime, one

of the higher modes René had been trying to access. Instantly, a log of past sessions pops up and Sam contemplates his next move, the only noise the low hum of the droning computers and his slow breathing. He is curious—there's been no session since two Augusts ago. It means, he realises, that he is a step ahead of Sonya and René.

He clicks on the very last session, and a thumbnail of a naked, sleeping couple appears. His lips take on a curl and he clicks *Play*. He shifts in his chair as he tries to increase the volume, but the clip has no sound. A shame, he thinks. Sonya stirs. She's not bad naked, he muses, if you like that sort of thing. The man, his arm resting across her stomach, is lying on his stomach. To Sam, he looks good… very good.

Clicking *Fast Forward*, he sees Sonya slide out from under the arm and the man roll over. Hmm… not bad at all. As she stands, her breasts give a small bounce but Sam's attention is elsewhere, even when she stretches a reddish-coloured leotard over her body and tip-toes out of the room.

Nothing much happens, not even in fast forward, apart from the man's small jerky movements: an arm splaying here, a leg bending there. The clip speeds on and on, until seemingly out of nowhere two men materialise beside the bed. With a vaguely military bearing, they're dressed in grey, tight-fitting but otherwise nondescript suits.

Suspecting fast forward had skipped the moment the pair entered the bedroom, Sam rewinds the last minute and replays it at normal speed. But it is no illusion: the two men emerge as if out of nowhere. One of them leans over to shake the man awake… and the screen flickers.

46

RENÉ PEERED INTO the gloom of the unlit Princeton backstreet as the dark majesty of the university loomed at him. He slowed, his wiper scraping aside the fresh fluff of snow on the driver's side of the window.

Suddenly, he braked, skidding the car on the icy roadway. Erica and Sonya, who'd both dozed off, snapped open their eyes and saw it up ahead, right outside CICRS. René's headlights were spot-lighting a Harley-Davidson.

"It's a Fatboy," said Sonya without thinking though, René noticed, with respect.

He nudged forward next to the bike. The trio squeaked open the car doors and clambered out. Steam rose from the Harley where the snowflakes melted on contact, but Sonya still leant over to touch it; she couldn't help herself. Her skin always crawled in the proximity of a Fatboy's 1450cc of in-your-face muscle. Her gloves were still in her hand and she rubbed the giant chrome headlamp. It too was warm. Sam couldn't be all bad. She hoped so.

Looking round, she saw she'd have to catch up with the others; they were already pushing on CICRS's front doors.

It wasn't in the plan they'd discussed, but she thought about slashing the bike's tyres, only briefly since she knew she couldn't, and not just because she didn't have a knife or a screw-driver, but because it was a Harley. Instead, she noted down its registration number from its plates and scurried after her companions.

She should have slashed the rubber.

Even before Erica and René entered the third-floor lab, they could make out Sam through the glass doors: he was in his white lab jacket, seated at a desk and focused intently on the computer screen ahead of him. To René it seemed so routine.

Sonya caught up, a little breathless, surprising given how fit she was. As she pulled open the door for them, a musty odour flew into her nostrils. She was about to jab René but his eyes met hers in confirmation, and feigning calm they pasted on smiles and casually walked in.

Sam was shoving something—the IcePaC?—into a drawer as he glanced up to greet them. "Ah, my dear friends. It's a bit early, isn't it?" he said, his dark eyes calm, as if their visit was not entirely unexpected. "And you bring another fine lady," he added as Erica walked in behind them. "Sam Sing," he said, pushing back his chair and standing, his hand outstretched.

Sam was such a charmer, thought Sonya, recalling his hospitality over dinner. Erica could be right: that it was all mere coincidence, yet the familiar smell and his suspicious manoeuvre with his drawer pointed against him. Keeping to their agreed script, she introduced Erica.

His gold molar, an adornment Sonya was surprised she'd missed previously, glinted through his smile. He sat back down, and focused on his computer screen, a dismissal that would normally signal the others to leave.

Erica observed him closely. In other circumstances, she thought, she would've found Sam beguiling. But when her eyes fell to below the desk, she noticed his hand-tooled boots were cradling a shiny bike helmet between them, also black. If she wasn't mistaken, it was identical to the one that had concealed the face of the drive-by thief.

Sam waited, his fingers poised over his keyboard in almost polite impatience.

Erica watched René take the lead, as planned. He slipped his khaki nor'easter off his shoulders. Stay calm, she mentally reminded him. Hooking the lightweight Gore-tex coat over his finger, he stepped over to the closet to hang it and, on his way, asked, "What're you working on?"

Sam hesitated, first glaring at René, then sweeping his gaze across to Sonya, and finally to Erica. "Cyber porn," he laughed, feigning embarrassment, his hand coming to rest across his chest. "You've caught me out."

"Sam…" René insisted.

"Just the usual drudge," he said. "You know… boring paperwork," and he looked back down again, though less confidently, since it seemed René and his friends weren't going anywhere.

"Who calls it paperwork these days?" said René, straining to put a lightness into his voice. His head was almost inside the closet, his eyes scanning Sam's black leather jacket for the telltale signs, but it was hung so it faced to the left. He couldn't yank it out; that would be too obvious, so he groped inside for the sleeve on the right. He ran his fingers along it until they detected a square-shaped outline of torn threads, what he'd expect to find on the thief's jacket where Erica had ripped off his pocket. He nodded to the others.

Erica's heart started pounding as if in sympathy with René's. The plan, when they talked it through before, sounded simple, but now they were here...

Sam could see that not only weren't they budging, they were hovering. "It's pretty early," he said, raising one eyebrow in question. "What brings you three up here so bright and chirpy?"

Erica saw René fluster. He'd warned the two women he was a scientist, not a Sherlock Holmes, and she knew in a flash she had to intervene or all could be lost.

"Oh shit!" she exclaimed and, in as strong an Australian accent as her ten years away from home could manage, she added, "I just remembered I was supposed to call my mother. She's in Sydney," she added, the lie to explain why she'd be calling at such a strange hour. She pulled her mobile phone out of her pocket and dialled the number, but it wasn't her mother's; her companions knew that. It was the number for Sonya's stolen IcePaC.

If it was in this room—perhaps what Sam had hurriedly placed in his drawer—they'd have the proof. But all they heard was the hum of computer fans, the whoosh of the central heating and the repeated thumping of three hearts trying to crack their rib cages. There was no ring.

"I don't understand it," Erica said slowly, as if to make sure the others understood. "There's a recorded message... it says her phone's been disconnected."

René gave a small cough into his fist and ran his finger under his collar.

Sonya waited for him to speak, but again he said nothing. He'd either forgotten his lines or was frozen with fear. She drew her arms across her body, "Sam... the heating! How do you put up with it? God, it's cold."

Sonya realised how feeble this was. Maybe that was why René had hesitated.

She moved toward Sam and placed her gloves on his desk. The plan relied on how cold René had told them it had been when he'd run into his colleague Dave Jackson, but now it was different and Sonya was sweating under her coat. That maintenance had already fixed the thermostat following René's fault report wasn't something they'd factored in. But she had her script. "It's so ah... ah..." she sneezed. "Excuse me," she said, and wiped her hand across her nose. "It's so ICY!"

"Bless you," Sam said, a smile creeping onto his face until a muffled beep struggled out of his drawer.

With an almost imperceptible nod, René signalled to Erica. No one spoke. The air was dense, thick with the expectation of the unknown.

Calmly, almost casually, Sam's hand dropped to the drawer and silently slid it open, not completely, not enough for the others to see inside, but sufficient to slide his hand in. He extracted Sonya's tiny computer and set it down on his desktop. "Goodness me," he said, feigning surprise, "what's this?"

Sonya sensed an unnatural strength from the man, and when he reached into the drawer a second time, her entire body tensed. For someone like Sam, she now suspected, no movement was redundant. Remain vigilant, she counselled herself, and she inhaled deeply, her lungs pressing against her chest. What he pulled out wasn't so much cylindrical and lightweight, like her roll-up computer screen, it was matte black, and heavy. Her lungs again sucked for air and, from the slight wheeze she detected, Erica's were doing the same. The three pairs of startled eyes were fixed on the barrel of the handgun gripped in Sam's hand.

To them it was a gun, but to Sam it was a carefully chosen Glock 35, an Austrian-manufactured .40 calibre practical/tactical weapon. Fully-loaded—and Sam used 15-round clips instead of the standard 10—this Tenifer-treated, high-impact-resistant weapon was a hefty 36 ounces of pure hate in the wrong hands. And Sam's hands were just that.

"Meet my good friend, Herr Doctor Glock," he smirked. "Doc Glock," he laughed, the spark of light from his tooth a flash of the macabre, as if any were necessary.

René grimaced. Sam… with a gun? A fake? A joke? Surely…

"René," said Sam, "It's not just the dandy cowboy gear, pardner; that's just the fluff… the flummery… a furbelow. If you want to know the truth, my affair with the Ol' West is all about the guns." Sam's dark eyes were impenetrable and he aimed them narrowly along the barrel to show he was ready for any quick movement.

To Sonya's surprise, Erica spoke, "It's rude to point, Sam." And worrying the others, she stepped toward him.

The bravado of this woman patently wracked by cancer shocked everyone, including Sam, though not for long. As menace wiped the smirk off his face, he jabbed the barrel direct at her fragile chest, motioning her to back off.

47

ANOTHER SWEEP OF his pistol directed the trio to bunch at the wall but, as they took a step backwards, Sonya's heel grazed against the leg of a chair and she stumbled, falling to the floor.

As she toppled, René stepped sideways to help her but Sam grunted and motioned him back as he eyed her suspiciously. In the fall, her coat had draped open, the camel cashmere revealing a cobalt blue silk shirt with an embroidered pocket. Sam let his crooked smile linger, "Ah! A woman after my own heart; not that one has ever won it."

Sonya feigned a hurt foot, rubbing it as her mind churned, at once relieved she'd tracked down her IcePaC and *Know-Ware* yet panicked she'd brought herself and the others into confrontation with a seriously dangerous man.

René had a similar thought, and opened his hands wide, trying to force a smile as if the whole thing was a mistake, "Sam... what's happening here?"

Before Sam could retort with another smart answer, Sonya sprung herself forward, up off the floor, leaping headlong for the gun and amazingly managing to surprise him. But Sam's reflexes were good and he swivelled to the side so she missed her grab and sprawled on the floor empty-handed. Even so, she'd still been able to knock the pistol out of his hand with such a force it flew across the room and came to rest under a chair. She hadn't noticed, though all the others had, but the force of her move had bounced her left breast out of her silk top.

Sam, still standing, hovered above where Sonya had fallen and wound his leg right back to power up a vicious spring kick. "You kangaroo fuck," he spat, his foot poised mid-air behind him.

René was stunned. Not once had he heard Sam swear before. But he'd never seen him toting a gun either.

Sonya, a confused mess of anger and fright, scowled up at Sam. Unsure why he was delaying his kick, but glad for the chance, she swept her own leg out from beneath her, arced it wide and knocked him off balance. He swayed then fell to the floor next to her, giving her the opportunity to jab her fingers at his windpipe, a technique from a martial arts course she needed to take after her divorce from Charles.

"Want to play tough, do we?" Sam smirked as one hand blocked hers and his other twisted her nipple brutally till he drew blood.

His breath, so close to her now, had a familiar smell... hoi sin sauce.

And as he continued to twist, he said, "I meant to tell you before, you've got weird lobes."

Despite the excruciating pain, she kneed his crotch and in the instant he released her, she rolled to the side for whatever protection she could get.

"Your mother never told you that topless isn't for polite company?" he said, and punched at her lower back, heading square for her kidney.

But Sonya saw his reflection in the glass doors and rolled some more so that all Sam fisted was empty air. She gritted her teeth—her nipple was killing her—and she sprang to her feet, sprinting to his gun so quickly she got to it before he got himself up from the floor. With two hands, she swung up the Glock and stepped back to him, almost jamming the gun into his chest as he got up from his knees. The pistol was considerably heavier than she'd expected and she shook, at first struggling to direct the barrel level at him. "Stop," she trembled, but the absurdity of her exposed breast dripping blood down her silk shirt and her body quaking with fear undermined her authority.

Sam took his advantage. "Why? You've got the safety on."

She held his eye, refusing to fall for the obvious trick but Sam smiled and did a jig, confusing her. He snatched the moment and, with a swift upswing of his hand, flicked the gun out of her grip, leapt up to catch it mid-flight and fired it.

Sonya convulsed with the two blasts just inches from her ear and she fell backward. She lay still. René who'd been stepping forward from behind her, yelped and also slumped to the floor.

Erica's eyes flew between Sonya's lifeless shape and the blood spurting from beneath René. She was twisting her knitted cap in her hands as she also came forward but Sam motioned her to back off, "No funny business, baldy." She stayed back.

Sam poked the air with the pistol as he went over to René. With his free hand he nudged René's body over, and rolled him aside to reveal the source of the blood and laughed, "And now you've gone and shot yourself in the foot. You know, René, I've always hated those shoes." And waving the pistol, he added for everyone's benefit, "I didn't mean to hit anyone, but next time…"

Erica was stunned. The frail woman stood limp, staring at Sonya's body lying motionless on the hard floor, praying for a rise in her chest… a movement… anything.

"I didn't hit her," Sam said. "She's in shock, and he… he's just a fucking wimp."

Sam stepped back to his desk and stuffed the two IcePaC components into his side pockets and shoved Sonya's gloves so they were hanging out of his back pocket. He moved over to the closet, keeping the gun barrel pointed toward the others and slipped his leather jacket off the hanger. He returned to his desk with it, and now Erica could also see the dark patch on the sleeve where she'd torn off the pocket. He placed the jacket on his desk and bent his knees, keeping his head up, and tapped around the floor with his free hand until he located his bike helmet.

René came to, squirming with the pain. "Sam?" he said. "We're… friends…"

"Friends?" he laughed as he put on his helmet. "Sorry 'bout your widdle foot, ol' pal o' mine. Is that friendly enough?" He backed himself toward the doors and sloughed off his lab coat, slid his arms one-by-one into his riding jacket, swapping the gun from one hand to the other as he did it, then spun round and bolted, the doors swinging the only farewell.

Erica rushed toward Sonya but almost instantly Sonya jumped to her feet.

Erica dropped her cap and grabbed onto Sonya's arm, gripping it as tightly as she could. "He has a gun!" Erica screamed, but Sonya squirmed and escaped her hold. "Sonya, we've got enough trouble without making more," she added, indicating the blood pooling around René's foot.

"Ears ringing," said Sonya, pointing to her head as she moved away, but winced as she peeled her shirt back over her nipple. "Call René an ambulance," she yelled and she sprinted to the door.

She was running so fast she almost slid into the front entrance doors and saw Sam's bike screech off. She picked up one of her gloves—it had fallen out of Sam's pocket—and angrily slapped the glass with it, not only because she hadn't slashed his tyres when she'd had the chance, but for not grabbing René's car keys. She slipped on the glove and pushed open the doors, taking the steps to the roadway two at a time and running after him, but it was futile. Sam easily put more and more distance between them, waving cheekily at her just as he reached the corner and fish-tailed his bike round it on the icy surface, only the cloud of blue smoke left behind.

Uselessly, she pursued him round the corner and up Nassau Street. One corner more and she was beat, puffed, bent over in the middle of the road huffing violently. Her mouth sucked in the burning cold air and blasted out hot anxious steam.

Over the clanging in her ear, she thought she heard a bike tearing up behind her and she straightened and turned, worried it was Sam circling back to finish her off. It didn't sound like a Harley but with her ears ringing, she couldn't be certain. She shivered in the cold, and twisted left and right to search for an escape route, but it was too late... the two wheels whizzed round the corner and headed right for her.

It wasn't Sam. From the rider's casual posture, she suspected he was a student or a young tutor. She ran straight at the oncoming bike like a bull to a toreador, her camel-coloured coat billowing behind her as the distance between them closed rapidly. He blasted his horn at her and skidded sideways in a scatter of snow, finishing inches short of her.

"Are you nuts?" he shouted through his helmet.

"Nuts," she said coldly as she shoved him off the bike. "Sorry," she added as she swung her leg over the saddle, revved the engine into the red, and spun the bike round to head after Sam. Despite the ice, she burned rubber... a black flash in a blue cloud.

The light snow had one advantage; it helped her track him. His fat treads were unmistakable and the morning traffic still hadn't built up to confuse them. It took only a minute's hard riding before her eyes, burning from the icy chill, spied him ahead of her. She powered up, but the wind cut raw into her skin. No matter how much she squinted, her eyes stung almost as much as her breast did, and the ungloved fingers of her right hand started to ache as the bitter wind rasped over the handlebars.

Out on Princeton's main streets, the morning traffic was still a trickle. She knew there was no way she could keep up the pace in these freezing conditions without a helmet and goggles, and only one glove. Having to squint from the wind and her various pains, she continuously risked sliding, whether into a wall or an oncoming vehicle.

Up ahead, a taxi's red brake lights were pulling to a stop outside a bank, just before where Sam swung his next turn, a right. The cab driver strained his bulky frame out from behind the wheel. He left his engine running—Sonya could tell from the exhaust still puffing out of the tailpipe. Needing change for a fifty, he hot-footed over to the cash machine. Sonya screeched to a stop beside the driver's door, set the borrowed bike on its stand, and slid inside the cab. She shoved the gear stick into Drive and floored it to squeal round the corner, waving an apology to the screaming driver through the rear window.

"Hey," shouted the passenger who'd been reading emails on his BlackBerry in the back seat, shocked by this crazy woman car-jacking his ride. Sonya checked the rear-view mirror again and skidded to a stop, swerving on the ice sharply all the way. The passenger was being thrown side-to-side and she clenched the steering wheel in fear of a smash. Stopped and safe, she lingered in silence a second too long.

"Hey," the passenger repeated with added urgency.

Sonya saw him clasp his black leather briefcase to his chest. "This is an emergency," she said. "The man on the bike... Please, get out of this cab."

The businessman—a give-away in his blue Brooks Brothers shirt, yacht-club striped silk tie, heavy grey woollen suit and Burberry coat—didn't budge. Then he spoke, "This is my hire, lady. You're making me late for my train."

Sonya spun round on her seat and up on her knees so she towered over him and glowered with the meanest sneer she could muster. "This is an emergency." He didn't move. She lowered her voice and with a deliberate whisper spelled it for him, "O-U-T," but still he didn't budge, though his eyes did dwell on the blood stain seeping across her chest.

Sonya very deliberately swung her door open, wide. This time he picked up on her don't-fuck-with-me vibe. "Forget it," he sighed, throwing his own door open and sliding himself out. He stood in the middle of the road watching her speed off with his door still swinging. "Crazy fucking bitch," he shouted at her, a lion in her absence. He flicked back his fringe and buttoned his coat, frustrated by how many risks he had to shoulder these days for a fraction of the pay he used to pull. He'd mention it at bonus time, if there was one this year.

Where was Sam…? Sonya saw him taking a left five, no six blocks down. She swerved the cab a couple of times to get the passenger's door to slam itself closed, then thumped her foot flat to the floor. Though she was a first-class biker, a cab had to be safer in these conditions. It wasn't just that four wheels were better than two, simply that without goggles and on slippery roads with a pounding ear and pumping heart she was jumpy as hell she might kill somebody, possibly herself.

She hung a left to follow Sam and freaked when, too late, she saw it was a one-way street and they were both heading the wrong way. Sam cut down the sidewalk, easy on a bike, and he knew it. The traffic was sparse and she used the indicator stalk to flash her headlights at oncoming cars but snapped it off in the stress. She hunted round the dash for the hazard lights and got them flashing.

Snatching up the cab's microphone, she tried to radio the base. No answer. She turned the knob. "Hello? Help. Anyone there?" She was doing something wrong, but she didn't know what.

Suddenly, static started out of the radio. "Emergency," she screamed.

"Car 863... Harry? What's the problem?"

"It's not Harry... I've, er, ah, borrowed his cab. I'm chasing a guy on a Harley Fatboy. He's just shot my friend."

"Your name?"

"Sonya Wh... just a minute," she said, taking a corner swerve. "Shit!" She had screamed round a corner to follow Sam and the cab slid widely, missing a parked car by barely a wing mirror.

"Sonya who?"

She didn't respond.

"Ma'am, hello.... where are you?"

"No idea. First time in Princeton. Nice town... must come back." She dropped the microphone into her lap and swung the wheel hard right to take the turn.

ERICA could see René was draining, his face already paler than the walls, and his body shaking. She rummaged around and, in a closet, found a blanket she guessed was used by over-keen scientists who would rather take a nap than go home while the chugging computers spent all night testing their world-changing hypotheses. After tucking the blanket round him, she focused on his blood flow, stemming it with a bandage from the kitchen's first-aid kit. Loath to remove his shoe, she wrapped the bandage round it. He was wheezing so she reached into his pocket hoping to find an inhaler, and forced a couple of puffs into him before sitting with him on the floor, pressing a wet towel compress on his forehead as they waited.

Only minutes after the paramedics arrived, a couple of uniformed police officers joined them and, while René was being bundled up and lifted onto a gurney, Erica raced the police through the night's events. When she reached the part she'd previously told the 911 operator, about Sonya chasing Sam, one of them interrupted her. "We know. She's, er, stolen a cab to chase him."

"But he's got a gun."

SONYA had made up some of the gap but Sam, still a couple of blocks distant, was pulling away again, as if up to now he'd only been teasing. She bit her lip in frustration when she saw him turn onto the overloop to Freeway One. No way she'd be able to keep this old cab revved up to match a Harley on a freeway. She picked the radio microphone up off her lap, "You still there?" The one concession she'd made to the cab company and the police was to leave the line open. "I've lost him. He's taking the freeway… the sign says it's north toward New Brunswick. I'm done here."

Her rear-view mirror showed three police cars approaching fast, and moments later, the flashing red, blue, red, blue lights sped past her.

She wasn't sure, but she thought one of them gave her a salute of thanks.

48

THE BULLET HAD ripped through muscle and flesh in René's foot, nicking a nerve but bypassing major bones. While it took the hospital little time to patch him, the shock and the painkillers kept his body shut down for a few hours.

When he first opened his eyes around ten he was oblivious to his surroundings. Hazy, his head turned to the side and he saw Sonya's outline. Blindly, he patted his hand around the bedside table till he connected with his spectacles and wound them round his ears. She was dozing, perched precipitously on the front edge of a white plastic visitor's chair. As his eyes unfogged, he took time to study her. Salty channels of dried tears crusted her cheeks and her hand was clasping a crumpled Kleenex tissue.

He grabbed a pillow and placed it ready at the edge of his bed nearest her. Delicately, he tugged her arm so she dropped her head slowly forward to rest on it and she snuggled woozily into the softness.

WHEN Sonya had driven back to return the taxi, the cab-driver was still fuming. The police patrolmen, who had been trying to mollify him by explaining the circumstances, were at the point of giving up to his rants.

The driver spat a gob of yellow phlegm at Sonya's feet as she slid out of his cab. "If you've so much as scratched my vehicle, you'll pay big time," he said, his ample flesh rippling with rage. Sonya could almost smell his anger.

"Cool it," one of the cops cautioned him, placing his hand on the man's shoulder.

"Cool it?" he yelled, shaking off the cop's hand. "This is my damn fucking livelihood. Arrest the thieving bitch. Arrest her!"

"Your vehicle seems fine, sir."

"I want to press charges." The cab-driver looked through the side window into the back seat, "And where the hell is my fare-paying passenger?"

"He got out," said Sonya, "I'm sorry."

The driver refused to look directly at her, keeping his glare fixed on the senior of the two cops. "He got out? A hundred-buck fare," he lied. "You don't get start-of-shift jobs like that in this town every day, lady." He slammed his fist on the cab roof, potentially damaging it more than she had.

She penitently held out some bills to him.

"I don't want your fucking money," he said as he snatched them from her, walked round the cab and crammed his mass back into the driver's seat. He shot a filthy look at her, then at the police, and took off.

Sonya and the two officers stood silently till he swerved round the corner. "I should return the bike, too," she half-smiled, edging toward it.

"We've got a patrol car bringing the owner here to get it," the police officer reassured her before explaining she'd have to accompany him back to the precinct.

En route to the station, the cops tuned their radio into the chase frequency, even though it was a breach of protocol with a civilian in the squad car:

> "… jumped the centre-strip and he's swinging round to head south toward Trenton. We can't get over the hump… it's too high… we'll have to go on till we hit a safety zone. Hang onto your hats…"

By the time they did jump the median, Sam had already sped off at the next exit ramp.

"We lost him."

49

MICHAEL WAS HUMMING *the tune from* Les Misérables, One Day More.

Soon, it would really be over, by his calculations, just one day; but what was out there for him now? And when would he go to, assuming he still could?

It mattered, of course... what Sonya would be doing... where she'd be... whether he'd even be able to find her. To do that, he'd have to break the rules again, he knew that. And he could easily land up here again, or somewhere worse.

Just one day more.

It was odd, he knew, for a song to have kept him sane—or close enough to it—all these years. For the millionth time, he hummed it to himself, or so he thought: "One day more..."

One of the warders keeping watch of the surveillance screens sighed. "Here he goes again, top of his damn fucking voice."

"Turn down the volume."

"We must have heard it from him three zillion times."

"Yeah, just one more day till he's out of here and," sneered one of the guards, *"then we don't have to listen to this crap anymore."*

50

"Tonight's main story again...," said the FOX News anchorman opening in front of a restful backdrop of light snow falling onto a vine-covered wall, "...*An Ivy League campus is rocked by scandal... with an eccentric Princeton University scientist on the run from police following a dramatic on-campus shooting... and Washington is asking why.*"

The backdrop switched over to some library footage of Sam, clad in his trademark cowboy garb, gesticulating in front of a lecture hall full of students.

> "Professor Sam Sing, though born in mainland China, has been working in the United States for twenty years. Today's shock revelation is that using his own state-of-the-art software, he has been spying on his many academic colleagues working on top-secret government projects.
>
> "This morning, Sing allegedly shot another scientist, physics professor René Zontsmann, before eluding police in a chase across state lines.

> "Police sources claim that Sing enjoyed an opulent lifestyle far beyond his Princeton pay cheque, with five luxury homes around the globe, a fleet of high-powered motorbikes and an extraordinary art collection, including original Picassos, Henry Moores and Monets."

A close-up of Dave Jackson, clearly unused to a shirt and tie, flashed up next, the text bar naming him as 'Professor David Jackson, Princeton University'.

> "Sam said he got his money consulting to Fortune 500 corporations," said Dave. "But spying on us? I don't get it."

Next, followed the bulletin's dog-story:

> "In Illinois today, a judge slapped an 18-year-old rap fan with an unusual penalty after he was caught playing his car stereo too loudly in breach of Chicago noise ordinances. Instead of ordering a $500 fine, the judge sentenced Peter Ford to spend six hours a day listening to Wayne Newton albums."

Just after Newton's syrupy signature song, *Danke Schoen*, cued in, a man wearing a headset briefly appeared on camera to hand a sheet of paper to the anchor. The newsreader skimmed it with a deep-vee earnestness intended to convey the gravitas of a breaking news item, even though it had really broken five minutes earlier. The producer had decided this had more drama.

In truth, the page was blank apart from the words 'look serious' typed on it. The real text was already loaded on the autocue.

"Just in... more scandal unfolds at an Ivy League university. Princeton University president, Barry Winters, has just revealed that Sam Sing, the missing professor at the centre of a spy scandal, had faked his academic qualifications..."

51

IT WAS BAD enough for Sonya but she couldn't have imagined how things could turn for Erica, yet they had. "You're kidding me," she said, her voice low.

"I wish," said Erica, holding her phone away from her.

The two women were outside René's room in the hospital corridor. Erica had just taken a call from her uncle in LA who'd broken the news that her mother had been injured in a six-car pile-up and was on the critical list.

Erica had been hanging out for her mother's visit but, according to her uncle, even if she survived her injuries, no way would she be travelling any time soon. And that, as Sonya didn't need Erica to tell her, wasn't going to be soon enough.

Erica let her scarf drop to the floor and pushed open the door to René's room and started explaining the news to him until her face broke and the tears rolled down her cheeks.

Sonya picked up the scarf and wrapped it around her friend's shoulders and hugged her, "Erica, you've got to go see her."

"I... I know, but... the doctors... my doctors." She sank onto René's bed, careful to avoid his foot. "I couldn't..."

"I'll come with you."

"Sonya, no!" Erica said, her eyes suddenly large. "You need to stay here."

Sonya patted down the dressing on her breast to make it more comfortable and cleared her throat. "Your mother needs you, Erica," she said, knowing the reverse was just as true. "I'll fly there with you."

"You can't," said Erica.

René tried too. It wasn't only that his potential Nobel Prize was slipping away, though that did press on him. He also sensed something developing between him and Sonya and hoped she might be feeling it too. "Sonya, *Know-Ware*... we're on the cusp of..."

"We could all have been killed. I need time to think, René. I'm going to LA with Erica, and that's that."

The determination in her eyes made him hold his tongue. The holy grail of what, or who, was behind *Know-Ware* was slipping away from him.

As was Sonya.

52

ANTS' NESTS OF travellers jostled each other, bumping their wheelie bags and luggage carts, racing from one side of JFK airport to the other for connecting planes, cabs, car service greeting signs and coffees.

Once into the passenger-only zone, Sonya and Erica passed by scattered islands of singles, all dawdling for those vital last-minute purchases that moments earlier none of them knew they pined for; and the magazine-shufflers and novel-flickers, tripping over each other's bags in the bookshops as they went about selecting their flight reading. The clock on the wall told Sonya they still had a few minutes, so she nodded toward the magazines and elbowed herself into a convenient spot. Erica waited near the cash register; her treatments meant her eyes weren't so good these days and reading had ceased being a pleasure, a double tragedy for someone who'd risen to become one of New York's star book editors.

The man next to Sonya was skimming a copy of *The Economist* and until now, René's interview at the conference had slipped her mind. He hadn't mentioned anything about it being published so maybe it hadn't been. She pulled down a copy, and "Yes!" she exclaimed, though it unsettled the man next to her, who shuffled his feet uneasily. Sonya noticed his quizzical eye, no doubt thinking that *The Economist* wasn't a publication that normally enticed the class of readers who had air-punch reactions. She flicked to the article, feeling a warm glow of reflected pride in René's new notoriety, even though understandably it made no mention of either his more recent heroism or Sam's treachery.

She headed toward Erica and the checkout counter, past a low crouched table weighed down with stacks of 'classics' with 'heavily reduced prices', books like George Orwell's *1984* and Jane Austen's *Pride and Prejudice*. All were books that if you asked someone: "*Have you read…*" they'd raise a hurt eyebrow which in most cases translated as: "Well, I did see the movie." One stack caught her eye: a pile of H.G. Wells's *The Time Machine*. Synchronicity, maybe? Her lip curled. She'd read it years ago, of course—truly read it, not just seen the movie— but now the need to refresh her acquaintance with it suddenly charged at her like a bull.

As she snatched up a copy, the airport public address system announced their flight was on final call, so she paid with cash to save time, and took Erica by the arm to head to the gate. As always seems to happen if you're in a rush, their gate was at the far end of the airport, and the moving footways that should've been rolling with them were quite unmoved by their need for speed.

A second announcement added more pressure, "All passengers on Flight 386 to Los Angeles, your plane is now ready for takeoff. Please..." Sonya could have made a run for it, but not Erica. They strode ahead for five hard and long minutes, and when the gate finally came into their sights they were breathless. Still up ahead was a long line of passengers, snaking back out of the gate. So much for being ready for takeoff.

Erica was especially puffed, small beads of sweat breaking out all over her shaven head. Sonya rested her belongings on a payphone shelf and, as she hiked up her slacks, observed to Erica, "The line's still got a few minutes in it. I should ring René... you know, to congratulate him on his fame and glory," she said, pointing to *The Economist* which was poking out of one of her plastic bags. "Make him feel better."

Erica thought she noticed the slightest of glows in Sonya's cheeks and wondered who the call was really intended to make feel better.

Since Sonya was temporarily phone-free—in all the panic and rush, she hadn't bought a replacement—Erica passed over her own mobile. "Here, make the call."

But René's line was busy.

"THANKS for the invitation, Anna," René answered after limping to the phone, "but I'm none too mobile. I'll be staying in a bit."

"Feel like staying in me tonight, maybe?"

He knew Sonya would be boarding about now but didn't know what to say. "Ah, I guess..."

Anna hung up on him.

Her double-entendres were hard going, and he hadn't really wanted to see her, or sleep with her, but....

When she arrived, she pointed to his walking stick. "René! A mighty fine crutch you've got there," she laughed. "Sam might have done us both a favour. Now," she said, putting her boots up on the arm of his sofa, "tell me about this Holovision thingy that everyone's babbling about."

SONYA was about to hand Erica back her phone, when it occurred to her that she should have heard from Al by now. Damn! Why didn't I give him Erica's mobile number? she asked herself. As she was about to ask if Erica would mind her calling Australia, she did a quick mental calculation of the time difference. It was too early. She'd have to wait till they landed in LA.

LETTING Erica board ahead of her, Sonya held back to assist a young family of five struggling through the gate with their clumsy assortment of overflowing bags, toys, stroller and whatever else they'd cobbled together to keep a six-year-old, a four-year-old and a ten-month baby amused for the six tortuous flying hours ahead of them.

The four-year-old started screaming, for no reason apparently than he hadn't done it for five minutes. As the father tried to console him, their boarding passes slipped out of his hand. Sonya reached down for them, breathing just a little easier after she saw their seat numbers; the family would be sitting down the back of the plane nowhere near her.

THEIR flight west to Los Angeles took off from JFK at 5 PM, twenty minutes late. Sonya and Erica each snuggled into their seats, one in front of the other. The idea of travelling First Class always seemed such a wanton extravagance when she couldn't afford it, thought Sonya, but now it seemed just dandy, and she was delighted to have stumped Erica for the fare, too.

Her stomach rumbled almost as soon as they stepped on board and thankfully, even before take-off, the airline had her nibbling on macadamia nuts and sipping a lightly frothing flute of a Napa Valley sparkling wine, a pinot chardonnay.

With the wheels up, the attendants invited their premier passengers to pile up floury potato blinis with silver spoonfuls of salmon caviar, chopped onion and cream cheese. Sonya passed on the onion and imagined that Erica was doing likewise although if she'd turned round, she would have seen that she had already dropped off to sleep, exhausted by the rush to get on board. The tiny pancake slipped into her mouth almost by itself, and her eyes closed in bliss as she popped the small orange eggs, one-by-one. Money didn't buy happiness, she of all people knew that, but this was hardly misery.

53

LEX TALIONIS, AL's criminal law partner, barged into his office ignoring the fact that Al was on his speakerphone. "Al, you won't believe this."

Al waved to signal him to be quiet while he finished the call.

"What's that?" said Al's client in London.

"Sorry, Bill, one of my partners just walked in. Something urgent. I'll call you back in five minutes, okay?"

Talionis was tugging on his already ample lower lip when Al ended the call. Protruding naturally, the lip made him seem thoughtful, not greedy, a handy asset for a litigator. "The arson," he said. "They made an arrest."

"Tell me it's not Michael Hunt," said Al, just as Karen Longly pushed open the door. She had been on the call with Al but had left to bring a document from her office. "Karen, it's the arson case... they've arrested someone," he told her.

"Not Hunt? Surely..."

"What if it was?" said Talionis, barely concealing a smile.

Karen had suffered Lex's twisted sense of humour many times when she'd been working with him. It was one of the reasons she'd asked for a move, though Al's, she'd discovered, was little better. "It's not Hunt. It's Klim, isn't it?" she said.

Nathan Klim had been the CEO who ZipChip had fired just before hiring Tito Wells and, like Michael, he'd been a suspect but until now the police had insufficient evidence.

Talionis crossed his arms. "Not Hunt. Not Klim."

"What is this? Twenty questions? Just give it to us," said Al, looking at his watch, keen to find out but also intent on keeping his five-minute promise to his client.

"Carmen Lynch and Tito Wells die in each other's arms, right? She was a bit of a bed hopper when it came to CEOs. Apparently she has an affair with Klim then trades up to Wells as soon as Klim stops being of use to her. Previously, the cops thought it was Klim, part vengeance, part jealousy. But it turns out it was his wife…"

"The firebomb? His wife?"

"Just before he's fired, Klim confesses about the affair… she snaps and tosses him out of the house. A nut job, she starts stalking the mistress… the ex-mistress now… to find out if Klim is lying and still seeing her but then, when he's fired and Lynch starts seeing the new guy, Wells, she decides to get them both at the same time. They'd both screwed her husb… sorry, I mean…. well, you know what I mean, and so she was going to screw them back."

"But the forensic report…" Al noted. "The firebomb was sophisticated…"

"No big deal, not for Mrs Klim. Before she and Klim got hitched and she got into the whole nice dress, big hair, corporate wife thing, she was an industrial chemist. Whatever you need to know about explosives, she knew it all."

54

TWO HOURS INTO the flight, an attendant cleared away the dinner settings, leaving Sonya with the vase and its two petite daisies, and a plate of chocolate truffles with her coffee. The flowers jiggled at something in her brain but it remained out of reach, inaccessible, like an old friend's hand stretched out from the wharf as your boat pulls away.

She elevated her backrest and skimmed the airline magazine a second time, hoping that reading something she'd already read once would flip her over into the sleep zone, but by the time she got to the end, the page with the shapes and sizes of each aircraft type in the fleet, she was still wide awake.

She then shuffled through the bag of reading material she'd bought at JFK musing how it must be twenty years, perhaps more, since she'd read anything by H.G. Wells. The Introduction did the trick. Written by some smug noteworthy, it was so turgid she only had to wade through three pages before she dropped off.

AFTER a few waking blinks, Sonya lifted the novel from her lap where it had been resting. The book, a steady seller ever since it was published in 1895, was no heavyweight in the length stakes coming in at only eighty pages.

"Two hours to landing, Dr Wheen. Would you care for anything else?"

The peppermint tea, in its own glass plunger, would give her reading a fresh spice, she decided, and this time she skipped the Introduction, determined to let Wells speak for himself. But she was unprepared for what was about to slap her in the face.

It wasn't the words, or the writing. It was the portrait Wells had painted of his hero. Known in the novel only as the Time Traveller ("*for so it will be convenient to speak of him*"), Wells's brush-strokes were hauntingly recognisable:

> "His grey eyes shone and twinkled, and his usually pale face was flushed and animated... Then, getting up, he went to the tobacco jar on the mantel, and with his back to us began to fill his pipe."

A small tea leaf caught between her teeth, and she tried sucking it out till it rested on the tip of her tongue, just like a stray flake of tobacco. Michael had grey eyes, a pale face and, of course, smoked a pipe. She spat the leaf into the palm of her hand and examined it, as if it would reveal something. Suddenly, Sonya was beginning to detest this flight.

As she read on, she visualised Michael and, no matter how hard she tried, she couldn't peel his face off Wells's imaginary character. Several times, distressed, she had to put the book down but after chiding herself it was only a novel, and one written well over a century ago, she forced herself to plough on. Yet, Michael kept poking his head out of the book at her: his haughty humour... his disdainful honesty. Sonya's hands were trembling so much, she could only continue reading by propping the book on her lap.

> "... The Time Traveller was one of those men who are too clever to be believed: you never felt that you saw all round him; you always suspected some subtle reserve, some ingenuity in ambush, behind his lucid frankness."

Get a grip, she thought. Her imagination was surely working overtime. What about the newspaper and magazine articles René had found? She reread the passage; it was Michael to a tee. And the similarities didn't end there. As she tore through the short book she found it was scattered with them. Whenever the hero returned from the distant future, he was unkempt... dusty and dirty... exhausted... dishevelled... haggard and drawn. She smacked her hand down on the armrest. How many of Michael's so-called overseas trips had ended with him bedraggled like that?

And what were those trips? Slowly Sonya pushed her head back. Those trips... as the police claimed... when he'd never left the country.

"More tea?"

"Whisky. Please. With ice. A single malt, if you have one. Actually, a double." A single double, she sniggered to herself. Or was it a double single? Whatever. She ignored the unprofessionally raised eyebrow.

> "His chin had a brown cut on it—a cut half healed."

Sonya looked up and almost saw the scar on the flight attendant's own chin as if Michael was delivering her drink. She took a slug and delved further, the pages yanking her forward like a medieval prisoner tied to the back of her captor's horse, struggling to keep on her feet, knowing that tripping meant death.

She almost choked on the *"scars on his knuckles"*. How often she'd run her lips over the pocks and puckers on the back of Michael's hand, trying to imagine their cause. He would never explain them: "A gentleman never tells," he'd smile before changing the subject.

She turned the book face down on her lap and stared out her window. It was still dark outside but for the mesmerising flashing white light on the wing tip of another plane passing in the distance. Fiction. Fact. Fiction. Fact.

A book she'd picked up by chance, one over a century old that described Michael right down to his most private mannerisms and habits and even his identifying marks. Not quite all of them, she remembered, though she wasn't even close to a smile.

Her mind searched for explanations... rationalisations. Perhaps he was a copycat? Michael was well-read so if he'd been a fan of Wells—though he'd never mentioned it—he couldn't have missed that he shared physical characteristics with the fictional hero, and maybe, initially for a laugh he sculpted his own traits into those Wells had crafted as fiction? She'd read about people who did such things... an unusual manifestation of literary worship, for sure, but it was at least an explanation. Sonya let the notion mull while she swirled her Scotch around in her glass, oblivious that the ice had melted.

"I don't recall it was an especially sad book."

Sonya looked up to the steward with a vacant but blurry stare. "Wha..." She dabbed her eye with the napkin the steward had held out to her.

"More Scotch?" the steward asked, a kind smile saving the embarrassment of further conversation.

Yes, she decided, and she stretched round to see that Erica was watching a movie.

No. The explanation didn't fit. Michael was too much an individual to descend to appropriating anyone else's character, let alone a fictional one. It wasn't his way, not even for cocky self-amusement.

Yet, she wavered. Had it all been part of a role? An act? Everything. For ten years.

This copycat theory though patently ludicrous was more palatable than the alternative her mind was trying to smother: that Michael actually *was* Wells's character, in the flesh... that the book in her lap wasn't fiction... and had never been.

She picked it up again and forced herself to read on, searching for something, a tidbit, anything, that would prove her wrong; some divergence to cleave the two men apart. Yet the more her finger ran on, the more Michael merged into the character Wells had created in 1895—or was the correct term 'portrayed'.

Some way into the book—she no longer dared label it a novel—the Time Traveller emerged into the year "Eight Hundred and Two Thousand, Seven Hundred and One A.D." The date had a troubling echo, but she couldn't pin it down. If it had been written in numbers—802,701—it might have been a more obvious trigger, and eventually she would have recognised it from *Know-Ware's* copyright statement.

The Time Traveller, she read on, was sojourning with two races, both barely human, who had survived the Earth after a holocaust, if you could grace it as a survival: the shadowy, dangerous Morlocks and the striking Elois, his girlfriend, Weena, one of them.

Weena.

"Dr Wheen, your Scotch?"

Sonya gulped it down straight and handed the glass back to the steward. "Another, please." She forged on, hardly prepared for the passage about to creep up on her:

> "'My pockets had always puzzled Weena, but at the last she had concluded that they were an eccentric kind of vase for floral decoration. At least she utilised them for that purpose. And that reminds me! In changing my jacket I found...'
>
> "The Time Traveller paused, put his hand into his pocket, and silently placed two withered flowers, not unlike very large white mallows, upon the little table. Then he resumed his narrative. His eye fell with a mute inquiry upon the withered white flowers upon the little table."

Sonya leant back and deeply inhaled. Two white flowers, just like the two in the vase on her tray table.

> "They were put into my pocket by Weena, when I travelled into Time."

Sonya's mind darted back to New York ten, eleven years ago when she'd taken a peek at Michael's passport, when the shrivelled... withered... white flower slipped out; the dead white daisy, she'd thought, but maybe it was a mallow, whatever they looked like.

What, she wondered, had happened to Weena's second flower? Straightening herself up in her seat, she almost huffed, "Get a grip... this is fantasy."

Fiction!

Even so, the void of Michael's past floated back to haunt her. He'd only ever skated over it; not once had she ever been able to draw details out of him, no matter how hard she pressed.

> *"The Time Traveller vanished three years ago," she read. "And, as everybody knows now, he has never returned."*

Her stomach went cold, empty, and she felt as if the plane had plunged suddenly beneath her. She gripped her armrests and, carelessly, the remnants of the white petals she'd crushed in her hand fell to the floor. She swung her head around, but no one else seemed to be fretting. It wasn't the plane falling, she was.

The thin volume, as if suddenly charged with an electric shock, shot from her fingers and flew to the floor, landing just out of reach. Even her feet recoiled from it.

55

"YOU *ARE* OKAY, Dr Wheen?" asked a flight attendant, stressing his concern with a touch on her sleeve.

"I'll be fine," Sonya said and tried for a tissue from her handbag, which was clasped as tightly as she was.

"If there's anything…" The attendant squatted down to pick up Sonya's book for her.

"Leave it!" she said, too brusquely, causing him to recoil. Sonya poked her head into her purse, more to take cover from the attendant's surprise, found a tissue and dabbed her eyes.

René! She felt a sudden urge to speak to him. Once she swiped her credit card in the armrest skyphone, she keyed in his number.

"Oh," she weakly smiled at the attendant. "Thank you, I will," she added, accepting another tumbler of single malt, but this time she left it on her tray table. She held the phone to her ear, and waited… and waited… only to hear the call fail. She tried again, but got the same result.

She craned her head round but Erica was asleep again, her headphones dangling round her neck.

She took a sip of the whisky and, placing it on her window ledge, dropped her head back but she knew it was useless; she'd never sleep now. Her hands fidgeted with the cord of her headphones and she adjusted the lumbar support in her seat. She lowered it to sleep position, but after a fidgety minute she raised it back up again.

The passenger across the other side of the plane, in window seat 1K, was tapping on his laptop, a cable snaking from it to a power outlet located below his armrest. Sonya lifted the cover plate on hers, and yes, her seat also came equipped with a complement of outlets: one for power and two connection ports.

She rubbed her chin and squeezed her neck, pulling at the skin as if that could help her. Maybe... if she could load up *Know-Ware*...

Passing up the rest of the whisky, she buzzed for a hot chocolate. The first swallow warmed her through, making her eyelids heavy, droopy. Sleep was suddenly seductive but a session of *Know-Ware* was more so.

Maybe it would give her a clue. She almost laughed as she pulled the flash drive off her pendant and it jangled her charm bracelet. Unclipping the bracelet, in case she did nod off, she dropped it into her handbag.

Once she'd slotted in the flash drive, she wiggled more comfort into her seat and adjusted her backrest for a better angle to see the small TV screen. Through her headphones, the usual drumbeat started up... but this time she didn't need to brace herself, she was already well buckled in, and she welcomed the familiarity. She took another sip of chocolate, inhaling the aroma of thick cocoa.

Should she even bother attempting Realtime or go straight for the usual, 3D? Wondering if the airplane computer system had sufficient power—wishful thinking, she knew—she went for the higher level.

The hourglass icon floated up on her screen, thinking, waiting for the various checks to complete. It would be a waste of time, most likely, but what harm could it do?

Far more than she knew.

Suddenly, the Boeing 747-400 jolted and Sonya slammed forward in her seat, the strap cutting sharp into her lap and her head whipping itself back onto her headrest. One hand, almost in reflex, jumped for the mug of chocolate to stop it flying but missed, and her other gripped the armrest, white-knuckled, ready for the next quake.

"Ladies and Gentlemen. This is your pilot. Please ensure your seat belts are strapped on firmly and be sure to remain in your seats. I apologise for the unexpected turbulence. If you need assistance, please press your call button for a member of the flight crew."

The crew scurried around the cabin checking no one was hurt, tightening belts and cleaning up the items that had been tossed around. Sonya's hot chocolate had smashed against the wall ahead of her, the thick brown liquid oozing down the surface like old blood. She unclasped her seatbelt and leant forward to pick up the pieces but a firmly polite hand on her shoulder pressed her back into her seat while the steward attended to the mess. Children were crying, she thought it was children, somewhere back behind her. It would be pandemonium back in Coach, she thought. She twisted round to Erica, whose face was white, drained of colour, apart from the scarf she was biting into. It was pointless to say anything calming above the noise, and any attempt at a signal not to worry would have been lost since her eyes were clamped shut.

Sonya took a deep breath and turned back, settling into her seat, but the breath caught in her lungs when she noticed the warning flashing on her screen:

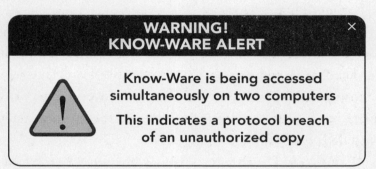

Sonya knew she had the only copy here on the plane. Sam had the other, but he was thousands of miles away.

The warning became more specific:

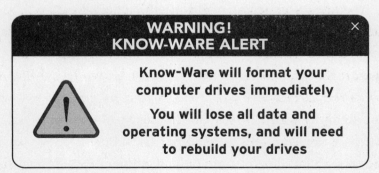

Shit! No... good, she decided... great! That bastard Sam would get his comeuppance. But no way was she going to let her flash drive get wiped clean. She pressed the *Stop* button on the console.

Nothing happened.

She jabbed at it as if her life depended on it, pumping her finger repeatedly but the alert continued to glare at her. She tried to pull the drive out of the port, but her fingers, moist from fear, slipped off the smooth silver case. After wiping her fingers on her seat, she succeeded, but the relief was momentary.

Her reading light began to flicker.

As did the cabin lights.

In total disbelief, she watched the screen stutter and with only a second before it spluttered out completely she reread it: "*Know-Ware* will format your computer drives," it said. Drives. Plural.

She froze with the sweat of terror as she tried to scream but couldn't.

The entertainment system was run by the plane's central computer but, she prayed, surely there'd be a firewall between them? If *Know-Ware* wiped all the plane's drives clean…

She pressed her call button for a flight attendant but there was no *ping!* She glanced up, half-afraid to look, and there was no orange bulb glowing above her.

"Ladies and Gentlemen. We are experiencing prob… with the electron… Please rem… your seats and keep your seat b… All crew please strap in immediat… We will communicate agai…" The public address fizzled.

She swung round to wave for a crewmember, only to see they were all strapping themselves into their seats back in the galley. Sonya's fingers unconsciously fiddled with her silver charm bracelet.

Erica's mouth was open and Sonya tried to lip-read. "What... the... hell..."

Throughout the plane, passengers fidgeted, uneasy. They turned to their neighbours, people they'd been avoiding talking to. What's wrong with the public address system? Why is the plane bucking? Why aren't the lights working? Why... Some tugged at their own seat belts and those of their loved ones. Many had filled their lungs with so much air it hurt to keep holding their breath. Others, to keep their minds from panic, packed and rezipped the cabin baggage at their feet. Mothers crooked their arms around their children to comfort them, and stroked their frightened faces. "The movie's stopped. I want to see it." "It'll start again soon, darling." People bent forward to pull on their shoes and tie their laces, as if it mattered. Others crossed themselves, Catholic or not. Scattered men and women scratched words on any available scrap of paper: futile messages to loved ones? Knuckles were being chewed, lips bitten.

An audible gasp of relief echoed throughout the plane when the cabin lights flickered on, but when they sputtered out again... for the last time... it was as if the entire plane sucked in its collective breath.

People in window seats slid open the shades to let in the outside light, to see... something, anything... to get comfort from the outside world. But it was black outside, except for the white strobe flashing on the wingtips for those positioned to see it.

The flashing was hypnotic.

Until it stopped.

Passengers could hear what they assumed were the oxygen masks dropping from above. "How do you put them on if you can't see," one woman screamed.

"That's mine; give it here," yelled another, using the light from his cellphone.

The pandemonium swelled until someone shouted: "Listen!"

"Listen to what?"

"I can't hear the engines."

The silence momentarily roaring through the plane was deafening—passengers up and down the aisles strained their ears toward the windows desperate for the comforting whine of the Pratt & Whitney PW4000s. Aviation aficionados knew these engines as high-hush propulsion machines but, for these unfortunates, whisper-quiet had become a jarring obscenity.

In a single atavistic reflex, the planeload of passengers kept in their breaths, until a four-year old boy, the one whose family Sonya had helped when she boarded, broke the silence: "Daddy, are we going to die?"

56

"WHAT DO YOU mean, dead?" Sam grunted in response as he pointlessly tried rebooting Sonya's IcePaC for the third time. He knew what formatting a drive meant... obliterating, wiping, killing every single bit of data and every program on the computer. Sam started to pull at the lace of his bolo tie, unaware his nerves were starting to show through his bravado. He caught a glimpse of his string tie in his handler's spectacles and for an instant imagined a noose.

Sam's academic life was over. It was an eventual outcome he'd resigned himself to years ago; one he had planned for. Given what he'd been doing, and for whom, he knew he'd pay a price some day.

But not this. He'd blown his cover, fine... *Know-Ware* was worth it... yet now, without the prize, his years of work would amount to little.

"Details about the crash of Flight 836 into the Californian desert west of Los Angeles remain sketchy.

"Though a rescue effort has been mounted, officials say relatives should expect the worse, that hope of finding survivors is slim.

"Moments prior to radio silence, according to aviation sources, the pilot of Flight 836 broadcast a may-day that the plane's entire power systems, including backups, were failing.

"We're crossing now live to Casey Macdonald, on board a rescue helicopter..."

57

AL MACANTAR POKED the tip of his letter-opener into the fold and slowly slit open the buff envelope, as if his reluctance could bring Sonya back. When she had left it with him for safekeeping, he'd dismissed her hand-written words on the front as melodramatic, but now they were repulsive. "To Al MacAntar: Please open after my death. Sonya Wheen."

He'd expected her Will, but all that was inside was an unmarked disk and a note, also in Sonya's hand:

> "My dearest Al,
>
> Thank you for everything.
>
> I have one more favour to ask.
>
> Please keep this disk safe for Michael for when he returns.
>
> Take care.
>
> Love, Sonya."

His eyes lingered over the last two words... unable to leave them... reading them again and again... even when the ink started to run with his tears.

For minutes, he clasped the disk, at first steely cold, in his fingers.

A shiver ran up his spine, and when it left him through his eyes, he felt empty.

Almost robotically, he slid the disk into his computer and clicked it open. He knew he shouldn't.

A game? What the...

He couldn't believe this. Not now. He was in no mood, no condition...

She'd left Michael a stupid computer game? What was she thinking?

Then he realised: she must have slipped the wrong disk inside the envelope. The poignancy depressed him even more.

He clicked *Eject* and watched as the tray slid out, slowly, like a hand making an offering. A sacrifice.

58

FRESH AIR. FOR the first time in twenty years, Michael breathes air that doesn't stink of him... that tickles his nostrils. Air that's clean and crisp. Sharp, like the flutter of snow that's falling on his cheeks as he holds his head up to the sky, his eyes closed.

He always knew he shouldn't go back to fix things. Travelling was one thing, but changing things... that was different, a crime. Yet, for him, almost broken, their threats are no longer of consequence.

He shuffles inside, asking for the bathroom, and after checking there is no surveillance he locks himself into a stall and jimmies the cap off his tooth. With a pin, he pops out the tiny quantum computer Quip he once secreted there and, without wasting a moment, presses the pin down onto the golden dot on its top. When it glows amber, a slight smile cracks his gaunt and weary face though it never quite reaches his eyes, still anxious that they will somehow jam the Quip from sucking the computer power from all networks within a one-mile radius.

Five long seconds later, the dot glows green in his palm and he clears his throat and speaks to it.

59

THE PASSENGER IN Seat 3E leant forward to slot his magazine away, and his smoking pipe slipped out of his shirt pocket onto the floor. When he tried stretching to fetch it, the pain pinched his eyes. He slumped back in his seat and pushed his sunglasses up to rest against his sparse grey hair and took long, slow breaths. He'd ask the attendants to pick it up for him later. He had more important things to do. The cabin lights hurt so he kept his eyes closed.

He'd heard the attendants gossip about the elderly gentleman with the dark glasses and the pipe that he acknowledged—five times, he recalled—that he couldn't smoke on-board.

The manifest didn't list him as a famous actor or celebrity and given his pallid complexion and his feeble movements, they figured he was merely one of the fast decreasing population of aging nobodies who could still manage to pay for a First Class ticket.

He repositioned his sunglasses and squinted through them across to the woman in Seat 1A, but he couldn't make out what she was reading.

Twenty years... If only he could steal them back. He gently reclined his seat. The pressure had been exhausting and given the little reserve of strength he had, he decided to nod off for a few minutes.

HE woke with a start, jerking himself forward. He snatched a nervous look around the cabin. A flight attendant brushed past to serve a drink to the woman at the window two rows ahead of him; it smelled aromatic, sweet. Hot chocolate?

He rubbed the sagging skin under his glasses then unbuckled his seatbelt and stood, at first unsteadily. Relying on his walking cane as much as the seat backs, he moved himself slowly toward the bathroom at the rear of the First Class cabin. Whether it was the dehumidified air or the lights, he didn't know, but his aggravated eyes needed their drops.

When he returned to his seat, he remained standing in the aisle and continued to blink himself back into focus. As he gazed down at the top of the blonde woman's head, he reached for the flower he'd left on his seat.

He was breaking the rules, he accepted that. He was old and weak, with little time left. Little of life. But she... she could still have time.

He had to do this. And maybe explain, or maybe not. He hadn't decided that. Some things had to be left to fate. Fate! He laughed quietly and took a step forward.

The chief steward smiled too as he saw the kindly gentleman hovering quietly behind the woman. It was as if the old man was watching over her, guarding her.

Had the woman in seat 2A been awake, she would have found the man's presence next to her uncomfortable, claustrophobic. He glanced at her for a moment, and saw she'd removed the crimson knitted cap she'd previously had on. It was resting on her lap, on top of a scarf.

He smelled the sweet cocoa aroma from the woman in front's hot chocolate and he closed his eyes behind his glasses. As he exhaled and blinked them open he spotted the flash drive in her fingers and that she was unclipping her bracelet.

"Excuse me," he croaked, warily edging forward a little more.

Surprised and somewhat peeved by the interruption, she looked up and twisted round to where he was standing, a flicker of irritation reaching her face. "Yes?" Sonya was in no mood to chat.

"Apparently, there's a problem with the entertainment system," he tipped his head slightly back toward the crew.

She noticed his voice was scratchy, as if he hadn't used it for years and it had rusted over.

"You might corrupt your data if you slot that in."

"Oh!" she said, immediately folding her hand right round her flash drive, her other hand slapping at her chest in relief as the bracelet narrowly missed the mug of hot chocolate. "I'm a bit preoccupied," she said, shifting in her seat, trying to smile politely at him at an angle. "I didn't hear any announcement."

He stayed back just behind her, anxious not to intrude on her space. "The steward... he told me," he said, almost swivelling his aching body this time to point back in the direction of the galley, but the pain stopped him getting far.

Her annoyance softened into gratitude for the kindly old man's concern. She didn't want *Know-Ware* getting corrupted in the plane's maul. She may have left a copy with Al for safekeeping but she still needed to protect this one. It was odd, Sonya thought, someone wearing sunglasses on board, and only when the man was at her side did she notice his cane.

As she took him in, she wondered if this was how René might age, his hair so thin there'd be little to mask his freckled scalp. But the rest was different. The wrinkles above the man's speckled grey beard gouged into his face like cables rubbing against a lifetime of anguish. His hunched shoulders evoked a life of fallibility or emptiness. Physically, her considerate fellow passenger seemed a broken man. A simple gold band circled loose around his bony finger and she suspected that once, when his body had the bulk of earlier years, it would have looked elegant there. She glanced back and saw that next to his empty seat was a businessman poring over a thick pile of documents. The old man's wife must be dead, she decided.

"Any idea how long before they fix it?" she asked, the question as much a thank you—to keep the conversation alive and repay his thoughtfulness—as a genuine query.

Holding his cane, he raised his hand to his glasses. It lingered there a moment indecisively and finally he pushed the lenses up to rest against his forehead. For men of his generation, she understood, it was impolite to talk through dark lenses. She noticed his grey eyes were tired, but kind. Without thinking, she clipped her bracelet back on.

"May I sit a moment?" he said, rasping and a little breathless. He was pointing to the folding jump seat in front of her and as he moved forward, the toe of his shoe brushed the book on the floor, though he didn't notice.

When he reached to unfold the seat, she noticed the back of his hand. "Your knuckl…" she started, her stomach writhing. Her eyes darted to the book at his feet, and then to the flash drive still in her hand. They refused to look up, knowing what she'd see… uncertain that she'd want to. Seconds passed, time a shattered bond between them.

From behind his back he brought her the tulip, blood-red and, holding the long stem, he lightly placed it in her lap.

In his palm, which he opened flat for her, was her missing bracelet charm: the invisible hand.

"The torment of the future is that no one can see all of it," he said in part atonement.

"Yet the arrogance of men is they believe they can," she replied, leaving the charm to grow cold in his hand.

Author's Note

TRUTH CAN BE stranger than fiction, at times wretchedly.

I finished my first cut of this novel in August 2001, only two weeks before the September 11 terrorist attacks. A little earlier that year, in June, my Kiwi colleague Jim McLay and I were chomping on bagels and danishes at a boardroom breakfast on one of the World Trade Centre's top-most floors. That morning, our hosts were the top three executives of a New York-based investment bank.

Jim—today back in New York as New Zealand's Permanent Representative to the United Nations—had just tossed back a ristretto, his favoured morning kick-starter. As part of the chit-chat, he mentioned I was writing a novel, and that part of it involved blowing up their building (though later I cut that). It's perverse now, but their eyes lit up.

Their firm had been in the Twin Towers since before the first terrorist attack in 1993 and they began spilling story after story about what it had been like. It wasn't that they weren't scarred by the event, but rather, as the bank's president explained, adding some colour to my book could help honour the six people who died and the 1,042 who were injured.

He then stood, took my elbow and walked me and Jim on a tour of the office, even into his private bathroom, to help me enrich my novel with details of daily life in the building: the hub-bub, the furnishings, the art, and the views.

On September 11, 2001 two of the three men in that room were murdered, along with 66 of their co-workers and 2,905 others.

Two weeks later, an email I'd sent them on the fateful day bounced back. It came with an automated but distressing header: 'Permanent Fatal Error'.

YEARS later, I picked up my pen for a complete rewrite of *Nowhere Man*, unaware that another September catastrophe would complicate it.

Sonya's attempt to escape her vortex of sudden debt was always core to my story. After the dot.com crash in 2000, I dreamt up what I thought was an even wilder stock market bust to give Sonya a hell of a time. But the financial earthquake that ripped global markets apart in mid-September 2008 was exponentially higher on the Richter scale.

So, after the gut-wrenching shock of seeing my own investments in freefall—just like millions of other investors and savers around the world—I decided that this would be the time for Sonya to be trading and, forget the fiction, her buying and selling would precisely mimic what happened in real-time. The main stock she trades is Merrill Lynch, now part of Bank of America. It was hardly the crisis's only victim, but its wild, see-saw trajectory was perfect for the story. So, to those of my friends who still work there or did at the time, apologies for picking it out.

MY thanks to all these people: *The Economist* and its science and technology editor, Geoffrey Carr, for reviewing my *Economist* pastiche (Chapter 42*) to check it caught their style. He wondered if 42 was a nod to authors Douglas Adams or Lewis Carroll. It was just a coincidence, but I liked the notion so that's why it's Chapter 42*, even though several drafts later it's really chapter 33. Rob Hirst of Midnight Oil (and now new surf-rock band, The Break) for reviewing my chapter where René and Anna dance to one of their classics, *Power and the Passion*. Bill Thompson, urbane yet pushy New York book editor. Working with Bill on this book was like attending a gruelling yet rewarding writers' university; authors Stephen King and John Grisham said good things about him for a reason. Professor Paul Davies, physicist, writer and broadcaster, now of The Beyond Centre at Arizona State University for clarifying some science questions for me. Dr A. John Green (no relation), former head of *Macquarie Group's* quantitative applications division, for checking early versions of Sonya's options trading for authenticity and accuracy. If you're a markets expert and think any of it's wrong, don't blame him. For reasons of flow, I've simplified the trading and taken some liberties. At least that's my excuse. Alan Gold, Allan Lang, Harry M. Miller,

Wendy Cohen and Christopher Pearson for advice on earlier versions of this book. Eric Grinbaum in Paris, for French with jazz. Daniel Czerniewicz also in Paris, for Sam Sing but that's another story. Russell Staley for metastable. Professor David Dobkin, Princeton University's dean of the faculty and Rob Joyce (Princeton, computer science '02) for showing me round Princeton University's computer science labs. Clarence Da Gama Pinto, of Melbourne Business School, for helping me see I wanted to be a writer more than an investment banker. My friends and former colleagues at *Macquarie Group* for tolerating me, especially as my passion for writing overtook my passion for banking. Luke Causby for the book design. Graeme Jones, typesetter plus. The amazing team at *Simon & Schuster Australia*, especially Lou Johnson and Ed Petrie and their fabulous reps, and the bookstore you bought this book at.

Now my family. First, my sister Alex Warner with her sienna cake, her generous spirit and her fervour for life and family.

But especially my role-model wife for so many things, not least the light bulb moment she flicked on for me when she tossed in her own business career to become a full-time professional sculptor. Visit her website: www.jennygreen.net.

And our extraordinary two kids who, with my wife, have lived with this book and far, far more.

All three are passionate readers, fearless critics and friends. And we're also co-founders of *Pantera Press*, one of the most pull-your-hair-out, yet thrilling ventures I've ever been involved with.

SPOILER ALERT: DO NOT READ THIS BEFORE YOU READ THE BOOK!

IN PART, THIS book is in homage to the 1895 classic, H.G. Wells's *The Time Machine*. Even though it is out of copyright in Australia, NZ, the US and many parts of the world, I still acknowledge with thanks the cooperation and advice of the author's estate through its literary agents in London, A.P. Watt. Chapter 54 explicitly quotes the classic, but sleuths will detect a few other winks to it elsewhere in my book.

Quantum computers are not even close to existing commercially but all over the world in universities and labs, the race is on to make them work reliably and build them at scale. I needed a term for the quantum computer equivalent of the conventional computer *chip*, but I couldn't find one so I coined my own: *quip*.

Sonya's rollable computer screen is no mere fiction. It was inspired by a 1999 *New Scientist* article ("Don't watch it, wear it," by Karl Ziemelis, 10 July 1999) and a related *Nature* article, "Electroluminescence in Conjugated Polymers," about a collaboration between a Cambridge University spin-off, Cambridge Display Technology, and Seiko-Epson. These companies and others like Plastic Logic have since been developing this technology.

CICRS is a fictional successor to the PICASso Program at Princeton University. To emphasise the obvious: all the CICRS staff members, especially Sam Sing, are fictional.

The Princeton conference that Sonya attends on the science of time is modelled on actual university conferences: the *First, Second and Third International Conferences on the Nature and Ontology of Spacetime* at Concordia University, Montreal in 2004, 2006 and 2008 and the *Time's Arrows Today* conference at the University of Columbia in 1992.

OVER many years, I have devoured books, magazines, TV documentaries and movies about the physics and philosophy of time. A few of my favorites are listed on Pantera Press's website.

When you picked up this book, you let yourself into another world. For many, this joy may never be possible. Some kids are left behind their peers even before reaching school because they come from disadvantaged families where books are not enjoyed.

Let's Read is a national initiative that helps pre-school kids in regional, rural and metro communities across Australia to have fun reading with their parents. Research has shown that reading with young children is an important activity to develop a child's future literacy skills. As poor literacy skills are associated with lower education, earnings, health and social outcomes, teaching kids from socially and economically disadvantaged families to read is a vital step towards breaking the cycle of disadvantage.

Simply buying this book will help us support these kids. Want to do more? Make a personal donation to Let's Read. Visit: www.PanteraPress.com/donate

1 in 4 Aussie kids start school without the building blocks for literacy*

Over 20,000 students don't meet the national minimum reading standards*

The proportion of Indigenous students achieving this standard is significantly lower*

Alicia's Story
Let's Read Parent, Qld

"I attend an Indigenous playgroup in Nambour which a *Let's Read* trainer comes to regularly. She uses puppets to bring her reading to life and the kids love it. I have four children aged seven and under. *Let's Read* has encouraged me to read with the family at home, as well as at the play group. We've started reading together every night. It's a lot of fun and really opened my eyes to the point where I am now reading to my seven-month-old, which I wouldn't have done before. It's also helped my two-year-old with talking. Getting him to sit down is hard but he knows when it's reading time and now he wants to listen along with the other kids."

Let's Read was developed by the Centre for Community Child Health. Let's Read is being implemented across Australia in partnership with The Smith Family.

*Australian Institute of Health and Welfare AIHW[1], 2008.

For more great books visit
www.PanteraPress.com

KILLING RICHARD DAWSON

ROBIN BAKER

"The phone rings. It's Jesus. I listen to him speak and then hang up…"

In this darkly comic, slow-burn thriller, reality is blurred… nothing can be taken for granted.

A gripping and poignant black comedy about love, friendship, booze, morality, death… and a generation's casual dissatisfaction with modern life. Sometimes, redemption lies in the darkest of places.

"You don't need to die to destroy yourself."

Killing Richard Dawson is a brilliant fast-paced story with a surprising twist. The reader gets sucked into the contemporary university student narrator's inner and outer worlds as he navigates his way, with wit and humour, through the minefields of loss, friendship and unrequited love. Death is the only constant in his life, yet Robin Baker deals with it with an irreverence echoing Evelyn Waugh's classic satire.

What they're saying about
KILLING RICHARD DAWSON

'…somehow doesn't miss a beat, all the way to an ending that'll knock you sideways.'
– *Nick Earls, award-winning author*

'A startling, original voice on the crime scene… To die for… a new crime writer you simply have to read.'
– *Booktopia Buzz*

'*Killing Richard Dawson* takes the reader on an unsettling journey… A truly gripping read.'
– *Bookseller + Publisher magazine*

'*Catcher in the Rye* meets *Dexter*… a coming-of-age tale injected with black humour.'
– *Reader's comment*

A Few Right Thinking Men
SULARI GENTILL

In Australia's 1930s, the Sinclair name is respectable and influential, yet the youngest son Rowland - an artist - has a talent for scandal.

Even with the unemployed lining the streets, Rowland lives in a sheltered world... of wealth, culture & impeccable tailoring with the family fortune indulging his artistic passions & friends... a poet, a painter & a brazen sculptress.

Mounting political tensions fuelled by the Great Depression take Australia to the brink of revolution. Rowland Sinclair is indifferent to the politics... until a brutal murder exposes an extraordinary & treasonous conspiracy.

"*The real enemy is Labor's Jack Lang and the Communist hordes into whose hands he plays... What say I introduce you to some chaps?*"

"*What chaps?*"

"*Right thinking men. Loyalists who love this country... Rowland, I think you could be moving with the wrong crowd.*"

What they're saying about
A FEW RIGHT THINKING MEN

''Witty dialogue, lively characters, and a shrewd political awareness of the times.'
– *Marele Day, award-winning novelist*

'... historically correct, gripping, no-holds-barred novel... an enjoyable read for young and old.'
– *Bookseller + Publisher magazine*

BETRAYAL
THE UNDERBELLY OF AUSTRALIAN LABOR
SIMON BENSON
Senior Political Journalist

This is a story that some in the Australian Labor Party would prefer to keep buried. But to others, including former Labor giants, it's a story that needs to be told.

Betrayal is a shocking, often crude, even hilarious war-story about politics, policy and petty personal ambition.

Leading political reporter Simon Benson reveals nasty secrets about how the Labor Party is run today through his detailed exposé of an extraordinarily vicious, behind-the-scenes battle over a few clapped-out power stations in NSW... when the Labor Party machine brought down an elected premier and crippled Australia's most populous State.

But more importantly, it's about the train-wreck of the NSW Labor Party and the policy reform framework that past Labor leaders fought hard to make it stand for.

"...where goes NSW, so goes federal Labor."

– PAUL KEATING

WHY *vs* WHY
Nuclear Power
BARRY BROOK & IAN LOWE

WHY *vs* WHY™ is a unique series of small books that tackle both sides of the hot topics that confront, confuse or trouble most people.

Making sense of everything™. This series aims to present everything you need to know about a complex topic in an easy-to-read, jargon-free, 2-books-in-1 format… all in one handy, & pocket-sized place.

It's part of *Pantera Press's* push to foster debate in this rapidly changing & confusing world, covering a wide range of big issues… topics which for most of us have no simple, easy answers.

In WHY *vs* WHY™ *Nuclear Power*, two opposing activists & writers, Barry Brook & Ian Lowe, go head-to-head, each presenting 7 key reasons why you should say YES/NO to nuclear power.

After each author presents his arguments, his opponent tries to tear each of them apart, both in the book & on Pantera Press's website (with further rebuttals). For readers, this book aims to leave nothing unanswered.

Barry & Ian are strong writers with well-argued opinions.

Who will you agree with?
Will one of them change your mind?

Read the book & find out.

In WHY *vs* WHY™, you get both sides, so you can decide for yourself… The books are also a great tool to help you convince others, people who don't see the light the way you do. Buy them a copy!

WHY *vs* WHY
Gay Marriage
RODNEY CROOME & BILL MUEHLENBERG

WHY *vs* WHY™ is a unique series of small books that tackle both sides of the hot topics that confront, confuse or trouble most people.

Making sense of everything™. This series aims to present everything you need to know about a complex topic in an easy-to-read, jargon-free, 2-books-in-1 format... all in one handy, & pocket-sized place.

It's part of *Pantera Press's* push to foster debate in this rapidly changing & confusing world, covering a wide range of big issues... topics which for most of us have no simple, easy answers.

In WHY *vs* WHY™ *Gay Marriage*, two opposing activists & writers, Rodney Croome & Bill Muehlenberg, go head-to-head, each presenting 7 key reasons why you should say YES/NO to gay marriage.

After each author presents his arguments, his opponent tries to tear each of them apart, both in the book & on Pantera Press's website (with further rebuttals). For readers, this book aims to leave nothing unanswered.

Rodney & Bill are good writers with strong, well-argued opinions.

Who will you agree with?
Will one of them change your mind?

Read the book & find out.

In WHY *vs* WHY™, you get both sides, so you can decide for yourself... The books are also a great tool to help you convince others, people who don't see the light the way you do. Buy them a copy!

ABOUT JOHN M. GREEN

When it dawned on John that what got him up in the morning was writing not his day job, he quit the job. Until then he was an executive director in a leading investment bank. Much earlier he'd been a lawyer, a partner in two major law firms.

He is a well-known business writer and commentator and his writing has appeared in a variety of publications in Australia and overseas including: *The Australian, The Australian Financial Review, Company Director, Business Spectator, The Age, The Bulletin,* the UK's *Financial Times* and Canada's *Director Journal.*

Nowhere Man is John's first novel.

Today, as well as writing, he is a board member of two stock-exchange-listed corporations and some not-for-profits, as well as a co-founder of *Pantera Press.*

He lives with his wife, a sculptor, in Sydney. They have two adult children who share their passions for the arts, books, business and philanthropy, as well as for the shimmering waters of an extraordinary city.